Watercolors

Shari Cylinder

other books by Shari Cylinder
Making Waves
Kaleidoscope of Stars
Red, White, and You
Sands of Time

BACK COVER PHOTO OF AUTHOR
BY KRISTEN KIDD PHOTOGRAPHY

Published by
GTI Press
Huntingdon Valley, Pennsylvania

Paperback ISBN: 978-1-7369568-8-5
Library of Congress Control Number: 2024904537

Book format by Annette Murray

For Stacy

Thank you for helping me find my voice again when it felt lost, for showing me the importance of turning up the volume on mental health and living my dreams out loud, and for making a difference that will forever echo.

Acknowledgements

To Mom, Dad, and Marissa, for your love and support. Thank you for being champions not only for my writing, but for me. You have been cheerleaders for my books from day one, and I so appreciate all the time and tireless efforts you've put into helping with revisions and spreading the word – and, of course, everything else you do and are. How grateful I am to have you there every step of the way!

To Jasper, Bandy, Cha Cha, and Brownie, for bringing such light and laughter into my life. Love is indeed a four-legged word, and I am the luckiest Ma and Auntie to have your sweet snuggles, hoppy hour performances, and zealous zoomies to fill my days with joy. You are my sunshine!

To Annette, for once again working your magic in bringing this novel to life. From the front cover to the back, and everything in between (literally!), your attention to detail is extremely appreciated. Thank you for sharing your talent with me and my characters, and for turning my manuscripts into beautiful books.

To Grammy, for being so much of the heart and soul of Lillian's character. I miss you dearly, and it was a true "work of heart" to weave your love into the pages of this book.

To Caryn, for being one of the earliest readers and editors for this story. The insight and wisdom you shared throughout our "revision swap" added so much, and I am thankful not only for that, but for your encouragement and friendship along the way.

To Melinda, for sharing your incredible talent and your equally as incredible kindness (and Nashville tips!). From the time I met you at the *American Idol* tour (I will never forget how you refused to get back on the bus without seeing me), to our "mommy/daughter"

Zoom chat, and all the moments in between, I am thrilled to know you and to draw inspiration from your music and words.

To everyone who has joined me at concerts over the years, for being a part of such special memories – whether we were singing (and jumping!) along to Kelly Clarkson, selling merchandise for Rachel Platten, fulfilling a one time childhood dream by seeing the Spice Girls from the third row, or enjoying so many other shows – there is nothing like live music, and I'm so glad we got to experience that together!

To my family, friends, and the people who have come into my life and changed it for the better, for all the ways in which you brighten my days. Your support of my writing – and of me – means more than you will ever know. Thank you for everything, most of all for being you.

To all the music makers, for the hope, inspiration, solace, comfort, joy, and connection found amongst your lyrics and melodies. Thank you for sharing your talents and for helping people find so much purpose and possibility inside your songs.

And to anyone who reads *Watercolors* and travels alongside Eden on her journey, I hope her story strikes a chord. Like the lyrics to the song say, "A *ripple in the water, spreading circles wide. We can change the world, if only we try.*" Much as Eden found she was more than just one chapter, when she looked beyond the page, may you do the same - and may you always remember to listen to your own voice and to share it with the world, for often times the melodies we create together are the ones that resonate the loudest.

Table of Contents

Chapter 1 1

Chapter 2 11

Chapter 3 21

Chapter 4 33

Chapter 5 43

Chapter 6 55

Chapter 7 65

Chapter 8 77

Chapter 9 87

Chapter 10 97

Chapter 11 107

Chapter 12 117

Chapter 13 127

Chapter 14 137

Chapter 15 147

Chapter 16 157

Chapter 17 167

Chapter 18 177

Chapter 19 187

Chapter 20 197

Chapter 21 207

Chapter 22 217

Chapter 23 227

Chapter 24 237

Chapter 25 247

Chapter 26 257

Chapter 27 267

Chapter 28 277

Chapter 29 287

Chapter 30 299

Chapter 31 311

Chapter 32 321

Chapter 33 333

*T*ime is a conundrum. It starts, it stops, it ebbs, it flows. There are moments when it lets us live in its gift and others when it snatches the beauty away, robbing us of the past, the present, and the future, all in one crushing fell swoop. And isn't it ironic, how we never see the blow coming? In the heartbeats before everything changes, we're completely clueless.

"Look all around you," my grandmom said before I moved to Nashville. We were standing in her driveway, car keys dangling from my fingers as I prepared to make the twelve-hundred mile journey, and though it's been six years since that breezy July morning, I can still feel the way she wrapped her gentle hand around mine, wrapped it up like she was trying to hold on to her Jellybean – that's what she's called me since I was born – for just a bit longer. "Magic is everywhere," she said, "if we open our eyes to find it." She let go then, kissed my cheek and blinked back gossamer tears, and I made a point of memorizing her words of wisdom. They've been my guide.

Tonight is no exception. My head might be in the clouds as I walk home from the Bluebird Café, its music and melody lifting me higher, *pushing* me higher, but my feet are firmly on the ground and my gaze flits around. There's a flash of headlights from an SUV as it rolls down the street, a spinning of bike tires as a teenager rides by on the sidewalk, and a pop of fireworks in the distance before the sky lights up with a rainbow-colored sea of sparkles. Independence Day was yesterday, but we were hit by a storm, so most of the celebrations were delayed. I stop for a minute and watch, thinking of Grandmom. July Fourth is her favorite holiday. When I was younger, I used to help her deck out the house: candles that smelled like apple pie, fairy lights in shades of red, white, and blue, a flag in the living room window and a half dozen more in the yard.

I miss that.

I miss her.

I may be twenty-eight years old, but I'm still Grandmom's girl.

I pull out my phone to call her, and that's when I smell it. The whiff of smoke is faint at first, like its edges are advancing and then retreating, and it strikes me as odd, because surely those fireworks are far enough away that their residue can't travel all the way here. The odor gets stronger, though. More pungent. I glance along the road, searching for the source, but find nothing. On the outside, everything is as it should be.

Then I round the bend to my street.

Dark clouds stream out of my apartment building, billowing toward the inky sky. I stare in shock and horror, barely able to register the blaze of orange engulfing the second floor, *my* floor, before a wail from a fire truck cuts through the air.

Is this for real? It can't be. It feels more like a dream. A nightmare.

Firefighters are jumping down from their truck, running into the scorching halo, and at the same time, a door flings open and my neighbors start to fly out. There's Walter, the elderly man who lives at the end of my hall, and Cindy, the lawyer who lives in the penthouse. There's Evan, the six-year-old who challenges me to a game of kickball whenever he sees me, and his mother Leslie, who has him by the hand. Kristina. Where's Kristina? I scan the crowd, desperately looking for my roommate. Is she still in the burning building? Or did she have plans tonight? In the tumult and terror of the moment, I can't remember if she mentioned anything about going out this evening.

My phone is still in my hand, and with trembling fingers I punch in her number. *Pick up,* I silently plead. But she doesn't. Each ring sounds hollow in my ear, warning of danger and despair, and I just about scream when her voicemail clicks on. We aren't close, Kristina and I, but things like that don't matter in times like this. All I can think of is her being trapped, surrounded by smoldering debris. As Walter slows to a stop beside me, I reach out, latching on to his arm. "Have you seen Kristina?" I ask him. "She's not answering her phone. She could be stuck in our … "

He extracts his arm from my grasp and winds it around my shoulders. "She's fine," he says softly and holds me up as I slacken in relief. "She's at the movies with Robert. They left shortly after you." Robert. Usually her boyfriend's name makes me grimace, because he's loud, boisterous, and sloppy. Now I just want to hug the man for saving her.

"What happened?" I whisper, and I must be shaking, because Walter leads me over to the curb, where we sit. "How did it start? Did everyone get out?"

He can only shrug. "It started on our floor. That's all I know." The flames hiss against his words. I picture the apartment Kristina and I rent, with its shaggy rugs and plaques on the walls. It's small, but it's home. Or it was, I suppose. It'd take a miracle to survive this inferno. My mind flicks on the things I'll never see again, the pieces of my heart that are being incinerated. The photo albums, one for each year I lived in Portsmouth, New Hampshire. The *best* half of the necklace I shared with my childhood best friend Kayleigh. The Magic Nursery doll I got as a present from Mom and Dad when I was seven, right before they left for another overseas business trip. The guitar that belonged to my grandpa. The bookcases overflowing with colorful covers and creased spines. The turquoise blanket Grandmom crocheted for me. The framed diplomas from Berklee College of Music in Boston, where I studied songwriting, and Belmont University, where I earned my Masters degree.

A sob chokes my throat. I think I'm going to be sick.

My head drops to my knees and I can feel the cries ratcheting through my body. Walter rubs my back comfortingly, and I try to reassure myself, too. At least I have my two most prized possessions. That's something. That's everything. There's the locket around my neck – Grandmom's locket, that her mother gave her when she turned sixteen. She passed it down to me on the same birthday. The rose etched on it reminds me of her – Lillian Rose is her name – and inside I've put two pictures. On the left is Mom and Dad. On the right is Grandpa, who was killed in the Vietnam War. Carrying him close to me makes me feel like I'm not alone.

So does my songwriting journal. Thank God I brought it with me tonight. I wasn't performing or anything, but being around music always inspires me and I often take a detour to the park afterward to work on some lyrics. Suppose I hadn't done that tonight? Would I have been back already, inside the apartment when the first alarm sliced apart everybody's bubble of peaceful security? I jerk my gaze over to the furious flames. A firefighter carries Marlena, the nine-year-old from down the hall, out of the building, and another pushes us all back to a safe distance from the blaze. A gasp goes up as part of the roof comes crashing down – directly onto a row of parked cars, including mine.

Down, down, down.

Gone, gone, gone.

If only I'd driven to the Bluebird tonight instead of walking. But I didn't, so my car's in the line of fire.

"What are we going to do?" I hear Leslie ask her husband. "Where will we stay?"

A puff of smoke spits out a window toward us, and I cover my nose before it can sting my lungs. *Where will we stay?* Her words hit me hard. Because I don't have anywhere else to go. I don't have anyone here to take me in. It's the most surreal sensation. It's like ... I recognize it, but I can't begin to comprehend it.

Any of it. But especially the fact that I'm now homeless.

It takes several hours before the fire is under control, and because we all have ties to this place, because it's the thread that linked us together and turned strangers into neighbors, we feel a sense of compulsion to stay until the last ember is snuffed out. It's a sense of community, of having to see this through as a unit. And then the firefighters give a briefing, saying something about a match that wasn't extinguished, and a representative from the Red Cross appears, talking about emergency aid and financial assistance and I don't even know what else.

This is all too much, and yet, it's not enough.

I allow myself the quickest glance at the ruins – the roof that hangs in shreds, the windows that have been shattered, the bricks that are pitch black with soot – and suddenly I can't listen anymore. I can't hear it, can't absorb it, can't fathom it. I might not have had any power over what happened here tonight, I might not have been able to save the belongings that formed such important squares in the quilt of my life, but I can do something about this. I can control what comes next. I can make a choice to leave the scene of the fire before it leaves me *breathless*.

"Eden?" I hear Walter call my name as I take off, but I don't stop. I just raise my hand in a silent goodbye and disappear into the night. It's muggy, the air heavy with the kind of moisture you'd only find in the South, and it pushes against my chest as I sprint across sidewalks and catapult over fallen tree branches. Sweat beads along my temples, a throb squeezes my side, and the rapid tap-tap-tap of my pulse feels like a drumbeat. Still, I keep moving. Keep running. Nashville was supposed to be my happily-ever-after, my star in the sky and my harmony in a life riddled with uneven chords. Now this. Now a world that has literally gone up in smoke.

Now nothing.

Now ... what?

Eventually I have to stop sprinting, because my heart feels like it's going to burst and my head is pounding as though someone's taken a sledgehammer to it. I pull the hair tie from around my wrist and throw my long honey-colored locks into a messy bun. I have to get them away from my neck. I have to cool off and calm down. My eyes seek out the nearest place to sit and land on the beloved Ryman Auditorium. Honestly, I didn't even realize I'd fled back to Downtown, but I'm glad. It is the daydream, the fantasy, the wish. It's what first drew me to Music City, so where better to settle the onslaught of emotion slamming in a frenzy around my brain?

I plunk onto the steps and think of all the music industry icons who have graced the stage inside: Reba McEntire, Emmylou Harris, Garth Brooks, Willie Nelson, the list goes on and on. Kristina's lived in Nashville since she was a teenager, and I remember her telling me, on our first day as roommates, about seeing both Kelly Clarkson and Carrie Underwood here. We'd bonded over our shared love of the *American Idol* winners, and that's when I knew I made the right choice in answering her ad for a roommate. It wasn't always easy for a neat-freak like me to live with someone like her, who tosses her things wherever she pleases, but at least we had that tidbit in common.

Kristina.

I should call her again. She should hear about the fire from me. This time, thankfully, she picks up after the third ring.

"Eden, hi." Her voice is light and airy. "If this is about the ice cream carton I left on the counter, I'm sorry. I was about to put it away, but the doorbell rang and it was the UPS guy with the birthday present I ordered for my dad. I got distracted and didn't remember again until I was halfway to the movies – "

"No," I interrupt. "It's not about the ice cream. There's something important I have to tell you."

My tone must speak for me, because she immediately asks, "What's wrong?"

"There was a fire." The words taste like sawdust on my tongue. "I don't know all the details yet, just that it began in the apartment next to ours and – " A tear escapes from my eye and trails down my cheek.

"*What?*"

"The building's destroyed," I hear myself say. "They won't even let us in to see if we can salvage anything. It's too unsafe. Not like it matters for us, anyway." Another tear, this time over the curve of my other cheek. "Everything has to be gone. We were too close."

"I ... this ... oh God," she stammers. "Was anyone hurt?"

"Some burns and smoke inhalation, but nothing life-threatening, according to the fire chief."

It's the sole bright spot in the darkness.

"How's Mrs. Lindenburg?" Mrs. Lindenburg is the woman who lived next to us. With a tangle of salt-and-pepper curls, a collection of reading glasses in every color imaginable, and a propensity for absentmindedness – well, I hate to say this, but it isn't a surprise that the flames were first fanned in her apartment. Still, she's endearing, gifting flowers from her floral shop to everybody on our floor and inviting us to Sunday dinner, and Kristina heaves a sigh when I tell her that our neighbor is okay.

What about us? Will we be okay?

When Kristina says she's going to move in with Robert now – which I should've expected, seeing as how they're practically joined at the hip – I'm not so sure. I don't make enough money to afford my own place. What am I going to do? Even if I ask for an advance on my next paycheck … but wait. I can't do that. I can't even rely on my normal paycheck, because I worked as a receptionist for our building's landlord. Not only have I lost my home, I've lost my income. I dedicate evenings to trying to break into the music scene, networking with fellow songwriters, but that's more about exposure than financial stability.

"I've gotta go," I say hurriedly, and end the call before Kristina can respond. She has every right to live with her boyfriend. The lease we signed is null and void, and she certainly has no obligations to me. I lean my head back against the railing, closing my eyes to the world and flashing on the only options I have. There's Grandmom, but she's still in Portsmouth and she moved to an assisted living facility earlier this year. It's not like I could live with her even if I wanted to, and I know she'll worry constantly if I tell her what happened. I love her far too much to upset her like that. There are Mom and Dad, but they're always thousands of miles away, always aiding people in need, always too busy for their daughter. Who else? I could call Kayleigh in Manhattan. She'd loan me money, but I'd feel awkward taking it since our different lifestyles have opened a chasm between us. Everybody in my life comes with a 'but,' which means I will have to navigate this scorched earth on my own. The only person I can rely on right now is myself.

I open my eyes again and survey the night. Thinking about the future is too difficult, so I don't. I push aside tomorrow, and the next day, and the ones after that. Tonight is what's pressing. Where will I sleep?

There are homeless shelters in the city, wonderful ones that build people up when they've fallen down. I could go there. I should go there. But I can't move. My legs melt to jelly when I stand and I have to grab on to the railing before they betray me completely. Suddenly I'm exhausted. I'm so, so tired and afraid. Every ounce of energy has been zapped from my body, filtered out by an ominous sieve, and the idea of walking anywhere, even a few blocks, seems akin to climbing Mount Everest. I just ... can't.

And so I slide back to the concrete steps, letting my thoughts escape once again to all the shows that have been played inside. Ryman Auditorium is happiness personified. It's the pot of gold at the end of the rainbow and the dream realized. It's part of the reason why so many tourists journey to Nashville and why so many artists crave the chance to call this city their own.

Maybe that's why I stay.

Maybe I'm craving something, too.

Maybe this is the only place that offers a pillar of support in the topsy-turvy universe.

I check my shoulder bag to see what's inside: my phone, an old weathered copy of Jane Austen's *Pride and Prejudice*, a bottle of hand sanitizer, a green ballpoint pen, four sticks of chewing gum, my songwriting journal, a flash drive, a neatly folded purple cardigan, and my wallet, heavy from all the loose change. That's it.

I am numb.

No more tears. No more running.

Not tonight.

I settle the bag under my head, scrunch up on the step, and pray for sleep to find me.

OPEN HEARTS SHELTER

ABOUT US:

Eighteen years ago, the first family walked through our doors. Since then, thousands more have walked back out to a new future. Under the loving guidance of director Abigail Birnbaum, we offer a comprehensive and individually-tailored program that addresses both the immediate and long-term ramifications of homelessness. Our residents have access to board-certified clinical supervisors and job counselors. Staff and volunteers are available daily to assist in group and singular sessions. We strive to help anybody in Nashville who has fallen on hard times, because it's our fervent belief that what tumbles down can also be built up again. No need is too great and no need is too small. This is the philosophy our shelter was founded upon, and it extends to all of our transitional programs. We believe in the spirit of our community, both inside and outside the shelter walls, and in the power of healing from the past, taking charge of the present, and infusing hope into the future. Individuals or families, children or adults, victims of domestic and emotional abuse or twists of circumstantial fate, our doors are open to all. Our hearts are open to all.

OUR MISSION:

To compassionately address the pressing and continuing needs of homeless individuals, couples, and families by providing a safe shelter, basic necessities, educational and community outreach, and varied opportunities to once again achieve empowered, successful self-sufficiency.

"You can do it. We can help."
– Abigail Birnbaum, Founder and Executive Director

2

When I awaken to the pale cadet-blue shades of dawn, I'm greeted by a painful crick in my neck, an itchy red bug bite on my ankle, and a disturbing silence in my head. Horns honk and trash trucks rumble in the distance as Nashville shines its light on a new day, but for me, there's nothing. Where are the lyrics? I slowly raise myself into a sitting position, stretching muscles that whine back at me in protest after six hours of being curled into a tight ball, and listen again. Maybe I just need to clear the cobwebs. That's kind of what my brain feels like right now, all dusty and moldy and shrouded in the shadows of what used to be. Surely the words are still there, hiding behind the corners, waiting to be let out.

I sit motionless, the breeze kissing my chapped cheeks, and will the words to play, like they do every other morning. To play faster than my hands can keep up, faster than my pen's ink can splash onto the page, faster than I can even make sense of them. This is how I start each day: with lyrics to one of my songs humming in my head. Sometimes it's only a fragment. Other times it's a verse, chorus, or bridge.

Where *are* they?

I pull out my journal, hoping it will prompt those cobwebs to clear, and flip to a blank page. My fingers curl around a pen, acting almost on their own after so many years of this same routine, and I urge my brain to follow suit. More silence. More confusion. More frustration. "This is so not what I need today," I murmur, and make a futile attempt at forcing myself to write anyway. Ten minutes later, with the world's worst lyrics taunting me, I stop. If you ask some writers, they'll say it's best to work through the block. If you ask others, we'll say the opposite. Sometimes it's more beneficial to take a step back, even when – and, perhaps, especially when – we don't want to.

I stand up, give the Ryman a long look, and head off down the sidewalk in the direction of one of the city's shelters. As I pass a coffee shop, it occurs to me: if the shelter doesn't take me in, how am I going to eat? The small amount of money in my wallet won't last too long. Maybe I can find a café that donates their leftover food at the end of each day. Maybe I can go to Robert's house and ask if Kristina has her half of last month's rent, which I spotted her for since she didn't have it at the time. I pull out my phone and send her a quick text about it. Not even a minute later, her response pings back: *Sorry, I'm using it to buy new dishes for the house. Gotta bring my personality into it now that I'm living here, too. Robert's kitchen is in desperate need of a female touch!* As I read her message, a sense of betrayal settles over me. I get that she's giddy about starting this new chapter, but you'd think our three years of being roommates would count for something. Hasn't it occurred to her that she's left me high and dry?

The thought makes me cringe.

It also makes my eyes well up, and try as I might to blink back the curtain of saltwater, it finds its way out just the same. The further I walk, the more upset I get, and by the time I reach the shelter I am full-on bawling. I see this place sometimes when I'm out and about in the city, and it seems like my refuge now. But I can't go in there like this. It's humiliating. I spin on my heel, round the side of the brick building, and duck my head to conceal the rivers gushing down my face. *Breathe*, I remind myself. *Pull it together. There are people worse off than you. There are people who don't make it to a shelter, who huddle in alleys and sleep on the sidewalk vents. There are people who struggle with homelessness for weeks, months, years. You simply don't get to feel sorry for yourself after a single night.*

"Hey." A voice breaks into my thoughts. It's lilting, instrumental, lyrical.

I swat at my tears before meeting the gaze of the person staring in my direction. She looks to be my age, perhaps a year or two older, and she's standing just inside the fence that encircles the back of the shelter, her arms folded atop its slats. Something about her gives me pause. "Hi," I answer in return.

"You seem like you could use someone to talk to," she says.

"Oh, no, thanks, I'm fine."

She raises an eyebrow, but doesn't contest my comment. "I'm Serena," she says instead. "And I don't normally strike up conversations with strangers, for the record, but I heard you crying and I'm sorry about ... well, whatever has you upset."

"Eden," I say, and then, for some inexplicable reason, I blurt out the entire story. It tumbles free in a waterfall of hiccups and anxiety, reminding me of a psychology class I took in my freshman year of college. My teacher presented us with a case study explaining why it's often easier for people to spill secrets to those they don't know, rather than those they do. I wasn't sure about it at the time, but now I see his point. Telling Grandmom about the fire feels impossible. Telling Serena?

I can handle that.

"Wow," she says quietly when I'm finished. "That's ... it's terrible."

I nod, sliding my thumb below my eyelashes to flatten the remaining tears.

"Is that why you're here?" She motions to the building behind her. "Do you want to come in? I can introduce you to the director. "

"I thought so, but ... " I readjust my bag over my shoulder. Kind as Serena is, her mere presence is making my nerves bristle. Why does she look so calm? Doesn't she feel trapped by the walls that confine her, the stigma that defines her? She unhooks a latch on the fence and walks out to join me on the sidewalk. Her clothes are big and baggy – gray yoga pants and an amber t-shirt that reflects the color of her eyes – and even though it sort of seems like she's hiding behind them, there's also a gentleness to her mannerisms, an acceptance.

"I know how it feels," she says. "To be trapped by your lack of choices. To be frozen in place by the unfairness of it all." Her fingers twist the gold band around her ring finger. "I've been here for a month, and I'm used to it now, but the first day I stood there for hours." She gestures to the bakery across the road. "Under that awning, as it rained and rained. It took a lot to get me here, but I just didn't realize until then that the last step is the hardest. I couldn't bring myself to go in."

"What changed?"

Her shoulders pop up, then down. "I don't think I can pinpoint it. I knew it was something I had to do, so I did."

She makes it seem so simple.

Too simple.

But simple sounds nice. It sounds like a relief, actually, and it isn't as though I have a plethora of other options. "Okay," I say. "Lead the way."

She takes me through the front door, instead of the back courtyard where she'd been standing and looking at the outside world, and I clutch onto the straps of my bag so tightly my knuckles turn white. This bag is my lifeline. So frequently, the homeless are lumped together as a group, like their only important quality is what they don't have instead of what they do, and within a minute of being inside the shelter, I can see how vital it is to have something unique to hold on to. I hope everybody here has that. Because yes, our roofs might've cracked over our heads, and our rugs might've been yanked out from beneath our feet, but that doesn't mean we're unworthy. It doesn't mean we have uniformly done anything wrong.

Each person is different.

Each person has their special something.

Each person has a reason to tie a knot when they come to the end of their rope.

At least, that's what I'm telling myself.

I sneak a couple surreptitious glances at the shelter's lobby as Serena ushers me along. The light is bright and warm, accented by a pair of stained glass lamps, and the carpeting is shaded in a pretty forest green. Rocking chairs are arranged in groups of four and the walls are decorated with framed pictures and letters. "Success stories," Serena explains, as we stop by an office door and she knocks lightly on it.

"Come in," a woman's voice calls.

I inch the door open, and the middle-aged lady sitting at the desk offers me a warm smile. She introduces herself as Abigail Birnbaum and gestures for me to take a seat, which I do, half in a daze. Ms. Birnbaum asks all kinds of questions, about the fire and insurance and annual income, and I try to clear the fog infiltrating my mind. But as she starts to spout a steady stream of information, this time about empty beds and training programs and a five month deadline for staying at the shelter, it just feels impossible to focus. Her words dart by, their arrows dangerous, like if I reach out and grab one, I'll get a puncture wound.

"I'm sorry," I say. "I'm grateful you're willing to take me in. I'm just overwhelmed. One second everything was there, and the next it was gone. It all happened so fast."

She nods slightly. "I lost my house to a flood when I was a child," she tells me. "It was similar to the way you describe. The water rose quickly and we had to be rescued by a boat. All we could take with us was what we could carry, and my parents were adamant that we each pick what meant the most to us. That's what I try to do here at Open Hearts. The goal is to provide everyone with what means the most during their rough patch."

"Is that why you opened the shelter?" I ask. "Since you know what it's like?"

"Yes." She leans back in her chair. "We stayed in a shelter for two months while we rebuilt. I'll never forget it. There was good, there was bad ... " She trails off and clears her throat. "Anyway, it inspired me to pay it forward and to hopefully make some positive changes along the way."

"Thank you." When I speak again, my voice is soft. "Thank you for letting me stay."

"Of course." She hands me a pile of paperwork, which I fill out, then she stands and motions for me to follow.

A ball of apprehension bounces in my stomach as we go through the lobby, by a dining area, up the stairs, past a library, and into a room with two dozen beds. It's a short walk, but we pass quite a few people. There are the girls with rosy cheeks, playing pick-up-sticks with drinking straws, and the toddler boy, clad in a sweatshirt and sweatpants, even though it's July. There's the woman pacing in the library, studying a thick math book, and the man sitting on a bed, arms linked around his knees, staring dully at the wall. But also, there is an elderly woman who sleeps peacefully, like it might be possible to finally relax, and a teenager who drums on a tabletop with tree branches, resourceful in her attempt to create music. There are the women in the dining room, setting up for breakfast, and the kind volunteer who shows me to a bed. The day's just started, but all I want is to fall into it and rest my weary head.

Twelve hours ago, I was in the middle of the crowded Bluebird, listening to a singing-songwriting duo who traveled from Albuquerque to grace the famous grounds. I was happy. And now? I'm in a homeless shelter. In this oversized bedroom with curtains on the windows and rows of paintings on the walls, with bunks on one side and singles on the other, with courageous spirit and zero privacy. I don't know whether to laugh or cry. Maybe both.

"Eden." Serena looks up from the sketchpad she's drawing on and waves me over. I drop onto the free bed next to hers, suddenly too drained to move any farther.

"How do you manage?" I ask her. "How can you sleep here? How can you live here?" *How can you thrive here? How can you survive here?* Sometimes the unasked questions are the ones that eat away at us most.

"It's a learning curve," she acknowledges. "Give it time. Be patient with yourself."

"I'll try."

She must hear the doubt in my voice. "I manage because I have to," she tells me, "because once I made the decision to come here, there was no turning back." She keeps chatting, sharing tidbits of information about mealtime ("They always have two options, regular and vegetarian."), job training ("There are counselors to help us prepare for interviews."), the courtyard ("The fountain out there is so calming."), and service projects ("Ms. Birnbaum believes in doing good for others, even if we feel like the world isn't doing the same for us."). I make every attempt to keep up, but my concentration is a nomad today and my eyes wander toward the shelf above her bed.

"Is that your family?" I ask, and she answers without even turning to look at the picture of four people, all with platinum blonde hair. Their arms are linked around one another, their mouths wide with dimpled grins.

"My parents, twin sister, and me," she says. "During happier days."

She doesn't offer anything more, so I don't push the issue. It's weird, though. I feel this kinship with her, and I have no clue why. It reminds me of the way Kayleigh and I used to be.

"I hope things get better for you," I say, and she nods.

"Me too," she answers. "I hope things get better for all of us."

She goes back to her sketchpad then and I shift my focus to the bag resting by my side. Maybe I'll give the lyrics another go. I've been working on this song for three weeks now and only have the chorus left to write. My college classmates always chuckled at my process, how I flit between verse and bridge, words and melody, but it's what works best for me and I've learned to embrace it. I am not a chronological type of person. I go where the chords take me and let them lead the way. Most of the time, it's an awe-inspiring experience. To create something from nothing, to give breath to all my innermost dreams, is my absolute favorite part of being a songwriter. It's a gift, a passion, a joy unlike any other.

Except for when it's not.

I listen carefully, straining to hear the chord that'll start off the chorus, and am just beginning to make out its faint edges when a crash comes from across the room, followed by high-pitched giggles from the little boy who knocked over his tower of blocks. I try again. This time, a baby's wail breaks into my thoughts. And so it goes, over and over. I must scribble down ten different choruses before scratching them out and shoving the journal away. If I thought I had trouble earlier, it doesn't come close to the brick wall now. I can't lose myself in the music with so many people around me. I can't hear my voice with others drowning it out.

A swell of fear rises in me. Suppose it's always this way?

I'm terrified the shelter is going to swallow me up.

I train my eyes on the water-stained ceiling. How is everyone else? Walter, Cindy, Evan, Leslie? Did they go with that woman from the Red Cross? Are they staying with friends? It's odd to think of them out there, separated and alone. Diaspora. We learned about that in my twelfth grade history class. A scattered population that shares a common origin. That's what the residents of Cedarwood Apartments have become. And what about the residents of Open Hearts? Where did they all come from? What are their stories? I want to know, but I also don't.

I swivel my head toward the window. I can see the fountain from here, with its crystalline water splashing down in nearly perfect arcs. It seems out of place, too pretty for somewhere like this, but I like it despite that, maybe even because of it.

Since I feel out of place, too.

Eden Abraham

310 Peabody Street • Nashville, TN 37210 • 603-555-1018

edenmabraham@gmail.com

OBJECTIVE: To obtain a position in songwriting.

EDUCATION:

Belmont University Nashville, Tennessee
MM in Commercial Music **GPA: 3.925**
Graduated May 2013

Berklee College of Music Boston, Massachusetts
BA in Songwriting **GPA: 3.902**
Graduated May 2007

EXPERIENCE:

Cedarwood Apartments Nashville, Tennessee

<u>Executive Assistant</u>: Roles include acting as liaison between the landlord and his tenants; fielding inquiries in person, over the phone, and via email; overseeing database management; filing rent checks; and providing receipts. *April 2011 – July 2014*

Belmont University Songwriters' Association Nashville, Tennessee

<u>Vice President</u>: Roles include networking with industry officials, including those in the Nashville Songwriters' Association; arranging on-campus showcases and pitch meetings; and hosting renowned songwriters for a continuing Q&A series. *September 2012 – May 2013*

We've Got the Beat Nashville, Tennessee

<u>Apprentice</u>: Roles include meeting with local performers to brainstorm ideas for future songs; drafting lyrics and melodies for commissioned work; and initiating correspondence with both record labels and music publishing companies. *January – May 2013*

Chords of Love Boston, Massachusetts

<u>Volunteer</u>: Roles include leading an afterschool music program for students ages five through eleven; preparing the students to perform at an area nursing home; and assisting in the creation of weekly "learn and play" sessions for residents at the home interested in exploring a variety of musical instruments. *January 2005 – May 2007*

HONORS & AWARDS:

Member of the music honor society Pi Kappa Lambda
Graduated with Summa Cum Laude and Dept. honors

REFERENCES:

Ms. Jenny Cahill, Founder and Songwriter, We've Got The Beat / 615-555-1234

Mr. Norman Jenkinson, Landlord, Cedarwood Apartments / 615-555-8612

Mrs. Lisa Worthington, Volunteer Coordinator, Chords of Love / 617-555-0913

3

How many times are we taught about charity? How many times do we read a news story about a local food drive, or donate money when Mother Nature asserts her strength in catastrophic ways, or run races to raise funds for medical research? Giving to others is an omnipresent part of society. It's consistently vital and vitally consistent. Grandmom has a mantra – "It's lovely to do well, but it's even better to do good." – that she instilled in me from a young age, so I've done my fair share over the years. I've always felt hopeful about it, like what I was doing made a real impact.

But what sort of impact? Did I ever stop to consider how it felt on the other side? Actually, was that even a possibility? How can you walk a mile in someone else's shoes if they don't fit your feet? These are the things I think about now. Each day at the shelter, or maybe it's less than that, maybe it's each hour, or each minute, skews my perspective. I see things I never would have imagined, not because I was close-minded, but just because this wasn't my world.

Now, a week after arriving at Open Hearts, it is.

"Want company?" Before I can respond, Serena sits down across from me at one of the circular tables in the dining room. She does this every morning, a persistent friendly face among the others that still remain a mystery, and though the last thing I feel like doing is making conversation, I decide to give it a try anyway. Maybe Serena could use a friendly face, too.

I offer a tentative smile. "Sure," I say.

"Great," she says, stirring berries and brown sugar into her oatmeal. "So ... how are you holding up?" It's a simple question, but the answer still eludes me.

"I'm tired," I tell her, after thinking about it for a minute. It seems like the best reply. Physically, emotionally, and mentally, I feel like the energy is slowly being syphoned out of me. "I can't believe I've been here a week already. It's been the longest week of my life, and the next one will probably be even worse."

"Only if you let it be."

"I don't get it." I regard her quizzically. "How are you so blasé about this?"

"I'm not." She spoons the oatmeal into her mouth. "I'm thankful. Is this the Four Seasons? No. It beats the alternative, though. I'm safe here. I don't have to walk on eggshells." She fidgets with the sleeve of her olive green t-shirt. "I don't have to be anybody but me."

We couldn't be more different. While she works to bring her true colors back out, I'm just trying not to let mine fade away.

"No one knows I'm here," I confess after a measured pause.

"Ditto." She sips from her mug of coffee. "I need to work on myself before I let anyone in again. For the time being, the anonymity is soothing. What about you? Why haven't you told your family about the fire?"

An image of Grandmom floats into my head, complete with the wedding ring she still wears and the hair combs she uses on her silver-streaked locks, and something hot stings behind my eyes. "It's just me and my grandmom," I tell Serena, deciding to take a chance and open up a bit. "She's raised me since I was four. My mom and dad work for an international children's charity – it's called Hands of Hope, maybe you've heard of it? They're overseas nine months a year."

"That must be hard," she says, and I nod, because it is.

"I mean, I know they do a lot," I say. "And I know it's for deserving people and worthy causes. It isn't like I'm begrudging them that. I'm proud, actually. But when everybody in my Girl Scout troop had a parent there for our promotion ceremony ... and when I won a gold medal in my eighth grade gymnastics meet ... and when I graduated college ... it killed me that they weren't there."

"Not even for your college graduation?" She sounds incredulous.

"Well, to be fair, they were trying to make that one," I allow. "But they missed their connecting flight home and got stuck in London." The memory springs to mind, never far from the surface. "I'd told all my friends they were going to be there, and the thing is, I truly believed it. Even though they had let me down over and over, I knew that time would be different."

She winces. "And then it wasn't."

"No," I echo hollowly, "it wasn't. Grandmom did everything in her power to make up for it. She *always* does everything in her power to make up for them. That's why I can't tell her about the fire. She's in an assisted living facility, so I wouldn't be allowed to live there with her long-term. Plus, all her savings pretty much go toward that. She can't afford to send me rent money every month, and the last thing I want is for her to feel helpless." That burning sensation returns to my retinas. I talk to Grandmom almost every day, and she'd be so upset if she knew the lies my calls have held lately. But I have to do this. I have to protect her like she's done for me. Because I know how helplessness can worm its way into your bloodstream, and if I'm sure of anything anymore, it's that I never want her, my sweet grandmom who ends our conversations with 'love you more,' to experience that kind of vulnerability. Better me than her.

"What about your parents?" Serena asks. "Obviously they aren't – "

"No." I cut her off before she can say it.

"Okay." Something unreadable passes over her china-doll features. "Well, I better get going. It was nice talking with you. See you around?"

"See you around," I parrot. I've been doing a lot of that the past week: a lot of seeing, of looking and observing. I scout out empty tables during mealtime so I don't have to join the groups of people eating hungrily, I hang back when a volunteer brings in clothing donations and let others pick first, I go outside to the courtyard and stare at all the pennies in the fountain. They're stuck there, tossed aside and left to tarnish.

Grandmom was wrong. There isn't magic everywhere.

The one exception to my attempts at blending into the background?

Job training.

Grateful as I am for the shelter, and to Ms. Birnbaum for welcoming me in, I'm desperate to get out of Open Hearts as soon as possible. I'm anxious to take my life back, to remind myself of who I am and who I want to be. If these sessions with a career counselor will help, then I am all for it. So far we've learned about creating a budget, "dressing for success," and sprucing up our resumés – all things I've had practice in already, but I gladly sit in the community room with the others and write down notes on the legal pad the counselor handed out. Today we're holding mock interviews, first with each other and then with Jillian, the counselor. I'm looking forward to it, especially since I have an actual interview tomorrow at the Country Music Hall of Fame.

"Interviews have never been my strong suit," I tell Serena as we pair up for the exercise. "They make me so nervous. I feel like I can't express myself properly."

She nods her agreement. "I need some help with them, too. I've spent so long letting someone else dictate my feelings that – " She breaks off, shakes her head abruptly. "Anyway," she says, "let's get started. Do you want to go first, or should I?"

"You can."

We spend the next hour interviewing one another for a variety of jobs, everything from clerical work to positions in the music industry, and by the time I'm sitting across from Jillian, answering her questions about my strengths and weaknesses, I actually feel like I might be able to do this for real. Like I might be able to get a new job, despite having nearly nothing to my name. Like I might be able to overcome this ball of messy emotions rolling around inside me, and turn the sadness, the despair, the fear, into something good.

Something hopeful.

When the session is over, I go outside to the courtyard, shuffle through my bag – it never leaves my side these days – and pull out a penny.

Make a wish.

I used to do this all the time. Portsmouth has a handful of fountains around town and whenever Grandmom and I would be out and about, my little fingers tucked tightly into hers, she'd stop by one and ask if I wanted to throw in a coin. "It's good luck," she said. "Give it a try, Jellybean." So I did. I pinched my eyes closed, rubbed the penny between my palms until they smelled metallic, and wished with all my soul.

It's been a long time since I've left my fortune up to fate.

It's been a long time since I've believed in luck.

I flip the penny back and forth, running my nail along its edge, thinking about what Serena said about my parents and contemplating sending Lincoln to join all his friends. But I don't. Instead I slip the coin back inside, tuck it safely away. I need to save every cent now, and besides, I don't believe my wish would come true any more than I believe my parents would fly to my rescue if I let them in on the recent developments in my life. It's better to keep them in the dark. Better to let myself at least hope they might help than to reach out, only to get my faith crushed.

Better to take no risk than to let a risk defeat me.

I sigh and replace the penny with my journal.

Let's try this again.

* * *

When Kayleigh and I were in fourth grade, we dreamed up this plan called Sleepover Saturdays. She lived down the block from Grandmom's waterfront cottage, and each weekend, we'd take turns spending the night at one another's house. We'd watch movies, make popcorn, polish our nails, and zip through a stack of board games. My favorite part was our clothing swap, though. Whoever was visiting would bring a shirt, or headband, or whatever, and exchange it for something in the other's closet. Then we'd wear the items to school on Monday. I think of those days while I get dressed the next morning, the fabric of my dress foreign against my shoulders and the heels on my shoes making my legs wobble. *My* dress. *My* shoes. It seems strange to label them like that, and unsettling, too, because this is the first time I've ever worn these clothes in my life.

Who did they belong to before? Whose closet did they reside in? Did the previous owner wear them for a job interview, like I am? Did they come from the same person, or are they from separate lives? The notion prickles the hair at the back of my neck. We don't consider these things when we have a normal home, a normal agenda, a normal existence. Now I can't help dwelling on them. It's sorta cool, I suppose, to picture my outfit as a puzzle, each piece fitting together in the most unlikely way. But it's also demoralizing.

"You look fabulous," the woman next to me says as I brush the waves in my hair and pull it back with a clip.

I manage a smile. "Thank you."

Her name's Ruby, and she reminds me a lot of Grandmom, with the lines around her eyes and a beauty mark on her cheek, which is probably why I'm drawn to her. With most everyone else here, I shy away from conversation. With Ruby, I welcome it.

"I'm hoping to find a job today," I tell her.

"How many interviews do you have lined up?"

"Only one, but I'm going to take my resumé other places, too. Someone has to be hiring, right?"

Ha. Ha. Ha. Naiveté, thy name is Eden.

My interview at the Country Music Hall of Fame isn't until eleven o'clock, so after picking up my last paycheck from my old boss and landlord, I spend a couple hours popping into every restaurant, store, and music venue I can find. For six years now, I've been applying for each music-related job I come across, but at this point, I don't care where I work. I'll do whatever it takes to put money back in my bank account. I just need someone to take a chance on me.

"We'll call you," the manager at a café on Twelfth Avenue says.

"I'll be in touch," the manager of a souvenir shop on Demonbruen says.

"I can put you on a waiting list," the manager at a club on Broadway says.

Empty words? It's hard to tell.

The shelter has computers in the library room, and I was up late last night, tweaking my resumé according to the feedback from Jillian and printing multiple copies. I hand them out now, trying to gauge the expressions on people's faces as they skim my contact information. Do they know that the address belongs to a homeless shelter? It isn't like there are any other residential places on that street. Do I detect a slight purse of the lips, a quick raising of eyebrows, or is it only my imagination? I ponder that as I push open the door of a record shop and emerge into the warm sunshine. Are the reactions an indisputable perception of homelessness, or simply a reflection of my own insecurities? And if so, suppose they carry over into my interview?

I only have this interview thanks to Ms. Birnbaum. Her brother-in-law works at the Hall of Fame, and she was able to pull some strings to get me in. It pained me to accept. I detest the idea of being given a job instead of earning it on my own merits. Every time Kayleigh talks about her company, an impressive, high-powered business firm that has its offices in a forty-five floor skyscraper, I mentally cringe. Kayleigh got her associate position thanks to a perfect GPA, leadership roles in her college's business sorority, and her sixth sense for the industry. But some of her colleagues? Let's just say it's not always what you know, but whom.

Never have I used a connection to get ahead. Never have I accepted charity.

Funny how things change when we're up against the wall.

Funny how our pride is forced to take a backseat.

Grandmom calls right as I walk up to the building designed to look like a towering piano. I stare at the phone for a second, gnawing my bottom lip until I feel a sheen of sticky lip gloss on my teeth, and contemplate what to do. Never have I ignored her call, not even when she rang as I was walking out the door for a date with the cutest guy in my Recording Technology course. His name was Jared, he had a smile that made me go weak in the knees, and our date turned out to be the precursor to a year-long relationship. I was over the moon when he asked me out, I had excited nerves bubbling in my stomach, yet I still took a minute to talk to Grandmom first.

Accept or reject? I eye the options on my phone.

And then I hit the red button.

I can't do this now. I can't tell Grandmom about the interview, because then she'll want to hear the details, and that would mean either 'fessing up or outright lying to her. So far, they've been lies of omission, and those have been guilt-inducing enough. Actually twisting the truth to deceive her? I just can't.

"You'll call her later," I tell myself. "Everything will be fine."

I silence the phone and head inside.

"Ms. Abraham." A man greets me in the lobby, his hand extended for a shake. "I'm Bill. Nice to meet you. Abigail said you'd be a wonderful addition to our staff."

"She did?" *Idiot. Way to put your foot in your mouth.* "I mean, how kind of her. I've lived here for six years and have always loved visiting the Hall of Fame. It would be an honor to join your team. Country music is in my heart. I was born up in New Hampshire, but my ex-boyfriend used to say I'm a southerner in spirit." *Ex-boyfriend. Brilliant move. Now he'll wonder why you split. Quick, fix this before it's too late.*

But Bill doesn't seem bothered. "Southerner in spirit, that's what I like to hear." He motions for me to follow him back to his office. "So tell me," he says, once we are seated, "what experience do you have in marketing?"

Um, none. Zero. Zilch. Nada.

"I ... well ... the thing is ... " I take a long breath and try again. "I haven't had a chance to explore marketing in too much detail yet, because I've been so focused on songwriting. I know there's not a huge overlap between the two fields, but I really feel like they could work in tandem if ... " I fumble for words as an image comes into my mind: the recent pages in my journal, riddled with cross-outs. Just thinking about it makes my brain hurt. My heart hurt.

Where is my muse? Did it go up in flames when my apartment did?

For what feels like the millionth time lately, tears blur my vision. This time, though, I blink them away. I push aside the image, refusing to let it haunt me, and look straight into Bill's eyes. "I really feel like they could work in tandem if given the proper channels," I continue. "For example, maybe you could use an artist's lyrics as part of a new promotional campaign."

I'm proud of myself for not giving in. For not giving up.

But it doesn't seem to matter. Because that image *does* still haunt me, even with all my efforts to block it out, and I fumble for words with almost every subsequent question. Bill keeps going with the interview, but I can tell I've bungled any chance at landing this job. It's depressing. Frustrating. I know I can do better. And so, when the interview's over and Bill thanks me for my time but adds in something about going with an applicant who has more experience, I'm not remotely surprised. The writing was on the wall, and I'm the one who scrawled it there.

I walk dejectedly back to the shelter and into the courtyard. What will I tell Ms. Birnbaum? She stuck her neck out for me, and I blew the opportunity.

Five months. I have five months to get myself out of this shelter before I'm forced to leave. And then I really *will* have no place else to go. This job could have been my ticket out, but not anymore. Not possible.

I plunk down on the fountain's ledge and bury my head in my

hands. Block it out. Block it all out.

"Dammit," I mutter under my breath, the word staccato, fierce, exasperated.

That's when I hear it, the munchkin voice next to me: "I wish I may, I wish I might, have the wish I wish tonight." A giggle. "I mean … today, not tonight."

I slowly peek over and see a curly-topped little boy, all of four or five years old.

And, immediately, I know. I know that something good can still come out of today. I know why I was meant to be at the shelter at this very moment. I know what comes next.

TOMMY AND SHERRI

The first time there was a round of layoffs at Mark's job, his bosses swore he was safe. The next time, they admitted it was looking precarious. The engineering firm was downsizing, cutting a third of its employees and consolidating responsibilities among the rest, and to say things were tense is a colossal understatement. With apt reason, too – because the third time around, Mark's job was on the chopping block.

The family tried to stay optimistic. Sherri had been a stay-at-home mom to Tommy, but since he was starting kindergarten the coming August, she could go back to work as a graphic designer. Mark would pound the pavement and find a position with another company. Except his firm wasn't alone in reducing its work force. Except the jobs Sherri interviewed for were given to younger candidates, fresh out of school and well-versed in the latest computer programs. Except … their life became one giant 'except.' When the bills piled up, they couldn't pay them. When the mortgage on their house became too much, they had to say goodbye to their home of six years. When Mark sank into a deep depression, he turned to alcohol as an escape. When his drinking threatened the very fabric of their family, Sherri issued an ultimatum: get help or get a divorce. Mark began in-patient counseling, and Sherri, with no other options and a little boy depending on her, moved to the shelter and started the lengthy process of rebuilding.

Some days she worries things will never get better. Some nights she cries herself to sleep. With Tommy tucked against her side, still too scared – or maybe just too sad – to stay in his own bed, rest is often hard to come by. But they muddle through. They find the positives when possible and trust that the negatives will, at some point, become a distant memory. Because really, what else can they do?

4

"I want a boat," the boy declares, and takes a penny from the woman standing next to him. She watches as he lets the copper disc fly. "One that's my size so I can play in the bathtub with it. When we get a house again, Mommy, will it have a tub, or will it just have a shower, like this place? I can't make a boat zoom in a shower."

She smiles wearily at her son. "I'll see what I can do, Tommy. But remember our motto, buddy, okay?"

"No promises; we just try our best." He recites it alongside her. Then, without warning, his face crumples, nose scrunching up and eyes narrowing to slits. "Oh no, I ruined it! I ruined the wish and now it won't come true."

She looks perplexed. "What do you mean? You didn't ruin anything."

"I did," he says woefully, bursting into tears. "It won't happen, 'cause I told you about it. That's what my friend Brendan says. We have to hold our wishes inside our mouths or somebody will steal them." His slender shoulders are shaking, hiccups popping from his body and streams flowing down his freckled cheeks, and I just want to give him a hug and assure him his boat will be safe and sound. But I can't do that. I can't offer comfort to this child who should be playing at a summer camp now, maybe swimming in the pool or paddling a boat in the lake with his counselor, and is instead living in a shelter. Why are they here? Is it just Tommy and his mother, or are there other kids and a father? Again, I think about the people who have found a haven at Open Hearts. I want to know what their heart-songs are.

I want to give those songs a voice.

I don't wait to hear how the woman reassures her son. Instead, I slip away and go inside. It's a busy time of day at the shelter, people congregating around tables for lunch, and for a moment, I'm struck by the normalcy of it all. The way a man scoops macaroni and cheese onto a plate, the way a father tucks napkins into his kids' shirts so they don't spill anything on the donated clothes, the way Serena drizzles dressing on her salad and Ruby accepts a cup of iced tea from one of the volunteers ... it's a scene you could see anywhere.

"Hey, how'd the interview go?" Serena catches my eye as I walk over to grab a handful of green napkins.

"I'd rather not talk about it." What else can I use to make that little boy a boat? I scan the area for items.

"Yikes." Sympathy fills her face. "Well, whatever happened, try not to worry. We tend to think the worst when it actually isn't that bad. I remember this one audition Seth and I went on last year, and we were positive we'd bombed it. Turns out we got the gig." Something about her tone makes me quit looking for boat-building materials and focus on her instead. There's a ghostly, eerie quality to her cadence.

"Who's Seth?"

Her fringe of bangs flutters as she shakes her head. "The reason I'm here." But that's it. It's like a steel cage snaps closed around her, preventing her from elaborating. "Don't sweat it, is what I'm saying. If you don't get that job, you'll find one someplace else instead."

If only I was as sure of that as her.

I'm not expecting my phone to ring anytime soon. I'm not expecting an easy fix for my life.

But Tommy's? I can tack a band-aid over his wounds.

Some modeling clay from the kids' playroom is all it takes to make his wish come true. I mold it deftly, easing the edges into a boat shape, and press my thumbs into the squishy dough until it feels solid and dry. Then I snip a plastic drinking straw in half, cut a napkin into triangles of different sizes, and attach one as a sail. It's no artistic masterpiece, but it should work. I add a name – SS Tommy – to the sail, and carry it outside.

The boy and his mother are still there, sitting on a bench now and reading one of the beaten-up books from the shelves inside, and I wait until they're finished, not wanting to interrupt. Honestly, I don't know how to go about doing this. I hope they don't think I'm overstepping. "Excuse me," I say quietly, and inch forward a few steps. "I couldn't help overhearing before – " That's as far as I get. Tommy glances up, notices the boat, and lets out a whoop of joy.

"Mommy, look!" he squeals. "She has a boat! And it's got a sail and everything! Can we buy it? I know we don't have lots of money, but I can give her all the quarters in my piggy bank."

"Oh no," I say hurriedly. "You don't have to pay me. I made this boat especially for you." I offer it to him and his jaw drops, like he can't possibly believe his good fortune. "You have to be careful," I add. "Clay breaks easily, but even if that happens, we can patch it up again."

"Thank you!" His happy yelp reverberates through the air. "Can we try it in the fountain, pretty please with a cherry on top?"

I look to his mother, who nods. "Of course," she says.

Tommy grabs my hand and practically drags me over. "This is the best day *ever*," he proclaims.

Forget the way I screwed up earlier. This compensates. This heals.

We must sit there for an hour, pushing the boat through the fountain, and the entire time, I feel Tommy's mother watching us. Warmth, relief, exhaustion, and mostly a reignited faith that there is good in the world after all, that there are pinpricks of light even amidst the darkness ... this is what I feel from her. "Thanks," she says, coming over to me after Tommy's lifted the boat out and carried it to the sunny patch by the maple tree for it to dry. "It was so sweet of you to do that for him. Your kindness is most appreciated."

"My pleasure. I'm glad I could help."

"I'm Sherri, by the way," she says. "And you did more than help. Tommy and I have been here for five weeks, and this is the first time I've seen him let go like that." She tells me a bit about their situation and almost chokes on her words. "I never thought it would come to this. Open Hearts has been great. They have a learning program Tommy loves and the job counselors are working with me so I can train for a position in HR. But still, I hate that Tommy doesn't have a house to grow up in. I hate that he's afraid to go to school in the fall because the children might tease him. Sometimes he plays with the kids here, and there's an acceptance you don't always find outside these walls, but it hurts to see how the light in his eyes has dimmed. You brought it back." Her voice quivers. "Today, he was happy. He was whole again."

I did that? Me?

I left a handprint?

Piece by piece, we arrange a different puzzle.

The lyric slams unexpectedly into my brain.

It has zero to do with the song I've been trying to work on, but that's okay. I can't forget it, can't ignore it, can't let its message disappear into the ether. I don't know yet if it will make it into a song, or even what the accompanying melody is, but still, I excuse myself to scribble the line across a new page in my journal. When I return to the conversation with Sherri, she thanks me again for "all I've done for Tommy."

I want to tell her that I didn't do anything at all, not really.

I want to tell her that it brought me as much delight as Tommy.

I want to tell her that it was so nice, so refreshing, to share in something good. This shelter has a different aura. People's smiles don't reach their eyes here. There's faith, but also concern. Hope, but also defeatism. Diligence, but also uncertainty. There's pain and sadness and despair.

Why not erase it, even if only for an hour?

So many pennies in the fountain.

So many wishes made.

Why not turn them into reality?

The idea implants itself into my thoughts, a seed begging for enough water to make it grow. It's there as I eat a late lunch, as I creep past Ms. Birnbaum's door on my way out of the shelter, and as I go to Cumberland Park and walk along the Explorer Trail. It's one of my favorite places in the entire city. The stone path is speckled through a seemingly endless meadow, and butterflies glide through the air, wings fluttering as they perch on flowers. I come here to write sometimes. Today, though, I keep on moving. Sitting still doesn't work for me anymore. It means too much time inside my head. To the contrary, putting one foot in front of the other means I get to set the pace ... or at least keep up with it.

I can do that.

What I can't do is answer the phone when Kayleigh calls.

I gaze at the picture lighting up the screen, the two of us in another lifetime. It was seven years ago, the summer after we graduated college. Kayleigh was home from Carnegie Mellon for only two weeks before she moved to New York for work. Maybe we'd started drifting apart prior to that, but this is when the rift really cracked open. She was leaving Portsmouth; I was staying. She was buying suits and stilettos; I was wearing long, flowy skirts and patterned scarves. She was looking ahead to marriage and children; I was still content to live with Grandmom.

"Promise you'll visit," she said, the day before she left. We were hanging out by the Piscataqua River, watching boats chug by as we sat on the harbor deck. I can't even count how many times we had done that since childhood. But this was different. This had a sense of finality that neither of us wanted to acknowledge.

"Sure," I said. "And you promise you'll come back sometimes, too."

"It's a deal," she answered, but I think we both knew it wasn't, not really. Kayleigh had a whole new life waiting for her, and ever since her parents had gotten divorced when we were sophomores in high school, there wasn't much to hold her in Portsmouth. It was a nasty split, and I'd wager any amount of money it was why she went to college so far away and why she instantly accepted the job offer in Manhattan. Once she was away, she wanted to stay away.

I miss her. I miss the way we used to be.

I wonder if she misses me, too, if that's why she's phoning. It's been months since we've talked and over a year since we've seen one another. She flew down for my graduation from Belmont and stayed in Nashville for an entire week. For awhile, it was almost like old times. I showed her all the touristy places: the Bluebird, Music Row, the Grand Ole Opry, and more. We took pictures by the honky-tonk music venues on Broadway and next to Reba's star on the Walk of Fame. Kayleigh even bought a pair of rhinestone-studded cowgirl boots. They were not remotely her style, which made it more fun. I smile as I think of the way she strutted down the sidewalk in them, heels clicking as the sun gleamed in her almond-shaped eyes and off her curtain of black hair. If I let myself forget about the rest of it, those seven days would be perfect.

Except I can't forget, and they weren't perfect. Because although my parents actually managed to attend this graduation, they spent half the ceremony checking their phones and discreetly texting back and forth with one of their colleagues in Cambodia. And though they took me out for dinner to celebrate, though they hugged me and said how proud they were, it was more a lesson in formality than affection. Maybe I was asking for too much. Maybe I just should've been grateful they'd come at all.

The tinkling of my voicemail alert snaps me out of my thoughts and I plop down on the dry grass to listen to the message. "Hi, it's me," her voice says. "I hate to do this over voicemail, but I'll be in meetings for the rest of the day and I'm leaving for a three-week business trip to London tomorrow. Otherwise I'd wait until we could chat properly." She sounds giddy. Euphoric. "Okay, so it's official: Gary and I are getting married! He popped the question this morning, up on the roof of our building as the sun rose over the city, and oh my gosh, Eden, it was the most romantic thing. We already set a date: Valentine's Day of next year. I know it's soon, and we're being kinda cliché with the day, but we want to hurry up and tie the knot so we can finally be husband and wife. I was hoping you'd be a bridesmaid in the wedding. I know things have been … " A pause. " … strained between us lately, but I really want you to be there. Please? Think about it, alright?"

The message clicks off then, and I sit there, staring at the phone in shock.

I don't know why this comes as a surprise. I knew she and Gary were serious. I knew they were planning to get married. I know they'll have a picture-perfect wedding, like something you'd see on television. I know they'll raise a beautiful family and send the type of holiday cards that would make even the most zealous Pinterest enthusiast jealous. It's who they are, who Kayleigh's become, who they turned into together.

"Congratulations, Kay," I say softly, and glance at the phone one more time before sliding it into my bag. Part of me wishes the shelter didn't have a box full of chargers. It's in the community room – right next to the bowl with pennies, which is where the ones in the fountain originate from – and it is generous, of course, but here's the thing: if I had just let the battery die, I wouldn't have to worry about this. I wouldn't have to decide whether to accept the invitation. How could I afford it? Trips to New York, a bridesmaid dress, shower gifts and wedding presents ... there's no chance. How do I tell Kayleigh? *Hey, I know things have been awkward between us, but this should break the ice: my apartment burned to the ground and I'm living in a shelter, so I'll have to pass on being a bridesmaid because the little money left in my bank account has to go for necessities instead.*

Ugh.

And honestly, do I even *want* to be in her wedding?

I hope they have the most incredible day, I hope it's everything she dreams of and more, but do I have a place in it? Our bond is a shell of its former self. Somehow we've lost each other along the way. She is sweet to reach out, and maybe she's trying to close the gap, but can something that has been broken down brick by brick, not in one crushing fell swoop, ever be fully pieced back together?

As always, I turn to Grandmom for advice.

I return her call from earlier as I head back to the shelter and take solace in the comfort only she is able to provide. "It depends, honey," she says, "on how much you want it. If you're willing to put in time and effort, then yes, I believe any hole is reparable."

"Or maybe this is when I respect our friendship enough to let it go." Saying it makes me sad. "It won't be the same, it can't be."

"You'll never know unless you try." It's her favorite phrase.

She's been reminding me of it for as long as I can remember. The Zoobilee Zoo puzzle I didn't think I could tackle as a five-year-old? The AP English class I was intimidated by in high school? The move to Nashville, this city of opportunity I saw as the answer to my prayers? Whenever I was hesitant, Grandmom gave me a gentle push. "So tell me," she says, "what's new with my favorite girl?"

"We just talked yesterday." I let myself laugh a bit. "Life isn't always exciting here, you know."

Another lie of omission. Another stab of guilt.

"Well, things *have* been exciting here," she says. "Margaret made the biggest sale of the year so far: five dresses, a shawl, seven pairs of slacks, and an afghan, all to the same customer!" Even from a thousand miles away, I can see her glow. It's the same one she gets whenever she talks about her store. She opened it not long after my grandfather died, something positive to channel her emotion into, and the boutique, Sew Stylish, has been in Portsmouth ever since. For years, it spotlighted her own creations, hand-sewn with love, and even now, after she's turned it over to a new manager to run because it simply became too much for her, she still knits some of the items.

"That's excellent!" I cheer. "Tell me more! Which afghan?" I try to keep her talking, try to keep the conversation centered around her and not me. It works. She relays stories about her shop, and the mahjong group she joined at the assisted living home, and the man she met there who takes her to the movies and dinner, and I just can't tell her my truth. It was a struggle to convince Grandmom to sell the cottage and move, even though she can sometimes use the helping hand these days, and she finally seems content. I'd hate myself for taking that away.

Long after we've hung up, I find that Grandmom's voice still echoes.

You'll never know unless you try.

Piece by piece, we arrange a different puzzle.

I haven't been able to write any more since those lyrics, but they're a start. The music is inching its way back. The inspiration is peeking out from behind a corner. I think of Grandmom, of Tommy, of Sherri. There's a common thread tying them together, this understanding that sometimes it's the little things which mean the most.

Maybe I can learn from that. Maybe I can learn from them.

Maybe, just maybe, all is not lost.

RUBY AND FRED

Nashville is in Ruby's blood. It's in her soul. The eighty-six-year-old has lived in Music City since she was a child and is head-over-heels for its charm. Her eyes light up as she talks about her college days at Vanderbilt, where she met Fred in one of her classes, and about her career at an elementary school nearby, where she taught fourth grade for thirty years before becoming the principal. This is her place in the world. So when Fred fell ill? When her husband's heart no longer ticked how it was supposed to? When the doctor recommended surgery? It didn't matter that the elderly couple had no family in the area, or that Ruby, who never learned to drive, would be hard-pressed to get to the hospital since Fred normally drove her where she needed to go. His doctor was in Nashville. This is where he'd get the best care. This is where they'd stay.

Before long, the bills began to add up. Ruby and Fred, who had taught in the same school as his wife, had been retired for seventeen years. Their income was small and their health insurance plan reflected that. As the costs rose, their savings plunged, and the couple found themselves faced with the worst decision: sell their home of sixty years or file for bankruptcy. In the end, they did neither. They moved into Open Hearts, praying for the day when Fred would be good as new and they would once again be able to afford the most basic commodities, things like electricity and heat and running water in their Victorian-style house.

Fred is in the hospital now, and Ruby dreams of the day they'll continue making new memories together. A cruise to the Caribbean. A Christmas spent in the Appalachian mountains. A chance to start their own children's charity. The stars Ruby's shooting for are far away, but she believes they'll reach them anyway.

❧ 5 ❧

For the first time since arriving at the shelter, I actually sleep fairly well that night. No noises jar me from my slumber, no aches spread across my back from the squishy mattress, and best of all, no nightmares torture my subconscious. It feels like a milestone. Like a miracle. Like an affirmation of my decision.

And so, when I wake up the following morning, I listen. I lie still, relaxing my mind, and hold my breath as I wait to see whether the melody will rise up again. But instead of a song, a memory flicks around in my thoughts: my first mentoring session through NSAI. I joined the Nashville Songwriters Association International when I moved here. With stars in my eyes and a song in my heart, I forked over the fee and considered it to be an investment in my future.

That first session ... let's just say it wasn't the grand success I'd hoped it would be. The producer I met with was kind and he framed his remarks with benevolence, but his evaluation of my song still whipped off my rose-colored glasses. I remember sitting in his office, staring at the framed painting behind his desk as my cheeks flushed fire-engine red and I willed myself not to cry. I had graduated with a degree in songwriting. I'd received praise from my professors, had been told I had real talent, had left everything I'd ever known and relocated to the music mecca. For what? To hear that eighty percent of my song didn't work?

I still have that song today. It's tucked into my journal, a reminder of how far I've come and how far I have to go. It wasn't bad, but the producer was right: it needed a lot of revision. I think it's the same with any sort of writing. You can go to school for it, you can study the intricacies and rhythms, you can practice and practice until you think you've achieved your personal best, but once you're in the real world it's a whole other ballgame. The frustrating thing, and also the incredible thing, about writing is that there's always room for improvement. We can always learn more, push more, grow more, explore more.

Except when a fire scorches the creativity and leaves behind a pile of smudgy, streaky soot.

Silence.

Again.

Still.

"Don't force it," I whisper, and heave myself out of bed. Breakfast will just be getting started in the dining room and if I don't hurry, I'll miss out on the scrambled eggs and home fries. I quickly get dressed, careful to avoid the mirror hanging between my bed and Ruby's. It still creeps me out a bit to see my reflection clad in clothes that once belonged to somebody else. It's like I've morphed into another person.

"Good morning," Ms. Birnbaum chirps as I walk into the dining room, and I answer hastily before ducking my head and speeding toward the drink table. It's rude and I know it – and I'm ashamed of myself for acting this way – but I can't bring myself to linger in her presence. She must've talked to her brother-in-law about my interview by now, and I'm so embarrassed to have a conversation with her about it.

"Grape juice?" A man smiles at me as I reach the table, offering the jug in his hand.

"Sure, thanks."

I'm about to pour it into a plastic cup when someone tugs the bottom of my shirt. "Miss Eden?" Tommy. Where did he come from? He's suddenly standing at my side, mouth covered in powdered sugar from French toast and the boat held to his chest. "Apple juice is yummier. You helped me out yesterday by giving me this boat, and I wanna help you, too."

Something bursts open inside my chest. "Thank you, little guy," I say, ruffling his hair. "I'll keep that in mind." He darts off to his table then, and I watch as he slides the boat around, stopping only to eat the circles of banana Sherri slices onto his dish. When I re-focus my attention on the drinks in front of me, I opt for the apple instead of grape. He's right. It's better. I add a bowl of berries to my tray and make my way to Serena. An empty table seems too lonely. Today, I'm going to sit with her. Today I'm going to try.

"Do you like country music?" I ask. It is, I realize, the most inane of questions, because probably ninety percent of the people living in Nashville are drawn to the twangy tunes, but it feels like a safe place to begin.

She laughs. "Is the Pope Catholic?"

"Who's your favorite singer?"

She twirls the band around her ring finger. She does this a lot, I've noticed. "Tough call. It used to be Garth Brooks, but I can't listen to his music now. It's too much of a reminder." She hesitates, and nervousness pokes at me. What am I supposed to do with that? Ask what it's a reminder of, or change the subject?

"A reminder of your family?" I guess, remembering the framed picture of them by her bed.

"Seth."

Seth. The reason she's here, that's how she described him.

She stops fidgeting with the ring and moves on to the sleeve of her shirt. It must be hers, all of her clothes must be, because there's a common denominator that sets them apart. They are baggy, earthy, dull. Camouflage. "Seth was my husband. Still is, actually. He was also my singing partner." So the ring is a wedding band. And the audition she mentioned to me yesterday was for ... what? A recording contract? A deal with one of the clubs in town? What's her definition of 'gig,' and why is she living in a shelter instead of with her husband?

"It must be fun to be part of a duo." Again, I opt for the route least riddled with risk.

"It was. We grew up together in Pennsylvania, just outside of Philadelphia. Seth is a year older, so we didn't have any classes together except band and chorus. That's when we really got to know each other."

"How did you end up in Nashville? It's a long way from Philadelphia."

Something desolate darkens the amber in her eyes for a moment, then it lightens. "Music was a passion for us," she says. "You know how a relationship can be super intense when it's formed over a common interest? Well, that's what happened with Seth and me. We fell in love over drumbeats and crescendos, and by the time we graduated, we knew we wanted to postpone college and focus on singing instead." She stares past me, seeing something no one else can. "We spent the summer in Seth's basement, putting our spin on every song imaginable. I played the guitar and he played the piano, and we'd literally stay there from sunup to sundown, practicing until our vocal chords felt like they were going to bleed."

"Wow. Talk about dedication."

"My parents were furious when I told them I wasn't going to college," Serena continues, on auto pilot now. "Our relationship hasn't been the same ever since then. Melanie – she's my twin sister – and I were both accepted to Princeton, and they didn't understand how I could give it up. They tried to reason with me, but I was certain I knew better." She clucks her tongue. "I was stupid."

"I wouldn't call that stupid. Determined, maybe."

Her hands tighten around her coffee mug until I'm sure it's going to shatter into a million shards. "I was reckless," she says. "Strong-headed and strong-willed." Her gaze slinks downwards. "I used to think it was my fault. That I deserved it. That I'd dealt my cards and had to live with the way they fell."

I don't want to ask what she means by that.

Because as she bends to pick up the napkin she accidentally knocked off the table, the sleeve of her oversized shirt slips a bit, exposing her left shoulder. An angry scar glares up from her skin, ugly and jagged and red. It is a singed lightning bolt, a brutal battle wound.

The reason she's here.

Oh my God. Did Seth do that to her?

She straightens in her chair and the sleeve falls back into place, and I'm trying to figure out what to do, what to say and what *not* to say, when she catches sight of my face. "You're pale as a ghost," she says, oblivious to what I've seen. "Everything okay?"

"Fine," I say quickly, but my eyes sneak involuntarily toward her shoulder, and she notices. She gets it. For a second, her hand flits in the air, as if it's making a move to cover the offending spot, to conceal its truth, and then she gives up entirely. "You don't have to – " I start to say as she leaps up, and then stop, because she's already gone.

It's weird. I'm usually able to control my own emotions, to box them into a small crevice inside my chest. When it comes to my reactions, though, I wear my heart on my sleeve. Grandmom says it is a good thing. I beg to differ. All those times when Mom and Dad failed to show up? The broken promises? The static-laden phone calls and crisp letters from abroad? Try as I might, I couldn't ever hide my disappointment. You'd think I would have hardened to it over the years, would have put up walls to protect myself, and I suppose I did to some extent. Eventually I accepted it. But sometimes the pain creeps back.

I used to think it was my fault.

That's what Serena said, but it may as well have come from my mouth. "What did I do wrong?" I remember asking Grandmom. "Am I a bad girl? Is that why Mommy and Daddy always fly away?" And my sweet grandmother, forever my shield, would sit me on her lap, brush my hair back from my face, and kiss the top of my head.

"No, my love," she'd answer. "You are the best girl. You're *my* best girl. Mommy and Daddy fly away because they have an important job that takes them all around the world. They help children who don't have a house to live in, or food to eat, or a school to attend. They make it better for their families."

"What about our family?" I'd persist. "Do those other kids take up so much room in their hearts that there isn't enough for me?"

I don't know how Grandmom got through those conversations. She was steady and still soft, my hope and warmth and sanctuary all wrapped into one. I know now how strongly she disagreed with Mom and Dad. I know now what the hushed arguments were about, the ones late at night with her bedroom door closed so I wouldn't hear her on the phone. I know now, despite Grandmom's effort to keep the story locked away, that they didn't even ask her first before sneaking out of town when I was sleeping over at her cottage. "We'll see you tomorrow, Eden," Mom said as she dropped me off and kissed me goodbye. She watched me skip across the lawn, waved to Grandmom as she opened the door, and drove off down the street.

Tomorrow turned into a week, then a month, then many months.

Even when they were home, I still lived at Grandmom's house. Mariah and Joel Abraham might be my parents, but my grandmother is the one who showed me what a family can be.

As I gather up Serena's breakfast plates along with mine and toss them in the trash, I wonder if it'd help her to hear about my parents. Whatever happened with Seth, whether my suspicion's right or entirely off-base, it's obvious that she's finding her footing again on her own terms. Could that be why she's been trying so hard to be my friend, because she feels alone? I consider the possibility. I understand that loneliness. Isn't that why I wear Grandmom's locket? It's my constant. My failsafe. Serena doesn't seem to have one of those anymore, and I'd like to help. I check everywhere for her: the library, the lobby, the community room. No luck. I go to the courtyard next, remembering what she said about how calming the fountain is. Nothing. I guess she wants to be alone, or she wouldn't have hidden herself this thoroughly. I respect that, so when I come upon Ruby in the courtyard and she invites me to join her, I agree.

"It's a lovely day, don't you think?" She tilts her face toward the sun.

I keep mine in the shadow of the accompanying clouds.

"Yes," I agree. It *is* lovely, if we're talking about the weather. Mornings are the best part of the summer here, before humidity soaks the air, and today the sky is a pretty shade of robin's-egg blue. The clouds are puffy, and I hear the strum of a street musician's guitar carry over from the sidewalk. I adore that about this place. Wherever you go, music follows. Normally I stop to listen and throw a few dollars into the performers' instrument cases. That's what makes this day less than lovely. The change in my wallet can no longer be shared. It must be saved.

"Things will get better," Ruby assures quietly, hearing the words I don't speak. It reminds me of something Grandmom would say. Sitting with Ruby makes me miss her even more, and for a minute I contemplate the idea of returning to Portsmouth. I could probably get a job at the music hall or in one of the theaters. The outfits I wear, the shampoo I use, the books I read ... they could all be mine again. I could be me again. I can't deny how appealing that is. But what about everything I'd have to leave behind? The walks down Broadway when you hear music spilling out from every storefront, blending together to create a symphony unique to that specific moment in time, the Opryland hotel and its magical holiday displays, the Cheekwood Botanical Garden with its sea of tulips and winding sculpture trail, the country songs that play just about everywhere you go, whether it's the airport or the dentist's office ... there's so much I cherish about this place. The people here, they're a different breed. They're *my* breed. They hum with the same inspiration I do.

"How long have you been in Nashville?" I ask Ruby.

"Since I was nine. I even met my husband at Vanderbilt and convinced him to stay after college. We lived in Germantown for decades. Hopefully we'll get back there someday. He's in the hospital, has been for weeks," she says, answering the question I'm too reluctant to ask. "All our money goes to medical bills, so they had to shut off the electricity and water in our house."

"Do you visit him often?"

I rarely see her leave the shelter. Why isn't she there with him each day?

"I have to rely on my cousin," she explains. "She lives in Chattanooga, but bless her heart, every Friday she comes up and takes me to see my Fred. I don't drive, so it's the only option I have. Cabs get too expensive and walking to the bus stop is difficult with my arthritis."

"Oh, that must be awful, knowing he's across town but being separated."

"It's the worst. Next Sunday is our sixtieth anniversary. I wish we could spend it together."

The light bulb flash is blinding.

Before Ruby can say anything else, I'm on my feet, hurrying into the shelter and returning with a penny from the bowl inside. I press it into her wrinkled palm. "Here," I say, a little breathless, "why don't you throw it into the fountain and put your wish out there in the universe?" She gives me an amused look, like she knows it won't make any difference, but I'm so intent on it that she agrees just to appease me.

She doesn't think anything will come of it. She can't fathom what will change.

Which makes her reaction even sweeter when, the following Sunday morning, I'm waiting in the dining room for her, phone in hand. "You can't have breakfast alone on your anniversary," I say, and take her by the arm. I guide her to the lobby, settle her in a rocking chair, and turn on the video app on my phone. Then I scan the contacts until I reach Kristina and click it to connect. She's a nurse at the hospital where Fred is recovering from his triple bypass surgery, and although we hadn't been in touch since the morning after the fire, making the call was worth it to see Ruby happy. "Oh my good Lord," she whispers, as Fred's face appears on the phone.

"Happy Anniversary," I say.

Time is a treasure from the universe's jewelry box.

The lyric doesn't slam into my brain this time. It floats through.
And, like Ruby as she talks to her beloved, I smile.

Sensations Café Menu

where music meets munchies

BREAKFAST

*Each platter is served with warm biscuits and your choice
of grits, hash browns, or home fries.*

Pancakes (3) $5.95
   with fresh strawberries, blueberries, or bananas $6.95

Belgium Waffle $6.50
   with fresh strawberries, blueberries, or bananas $7.50

Challah French Toast...$6.50

Eggs (3) and Cinnamon Toast...$6.75

Southern Omelet
   – diced tomatoes, onions, bell peppers, and cheddar cheese...............$8.75

Country Fried Steak and (2) Egg $11.50

LUNCH & DINNER

Soups of the Day
   – ask your server about our selections! .... *Cup* $3.00 *Bowl* $4.00

Grilled Cheese Sandwich
   – your choice of American, Swiss, or Cheddar $6.75

Salad Your Way
   – your choice of six toppings and dressing $9.00

Fried Chicken Salad
   – savory chicken on a bed of lettuce, cucumber, tomato, and walnuts $9.25

BLT
   – served with your choice of French Fries or potato chips $7.00

Grilled Chicken Sandwich
   – served with your choice of French Fries or potato chips....................$8.00

Chicken & Dumpling $9.95

Hand-Breaded Chicken Fingers
   – served with biscuits and your choice of two side dishes $11.00

Fried Catfish
   – served with biscuits and your choice of two side dishes $15.00

Shrimp & Grits $14.50

Classic Spaghetti and Meatballs
   – served with marinara sauce and garlic bread $11.50

SIDE DISHES

A la Carte, $3.50 each

Mashed Potatoes	Fried Green Tomatoes	Corn Bread
Baked Potato	Green Beans with Almonds	Fried Pickles
Sweet Potato	Grits	Collard Greens
French Fries	Macaroni & Cheese	Caramelized Carrots
Hush Puppies	Coleslaw	Catfish Cubes

BEVERAGES

Coffee, Sweet Tea, or Hot Chocolate $2.25

Iced Sweet Tea and Assorted Soft Drinks $2.25

Juice
  – apple, orange, grapefruit, cranberry, or tomato $2.50

Milk...$2.00

DESSERTS

Homemade Pie or Cobbler
  – ask your server about our selections!..$3.25

Banana or Chocolate Pudding $2.75

Ice Cream
  – your choice of vanilla, chocolate, strawberry, or Oreo....................$3.00

Milkshake..$3.95

Banana Split...$4.50

"You must be a saint," Ruby says when she walks into the library an hour later. I'm printing off a new batch of resumés since I haven't heard anything from the others I dropped off, and I look up as Ruby settles into the chair next to me.

"Nothing of the sort," I answer, chuckling, "but I'm glad I could help. Kristina – she and I used to live together, before the fire – she is a nurse on the pediatric floor. She was happy to visit Fred and lend him her phone."

"Please pass along my appreciation to her too, then," she says. "Fred looks good. There's more color in his cheeks." She hums quietly, almost imperceptibly, under her breath. "I talk to him every day, of course, and I speak with his doctors, but seeing him is different. It's the best anniversary gift I could have gotten. How can I thank you?"

"No thanks necessary."

I'm glad I could help.

It's what I said to Sherri, what I'm saying to Ruby, and it's true. The most difficult part of living in the shelter isn't the lack of privacy, or the wait for a shower, or the old paint on the walls. It's seeing the mouths that have lost their upward slant and the eyes that have lost their luster. That scares me to the core, because when I look in the mirror now, I see the beginnings of the same dullness. I used to love my eyes. They're aquamarine, like Grandmom's. "Like the sea on a clear summer morning," is how she describes them. But the sun no longer glints on their water. The diamonds have become coal.

I hate that.

I hate it for all of us, so if I can bring back the light briefly, why not give it a shot? It feels so good to make a difference – and, for the first time in forever, it also feels like my presence matters. Like I have a purpose. Like I can guide others' melodies from the diminuendo to the crescendo. Will these wishes have a lasting impact? I don't know, but for now, during this period when each day is a fight, a struggle, a reminder of what used to be, maybe I can use them to bring a sliver of happiness. The thought of it keeps me hanging on.

Forget the voicemail from Kayleigh I still haven't answered.

Forget the evasion from Serena, who speedily turned away when I joined the sing-along she was leading in the kids' playroom yesterday. She's avoided all contact with me since that morning in the dining room.

Forget the empathy from Ms. Birnbaum. She finally cornered me the other day, sliding into the opposite seat while I was waiting to meet with Jillian. "I talked to Bill," she said softly. "He told me things didn't go so well with the interview." She tilted her head a little. "Actually, he said to be sure you're okay, because you hurried out of there afterwards like you were being chased."

In a way, I was being chased. By my failures, my inadequacies, my life. But I didn't tell her that. I only apologized.

Forget all of it.

Remember Ruby's crinkly smile. Remember that something is better than nothing.

This is what I must focus on. This is where my heart must beat.

Before I continue my job search, I stop in the community room, pick up the bowl of pennies that the shelter staff keeps on hand for people to use in the fountain, and bring it outside. Hopefully it'll inspire more people to make a wish. I feel a zing of determination simply thinking about it, a resolve that pushes me onto the streets and off to the café I saw a posting for on the shelter's 'help wanted' bulletin board. It's no Bluebird or 3rd & Lindsley, but the minute I step inside, I like it. The wooden floor is slatted, the walls are painted a warm buttery color, and the ceiling is high with crisscrossing beams. Stained glass lanterns hang over the tables, and the back half of the place is a performance area. There are stools, microphone stands, and a set of speakers. Instead of a stage, there's a semi-circle of chairs, and though no one's sitting in them now, I can picture how intimate it must be when a singer is up there.

I would give anything to hear one of my songs performed here.

I would give anything for my words to have an audience.

Will I ever be good enough for that?

"May I help you?"

I'm so lost in my daydreams that I jump when a woman approaches. "Yes, please," I say quickly. "I was hoping to fill out an application for the hostess position you have open. This is a great place, by the way."

"Thank you." She smiles amicably. "I can interview you now, if that's okay. I'm Dina," she adds, "the manager."

Seriously, she'll interview me now? When the other places with my resumé haven't so much as called? My mind explodes into a momentary bout of panic, but I breathe in deeply and shove aside the nerves. "That'd be wonderful," I say, and Dina motions for me to join her in a booth.

"So what brings you to Sensations?" she asks.

"I adore the name," I tell her. I really do. It makes me think of the myriad sensations that course through me upon hearing a song for the first time. I think it's the closest we can get to heaven here on Earth, that breath when the music starts to resonate. "I used to work as a receptionist for the landlord at my apartment complex," I explain. "But it went up in flames and the building is basically demolished, so I'm looking for a new job."

"Oh, I'm so sorry. Is this the fire I heard about on the news? Cedarwood Apartments?"

"We were on the news?" I gape at her. Why this comes as a surprise, I don't know. How many times have I seen flames cannonball up, listened to the anchor give details on causes and alarms and injuries? Local stations always cover stories like this, and yet, when I was part of the tale, television cameras and reporters were the farthest thing from my mind. When something happens to you, not around you, everything is different.

"Yes," Dina confirms. "It looked incredibly scary. I'm glad the firefighters got everyone out."

"Me too." My voice cracks unexpectedly.

"Do you have family in the area?"

Shoot. I know where this train is going, and I'm frantic to switch its track.

"No, but I'm staying with friends until I'm back on my feet." Since she hasn't asked for a resumé – which has the shelter's address on it – it seems like the wisest course of action to avoid telling her about it. She doesn't appear to be judgmental, but still, it's better to play it safe. Better to leave the stereotypes in the shadows. Better to alter my reality than let my reality alter me. Though, really, is that not happening already?

"How kind of them to support you," Dina says. "Alrighty, moving on: have you ever worked in a restaurant before?"

"No, but I'm willing to learn. I'm detail-oriented and meticulous, so I'd be good at keeping a log of reservations, and I'm well-versed in the music scene, which seems to be a great fit for your café." I gesture to the microphones and stools. "I worked with tenants each day at the apartment building, and although this is different, of course, I think that interaction is decent preparation for the contact a hostess has with the customers."

Dina asks a few more questions, jotting down notes as I talk, and promises to be in touch soon. The tiniest frisson of excitement uncoils from my shoulders as I head back out onto the sidewalk and stand there, drinking in the soupy air. Low clouds skim the sky, hiding the top of the AT&T building, and I smell the rain gathering in their folds. I should really get going, since I don't have an umbrella. Clothes, toiletries, blankets ... these are the things people think of to donate. Weather gear? Not so much. I don't care, though. If I get soaked, so be it. If the navy skirt I'm wearing bleeds all over the cream shirt, that's okay. If I slip on the wet pavement in these shoes which are half a size too big, I'll deal. I want to celebrate the fact that I didn't bomb the interview. A slow grin curves my mouth as I look at the vintage music store across the street.

I know exactly the way to do it.

The bells on the door tinkle merrily as I push it open, announcing my arrival, and the man at the cash register raises a hand in greeting. "Hello there," he says. "Anything I can help you with today?"

"Just browsing," I call.

It's my favorite thing to do in music shops. Getting lost inside, wandering the aisles and looking at row after glorious row of albums, is an oasis. One of the most truly beautiful things about music is its diversity. You never know what will speak to you at any given time.

For an hour, I explore the selection. It's a tiny store, and the shelves are packed tight as can be. CDs, old-time vinyl records and cassettes, sheet music, concert posters from the fifties and sixties … I want to buy it all. My fingers brush the cases as I meander along, and I smile, thinking back to when Grandmom let me choose which singers would grace her record player. "One at a time, Jellybean," she'd laugh, after I searched through the cabinet and brought her a teetering tower. "Pick your very favorite for us to listen to first."

"But they're *all* my favorites," I'd proclaim, and then rattle off a list of reasons why. Sometimes it was the song titles, sometimes it was the cover art, sometimes it was a remembered swell of bass from the last time we'd given a particular record a try. Grandmom said I had a mind like an elephant – which is true, but only when it comes to music. Ask me what I ate for dinner yesterday, or where I visited last weekend, and it'll take me a minute. Ask me about the bridge of the Beatles' "Let It Be," or the chorus of Patsy Cline's "I Fall to Pieces," or the verses of Mazzy Star's "Fade Into You," and I'll instantly offer up a steady stream of information.

You know how the ocean makes people feel big and small at the same time?

That's what music does for me.

All its possibilities, these stories waiting to be heard, these harmonies waiting to intertwine, it's remarkable. It's almost overwhelming. Sometimes a twist of sadness unleashes inside me when I'm in a store like this, because the sea of selections makes me realize how many songs I'll never know. I wish there were a way to listen to every one.

For now, I decide on a country CD from the clearance bin. It's the only way I can justify shelling out even a few of my remaining dollars. I wrap my hand around this square-shaped treasure as I go to pay. How will it sound on the shelter's CD player? It'll be strange, listening with a bunch of other people around, but my iPod fell victim to the fire, and I'd rather it be a community experience than a non-existent one.

"Will that be all?" the man asks, as I hand over the CD. I wish it weren't. I wish I could buy this whole place.

"That's all," I confirm. My fingertips graze the crisp dollar bills I've pulled from my wallet. This is foolish. I should be saving money, not spending it. And yet I can't help it. I need something to stop my internal flame from extinguishing. I need something to look forward to again. I need something to remind me of who I am.

"Have a great day," the man says, giving me my change, and instead of pocketing it, I release the coins into the jar by the register. It's for a charity that funds music programs in area schools.

"You, too," I answer.

It is indeed pouring when I get back outside, so I tuck the CD in my bag and make a mad dash for it. Raindrops pelt my arms and plaster my hair against my neck, and a roll of thunder rumbles in the distance. By the time I get to the corner, I'm sliding all over in the too-big shoes and rivers of water are finding their way inside my shirt. I have to laugh at the absurdity of it. It's a barking laugh first, then an uncontrollable one. How is this my life? How am I standing at the intersection of Broadway and Second Avenue, waiting for the traffic light to blink green, while the sky's waterfall unleashes in torrents?

"Are you okay, Miss?" the woman next to me asks. She's corralling a gaggle of kids beneath an oversized bubble umbrella and still manages to fish around in her purse to retrieve a grocery bag. "I know it's not much," she allows, "but you're welcome to it, if you want something to hold over your head."

"You look like you took a shower with your clothes on!" one of her children giggles.

This brings back my own hysteria.

"Yes," I say, giving a quick wink, "I suppose I do."

The light changes and we cross the street, and although it would probably be wise to take shelter under an awning until the summer storm lets up, I move on. I play on. It's cathartic in a way. There is something equalizing about the rain. It washes away the outer layer and morphs us into our most natural selves. The man striding in the opposite direction, whose expensive suit and shoes are now soaked? The woman fighting with her umbrella as a gust of wind blows it inside-out? The kids from before, inching forward as a group while their mother sacrifices her dryness to ensure theirs? We're all in this together.

I must resemble a drowned rat as I approach the shelter, but still, the first thing I do is check the courtyard. Nobody's there. Of course they aren't. Who would sit outside in a monsoon? Logically, I know that'd be ridiculous. But I can't help feeling disappointed. It's been a good day and I want to share it with somebody. I want to make a wish come true. So, beneath the shelter of the overhang, I wring out my hair and wait for someone to come through that door, to pick up a penny.

Eventually I give up and go back inside. Serena's with the kids again, providing a soundtrack for a game of musical chairs, and her eyes widen as I pass by the playroom, which is really just an alcove off a bigger area. "What happened?" she questions.

"Got caught without an umbrella."

"Miss Eden!" Tommy leaps out of his chair and makes a beeline for me. "Come play with us!"

I glance at Serena and she shrugs.

The waves in my hair are coiling into damp curls, my skirt's literally stuck to my legs, and my feet are aching. I should take a shower. I should listen to the CD. I should charge my phone in case Dina calls with a job offer. But I don't do any of those things. "I'll be back," I tell Tommy. "Let me change into dry clothes first."

Around and around and around we walk, circling the seats as Serena churns out a perky, upbeat tune. When she stops mid-chord, the kids dart for the chairs. A little girl named Angelica and I head for the same one at the same time, and I'm fully prepared to let her win, of course, when she judges the distance incorrectly and ends up flinging herself into my leg. We both fall onto the thin, fraying carpet, and Angelica starts to spew such high-pitched giggles that I actually think she's crying. Once I realize she's not, I join in too, and then, before I know it, the whole group of kids is piling on top of me.

"Careful," Serena cautions. "We don't want to hurt Eden, right?" She says it lightly, but I catch the strain behind her words.

"I'm fine." I prop myself up on my elbows. "No worries. They're just being kids."

She frowns slightly. "Still. Sometimes we don't see the danger in a situation until it's too late."

We? Or she?

I do a rapid inventory of the playroom. Checkered carpeting, with blocks of blue and gold. Bean bag chairs below the window. A single bookcase with only two of its three shelves in use. A toy box with its lid open and a zoo of worn stuffed animals peeking out. A handful of board games, spinners held together with tape and playing pieces mismatched. The alcove isn't bigger than my living room used to be, and yet there's a dozen kids here. Are they happy? In this moment, pulling one another up so we can begin playing again, they seem to be. But what about the toddler girl who cries for her daddy at night? What about the brown-haired boy who carries a teddy bear with its stuffing falling out? What about all of them? Do they understand the shelter is temporary? Or does it not matter? How does life differ when looked at through a child's eyes?

So many questions.

So few answers.

I'm still pondering them when my phone rings. I'd put it atop the bookcase so I'd hear it if Dina called. I jump up to grab it, praying the battery will hold out, and stop dead in my tracks as I see the number on the screen. It isn't a Nashville area code. It's a

Portsmouth one. The digits I used to dial relentlessly.

Mom and Dad.

The two people in this world who have always left me searching for more.

COLTON

When Colton first sat down in his tenth grade American History class, he didn't know it'd change his life. He didn't know what a connection he'd feel with the veterans he learned about, the valiant soldiers who fought for their country and made it a better, safer place. Reading about the battles in his textbook, listening with rapt attention to the guest speakers who told stories of World War II and Korea, patriotism surged in Colton's chest. He wanted to be just like the Army lieutenants, the Navy Seals, the Air Force pilots.

The day after graduation, Colton enlisted, much to his parents' dismay. They'd wanted their son to be a doctor. It had been the family way for three generations. But Colton swore that this was his calling. In time, his parents warmed to the idea and even displayed an American flag proudly in the front window. Their son might not be nearby, they figured, but he was thriving on a military base in North Carolina. Though it wasn't their first choice for their only child, they respected his dedication, loyalty, and courage … until the Persian Gulf War turned it all upside-down.

Almost twenty-five years later, Colton can't escape the experience. The atrocities he witnessed will forever be emblazoned on his mind, the losses he suffered will forever haunt his nightmares, the comrades he watched fall will forever remind him of the ultimate sacrifice. "Why them and not me? How did I make it home when so many didn't?" He still asks these questions. He still struggles with post-traumatic stress disorder. He still mourns. Keeping a steady job has been difficult, because his military training doesn't always jive with the civilian workforce, and when he was fired from a recent bartending job, he simply gave up. Open Hearts has gotten him off the street, where he slept every night, but it hasn't yet gotten him out of his head. That's where his soul still lives. That's where the memories still lie.

My first instinct is to ignore the call. To ignore Mom and Dad, just as they so frequently do with me. Sometimes I think about the times we spent together before they left. I'd mix the waffle batter when Mom made breakfast, or help Dad plant geraniums in the big flower pots by the front door, or drag a dusty piece of chalk down the driveway, sketching a hopscotch court so we could play. Never once did I think it would all vanish. Never once did I stop to consider how different life would be if a job offer stole my parents away. And why should I have? It's not like there was an indication ahead of time. The upheaval was so fast. Normal existence one day; disappearing act the next.

I used to be transported back in time whenever my parents would call. It didn't matter where I was, or what I'd been doing. The second that number flashed in front of my eyes, I was a four-year-old again. Kissing my mother goodbye when she dropped me off for what I thought was a one-night sleepover. Eavesdropping on Grandmom's conversation with my father when he called the next day to explain. Crying in my bedroom late at night, arms wrapped tightly around my stuffed polar bear, and wondering why Mommy and Daddy didn't love me enough to come home. For years, these are the memories which tormented me. Sometimes they still do.

"Aren't you going to answer?" Serena, surrounded by the kids now, glances over with eyebrows raised.

I'd rather not. The digits on the screen mean my parents are home from their latest expedition. They mean it's time for the customary once-per-year visit, where we sit across from each other in an awkward silence, trying to figure out where to even start, and then realizing, all over again, how that bridge has become impossible to cross. And yet … "I guess," I tell Serena, then traverse the room to head for the lobby. I don't want an audience while I talk to them.

I brace myself and push the button. "Hello?"

"Eden," Mom says. "Hi. How are you?"

"Fine, thanks. How about you and Dad? When did you get back?"

"Early this morning. Flew in to Boston Logan this time instead of Manchester."

I wait for her to say more, but she doesn't, so I jump in to break the silence before it drones on a beat too long. "How did the job go?" I ask.

She tells me a bit about their latest endeavor – building a high school for the teenagers who are often overlooked, who often go without so their younger siblings can have a chance at a brighter life – and then tosses the ball back in my direction. "How's Nashville?" she asks. "It must be humid this time of year."

"Oh, yeah," I agree. "There are days when you can literally see the moisture hanging in the air. I got caught in a torrential downpour earlier. Lots of pop-up thunderstorms in the summer." I shake my head. Nothing says warm and fuzzy family reunion like a conversation about the weather, right? Not that I'm expecting anything more. This is always how it goes.

Always how it fails.

"So we'll be in New Hampshire until the end of October," Mom says. "When can we see you?"

Here we go.

"You know, life's been crazy lately," I tell her, glad for the ability to color this lie of omission with a sliver of truth. "I'm not sure I'll have a chance to get away before you leave again for ... where are you going next time?"

"Haiti. We'll work on rebuilding some of the schools leveled by that horrible earthquake. There really is a lot to be done still. But we'd like to spend time with you first. Maybe we can come to you if you can't make it to Portsmouth."

What?

Is she for real?

The fire. The shelter. The mountain of truth hiding behind that sliver.

They can't set foot in Tennessee.

"I thought you didn't like Nashville. Didn't you say it was congested?"

"Well, yes," she allows. "It's definitely more hustle-and-bustle than Portsmouth, not to mention the towns and villages your father and I live in for most of the year. But you love it there, obviously. Have you secured a spot at that café yet? I'm drawing a blank on its name … the Cardinal? No, that isn't right – "

The tiniest smile plays around my mouth. "The Bluebird," I tell her, "and no, not yet." Probably not ever, at the rate I'm going. Something pinches my temples as I think of my songwriting journal's remaining pages. Will they ever be filled? And even if so, will I feel comfortable enough to audition for the cafe's Sunday Writers' Nights, when songwriters sing their songs? After my first – and last – performance at a different café in town, I doubt it. The open mic night was a requirement for one of my graduate courses, and it's an experience I've tried to block from my mind. "Listen, Mom," I say, before the disastrous night can make a reappearance in my thoughts, "I'll call you tomorrow, okay? My head's pounding and I have to go lie down. Tell Dad I say hello."

Then I disconnect the call.

I don't know what to do. The stilted conversation, I can handle. The odd juxtaposition of feeling like a stranger in the house I lived in for the first four years of my life, I can handle. Flipping through photos of the sweet kids my parents have helped, I can handle. But not this. The thought of sharing my life with them now makes my stomach turn. Because they wouldn't stay in Nashville to help me get back on my feet. They wouldn't postpone their next work project until they knew I was alright. No part of me believes they'd put their daughter first. That's simply not who they are and I refuse to fall into the trap of thinking otherwise.

Ugh.

It feels like something's compressing my forehead.

I think I really do have to lie down.

The bedroom is silent, empty for perhaps the first time since I got to the shelter two weeks ago, and I shuffle across the floor until I reach my bed. It's neatly made, the striped quilt tucked beneath the pillows. When Kristina and I lived together, my room always had everything in its place and hers looked like a tornado had blown through. "Why bother making the bed if I'm just going to sleep in it again tonight?" she'd say. I craved the organization, though, and I feel the urgency even more here. I might not have a room to call my own anymore, I might not have a closet to hang my clothes in or a window seat to curl up on, strumming my guitar in time with the lyrics in my head, but I have this. I can control this.

Purple cardigan, *Pride and Prejudice*, and now the CD from that little music shop. These are the items on the shelf above my bed. I stoop down, reach beneath the soft fabric of the quilt, and free my journal from underneath the mattress. It feels safer to keep it hidden there, away from people's inquisitive eyes. It's the same reason I never take off Grandmom's locket now. I want to make sure they're protected, always. "One day," I whisper, stroking the journal, "you'll be a symbol of what is, instead of what could be."

"One day?" My back is to the door, but I know it's Serena. "Why not this day?"

When I turn around, I see her lingering at the threshold, guitar strap slung across her shoulder. I guess playtime with the kids is over and she's putting it away. "Look," I say, taking advantage of her presence to finally speak the words I've been trying to say for days, "I'm so sorry about last week. I wasn't prying, but the scar – "

"Please, stop. Is that your songwriting journal?" She gestures to her guitar. "Let's do one of the songs."

"Oh no, I couldn't." I avert my gaze to the window.

The floorboards creak as she moves over them. "You could. You should. You can."

She holds the instrument out and a memory lights up my mind: my first morning here, stumbling upon her in the courtyard and confiding my story, all of it, including how crushed I was about losing Grandpa's guitar. That was my link to him. Grandmom says he loved to play as much as I do. And now Serena's offering to let me use her guitar? It might seem like a simple gesture, but it's not. It's the world.

She nods at the journal in my hand. "Why don't you choose a song? Run through it once to give me an idea how it goes, then I'll join in." She perches on her bed, careful not to jostle the sleeve of her XL t-shirt as she settles into a cross-legged position, and I stand there, biting my lip as I consider. When was the last time I shared my lyrics with someone who wasn't from the Nashville Songwriters Association? Or interviewing me for a job? Or Grandmom?

When I first came to Nashville, I was buoyant with ambition, fueled by adrenaline. This was it! I would take Music City by storm! All my life, I'd been driven by the music in me, and now I would be in the one place where everyone else felt the same way! I'd force those doors to open by the sheer strength of my determination! Collaborations with other songwriters, with singers, with people who pushed me and inspired me and understood me! How lucky was I? But, see, the thing about buoys? By nature, they are unsinkable. They just bob along, floating atop the water and barely skimming its surface. You'd think that's good, right? They're always above it all. But I've learned that sometimes you have to dive in. Sometimes it's not enough to skim the surface.

And sometimes sharks are lurking underneath.

The producer I managed to get a meeting with, who told me I wasn't "quite there yet in terms of relatability" and then poached a line from the song I'd submitted. The A&R executive who made my day – heck, my entire month – when she called as a follow-up to the resumé I sent in, only to cancel the interview at the last minute because the position had already been filled. The girl from Belmont who beat me out for a job at We've Got the Beat after we both interned at the company during grad school. The demons in my head, who taunt me with fears that I'll never be good enough. Some are sharks by choice. Others never even realize the wounds they've inflicted.

Serena seems safe, though.

"Okay," I say, more to myself than to her. "Okay."

I sit down, flip through the pages until I reach my favorite song, and sing it so Serena can hear its melody. Then I pass over the journal. As she skims the lyrics, I wonder: what kind of music did she used to sing with Seth? Is it odd for her to be a solo artist now after being part of a duo for so long? And how will it feel to hear her give breath to my words?

Eerie. That's how it feels. But also uplifting.

"What do you think about, half a world away? Do you ever think of me and how l wanted you to stay?" Serena's singing voice is every bit as lilting as her speaking one, full of baby's breath and fluff from dandelions. It's the type of voice no producer would dream of auto-tuning, because to do that would be to lose the nuances, the intricacies, the velvety texture twisted into something delicate. In Serena, I hear how I always meant this song to sound. "I love you, I miss you, I still keep you close to my heart. But yesterday must end. Tomorrow's my start."

My fingers pluck the guitar strings, moving by memory, moving all on their own, and it's so great to sense the vibration again that my eyes fill with tears. "Thank you," I whisper, after Serena's sung the last note. "This was … it's … I can't even … your kindness is more appreciated than you will ever know."

She reaches over and gives my hand a squeeze. "This is about your parents, isn't it? You should share it with them. Some people can't see what's right in front of them until we open up their eyes. Think about it." And then she taps an oval-shaped nail against the neck of her guitar. "Keep this for awhile. Play all you want." Before I can say anything, she stands up to leave. "Oh, and Eden? It's a beautiful song. Exactly the sort of thing I like to sing."

* * *

I can't sleep that night. Moonlight glows through the curtains, illuminating shadows that dance on the walls, and as I watch their silhouettes, my thoughts continuously return to what Serena said. My song is the sort of thing she likes to sing. How many times have I heard the opposite, that I need to be more commercial, more marketable, more in tune with what's playing on the radio? Music is an art, but recording is an industry.

Could this song make the cut?

It's called "Voyage of the Heart," and I'm going to use it for an interview I have with a publisher on Thursday. It's been scheduled for awhile – since before the fire – and I'd rather have submitted a new song, but I can't seem to draft anything unless it's connected to a wish. Even then, it's only one or two lines. Unless this is the turning point? Quietly, cautiously, so as not to awaken anyone else, I grab my journal, slide my feet into the pair of flip-flops I rescued from the donation box, and tiptoe across the room, downstairs, and into the community room. I have the album, too, the one I bought after my interview with Dina, and I lower the volume on the CD player to its quietest setting before letting it spin. For fifty minutes, a blissful fifty minutes, a peaceful fifty minutes, I just sit on the floor and lose myself in the harmonies.

God, I miss this. The solitude. The serenity. The stillness. The sense of self.

The person I am now, can she ever be the same as before?

Without even thinking about it, I unclasp my locket and stare at its pictures. Mom and Dad, with their hands linked as they posed for a wedding shot. Grandpa Rick, his arm raised in a smart salute. "I wish you could have met him," Grandmom's said more than once. "You would have adored each other."

"What would you do?" I ask his photo. "How would you handle this? Am I wrong to hide it from everyone? If I tell Grandmom the truth, she'll want me to come back to Portsmouth. She'll want to take care of me like she always has. But I want to take care of her now, and I'm not ready to give up on Nashville, either. If I move back, my songwriting dreams are finished. Am I ready to admit defeat and wave the white flag?"

"There's no such thing as a white flag." I jump at the voice, whipping my head around to see the man just entering the room. He's tall, with close-cropped brown hair and days' worth of stubble on his face. "There's no such thing as surrender. You can't leave it behind; it follows you wherever you go." He's talking to me, that's obvious, but he refuses to so much as glance in my direction. Instead, he lumbers right on by, slides open the glass door to the courtyard, and disappears straight into the darkness.

Two weeks ago, I never would've chased after a stranger in the pitch black. Tonight, I switch off the CD player and follow him out. There's just something gripping about him. He is burly, muscular and broad-shouldered, but the way he hunches over makes it seem like he's attempting to become invisible. "I'm Eden," I say, joining him by the fountain and offering a smile. Then I take a coin from the bowl I set outside. "Penny for your thoughts?"

"No thanks," he says gruffly.

"Even if I promise not to talk about white flags?"

He shakes his head.

The more he stonewalls, the more I feel compelled to keep trying.

"Do you like music?"

"No."

I wrinkle my brow. "Not at all?" That seems ... unfathomable.

"Seven months, eight days, and nineteen minutes." He still won't look at me. "That's how long I was in the hospital after the Persian Gulf War. My parents played music for me each day, and I can't listen to it anymore now. None of it. Horrid memories. God-awful memories." That's when I notice the way his hand's resting on the edge of the fountain, fingers not quite able to grip its concrete. Oh ... a prosthetic. "Trust me, you don't want my thoughts. I don't even want them."

So much for making his wish come true.

So much for any lyrics about this man and his sad, sad situation.

I decide to leave him alone, give him some space, let him be.

But first, I bring out the CD and set it beside him.

He might not know it yet, but he needs the music in his life more than I do.

songwriting journal
winter and spring 2014

"Iceberg" (bridge):

> When the icebergs shimmer
> When the sun glints strong
> She finds a whisper of truth,
> who she was all along

"Voyage of the Heart" (first chorus):

> What do you think about
> Half a world away
> Do you ever think of me
> And how I wanted you to stay?
> Oceans divide us
> Water, clear and deep
> But the stars are the same
> As the memories we keep
> Voyage of the heart, it can take us anywhere
> But can it bring us home again?
> Is life ever fair?

"Once Upon a Midnight Dream"
(verse one):

Inky sky

Canvas of stars

Moon glowing gently

Down on their hearts

These are the snapshots

of their first midnight dream

Of their only midnight dream

Of their secrets

Of their souls

Of their pain

Of their holes

Of their life left unlived

Of their promise unabridged

8

By the time Thursday rolls around, I'm actually feeling semi-decent about things. I've called Dad and Mom to tell them I'll be able to visit, after all. I've called Kayleigh, even though she's in London, to thank her for extending such a sweet invitation and to, as gently as possible, turn it down. A knot forms in my chest whenever I think about being in the bridal party, and I must listen to my instincts. I hope she will understand. Oh, and I've made a third call, too: to my former boss and landlord, who seemed pleased to hear from me.

"Eden!" he exclaimed. "How are you? *Where* are you? Did you and Kristina find an apartment somewhere else?"

"It's a long story." It's not, it's really quite a short story, but he's the type of person who will try to rewrite its ending, and this is a journey I must pen on my own. "We're fine, though. I'm calling to check in on the others. How is everybody?" As he told me about them and about the plans to raze the complex and rebuild from the ground up, I felt oddly hopeful. Maybe things would never be the same again. Maybe the community we'd formed would never be together again. But maybe, also, that's how life unfolds, with all of us traveling from one place to the next, forming new connections with each chapter we turn the page on, new connections that don't erase the old ones, but just add to them instead.

As I make my way through the shelter on Thursday morning, that's where my mindset is. Clad in the same black and white houndstooth dress I wore to my interview at the Hall of Fame, it still feels like I'm a kid playing dress-up in a stranger's life, but this time I'm wearing my purple cardigan for a pop of color. Simple as it is, the choice makes a world of difference. Because it makes me feel more like myself, like someone who belongs at a meeting with a music publisher. I pause at the donation box in the lobby and sift through its neatly divided sections. Is there a scarf in there? Not a paisley print like I used to wear, but a solid that'll accentuate the dress?

No dice.

"Can't blame a girl for trying," I say to myself, then wonder … when did I become somebody who talks to herself? July sixth, that's when. The day Ms. Birnbaum welcomed me to the shelter. I don't think I even realized I was doing it until right now. It isn't that there's no one else to talk to here. In fact, it's the opposite – with dozens of people living in a building with only a few rooms, quiet is hard to come by. What I've learned, though, is that being surrounded by people can sometimes make for the loneliest situation of all. The juxtaposition of the ones who seek out attention, diversions, a very lifeline of sorts, and the ones who keep to themselves, lost in their dreams or, perhaps, nightmares … it's challenging to reconcile.

Is it like that for the others here, too?

How about Serena?

"Hey." She walks by on her way to breakfast and stops to wish me good luck. "She'll love your songs. I know it."

"Hopefully." I think of my mentoring sessions with the NSAI, of the song evaluations that, twice, have landed me in the top quarter of submissions. That meant my work was presented to a handful of publishers and A&R reps, but still, no one picked it up.

"'Voyage of the Heart' is special," Serena insists. "It's touching and personal." She pauses, then slides off the bracelet hiding beneath the cuff of her terracotta-colored shirt. "My sister gave this to me," she says, tracing her finger around its gold treble clef, "before I left Philadelphia. 'For luck,' she said. She was the only one in my family who tried to understand." Sadness washes over her face, but she blinks it aside. "Anyway, why don't you wear it for your meeting? Not that you need luck. Your talent speaks for itself."

Could she be right? I'm too close to my songs to be objective, too entwined in the notes to hear the fallacies, but Serena … she can listen with unbiased ears. She's clearly had at least some success in her career, if she and Seth were rocking auditions and landing gigs, so maybe I should believe her. Maybe I should step out of my own way.

"Thank you," I say, and slip the bracelet onto my wrist. "Fingers crossed."

"Fingers crossed," she repeats.

I walk out onto the sunny streets with my head held high. I can do this. I can stride into today's interview with poise and pride. Ginger Mattington is a musical idol of mine – not only does she sing the most resonating songs, but she writes her own material and founded a publishing company last year – and I could barely believe it when she called to say she was impressed by the samples I'd sent in with my resumé and cover letter.

Even if she doesn't sign me, I'll learn a lot simply by talking to her. When I first began to write, I thought every song was promising. Maybe I wasn't Dolly Parton or Kara DioGuardi, but I knew there was a spark. I knew this was my calling. I knew my words mattered. But everybody's words matter. That doesn't mean we're there yet. My songs are not perfect. I can always do better.

I always want to do better.

I always want my songs to be real – sometimes pretty, sometimes gritty, but above all else, *real*.

I always want music to be my voice when other words fail.

But I guess not everyone feels that way, because as I start off down the sidewalk, I catch sight of something in the trash can in front of the shelter. It's balancing right inside the rim, wedged in place between an empty take-out container and a broken toy. The CD. The present I thought I was giving to the veteran who suffers viciously in a never-ending battle. He tossed it out? Like an undeserving piece of junk?

It jolts me.

I wanted to help. Knowing he resents music hurt my heart. No one should associate something so special with a struggle so painful. Even if he can't tolerate it now, surely he'll be able to one day in the future. Surely his injured soul will heal enough, his holes will close enough, for the music to inch back in.

At least, that was my sheltered view. My foolish view. My arrogant view. Really, though, what do I know about this soldier? What do I know about the horrors he has witnessed, the losses he has suffered, the fights he has endured? How presumptuous to think I could even begin to understand those long, winding roads he's traveled. Suppose, instead of helping, I made it all worse? Suppose I brought the terrible memories back to the forefront?

The earth wobbles below me, and I reach a hand out to the wall of the shelter to steady myself. *What have I done?* We hear about PTSD, how traumatic events aren't over once the bloodshed has stopped, how all it takes is the most innocent trigger to force the past to conquer the present. *What have I done?* Did he listen to the CD, or trash it immediately? Actually, come to think of it, I haven't seen him around the shelter in days. *What have I done?*

Did I chase him away?

Did I chase my mom and dad away all those years ago?

Maybe it's me. Maybe it's always been me.

I grab the CD and take off at a run. Buildings streak past, tourists with cowboy hats and cameras jump out of my way, and the pages I printed this morning and stapled together rustle in my bag until their corners are dog-eared.

I have to get to my interview.

I have to get to something good.

Move faster, Eden.

Mostly, I have to get away from here.

Faster. Faster. Faster. Faster.

* * *

By the time I arrive at Ginger's house – she works out of a studio she built there – my cheeks are flushed a bright crimson and my mind's stopped focusing on the singular effort of running and gone back to the image of the CD, stuck at the edge of the trash can. Like it was on the brink. Like I'm on the brink. I take a minute to smooth out my dress and breathe some air back into my lungs. Having a panic attack now is simply not permissible.

"You can do this," I whisper. "You have to do this."

Before I can second guess myself, I raise my hand and knock on the door.

When Ginger opens it? It's like walking into paradise. Her studio's the stuff dreams are made of – oversized album covers hanging on the walls, microphones set up on stands, a mixing board by the window, a guitar leaning against the sofa, a keyboard next to the door. But it isn't only professional. It's also personal. A shaggy area rug covers part of the hardwoods, freshly cut flowers make it smell like spring, and between the album covers are pictures drawn by Ginger's five-year-old twins. "Ayla did that one," Ginger says, following my gaze as I smile at a depiction of her onstage. "My hair never looked better, right? Red marker suits me." She laughs, and I let myself do the same. I just got here a few minutes ago, but I already like her.

"It must be nice to work from home," I say, as we sit down. "Do the twins ever watch?"

"Only if I'm experimenting." She kicks off her sandals and curls a leg beneath her. "I used to let them play in here while I was working, but I had to put the kibosh on that when Anna decided to yell her heart out during a recording session for my last album." She grabs a pen off the coffee table and uses it to balance her red locks in a messy bun. "Enough about me. Let's chat about you. I was very intrigued by your writing samples. What songs did you bring today?" The atmosphere may be more informal than what I'm used to with interviews, but as Ginger fixes a steady gaze on me, I know that the stakes are every bit as high. I only have one chance to impress her. One chance for my songs to impress her.

Deep breath. It's go time.

I pass her the papers – "Voyage of the Heart" and two other songs I wrote last summer – and try hard to focus on what's happening in front of me, not in the recesses of my mind. I'm worried about that veteran. Where can I learn more about PTSD? Where can I learn about how much damage I've caused, so I can figure out a way to fix things? Would Kristina know, since she's a nurse? I close my eyes as the questions nag at my brain, doing everything in my power to wrangle them into a box and shut the lid. I'll get back to them later. I take another breath and open my eyes as Ginger stares at my work.

"Hmm," she says, her face blank, and the nerves begin their familiar tap dance in my stomach.

Is that a good hmm or a bad one?

My heart does a drumroll as I wait for Ginger to elaborate. I just ... I have no clue what to expect from her. She's so different from most of the people I've interviewed with, so laidback and relaxed. "These are quite good." Her hair tumbles from its bun as she looks up at me. "Especially 'Voyage of the Heart.' There's a simplicity to the lyrics which works well with the wistfulness of the message. It feels like ... " She drums her fingers against the back of the sofa, thinking. "Like I can hear the tears in your words, if that makes sense."

"Complete sense."

I let myself smile a little. She gets it. She really *gets* it.

"I assume this is autobiographical?"

I glance down at the rug for a moment, then up at Ginger. If I want to make it in this business, it is imperative that I wear my heart on my sleeve, even when it hurts. "It's about my parents. I could play it for you," I say, gesturing to her guitar, and am glad when she nods, because my favorite thing about the song is how its melody stays low and lilting until the bridge and then crescendos up into a powerful statement.

Maybe "Voyage of the Heart" will be my break. Maybe my parents will finally get the message if they hear it. Maybe Serena was right ... *Serena.* The moment her name pokes into my thoughts, my instinct settles on something. That light pressure around my wrist, I don't feel it anymore. I sneak a peek and am horrified to see the bracelet is gone.

Oh God.

First the CD; now this.

"Things are just that, things. It's the meaning behind them that counts." Serena said this during one of our conversations shortly after I arrived at the shelter, when I was telling her how upset I was at the thought of losing Grandpa's guitar and the quilt Grandmom crocheted for me. I used to keep it on my bed each night, even during the summer, when it sat folded at the bottom, because it was my way of having her close. Out of everything incinerated in the flames, those are what I miss most. Forget about the laptop, or the blue topaz earrings Jared gave me for my birthday two years ago, or even my music collection. The guitar and blanket left the largest hole, because they were a constant connection to my grandparents. Like Serena's bracelet was her connection to Melanie.

I think I'm going to be sick.

"Is everything okay?" Ginger asks, as my fingers slacken atop the guitar strings and I stop playing mid-chord.

"I ... it's ... I was just ... "

"The instrumental is beautiful," she says encouragingly.

"Thank you," I answer numbly. Serena let me use her guitar. She let me wear her bracelet. No matter what she claims, those aren't only things to her. They're treasured. What am I going to do? I could retrace my steps, but that's akin to finding a needle in a haystack. I try not to think about it, I try to listen to Ginger as she discusses what she calls a song's 'heartstring factor,' but her words are fuzzy against my eardrums.

"You nailed that part," she says, and, for the moment, it perks up something inside me. "These are the kind of songs that reach right into a person's soul and refuse to let go. On many levels, they are excellent. But I'm afraid they aren't debut material, which is what I'm looking for now as I build my company." She frowns as she says it, like she's angry at herself for having this perspective. "I'm genuinely sorry. The industry is just so focused on radio airplay. These songs won't jump-start your career the way you're hoping."

Of course not.

I can't believe I let myself think otherwise.

Hope is a reckless thing. A dangerous thing. Even though I do feel vindicated to know someone as well-respected as Ginger is a fan of my work, it doesn't change the fact that I'm stuck in the same quicksand. I'm still no closer to transforming songwriting from my life into my living. Why do I even bother?

"Thank you for your honesty and time," I say, and Ginger must see the way my shoulders droop, because she bows her head slightly, sadly. "I appreciate it."

I leave her house and walk, slowly and lowly, eyes trained on the ground. Part of me is tempted to call Kristina and pick her brain about PTSD, but I can't make myself punch in her number. I don't want to hear how much she adores living with Robert and I *really* don't want to know all the ways I might've sent that poor soldier spiraling into a black hole. I can't decide if I'm desperate to find him or too terrified.

On and on and on I walk.

Am I going in circles? Feels like it.

Eventually I glance up and realize I'm on Music Row. The irony's laughable.

This is the first place I came after moving to Nashville. I didn't even bother unpacking the car. I just drove straight here, parked on a side street, and spent hours meandering around. RCA Studio B, Sony Music Publishing, ASCAP, Great American Country, it was like wonderland. And now here I am, six years later, and really, what's changed? Grad courses, an apprenticeship, a handful of promising job leads that fizzled to ashes. When does it become futile? When do I give up? My tears encroach again and I slink down, beneath the Music Square West street sign, and let them out. Is this all that my life is destined to be? My cries deepen at the thought. I scrunch over on the sidewalk, wrapping my arms around my knees. A woman walking by gives me a weird look and hurries past, and I know I must seem like a mess, sitting here and sobbing, but I can't stop. I just can't.

I miss my apartment. I miss my security. I miss my muse. I miss my naiveté.

I miss so much it hurts.

"Help," I whisper. "Please help me."

And that's when I feel someone crash into me.

July 1, 2008

Dear Eden,

Well, here we are, my darling girl. In a few short hours, you'll be on your way to Nashville to make your dreams come true. I'll miss you, of course, more than words can express, but I am so happy you're following your heart. It's the greatest gift we can give ourselves. The journey might not be easy – most things worth having never are – but still, I know you will persevere. I know you will write your way into so many lives.

Paint your dreams boldly, Jellybean, with daring brushstrokes and vibrant colors. Remember to be grateful for every day, even the difficult ones, because it's exactly when things get tough that we find out what we're made of and who we are. But also keep in mind: your soul will need soothing sometimes. Take a trip; get lost in a book; go for a walk; have a "cookies and hot cocoa day," because chocolate has restorative powers. And above all else, believe in yourself. Believe in yourself like I believe in you. I am so proud of you, dear. You are the light in my life.

Love you forever and a day.

xoxo,

Grandmom

9

I let out a yelp of surprise and so does the person who tripped over me.

"Hey, are you okay?" he asks.

Four words. Four tiny words that, to my befuddled brain, sound like an answered prayer.

Then, before I can answer him, four more: "I am so sorry." He sits down next to me on the curb and holds up the camera in his hands. "I just finished a photo shoot and I was checking the shots to see how they came out." A sheepish smile curls across his mouth. "I guess I wasn't watching where I was going. Are you okay?" he repeats, with a twinge of a Southern accent, and for a second, I can't answer. I'm too distracted, taking in his dark blonde hair, his single dimple, and his eyes, which are the most spellbinding ones I've ever seen. They're hazel, mostly, but flecked with gold, like the sun has exploded and sprinkled down shimmering pixie dust. The type of eyes you could get lost in. The type of eyes I could write a song about ... you know, if I was actually capable of doing that anymore, which seems not to be the case.

"I'm ... I'm fine," I say haltingly. "And I'm sorry, too, because I shouldn't have just plopped down on the sidewalk like that. Talk about being a hazard." Hazard. As the word escapes my lips, a fresh batch of tears wells up beneath my eyelids. Because that's what I am. A hazard to this man. To that veteran. To myself.

"You don't look fine," he says gently. "Can I help? My mom taught me never to ignore a person in need, so ... "

I can't decide whether to be irked or touched. On the one hand, I loathe being lumped into that category, automatically needy because I happen to be shedding some tears. On the other hand, I'm not exactly a picture of stability and composure now, am I? He's right. I'm in need of a lot of things, too many things. "That's very nice of her," I say, sliding a finger under my eyes to dry them. "And of you, too. I'll be okay, though. Just having a bad day."

A "cookies and hot cocoa day," as Grandmom says.

"Wanna talk about it? Sometimes it helps to get things out."

This is odd. I mean, the South is known for hospitality, but this is unusual even for here. To take what appears to be a sincere interest in a complete stranger, to issue a time-out from his own life in favor of mine, to – as he does next – suggest we go grab coffee, it's like something out of a movie. I should turn him down. Logically, I'm aware of this. I know nothing about him, and I'm not at all the type of person who goes off with a guy after meeting him five minutes earlier. But something in his eyes draws me to him. It's the middle of the day, we're in an area with people walking by and music studios all around, and he isn't raising any suspicions. He just seems like a good guy who was raised right by his mother.

"Okay," I agree, surprising even myself as I stand up.

He suggests a nearby place, and we set off in silence. I sneak peeks at him while we walk and try to paint a picture of his personality. What sort of shoot was he on? Something for an assignment or more of a creative thing? Why was he talkative before but quiet now? Also, I can't help noticing how handsome he is. There's a thin film of scruff on his cheeks and chin, the start of a five o'clock shadow, and his t-shirt is loose enough not to hug his chest but snug enough to show how fit he is. And, I realize, as he holds the door open at the coffee shop, he smells like this intoxicating combination of spice and pine needles. It makes the hair on the back of my neck prickle.

The silence continues as we wait in line, but it's a comfortable kind, not awkward, and when he insists on paying for my drink to make up for tripping over me, I actually agree without an argument. Because it isn't charity. It isn't a reaction to me being homeless or to knowing that my bank account is shrinking by the day. It's nice to be with somebody who knows nothing about me. A blank page. A fresh slate.

"Thank you," I say, as we sit at a table by the front window.

"Welcome." His dimple creases his right cheek as he grins. "I'm Wilson, by the way. Figure you should probably know my name."

"Eden." I offer my hand and he shakes it. His grip is firm, warm. "Nice to meet you."

"Likewise."

We smile at each other, and I feel that prickle again.

"So," Wilson says, and clears his throat. A curlicue of steam rises from his cup of espresso as he lifts it to his mouth. "We don't have to talk about it. Whatever's upsetting you, I mean. It was rude of me to ask."

"No, no, you're right. Keeping things bottled up is a recipe for disaster. It might be good to get another perspective." I sip my hot cocoa – I listen to Grandmom's advice always – and try to decide how much to confide. Part of Wilson's allure is that he is oblivious to the realities awaiting me back at the shelter. I don't want to change that; I don't want his perception of me to shift. It's laughable, really, because it isn't like I'll ever see him again, but I think that may be part of the appeal, too.

"Consider me your sounding board," he offers.

"Well, first, let me say that public meltdowns aren't usual for me. It's just been too many things on top of one another today."

"Such as?"

"Well, for starters I was told the songs I write aren't what the industry's looking for, even though they're heartfelt and relatable and all that jazz. I also lost a bracelet that's important to somebody, and … " I trail off before mentioning the veteran. As it is, I didn't intend to confess this much. With Wilson's gaze fixed on me, with those eyes penetrating my defenses, it's like my voice has taken on a life of its own. "So," I sum up, "not the best day. Have you ever wanted to run away and not look back?"

"Not really." He squints into the stream of sunlight coming in through the window and bathing our table. "I prefer to tackle things head on. Besides, I couldn't run away even if I wanted to. I have too many responsibilities here. I'm sorry, though, for the lousy day you're having. For whatever it's worth, I'd rather listen to a heartfelt, relatable song than a bubblegum, auto-tuned one."

Hearing that is worth a lot, actually.

"Thank you. It sounds like things are tough for you, too, with all the responsibilities?"

He shakes his head slightly. "Not tough, just complicated sometimes. I wouldn't trade it for the world, though." He clears his throat. "So ... you're a singer?"

I decide not to push him about his life. If he changed the subject, he must've had a good reason. "A songwriter. I moved here six years ago, thinking it was my ticket to the career I loved."

"Ah, that explains it." He leans forward. "The lack of accent."

"I'm from New Hampshire," I tell him, "and sometimes I honestly wonder if not having an accent is doing me in. My songs are sort of a fusion between genres, but they favor country music the most and it's obvious whenever I open my mouth that I don't have a native kind of country vibe. You hear interviews with Faith Hill, or Miranda Lambert, or Martina McBride, and you can feel their ties to the South. Maybe I can't identify with – "

"Stop right there," he cuts me off. "I *am* from Tennessee, I've lived here all my life, and I can tell you that its spirit is infectious. Besides, where we're born doesn't dictate who we are."

It reminds me of something Jared, my ex, would've said. I allow myself a brief moment to think of him, to wonder how he's doing in Washington DC. Next month will be a year since he moved and it's still odd to imagine him anywhere other than here. He was so passionate about music while we were at Belmont together. "I'm going to produce something ground-breaking," he used to say, and I believe he would have, if he'd stuck with it. But one night, while we were eating dinner at Monell's, his phone flashed with an unfamiliar number. It was a hospital in DC, where his parents lived. They had been in a car crash and were in intensive care. He blanched this horrific shade of white, we paid the bill without finishing our meal, and headed right to the airport. "I don't know when I'll be back," he said, kissing me goodbye. "It's okay if you don't want to wait for me."

I did want to, though. I loved him. In a world full of unknowns, he was a constant.

Until he wasn't.

Until he spent so many hours at the hospital, sitting by his parents' bedsides as they healed, and fell in love with the occupational therapist assigned to his father's case. Until he decided he wanted to be a therapist, too. Until he found happiness without me.

"Eden?" Wilson taps my hand. "Is it something I said? I didn't mean to upset you."

"You didn't." I drain the rest of my cocoa and reach for my bag. "I'd like to stay and chat some more, but there's something I have to do." Someone I have to face. "Thanks again for the drink and for listening. Mostly, thanks for caring. Your mom would be proud."

"I'll make sure to tell her you think so." He gives a quick wink that'd be corny coming from most people, but is endearing on him. Then he takes out a pencil from the messenger bag he uses for his camera equipment and jots down a phone number on a paper napkin. "If you find yourself in need of a sounding board again ... "

There's a mystery in the way he trails off.

An intrigue. An invitation.

And even before I've left the coffee shop, I'm tempted to accept.

I want to know more about Wilson. I pause by the door, glancing back at him as he pulls out his phone. It'd be easy to rejoin him. To ask questions instead of answering them. To hide away from life a little longer. But then I think of Serena and know I can't stay. She's been a good friend to me, and I owe it to her to be truthful about what happened.

I just ... it fills me with dread.

My mood is temporarily brightened when, as I'm heading back to the shelter, Dina calls to offer me the hostess job at Sensations. "Oh, thank you!" I exclaim. Finally, I have good news. Finally, I'm able to take a step in the right direction. Finally, something is going right. But when I walk into the community room at Open Hearts, looking for Serena, I'm afraid that's all about to change. She's at a table, sitting cross legged as she writes furiously on a piece of loose-leaf paper. Her hair falls in front of her face, creating a platinum curtain, and it's obvious she's busy. This probably is not the time to interrupt, I reason. I'll seek her out later. There's a meeting this evening about our next community service project. I'll wait until after that. Yes. Good idea.

"Eden?"

I'm five seconds away from creeping out of the room when Serena realizes she's not alone.

I could still wait.

I could backtrack, I could find Ms. Birnbaum and talk to her about helping at the shelter's school program, which I've been meaning to do anyway, I could retreat to the courtyard and see if there's a wish to grant. But just because I could doesn't mean I should.

"Hi," I say. "Sorry, didn't mean to disturb you. Looks like you're writing something important?"

"A letter to Seth. Homework from my therapy session."

I don't know how to respond. I know she's been working with one of the therapists here, but it isn't something she mentions frequently and it's clear that her marriage is a sore spot.

"I hope it helps," I venture. "Writing can be cathartic."

"We'll see." She sets down the ballpoint pen and motions me over. "How did the interview go? I was sending good vibes." That makes me feel even worse. I hate that I'm about to ruin the closest thing I have to a friendship these days.

"It was okay," I say, hiding my hand beneath the table as I sit. Better for me to tell her about the bracelet than for her to notice on her own. "She was complimentary about the songs, but it was the same end result as always: she doesn't think they are commercial enough to be a single or a break-out hit."

"Do you really need that, though? Couldn't you approach it

from the opposite direction? Work on the quieter songs, the special ones an artist includes on an album as a thank you to the true fans instead of the bandwagon listeners ... then network with other writers and build your catalogue from there?"

"See, the thing is, I don't think I'll ever be able to write one of those anthems you hear every five minutes on the radio. I don't even think I'd want to. It's not my style. My songs have to mean a lot to me. I can't write simply for the sake of writing."

"I get it. I'm the same way with singing. Seth was willing to audition for anything, just to get our names out there, but I couldn't sing something with no integrity. Guess that should've been my first clue." She sighs and folds the notebook paper in half. "Anyway, I'll say to you the same thing I used to say to myself: don't give up and don't compromise. You never know what will be waiting for you around the bend."

Oh, the irony.

Before I can lose my nerve, I look her straight in the eye and confess. "There's something I have to tell you, and let me preface it by saying how deeply sorry I am. I swear, I'll do anything to make it up to you." I lift my wrist for her to see. "Your bracelet fell off this morning and I didn't realize until it was too late. I'm going to search for it, and if I can't find it, I promise I'll buy you a new one. I got that hostess job at Sensations. My first paycheck is all yours. I know it won't be the same, because Melanie's love is attached to the original, and again, I'm so sorry – "

"Stop apologizing." She holds up a hand. "It's okay. It wasn't your fault."

I stare at her.

"Of course it was," I say.

"It was an accident. These things happen." She's trying to be kind, but her eyes betray her. The amber is almost fiery with pain.

"It's okay to be mad at me," I tell her. "Go on and yell if you want to." I remember what Wilson said and repeat it. "It can help to get things out instead of burying the emotion into an unreachable place. And hey, I deserve it. You've been so nice," I say, "and this is how I repay you? I feel terrible. If there's anything else I can do – "

She forces a half-smile. "Don't beat yourself up, and please don't worry about paying me back." She slips her wedding band around her finger, its revolution slow and measured. "I should finish up this letter to Seth. See you at the meeting tonight?"

That's a cue to leave if I've ever heard one.

"Definitely," I say, rising so quickly I nearly knock over the chair. I apologize again and flee from the room. But I can't shake our conversation. As I go outside and comb the sidewalk, as I knock on Ms. Birnbaum's door and volunteer for the makeshift classroom, as I ask her about that veteran and am told he has transferred to another facility ... the whole time, I keep picturing that look in Serena's eyes and thinking about how it belied her words. Has she simply grown so accustomed to disguising her feelings that it's become second nature?

I wish I could help her.

But haven't I learned that my so-called help does more harm than good?

I ponder that as I take refuge by the fountain. Just a few days ago, I thought this place would be my salvation. I thought it would be my way of making a difference, of reigniting the flame that once burned so brightly inside me. I thought it would be a chance to make my life count. How wrong was I? How short-sighted and how deceived by the rose-colored glasses I was wearing? I watch intently as a man removes a penny from the bowl I set out and tosses the coin into the water. Part of me is seized by a need to ask about his wish and do everything possible to make it come true. It could be a redemption, of sorts. But the other part of me is petrified of miscalculating again and hurting yet another person.

What would Grandmom tell me to do?

I want to call her. I want to tell her everything. I want her to rescue me.

I want those things so fervently, I actually take out my phone and punch in her number. It rings once, twice, three times. She must be at dinner with the other residents on her floor. She'll call me back later, but by then the inclination will have cooled. I will focus, instead, on asking about her day. It'll weigh me down with guilt, spinning a web of deception, and yet I will still do it, I will still protect her at any cost. "Hi, Grandmom," I say when her answering machine clicks on. "It's me. I just called to say I love you. Hope you're having a great day."

I disconnect the call and scroll down through the list of contacts. Who else could be my answer? Kayleigh's still in England, plus I don't feel right about declining her bridesmaid invitation in one call and asking for advice in the next. Kristina is probably at work, and if I talk to her, I'll feel compelled to ask about PTSD and I don't think I can handle the answer right now. There are friends from home and school, and even Jared, who I know would be happy to hear from me, despite his new life, but I can't imagine opening up to any of them about this.

Then my eyes drift over another name.

Wilson.

If you find yourself in need of a sounding board again ...

I don't know why he cares.

He seems to, though, and so, not letting myself think twice, I do it. I call him.

Sensations Café

where music meets munchies

Employee Checklist:

- Always pass out menus to each person; do not simply set them on the table.

- There is a $10 minimum during all shows and open mic nights – please remind your customers about this up front.

- You are entitled to a half hour lunch/dinner break, plus two fifteen-minute breaks throughout your shift.

- Please wear your Sensations Café polo shirt during all work hours.

- No server may wait on more than six tables simultaneously.

- Gloves and hairnets must be worn by all kitchen staff, no exceptions.

- If you know in advance that you'll be missing a shift, please arrange coverage.

- Flowerpots should be on every table. Extras can be found in the back storage room.

- Customer complaints and/or special requests must be shared with the management staff and all necessary parties. Communication is key.

- Each patron should receive an "S" stamped chocolate square with the bill – a reminder of our sweet Southern hospitality!

- Enjoy! Cheerful and friendly employees create a cheerful and friendly atmosphere. Let's make Sensations the best café in Nashville!

10

"Hey, you've reached Wilson. I'm either off making memories or capturing somebody else's, but if you leave your name and number, I'll return your call as soon as possible. Y'all have a terrific day, and remember: embrace whatever develops."

I yank the phone away from my ear and hang up. It's a good thing he didn't answer. What was I thinking? I can't get close to this man. Better to chalk him up to a chance encounter and leave it at that. *Embrace whatever develops.* You can tell a lot about people by their voicemail message. Is it cut and dry? Creative and clever? Wilson's strikes me as both friendly and unique. And what about his coffee choice? I've always believed that can also be telling. Plain espresso with a dash of sugar. Simple, strong, sturdy, sweet. He didn't even look at the menu, so it must be his usual. I don't have a usual, but I wish I did.

Wish.

The man's still by the fountain, flipping through a wrinkled magazine, and I wage an internal war with myself: keep my distance or try to make amends? Not that granting this man's wish will negate the trouble I caused for the other one, but at least it'll swing the pendulum in the positive direction. Maybe I'll just see if he'd like to chat and take it from there. I move over slowly and steal a sidelong look at his magazine. *Bicycling Weekly.* "Do you ride?" I ask, and he startles.

"Didn't see you there," he says. "Yes, I do. How about yourself?"

I shake my head. I feel so small in this moment, mentally grasping for something, *anything*, that will engage this guy in conversation. When did I become this bold? I flash back over the past couple weeks – the mornings I wanted to hide beneath the covers, the afternoons I snuck away from group sessions, the evenings I tiptoed past the community room so no one would see me and ask if I knew how to play poker, or rummy, or whatever the card game of choice was that night. At first, forging a connection with the others just seemed like confirmation of my place here. And how could that be, when I didn't belong? This wasn't my life. This wasn't where I was supposed to be. It's still foreign to me at times, but mostly, I'm growing to accept it.

"Is that what you wished for?" I blurt out, gesturing to the magazine's cover. There's a blue bike on it, a helmeted man raised up from its seat as he races down a dirt road. "A bicycle like that one?" Why am I even bothering? It's not like I can afford to buy it if he says yes.

He looks at me quizzically. "What're you talking about?"

"Before, when you threw a penny into the fountain … I couldn't help noticing, and I just thought you might want to talk about your wish."

Now his look morphs from quizzical to wary. "I, uh, I'd rather keep that to myself," he says, and goes back to staring at the magazine. He's not going to be the one to save me from myself, I realize. I'm still a failure. I'm still an embarrassment. I'm still a songwriter who can't write and a genie who can't find a willing master.

I leave the man in peace and shuffle inside. Through the community room, where a boy plays a game of Go Fish with his mom. Up the steps, where I almost trip on a toy one of the kids must have dropped. By the library, where a light illuminates a row of turned-off computers, their dark screens like ominous black holes. Into the bedroom, where a young girl is skateboarding between the beds. I marvel at her, impressed by her ability to create fun in a situation like this. All I want is to close my eyes and block it out.

To pretend I'm anywhere else.

So I skip the community service meeting, even though Ms. Birnbaum asked everyone to be there for it. It's probably best to keep my distance from Serena for a little bit, anyway, because I know she is more upset about the bracelet than she let on.

I flop down on my bed instead, open my journal, and flip to

the page with that blasted ballad. I will finish its chorus tonight if it kills me. I let myself remember when I started this song, one stormy night in June when lightning electrified the sky and thunder grumbled like timpani drums, and I take time to really feel the lyrics. Then I get to work.

Butterfly of innocence
Butterfly of peace
Butterfly of faith, of love so intensely deep
No.

I groan, scratch it out, and try again.
Her wings are light, her flight serene
His catch is sturdy, his arms a peace
No.

Even worse.
She didn't know it then, but he was carving out a place
He didn't know it then, but she was memorizing his face
They didn't know it then, but –
"Watch out!"

I look up just in time to see the skateboard whizzing right at my head. Its lavender wheels whirl furiously, and as I fling my arms over my head and duck, it whooshes by and crashes into the wall. I feel the thud as it bounces back onto my pillow.

"I'm sorry," the little girl bawls. "Mommy told me to be careful and my ears didn't listen." She's standing at the foot of my bed, her nose like Rudolph's and her eyes sad. "I thought there would be a driveway here, because this is a mansion and mansions are supposed to have lots of room to play with your toys." She wipes the tears dripping down her cheeks.

"What Allie is trying to say is that she apologizes," the girl's mother interjects. "It won't happen again. Right, Allie?" She nods woefully. "Good. Now come along, we're late for the meeting." She shifts her baby boy in her arms, takes her daughter by the hand, and they file out. I sigh, then force my attention back to the journal.

She didn't know it then, but he was carving out a place
He didn't know it then, but she was memorizing his face

They didn't know it then, but –

But ... what? And does 'memorizing' have too many beats to it?

When did this become so hard?

When did this become so impossible?

She didn't know it then, but he was carving out a place

He didn't know it then, but she was memorizing his face

They didn't know it then, but tomorrow had begun

Forever was waiting for its threads to be spun

"Seriously?" I mutter. "What's with the rhyming? It's contrived."
I stare at the page, willing the right lyrics to materialize, as though
they're an apparition of some kind. Instead, the only thing that
comes to mind is a memory of the first song I wrote, when I was six.
Grandmom was so proud, she hung it up on the refrigerator, even
though the whole thing was about my My Little Pony collection. I
sigh. "Forget it." I rip the page from my journal, squeeze it into the
tightest ball I can manage, and arc it into the trashcan by the door.

Slam dunk.

The end.

I'm finished with this song, just not in the way I'd originally
intended.

The idea of starting a new one seems exhausting. I detest that.
Writing used to be the best part of me. Curling up on the window
seat each morning, greeting the days with a melody, and hurrying
home after work, eager to shed the nine-to-five lifestyle in favor
of an evening out, witnessing music come alive on stage ... I lived
for it. I breathed for it. Now I wake up to the stirrings of strangers
and my evenings are no longer spent on Broadway. To go from that
atmosphere to this one simply hurts too much.

Suppose I never get there? Suppose Nashville isn't my happily-
ever-after?

Serena's bracelet is gone. My apartment is gone. The joy I
found in writing is gone.

Or is it?

I heave my journal onto the end of my bed and it falls open to
the page where I jotted down the lyric inspired by Tommy's wish.

That moment, it was joyful. The moment when I helped Ruby and I was rewarded by another line, that was joyful. But, and I'm learning this more and more every day, you can't force moments like those. The whole beauty of them is in their authenticity.

I trace my fingers across the page, over the words.

I miss you, I think. *Please come back.*

* * *

When I wake up the following Monday, my mouth curves into a smile. It's the first day of my job at Sensations, and I'm excited. It's not that the position will be the American dream or a step up the musical ladder, but it *is* the first step on my journey to get back on my feet. I hop up, make the bed, and jump into the shower while everyone else is still in dreamland. The water is warm as it hits my back – a luxury here at the shelter – and I savor it for a few extra minutes. All those mornings I took a hot shower at my apartment, then dried my hair and moseyed into the kitchen to make breakfast, I didn't realize how good I had it. I guess sometimes we have to lose something before we can really understand.

Even that sense of loss can't knock me down today. The sun's shining, birds are chirping, and as I walk outside, the air feels light, refreshing. The streets are still quiet, and I take my time traversing them. I want to memorize the details of this morning. Like the car going by with a bass clef magnet on its trunk. Like the pigeon bobbing along with a piece of bread poking out from its beak. Like the stores and cafés shrouded in darkness, their treasures lying dormant until somebody flips the switch and illuminates them. Like the man standing on the corner, strumming a guitar, its case laying open at his feet.

I should keep going.

I should keep the five measly dollar bills left in my wallet in their place.

Instead, I stop. I watch him play – "God Bless the USA" is his song of choice – and let the dollars flutter into his guitar case. Maybe he's doing this merely for the entertainment. Maybe he loves to bring his music straight to the people. Or maybe he's found himself down on his luck. Maybe he's a widower, or maybe he's lost his job, or maybe the stock market stripped him not only of his money, but also his pride. Who knows? We don't ever really know, do we? Sometimes people smile just to disguise their pain. "Always be kind to everyone," Grandmom taught me. "It's nicer to be nice, and oftentimes our compassion is precisely the thing to turn a person's day around."

I hope he uses my five dollars to treat himself to something.

I hope they make a difference.

What would his wish be, I wonder, as I continue on my way. The teenager pedaling his bike, the woman going to work, the driver of that car with the magnet ... what would their wishes be? I'd ask them all if I could. I'd grant them all if I could. Maybe then I'd get back into my writing groove. How incredible it'd be to feel that rush again, that writer's high when it seems like you're right on top of the world. It's intrinsically connected to the wish granting at this point, which leaves me ... where? I either let my inspiration dry up or turn the fountain into my permanent residence.

Could I do that? Could I start over, this time without making unsubstantiated assumptions and jumping to faulty conclusions? Could I turn 'someday' to 'today' for the people who do believe, and respect the others enough to hold back?

I think so. I think I can help others and myself at the same time.

But first, work.

Sensations is quiet when I walk in. Dina's sitting at a table up front, sipping sweet tea as she fills out what appears to be order forms, and she smiles when she sees me.

"Morning," she says, then gestures for me to join her. "We'll start you off slow today. Mandy – she's our hostess who you'll be replacing – will train you."

"Sounds perfect," I say, inwardly breathing a sigh of relief. I don't think I'll have trouble with this job, but it's nice to have some time to learn the ropes. There's the reservation book, the credit card machine, the numeric setup of tables and the breakdown of how many a server can have, and much more. Mandy does her best to explain everything in between her interactions with customers, and I jot copious notes.

"We only take reservations for parties of five or more," she tells me. "The credit card machine is temperamental sometimes, but if you hold down the power button for ten seconds, it usually resets itself. We try to limit each server to five tables; never more than six. Business is usually brisk in the mornings, afternoons are normally slow, and evenings are the busiest because we host an open mic. Hmm, what else?" She taps her pen against the wooden hostess stand. "I'm sure Dina told you that you'll be taking the day shift. Bobbi's the evening hostess. She's a singer, and sometimes her shows interfere with work. She'll probably ask you to switch shifts at least once a week."

"Got it." I nod.

I'll be happy to switch with Bobbi whenever she wants. Getting paid to spend my evenings in an environment like this? Listening to singers while I work? It's my first day at Sensations, and already I love it. It's not the job of my dreams, but in comparison to where I've been, where I am headed is all shimmer and stardust. It's like the girl from the shelter, the one who described it as a mansion. I thought she was kidding when she said it, until I heard the swirl of awe in her voice. To her eyes, the two-story building is huge. Maybe her family lived in a one-room apartment before. Maybe they'd been sleeping in their car. Maybe they'd spent their days huddled on park benches, trying to ignore the double-takes people shot their way. Then, yes, Open Hearts would be a mansion in comparison. It's all in the eye of the beholder. The same reality can look so different to so many.

Mandy doesn't know I'm homeless.

Dina believes I'm staying with a friend.

Grandmom assumes nothing has changed.

Mom and Dad remain blind to the arrows they've shot, the cuts they've sliced into my soul.

Kayleigh thinks I let her down for no reason whatsoever.

Wilson – who must've thought it was a wrong number since he never called back – imagines me as a damsel in distress.

All these people have perceptions of who I am.

None is accurate. They see me the way I let them see me.

I am the gatekeeper.

But my heart? It knows the truth. It beats its own truth, camouflages it inside a steel cage.

I guess my question is: how can I change that? How do I melt the steel?

LAINEY AND RISA

It was a normal Saturday in the O'Donnell household. Lainey and Risa's parents had made them pancakes for breakfast, and after eating together, Lainey got lost in a book, Risa dove into a world of make-believe with her dolls, and their parents headed for the home improvement store to pick up a can of paint for the kitchen remodel. It was supposed to be a short excursion, only three miles each way. Nobody could've predicted it would turn into forever.

The car that hit MaryAnn and Timothy was a black BMW, a speeding bullet traveling far too fast. Sharp swerve. Shattered glass. Internal injuries. Hit-and-run. Ongoing investigation. Lainey can no longer hear these words without feeling violently ill. She can no longer look at a policeman without seeing the one who rang their doorbell. She can no longer wander around the house she's grown up in, because without her parents, it's not a home. Neither is Open Hearts, but for Lainey and Risa, it's a sanctuary. It's their holding cell, the safety net to catch them and keep them together.

They share a bed at the shelter, and Lainey hugs her little sister at night, swears that nobody will ever come between them. As they snuggle beneath the afghan – one MaryAnn knitted for the sofa in their living room – she tries to believe her own promise. She tries to believe that she did the right thing by running away, she tries to believe that the police commissioner, who Ms. Birnbaum phoned about her and Risa, won't force the sisters into separate families, she tries to believe that her mom's best friend Denise will adopt them. Sometimes she succeeds. Sometimes she fails. And always, she misses her parents. Always, both girls yearn for one more hug, one more kiss, one more day or even one more hour with them.

Always, they pray for things to be so very, very different.

11

The first thing I do when I get back to the shelter? March directly to the fountain. I am going to grant someone's wish. This is the key, I think, to turning things around. To changing the direction of my sails, because, even when we can't control life's currents, we can decide how to navigate them. An adjustment feels necessary right now.

The courtyard is pretty crowded. Tommy's playing tag with another boy, and Ruby sits at one of the patio tables, writing a note in her fancy cursive. A man sits across from her, reading a book with a creased spine, and over near the fence there's a group of kids trying to juggle acorns. A teenager – she must be seventeen or so – watches them with the slightest smile. "Great job, Risa," she says, as the smallest child manages to get three acorns into the air for all of five seconds before they tumble down again.

"No, it wasn't." The pint-sized redhead pouts, and her lower lip juts out.

"Hey now." The teenager kneels down to her level and lays her hands on the little girl's crossed arms. "Remember what Mom always taught us? Don't be sad when something doesn't go right. Be happy that – "

"You tried." Risa's gaze is fixed on the ground.

"Exactly. Mom would've been proud of you for giving it your best shot."

"Even though the acorns fell?"

"Even though the acorns fell," she says, then presses a kiss to her sister's forehead. "I bet Mom is watching, you know, from up there." She tips Risa's chin so she's looking at the sky. "An audience is your favorite thing, right? Can you imagine Mom and Daddy cheering for you up in heaven?" She swats away a tear, and my heart cracks. Those poor sisters. Losing both their parents? At so young an age?

It's blindingly unfair.

"Do you think they have friends in heaven?" Risa asks. "Not their friends from here, not like Mr. Tom or Mrs. Sandy, but like … friends who also had accidents and turned into angels?" This appears to be more than the older sister can take. She glances upward, and her lips move faintly, as though she's praying, or perhaps asking their parents for guidance.

"Absolutely," she says. "Mom and Daddy made friends wherever they went. I'm sure heaven is no exception." She hugs Risa and keeps her snug in the embrace. They stay like that, still as statues, but also leaning on each other, until a blonde-haired girl skips over and says something to Risa about teaching her to juggle.

"Can I?" She looks to her older sister for approval.

"Of course." She hugs her one more time, then waves her hand. "Go on. Have fun."

Oh, I want to help them.

I want this wish to be theirs.

And yet, even as I watch the older sister walk to the fountain and reach for the penny bowl – it's almost like she's reading my mind – I know that I'll never be able to give her the one thing she needs most. When she lets that copper coin fly, she's not going to wish for what a normal teenager would. She's going to wish for her parents to be here, or for the pain to stop pressing so heavy on her chest, or for a way to make things better for Risa. I should really let this one go. Another failed wish is the last thing I need. But I can't let it go. Because of my own parents. Because, although they are alive and well, I understand the sorrow of not being able to turn to the very people who brought you into this world. It's a different situation, clearly, and these sisters are experiencing a visceral grief unlike anything I can comprehend, but still, I feel drawn to them.

"Hi." I join her by the fountain. "I'm Eden."

"Lainey." She tilts her head and peers at me through long red eyelashes. "Are you new here? I haven't seen you around."

The thing about trying to blend into the background? Sometimes it makes you invisible. "Three weeks ago," I tell her, "that's when I moved in. How about you?" Even if I can't change Lainey's life, I can at least lend an ear.

"Five weeks, two days, one hour, and ... " She checks her watch. "Eleven minutes."

"Wow, you're really keeping track, huh?"

She tries to smile, but it stops at her eyes. "I used to do that with my grades. I'd record them all so I could stay on top of things. My dad would joke about it and say I must not trust my teachers to give ... " She trails off and shakes her head sharply. "Never mind."

I weigh my options: encourage her to open up or let it be? I swore I wouldn't push anymore and I meant it, but there's so much pain in Lainey's eyes. I want to help. And so I find a middle ground. "Loss is a terrible thing to deal with, especially when it's unexpected," I say gently, and Lainey raises a hand to the engagement ring dangling on a chain around her neck. It must be her mother's. Risa, too, wears a circle strung around her neck – their father's wedding band, it looks like.

"Terrible," Lainey echoes in a whisper.

"It's scary when your life's suddenly upended and everything that was normal becomes foreign. And the outside world keeps spinning, the people around you go on with their days as usual, and it's hard to make sense of it because your existence has changed drastically." I'm trying to tow a careful line here, balancing between not prying and still offering some solace.

My words hit a nerve.

"It isn't hard," she whispers, "it's impossible." Then the flood comes. "My parents were killed in a car crash. They went to a store to buy paint because we were redoing our kitchen and never came home." The color drains from her cheeks. "A policeman rang our doorbell to tell us what happened, and he was a really nice guy, but I had to lie. I said our grandparents lived with us, that they weren't home, and they'd be back from the grocery store soon. They aren't alive anymore, but I was scared the cop would take Risa and me down to the station if he figured out we didn't have anyone to look after us. Our parents didn't have siblings, so we don't have any aunts or uncles, either. I thought it would mean we'd go to foster care and be separated – I saw a story about that on the news not long ago – so that's why I couldn't tell the truth. The cop went to his car for a minute to call his chief, and that's when I grabbed Risa and we ran. We ended up here." Rain clouds thunder through her eyes. "Ms. Birnbaum said she can't let us keep staying alone since I don't turn eighteen for a couple more months, so I called our mom's best friend Denise, and I think she's going to adopt us. It's just taking a long time since she lives in South Carolina, and I guess the states have different adoption systems. Hopefully it'll go through soon."

By the time Lainey finally stops for a breath, her cheeks are no longer white, but fire engine red. She isn't crying, though. In fact, she seems relieved. Her shoulders slump, causing the chain around her neck to swing forward, and she grabs the ring, caresses it with the pad of her thumb. "It sucks," she laments. "I never thought I would be an orphan at seventeen, or worse, that Risa would be one at five. She doesn't really get it, what happened to our parents. She only knows they aren't coming back. I'm always telling her how much they loved us – and that they *still* love us – and I think maybe it helps. Or maybe not, I don't know. It's hard to make things better for her when I can't even make them better for myself."

I rest my hand on hers. "I'm so sorry for what you've gone through. You're doing a good job," I reassure her. "Not only are you keeping your parents' memory alive, you're also giving Risa the love and comfort she needs." I watch the little girl for a moment. She's juggling again, still not as well as the other kids, but an improvement from before. "And joy, too. You help her smile when she feels like crying. It takes a strong person to do that."

"Sometimes it hurts to be strong," Lainey says, lifting her gaze and staring at Risa. "Sometimes I wish I could have an hour to myself, without her hanging on my every move. Risa's my world, but I have to hide when I'm with her. I can't scream and cry and throw things. I can't let her see just how devastated I am."

This ... *this* is why she seems relieved. Because she was able to talk to me without censoring her anguish. Without sugarcoating her words. Without having to put on a brave face for the sister who now relies on her for everything. Lainey's had to grow up too fast. Maybe I can't grant her deepest, rawest wishes, but I can give her that hour. I can give her the freedom to break, to grieve, to mourn. "I'd be happy to keep an eye on Risa for awhile if you want some alone time," I offer. "We can read, or color, or do whatever she enjoys."

Lainey opens her mouth to answer, then closes it again. She watches her sister, who's gathering up the acorns she just dropped, but after a few seconds her gaze turns vacant. What is she seeing, if she's even seeing anything at all? I wonder if she's remembering the good times or if she is trapped in an endless cycle of the bad ones.

"That would be great," she says finally. "I'm not sure Risa will go for it, though. She doesn't like when I'm not within eyesight. She needs me."

"And you need a break."

Her mouth dips into a frown. "Does that make me a bad person?"

"Of course not. It makes you human. If you spend all your time holding someone else up, you'll end up falling down yourself. Take an hour. Take more, if you want. It doesn't mean you love Risa any less. Taking care of yourself is the best way to take care of her." Lainey doesn't answer, but she does sigh heavily. "It doesn't have to be today," I add. "Whenever you are ready, the offer will still stand."

Time to go.

I've put the suggestion out there. The choice is hers alone to make. Lainey is the only one who knows what's best for her and Risa.

When four become two, two become one.

This time it's bittersweet when the lyric drifts into my mind. I almost don't want to jot it down, because it feels too personal, too bound with pain, and yet I reach for my journal anyway. Music is a story, a journey, and it's only when the characters are organic that the listeners can relate. I know a song like this will never saturate the airwaves, but it's the kind that might sneak into a person's soul and stay awhile. I'd rather write one of those. I'd rather stay true to what drew me to music in the first place: the power it holds to make people feel like they aren't alone.

When four become two, two become one
Souls connected, hearts undone
Who do we turn to when the world grinds to a halt?
When tears run rampant and it all falls apart?

The words race at me faster than I can write them, and it takes my breath away, this emergence of something I'd feared was gone forever. It isn't enough for a verse or a chorus, but the beginning's there, and for the first time since the fire, a melody is, too. It's faint, the chords peeking uncertainly around a corner, and yet it seems like a victory.

I even tell Grandmom about it when she calls. "The notes are cautious," I explain. "It may take time before they trust me enough to play at full volume. But I love them already."

How amazing it is to say that again.

How rejuvenating.

"I reserve the right to hear it first," Grandmom says, and I smile, because this is what she always says.

"That's the perk of being my number one fan," I tease.

"Just you wait, pretty soon you'll have a whole legion of fans. Promise you won't forget your old grandmom when that happens?"

"You're not old, Grandmom, and you certainly aren't forgettable."

It's true. Grandmom is one of those women with classic beauty. With auburn hair, aquamarine eyes, and porcelain skin, she used to be the belle of the ball as a teenager and young adult. Her hair may be gray now, her eyes may have a few wrinkles around them, and her skin may be freckled, but she's still the epitome of elegance. Grandmom's beauty is much more than skin deep, though. She has a light inside her, this sweetness and love of life that would make anyone sit up and take notice. She is warmth and affection, confidence and support.

"I was looking through some photo albums today," she tells me. "Remember the summer when we had all those record high temperatures and we had to use spray fans every time we went to the beach?"

"And the zoo, and Sohier Park to see the lighthouse, and Water Country ... boy, were you a good sport to let me drag you everywhere. Thank you."

"Oh, honey, you never have to thank me. I loved doing those things with you."

"Right back at you."

"We should go again," she suggests. "To the park, when you visit. Maybe we can convince your parents to join us."

And maybe thousands of pigs are about to take flight. That'd probably be more likely, actually. Even when Mom and Dad are home, they're not really there. They're working on journal articles, or planning the next trip, or meeting with colleagues, or monitoring the progress of the kids they have helped ... it goes on and on. I wonder what would've happened if I took my mother up on her offer to come here. Would they have stayed holed up in the hotel room again, or would things have been different this time?

Stupid, Eden.

Things are never different. You know that.

"Yeah, maybe," I say noncommittally to Grandmom. As angry as she was with them for leaving, for just up and abandoning their life and family like they had no ties to Portsmouth, she still has this hope that they'll come around one day. I guess a mother has to believe in her daughter like that ... it frustrates me, though, because it'll never happen and she'll keep being disappointed over and over. "So I started a new job today," I say, suddenly desperate to change the subject. "It's at an awesome café called Sensations."

"Excellent!" she exclaims, and I picture her hand going to her chest, as it always does when she gets good news. "Tell me more."

So I do. I tell her about the stained glass lamps, and the delicious-sounding menu, and the stage area in the back. I tell her that tomorrow will be my first day seating diners and running the hostess stand on my own, and I tell her about the open mic nights and scheduled shows. But I don't tell her the rest. I don't tell her the *whys*, just the *whats*. I don't tell her that I'm hiding in the shelter lobby, where I go every night when we chat, so she won't hear the commotion and figure out something is amiss.

Serena walks in while I'm talking, her smile painted into a mauve curve and her eyes glimmering beneath their dusky-shaded lids, and I do such a double take I nearly fall out of the chair. I've never seen her wear anything except a barely-there coating of lip gloss. A chocolate brown shirt still hangs around her frame, but instead of yoga pants she has it paired with jeans.

"Hey," she says, raising a hand in greeting. "I'm going up to the library. Find me when you're off the phone, okay? I have an idea I want to run by you."

She floats out of the lobby before I can answer, but it's already too late.

"Was that Kristina?" Grandmom asks. "I'll let you go, dear, if you two have plans."

"No plans," I say tightly.

It's true, but also not. Honest, but also not.

Would it really be so bad if I told her what happened? She's eighty-one, but a strong eighty-one in many ways. Her mind is as sharp as ever, her heart is as full as ever, and maybe I'm not giving her enough credit. Just because she walks slower now, and grows tired more easily, and is comfortable with somebody else cooking her meals sometimes instead of whipping them up herself … it doesn't mean she can't handle whatever life throws her way. She'd be so upset if she knew I had been lying to her for weeks. "How could you shut me out?" she'd say. "I thought we were a team."

She'd be right.

We were a team. We *are* a team.

I take a breath.

"Grandmom?" I say. "There's something I have to tell you."

NOTEWORTHY

Want to perform at our restaurant three evenings per week?

Want exposure in front of hundreds?

Want your chance to break in to the Nashville music scene?

Want free admission to a singing showcase?

Want to help choose our new act?

Want to chart the course of someone's future?

Here's your chance!

NOTEWORTHY will be holding an **Open Mic night on Monday, July 28th** for anybody interested in joining our team. Doors open at 6:00PM, performances begin at 7:00, and after all the auditions have taken place, audience members can vote for their favorite. The winner will receive a place on our renowned roster. Don't miss out on this wonderful opportunity!

For more information, please contact Chelsie at 615-555-6914.

12

"What's on your mind?"

It's a simple question, yet I can't seem to force an answer past my lips. Where do I begin? How do I phrase this so that worry won't gather in my grandmom's veins? She is like a mama bear when it comes to me, and although this cub has been out on her own for quite awhile now, the inclination is still there.

"Sweetheart?" she prompts.

"Sorry," I say hastily. "It's just that ... well ... "

All of a sudden, a movie reel has started to play before my eyes. Grandmom teaching me to ride a bike, pastel ribbons flapping from the handlebars as I crept down the sidewalk. Grandmom setting up a checkers board on her front porch, each of us in a wicker chair with a glass of milk and plate of cookies for "brain power," as she called it. Grandmom making her delicious chicken soup – forever the smell of home to me – and explaining the steps as I stood on a stool to help. Grandmom cutting my hair, volunteering as homeroom mom, picking out seashells for my collection when we spent our summers on the beach. Grandmom showing up early to all my gymnastics meets, so she could sit in the front, and Grandmom adding pretzel sticks to my bowl of ice cream, because "it's simply better that way."

It's a movie reel that could go on forever, one I *want* to go on forever. Suppose I cut it short by telling her what's happening? Suppose it dissolves into a disagreement about if I should stay or go? And suppose she tells Mom and Dad? I know she'd want to, and I'm not sure I can persuade her to keep quiet. Is it even fair of me to put her in that position?

"Eden?" Grandmom's voice juts into my thoughts. "Are you there?"

"I'm here." And then, before I can stop myself: "I was just going to say I miss you, that's all."

Also true. Also honest.

Also a deception.

But I can't risk it. I can't risk Grandmom begging me to come back, me refusing, and us having a falling-out. I can't risk her lying in bed at night, staring at the ceiling as the clock's numbers glow an ethereal green from the nightstand next to her, and worrying nonstop about her only grandchild. Is my motivation selfless or selfish? It feels impossible to extricate the two sides of the spectrum from one another. They're too tangled. I'm too tangled.

"I miss you too," Grandmom says. "But we'll see each other soon."

October fourth. That's when I'm flying to New Hampshire for a week. I depleted the last of my savings account to buy a plane ticket. I resolve, right here and now, to be out of the shelter by then. Surely it'll be easier to talk about the experience once it's part of my backstory instead of my current chapter. It won't matter if Grandmom tells Mom and Dad at that point, because they'll no longer be able to let me down. They'll no longer be able to tack me onto the bottom of a to-do list or make a lot of empty promises we all know they have no intention of keeping.

Sixty-eight days.

I have sixty-eight days to turn things around.

Sensations is a good start, but deep down I know there must be more.

Where will I find it? How will I find it?

I consider that as I head up to the library to find Serena. My stomach ties itself into a knot when I see her sitting there. Should I apologize again about losing the bracelet? Or is it best to stay quiet? She appears to have put it behind her, but things aren't always what they seem. I don't know what to do.

"What's up?" I ask cautiously, taking the chair next to hers.

She twists around, and close-up, I notice she's wearing mascara, too. "Okay, so I just had a killer audition," she says, her voice pitching up an octave. "Ever since leaving Seth, I've ... well, it's been a harder transition than I thought. I'm so used to harmonizing with him." She flinches, but continues. "Anyhow, there's a restaurant on Demonbruen that was looking for a regular performer, somebody to sing three nights a week, and instead of holding auditions in front of the manager, they invited a crowd to listen. For the first time in months, I felt that spark again ... you know, the kind where you just sense a song is working."

Okay ... maybe she really isn't upset anymore. If she was, why would she be telling me this?

"That's awesome!" I exclaim, breathing a little easier.

I'm elated for her. When a song clicks, there's nothing like it.

"Thanks." She smiles. "So the manager asked the crowd to vote, and they chose me. Beginning next week, I'll be on stage every Tuesday, Friday, and Sunday night. But here's my problem: most of my catalogue is material Seth and I worked on together. The thought of having to sing the songs, of having his words come out of my mouth ... it makes me sick." She glares at her wedding band, and I wonder, not for the first time, why she doesn't take it off. Even if they're still legally married, she's clearly furious with him.

"I don't blame you," I say. "I'd feel the same way."

"Good. Because I need your help." Her smile grows a little wider. "I'd love to sing some of your songs instead."

To say I'm caught off-guard is an understatement. Never in a million years did I imagine she was leading up to that. I guess after hearing 'no' so many times, 'yes' feels out of reach. We can dream about it, we can pray for the day a door opens and we finally get to bound through, and at the same time, it's tough to let yourself believe the moment will come. At least, it's tough for me. But didn't I promise myself I was going to melt that steel cage? Letting people in has been, for the most part, an error. A miscalculation. Maybe the inevitable disappointment is worth it, though, to experience the temporary joy.

And what better way to make up, at least a bit, for losing Serena's bracelet?

"Of course you can sing them," I tell her. "I'd be honored."

We spend the rest of the evening studying my journal, me

playing the guitar to teach Serena the melodies and her jotting down notes about key changes, and when I wake up the next morning, I'm filled with a hope that feels almost foreign. Ruby's snoring in the next bed, wind-driven rain pounds against the roof, and a blast of icy air from the vent sends goosebumps down my arms. Nothing can ruin my mood today, though. I practically bounce out of bed, and the spring stays in my step all the way to Sensations.

"Good morning," I say cheerfully to Dina.

"Good morning." She peers over her glasses. "You're early."

I'm always early. I get it from Grandmom.

"Eager to get to work." I flash a smile that's loose, genuine. "Thanks again for the opportunity."

Pre-fire, I'd never have viewed a place like this as an opportunity.

It would have merely been a stop on the way to where I was going, not a stepping stone.

Now I'm grateful.

Even when the first customer of the day throws a wrench into all I've been taught by declining a menu, because she eats here every morning and always has the same omelet with grits. Even when I answer the phone and take a noontime reservation for seven people, only to have twelve show up. Even when the credit card machine jams, just like Mandy warned, and I have to call Dina to help. It's not the smoothest day, but I'll take it.

"Welcome to Sensations," I say, over and over. And, later, "Hope y'all enjoyed your meal. Have a great day." Sometimes I feel like an imposter when I say 'y'all.' Do people think I'm trying to fit in where I don't belong? Or does this sort of thing happen when a person moves to a different part of the country? Is it a natural assimilation? I often wonder how my parents cope with this. They're in another country every year, after all. I've seen the photos they bring back. I've watched the videos. I've heard about the schoolteachers, and doctors, and vendors who sell handmade jewelry. But I've always wanted to know more. Maybe I'll ask them this time. Maybe I'll keep an open mind. Maybe my skin is thick enough now that the puncture wounds won't hurt as much.

Sixty-seven days.

Then sixty-six, sixty-five, sixty-four, sixty-three.

By the time it's the weekend, I'm exhausted. Working six shifts – Bobbi did indeed have a show on Friday, so I covered for her – was a lot more draining than I expected. When I was a receptionist, I could sit all day. At Sensations, I'm constantly on my feet. It's a satisfying kind of tiredness, though. Still, it's a relief to sit out in the courtyard for awhile, eating breakfast as I dog-ear the pages in my journal that I want Serena to look at before Tuesday.

Each time I think about her up there on stage, sharing my songs with an audience, I'm consumed by exhilaration. It reminds me of the William Wordsworth quote I've always loved: "Fill your paper with the breathings of your heart." That's what songwriting is about. The songs work their way into my head and refuse to leave. That's where they're supposed to be. I don't write because I want to say something, but because I have to, because it takes a pastel world and turns it into an explosion of technicolor.

I want to do that for people.

I want to touch their lives like other songwriters do mine.

Like music does to me.

I've just marked a page in the journal – a song titled "White Dove" that I wrote in April – when a shadow falls over the paper. I look up to find Lainey, the girl I talked to earlier in the week. Her eyes are red, her hand around Risa's. "That offer you made," she says, barely audibly, "if it isn't too much trouble, I'd like to take you up on it now."

"Absolutely," I say, closing the journal. Then I hold out my hand to Risa. "Hi, I'm Eden."

She shrinks back behind her big sister.

"It's okay," Lainey says soothingly. "Eden's really nice."

She slowly peeks out from behind Lainey's legs.

I crouch down so Risa can look me in the eyes. "I like your shirt," I tell her. "The puppy dog is so cute, and turquoise is my favorite color. What's yours?" She still doesn't say anything, only regards me warily.

"Pink." Lainey answers for her. "Your favorite color is pink, right, kiddo?"

Risa nods her head a fraction of an inch. "'Cause Mommy said it makes me look like a Valentine, with my red hair."

"Your mommy sounds like a very special lady."

"She was the best. Daddy, too. He teached me how to play hopscotch and build block towers."

"Maybe you can teach me those things. What do you say?"

I watch her scuff the tip of her sneaker against the ground. Back and forth, back and forth, back and forth. The repetition seems calming for her. I don't know what to do next. Lainey is desperate for a time-out and Risa's petrified of one.

"I won't be far away," Lainey promises. "I just need to go for a walk. I'll be back before you can miss me."

"And you can call Lainey whenever you want," I add. "We'll put her number into my phone right now." Risa's cocoa brown eyes dart between us as Lainey inputs the digits and I do the same on her phone. Has she always been this cautious, or is it a new development? It saddens me to think she's been forced into timidity by life's unfair hand.

Eventually Lainey convinces her to give me a chance, and with a kiss on the little girl's forehead, she's off, nearly tripping over her own feet as she flees. What happened to precipitate this? Why is she willing to leave Risa today when she wasn't before? I get an answer in the picture Risa draws. It was her suggestion to color, after turning down everything I proposed – playing hopscotch, building with blocks, reading books, having a pick-up-sticks tournament – and I can't help sneaking peeks as we sit at the outdoor table with construction paper and crayons. "You're an awesome artist," I say. "Much better than me. I mean, look at this cherry tree I'm trying to draw. I think it looks more like a beach umbrella."

The tiniest of giggles escapes her mouth. "Or a ginormous mushroom!"

I purse my lips and try to put on an indignant face. "It does not."

Actually, it does. It really, really does. "You gotta make the leaves big," Risa says, taking a green crayon from the box. "And messy, not super neat, 'cause real trees grow in lots of directions." She slides my paper over and sets about fixing my error. This gives me time to appraise her own picture. There are two girls, both with red hair, and the taller one is holding a phone to her ear. The thought bubble percolating from her is jagged, and in it is printed a thick NO. Lainey had mentioned they're waiting for approval from the court about their mother's friend adopting them, and I instantly worry something's gone wrong. I don't want to ask Risa, though, so I go back to coloring instead and toss innocent questions at my once-again quiet companion. What's her favorite game? Does she like to play any sports? What's her favorite animal?

Hungry, Hungry Hippos.

Soccer.

Panda bears.

Her answers are clipped, closed-off, so I decide to try another tactic. "Can you help me out with my picture again?" I ask. "I want to add in swings and a slide – " It's exactly the wrong thing to say. Before I even finish the sentence, she jumps down, bolts across the yard, and slips through the gate as somebody opens it to enter from the other side. It all happens so fast I barely register her escape until she's already gone, and then I'm running after her, panic slamming in my chest. "Risa, wait!" I scream, but if she hears me, she ignores it.

Down the sidewalk she sprints. Right at the corner. Over the square of concrete that's cracked slightly. Across the lawn. Through another gate. This is when I lose sight of her, and I scream again, praying she'll listen this time. My God, if something happens to her … no, it won't. It can't. I swore to Lainey that I'd keep her safe. I slam through the gate after her, searching for a glimpse of light-up sneakers, a flash of red hair, a hint of turquoise fabric, and nearly drop in relief when I catch sight of all three. We're at a playground, one I never knew existed, and Risa's sitting on the seesaw, trying – and failing – to propel herself, even though there's nobody to counteract her weight.

I hang back by the fence, trying to force air into my burning lungs. I want to go over to her, but I feel like she needs some time to herself. There was something about my drawing that was a trigger, that brought her here. It's a cute place, with a castle-themed wooden jungle gym, swing-set, slides, and the seesaw, and all around me, kids are running wild and free. There's a whole group of them in the castle, squealing about dragons and sorcerers, and over on the swings, a woman pushes a set of identical twins. Older kids whiz down the slides, arms in the air like they're on a roller-coaster, and I watch as a pixie-sized girl toddles over to them. She must be three or so, with blonde ringlets which cascade down her back. And then there's Risa. She keeps her gaze fixed downward, hands clamped around the handlebar of the seesaw, and doesn't react at all as I balance her out on the other end. "Are you okay?" I ask softly.

Silence.

"Should we call Lainey?"

Silence.

"Do you like playgrounds?"

Silence.

Then, finally, she says, "Daddy took me to the playground every weekend. He pushed me super high on the swing and held me really tight when we zoomed down the slide and bounced his feet on the ground so I could fly up towards the sky when I was on the seesaw. Lainey says that's where he and Mommy live now, in the sky, so I thought if I tried really hard, I could send myself there to visit. Lainey brings me here to play sometimes and I remembered there was a seesaw." A tear slips out of her eye and trickles down her face. "But it isn't working. Don't they wanna hug me again? Can't they help me up?"

It's an arrow to the heart.

What would Grandmom say in this situation?

How would she make things better?

I'm still trying to formulate a response when someone helps me out.

"Close your eyes," the man says. "And wrap your arms around

yourself, snug as can be." I ease up from the seesaw so Risa will move closer to the ground, and to my surprise, she actually follows the instructions. "Now think of your parents, imagine them giving you their best bear hugs, the kind where you never want to let go. Can you feel it?"

I know that voice.

A slow smile crawls across Risa's face. "I feel it! Hi, Mommy! Hi, Daddy!"

I look over and meet those eyes, those mesmerizing eyes, and see the man who has handled this so much better than I ever could have.

Wilson.

But he's not alone this time. That little girl with the halo of blonde curls is in his arms.

"So we meet again," he says with a friendly nod.

"So we do. Thanks for the assist. I was ... I didn't ... this isn't my ..."

Somehow he understands what I'm trying to say.

"No problem." He gives Risa a wave as she stares at him. "Hi," he says. "I'm Wilson."

"Who's that?" she asks, pointing to the girl in his arms.

He smiles. "This," he says, shooting a sideways glance at me, "is Emmalyn. My daughter."

Second Chance Thrift Store
Shop • Donate • Volunteer

Want to update your clothes?

Unable to afford department store prices
or the high-end boutiques?

Looking for a large variety of quality merchandise?

Second Chance Thrift Store carries just what you need. Visit one of our two area locations and see for yourself that secondhand doesn't mean playing second fiddle. Eighty percent of our profits are donated to local charities, and we offer a wide range of clothing, accessories, and shoes.

Bring in this ad for

30% off
one regularly priced item.
Expires 12/31/14

Open Monday – Saturday, 11:00AM – 8:00PM

Donations accepted during business hours.

13

His daughter? He has a daughter?

I blink at him in surprise. He seemed so what-you-see-is-what-you-get that day. I'd never have guessed that one of his job titles is Daddy. But here we are, with Emmalyn circling her arms around his neck, and all it takes is a cursory glance to see what a mutual admiration society they have. Plus, the resemblance is clear: she has the same hazel eyes, the same dimple dotting her right cheek, and the same mouth, which swings up slightly at the corners, like there's always a reason to smile.

"You're super lucky," Risa tells Emmalyn. "I used to have a daddy, too, but he moved to heaven. I miss him lots." The smaller girl just blinks, eyes wide as saucers, and I look helplessly at Wilson, not knowing where to begin. Do I ask Risa not to talk about this, for fear of upsetting Emmalyn? Or is it good for her to speak her grief? Is that the best way to heal? My brain can't wrap itself around this; it's too busy responding to Wilson's revelation.

Never judge a book by its cover. First impressions are rarely what they seem.

You'd think I would have learned that by now, living in a homeless shelter and all. Serena, Ruby, Tommy, Sherri, Lainey, Risa … they're much more than their losses. We're so quick to define people before even knowing them. It's a judgment I've been terrified of having cast upon me. Maybe this is a reminder to practice what I preach.

"Risa, I think Emmalyn's too young to – " I start to say.

"I'm a big girl!" Emmalyn interrupts, and proudly displays three fingers.

"How did that happen?" Wilson tickles her and she giggles. "It seems like you were just born." He sets her down, straightens the ruffled bottom of her turquoise and white gingham sundress, and gestures to the sandbox. "Maybe you can show Risa your favorite part of the playground, Em. Does that sound like fun?"

She nods and holds out her hand to Risa. "Wanna play?"

Three years old. What a marvelous age to be. The world is all rainbows and roses, so innocent, so joyful, with no storms to overshadow the sun. How long can that last? How long can we build a bubble around these precious lives?

I look to Risa.

Not nearly long enough.

She does go off with Emmalyn, and I let some of the tension drain from my muscles. Maybe this is what she needs most, just to have a chance to be a kid again. It won't close her wounds, but it can tack a band-aid on them for a bit. I hope Lainey is doing the same, wherever she is.

"So ... " Wilson stuffs his hands into his pockets and rocks back on his heels a little. "Should I be insulted that you didn't call?"

Fire rushes into my cheeks. "I actually did, but I got your voicemail. You were already kind enough to listen to me ramble at the coffee shop, so to subject you to another round of it didn't feel fair and I hung up. I'm sure you have better things to do with your time. Like your photography and your daughter – " I clear my throat. "Anyway, how funny to run into you again."

"Fate must like our odds." He grins. "And for the record, I always have time for pretty women."

A beat later, he realizes how that sounds.

"Oh God, I didn't mean – " His face flushes almost as badly as mine. "I'm not a ... I don't date a lot ... it's just Em and me ... it's tough to have a personal life ... " He stops and shakes his head good-naturedly. "Let's try this again. I've been a single parent since Em was born, and you're right, other than work, I don't get out much, unless you count music class, story time, or Gymboree. I blame my astounding lack of charisma on that. It's been forever since I braved the dating world. I could make the time, though, for the right person." He smiles shyly, and it's such a departure from his take-the-reins foresight with Risa moments ago, that I don't quite know how to respond. I like him. I like him a lot.

And apparently he likes me, too.

"You were great before," I tell him, annoyed with myself for detouring the conversation, even as I make a conscious choice to do it because I'm nervous about where it may lead. "With Risa, I mean. Thank you. I didn't have a clue how to help her."

"Glad to do it. My heart broke when I overheard. That poor girl lost both her parents?"

"In a car accident. She and her older sister are staying at the same – "

Shoot.

"The same what?"

I'm not ready to tell him about the shelter yet.

"We were kinda thrown together by chance," I fumble. "I'm babysitting so Risa's sister can take a breather." My eyes flutter over to the sandbox, where the girls are playing side-by-side. Risa's not smiling, but she isn't crying, either, and maybe for now, that's all anyone can ask for. "You're such a natural with kids."

"You should have seen me the first couple months." Out pops his dimple. "There was the time I snapped her pajamas wrong and both her legs stuck out. There was also the time I forgot to put a new diaper on her after taking off the dirty one. Don't even ask how I managed that, except, in my defense, it was shortly after I brought her home from the hospital, and the world's a very fuzzy place when a person's sleep deprived. Oh, and my personal favorite: the time I had the wise idea to feed her while already dressed up for a wedding I had to shoot." He wiggles his eyebrows. "That went about as well as you'd imagine."

I let myself laugh. "She obviously adores you, though, so you're doing something right."

"I hope so." His whole expression softens.

I want to ask why Emmalyn's mother isn't in the picture.

I want to ask why he's doing this on his own.

Suddenly, I want to know so much about him.

Risa runs over then, her knees gritty with sand. "Wanna play?" she asks me. "We're pretending the sandbox is a castle for princesses to live in with their princes."

I love this. I love that her mind is still willing to fool itself into thinking of fairy tales, even though her own life has become the worst sort of horror story. And so I follow her lead, settling down into the sandbox. Emmalyn reaches over me, trying to pick up one of the shovels. She smells sweet, like a summer rain, and I dart out my arms to catch her when she knocks herself off balance and tumbles into my lap. Hands on my knees, head tossed back, cheeks rosy and eyes prismatic, she reminds me of a baby doll come to life: sugar and spice and everything nice.

I hope she never loses her sense of wonder. I hope her glass is always half-full.

Her father's, too.

He's standing outside the sandbox, watching us with this smile that makes my heart melt around the edges. "C'mon," I say. "Join us."

"Yeah, Daddy!" Emmalyn squeals. "Play with us!"

For a brief moment, I flash back to a similar scene twenty-three years ago. I was Risa's age, and Grandmom had bought a sandbox for our backyard. "For those days we can't make it to the beach," she explained. I loved that thing. I'd entertain myself in it for hours, while she cooked dinner and made clothes for the boutique, and when my parents came home in the fall, the first thing I did was drag them outside and plead with them to play. And they did. Mom on one side, Dad on the other, me in the middle ... we were back together again. Grandmom watched from the window, and when she tucked me into bed that night, I remember asking if they could stay this time, if we'd be a happy family again. "We make our own happiness, dear heart," was her response.

It took a long time for me to learn that lesson.

I think I'm still learning it.

So when, as we're leaving the playground a half hour later, Wilson asks if I'd like to do dinner or a movie sometime, I don't sabotage myself. I remember what Grandmom said. I inch out onto that limb. "Yes," I say. "I'd like that a lot."

* * *

I'm just finishing up my shift at Sensations on Tuesday when my phone rings. Serena. "Hello?" I ask, sandwiching it between my ear and shoulder as I jot down a reservation I took a minute before. Six people, plus three babies who need highchairs, for seven-thirty this evening.

"Are you busy? Please tell me you're not busy."

"Getting ready to clock out and head ho – head back," I quickly correct, jolted by my slip-up. Did I seriously almost refer to the shelter as home? What's gotten into me? "I have enough time, right? When are you leaving?" This is the night, Serena's Noteworthy debut, and I'm going both for moral support and to finally hear my songs make their way into the world. I don't know which one of us is more excited.

"Not until six," she says, "but I'm having a fashion crisis."

I choke down a staccato laugh as I survey my own wardrobe: the Sensations shirt, a pair of black pants I found in the latest donation box at the shelter, and matching flats that are pinching my toes. "You are welcome to anything I have," I tell her. "Other than the purple cardigan, though, none of it is actually mine." Not that I think she'd go for my regular clothes anyway. Patterned scarves, flowy skirts, and colorful jewelry don't seem like her style.

"And everything I have *is* mine. That's the problem. It's too attached to the memories." Serena is one of the people at Open Hearts who brought along a suitcase when she took shelter – I'd say it's probably split fifty-fifty between those who lost everything and those who still hang on to bits of the past – and though I haven't seen her in anything other than those loose, dull-colored clothes, I figure there must be other options. Or maybe not. "Can you meet me at the thrift store?" she asks. "The one down the street. Say, in twenty minutes?"

"Sure." I wave to Bobbi as she pushes through the door. "Be there soon."

"Where ya headed?"

It's only my second week of work, but I've already come to expect the third degree from Bobbi. Forget about a singer; she should be a detective. "Shopping," I tell her. "With a friend." The instant the words leave my mouth, they remind me of Kayleigh. How many times did we go to the Fox Run Mall? We'd wander around, browse the stores, and stop for something to eat.

How different today's excursion will be.

Serena is waiting outside the thrift shop when I arrive, blisters needling my heels from the walk and a whole day on my feet at work, and as she pulls the door open, I notice her nails are polished a pastel pink. "Thank you for coming," she says.

"No problem." I want to tell her it's a drop in the bucket compared to the kindness she's shown me. Instead I opt for, "that's what friends are for." Because she is a friend now.

Serena smiles. "Indeed."

And then she's off. Down one aisle, up another. Crouching to reach the lower shelves, standing on tiptoes to comb through the higher ones. I don't know if she's just really picky, or if she's looking for something in particular, but whatever the case, she rejects almost every single item I suggest. A long sleeve copper wrap dress? The v-neck is too deep. An aqua chiffon peasant top? The material is too sheer. A lavender eyelet skirt? The length is too short. Eventually I stop offering possibilities and simply trail after her, hoping she finds something soon, before we end up being late for her own show.

"Thoughts?" she asks, after we get to a table piled high with sweater dresses. She rifles through until she finds a teal one with sleeves that stretch to the elbow.

"Won't you be hot in it?"

"Better to be hot than cold." A strange expression passes across her face. "I have a pair of black leggings I can pair it with, and maybe some black boots?" She rushes off to the shoe section without even waiting for me to answer. Ten minutes later, we're back outside in the soupy air and Serena is chatting animatedly about the night ahead. I try to keep up, but the whole time I'm wondering why she picked an outfit – there's a plain black scarf and matching chandelier earrings to accompany the dress – more suited to March than August. It's her night, though. I'm just along for the ride.

Oh, and what a ride it is.

To look at it, Noteworthy seems like the polar opposite of Sensations. The brick walls are dotted with white fairy lights, and on each small circular table there sits a tiny votive candle lamp. It's dim, yet cozy. Autographed pictures hang sporadically, big name artists who performed here before the siren song of success called to them, and in the center of the restaurant is an oval-shaped platform, complete with a stool, microphone, guitar stand, and keyboard. Serena isn't due on for an hour and already the tables are filling up.

"Oh my God," I whisper. "I can't believe you're singing here. This is so cool. *So cool.*"

Even in the shadows, her eyes glitter. "I know, right?"

There's a bar at the side of the restaurant, and we inch our way over to the only two open seats. "What can I get you?" the bartender asks as Serena props her guitar between our stools. The menu is extensive – cabernet, white zinfandel, pinot noir, and a host of mixed drinks – but I don't give it a second glance.

"Ice water," I request. "With lemon, please."

Serena arches an eyebrow at me. "That's it? I'll have a margarita, please," she adds to the man behind the bar. I get the impression she brought a little money with her when she left Seth. It must be nice, to have the freedom to splurge on something she'll finish within a half hour. I'm not much of a drinker, just a glass of wine sometimes if I'm out, but a night like this is something to celebrate. I can't justify it, though. Not when that money could go into my savings instead. "Let me treat you," Serena offers, gesturing at the menu. "Consider it a thank you for lending me your words when my own have failed."

Is that how she views it? That the few songs she's written since leaving Seth are a failure?

"I'm fine, really."

She tilts her head, appraising me silently. "Well ... okay. Let me know if you change your mind." Her fingers go to her wedding ring for the umpteenth time and her foot taps against the rung of the barstool. One, two, three. Tap, tap, tap. It has a rhythm all its own and she's completely oblivious to it.

"Nervous?" I ask quietly.

She manages a smile. "Excited, mostly, but ... yes."

"You'll be awesome. Some people are born with music in their blood."

"And some people bleed their music."

Tap, tap, tap.

Her foot picks up tempo.

"Look, whatever happened with Seth, you can't let it define you," I tell her. "You can't let it – or him – control you. That's what tonight is about, right, taking your life back? Maybe it's not how you imagined things, maybe this is the hardest performance you'll ever give, but you can't move forward if you're standing still."

I think of Lainey, who was strong enough to take care of herself when every instinct told her not to. Of Risa, who reached out to her parents, but also reached out, just a little, to me. Of Fred, who's coming home from the hospital tomorrow and joining Ruby at the shelter until their bills are payable again. Of Wilson, who stepped up for Emmalyn when her mother either couldn't or wouldn't. And I think of myself. I think of that person, who, exactly a month ago today, watched her life go up in an agonizing blaze of flames. It's been a terrible month in so many ways, but it seems like things might be turning around now.

It seems like the notes are finally in tune.

July 2014

Seth,

I don't know where you are, what you're doing, or if you think about me as much as I can't help thinking about you. Maybe it was a wake-up call when I left, and you finally got the help you needed. Or maybe you are still in the same explosive place. I really don't have a clue, because the thing is ... I also don't know who you are anymore. You are not the boy I fell in love with or the man I married.

I'm furious with you for it. When I think of all the pain you inflicted, my blood runs cold. You said you loved me. So how could you hit me? Grab my arm so hard your fingers left imprints? Break open the skin on my face, and leave it bruised and blue? You stole part of my heart and crushed it to pieces. I thought I was to blame. I thought I could fix you. But I can't. Only you can do that. I want no part of it. I want no part of you.

You broke me, but I will piece myself back together. You knocked me down, but I will stand up again. You towered over me, so powerful, but I will find my own footing. My own strength.

You lose, Seth. I win.

Serena

14

Countless times, I've sat in a venue like this.

Countless times, I've blended in with the crowd, one face in a sea of many.

Countless times, I've closed my eyes and let the music wash over me, around me, through me.

Countless times, I've lost myself in the reverie of it all.

But never like tonight.

A line of goosebumps breaks out along my arms as Serena takes the stage. People are sitting on all sides of me – husbands with their wives, groups of friends, tourists who have come from far and wide to experience an authentic Nashville concert. I sit up tall, looking at them, at Serena, trying to memorize every detail. This is a memory I want to emblazon in my mind forever.

"Hi guys." Serena smiles demurely at the crowd. "Thanks for coming. It's truly an honor to play for you tonight. For those who don't know, my name's Serena and I won Noteworthy's performance contest last week. I'll be here each Tuesday, Thursday, and Sunday from eight to ten." She inhales a long, confidence-boosting breath, and I flash a discreet thumbs-up sign in her direction. "Okay, let's do this."

She begins with "White Dove," the song I wrote about a girl who grows up among the sadness of divorce, whose childhood is painted against a canvas of slamming doors and shattered glass. I based it on Kayleigh's family, even though her mom and dad didn't split until she was in high school, and as I listen to the words pass through Serena's mouth – sometimes harsh and cacophonous, sometimes haunting and low, sometimes serene and peaceful – I wonder how Kayleigh would react. Would she love this song? Hate it? "From heartache to heartbreak, she flies with wings spread wide.

How can she fix this? Should she have tried?" Serena's interpretation of my lyrics gives me chills. It doesn't matter that she was raised in a happy and loving home. Listening to her, you'd believe she had lived this broken path.

It is completely surreal, sitting here and hearing my own work. And wonderful.

Completely wonderful.

No matter what happens next with my music, I will remember tonight forever.

I sneak a peek around and try to gauge people's reactions. Are they enjoying the song? It's hard to read their expressions. But not the applause when Serena stops. That rings in my ears, loud and clear. "Thank you," she says, bowing her head slightly, then swiveling to smile at me. "And a special thanks to Eden Abraham, who wrote 'White Dove.' Actually, she wrote all the songs I'm singing here tonight."

She didn't have to mention me. I never asked for credit.

"Thank you," I mouth, blushing as people turn to look at me. It's weird to feel their eyes on me, to know they are noticing me for the first time, but it's also nice. I've been waiting a long time to be seen.

Serena nods, then segues into the next song. If her nerves are still jittery, nobody would know. Her voice floats through the restaurant, pure and transparent, and aside from the quickest glance at her ring finger as she's performing "Once Upon a Midnight Dream," she gives no indication that she is even thinking about Seth. She's strong, brave, standing on her own instead of propping herself up against somebody else. I'm proud of her.

Sometimes I leave concerts with tears in my eyes.

When will it be my turn?, I think.

Tonight, as Serena closes with "Voyage of the Heart," I feel the familiar swell below my eyelids.

But this time, they're grateful tears.

"Thank you again," I say, as we walk back to the shelter after the show. The streets are buzzing, awash in the fluorescent glows of neon signs that glisten down from the buildings and cast reflective rainbows onto the sidewalk, and it reminds me of why I came to Nashville in the first place. This city envelops you in its color.

"You're welcome," Serena says. "It was my pleasure."

"So how did it feel, being up there again?"

She tilts her head toward the stars. "Strange. Intimidating. Raw. Great." She searches the sky for something, I can't tell what. "I always told Seth that we needed to be vulnerable on stage, that if we wanted to be successful, our songs had to be windows into our souls. And I think we managed it to some degree, but not like tonight. Not like he forced me to do on my own."

"Do you wish he'd been there tonight?" I ask.

No penny. No fountain. No need to grant anything.

I'm simply curious.

"Yes and no. On the one hand, talk about poetic justice at its finest. On the other, I don't ever want to see him again. It took too long to break away. When I think of all the times I cowered to him – " A shudder overtakes her shoulders. "You were right," she says simply. "About my scar. The instant you looked at me, I knew you had figured it out."

"It's okay, we don't have to talk – "

"No." Her mouth flattens into a taut line. "It's not okay. What he did to me is so far from okay. I never talk about it, and that's not okay, either. The therapist I work with at the shelter, she keeps prodding me to open up, and I try, honestly, but I can't bring myself to say it aloud. That's why she suggested I write to Seth." I think of the way her pen cut across that paper. She wasn't cowering to him then. "It was cathartic beyond measure."

"Did you send it to him?"

"God, no. Though I won't lie, I was tempted." She sighs. "Not that it would've mattered. Seth sees things how he wants to see them. I bought into it at the beginning. I bought into this fairy tale of the life we thought we'd have. And then, even when things started to go south, I ... I wasn't ready to stop believing."

"How long did it take?"

Another sigh. "Until he put me in the hospital."

Something ugly twists my stomach. "He put you in the hospital? That's … " I struggle to find an appropriate word. "It's hideous. I'm so sorry. But you're okay? No lasting damage?"

"Just the scar you saw." We've reached Open Hearts now, but instead of going inside, she leans against the brick wall. "It's confusing, you know, when the feelings are that intense. It was love and lust and anger and stress, all jumbled into a mess of emotion. One minute we were screaming and the next we'd be planning our future. And it wasn't physical at first. We'd disagree over a song, a contract, a gig, a meeting, whatever. We both said things we regretted after the fact."

"That's not an excuse."

"No," she agrees, "it isn't. At the time, though, I was so desperate to hang onto him … or maybe to the life we had for the first few years, because it was a good life, it really was, especially after we moved here and got married … anyway, I couldn't face the reality of how things had changed. I gave up Princeton for this man. I gave up my family. So I had to make it count. I had to keep trying. And he always apologized. He'd get so into an argument, and he'd push my hand away a little too hard, or shove a little too forcefully, and when he realized what he'd done, he'd get all choked up and say how sorry he was. Like a fool, I accepted that. Even when it got worse." Disgust slithers into every syllable. "The thing is, he claimed it was because he loved me so much. He said I made him act that way because he adored me to the point of losing control. So I kept staying. I found an outlet in my sketchpad, because art was something I could do alone, something I could do only for me." Up and down, her voice wobbles. "And I hid the bruises, I invented excuses, I took him back over and over. In the end, it didn't only cost me my dignity, it also cost our baby its life."

A strangled sob claws its way from her throat and she doubles over, like the pain's too vicious to withstand. I should do something. I should put an arm around her, help her up, remind her that it's not her fault. But this admission stuns me into immobility.

"You ... you were pregnant?" I stutter, and immediately want to kick myself for being so stupid. Obviously she was pregnant if she said she'd lost the baby.

She's folded in half now, hands on her knees as she gulps in ragged breaths of air, and I'm angry with myself for letting the conversation veer in this direction. Tonight was supposed to be sunshine. Instead it's darkened into the most dangerous kind of storm.

"I ... I don't know what to say, other than I'm so sorry." I feel like a broken record.

"I had no idea," she whispers. "I'd been queasy for a few weeks, but I thought it was the stress. Things were especially bad with Seth then, so I wasn't eating well or sleeping much, and ... God, if I'd had a clue ... " A fresh flood of tears pours down her face. "I have nightmares about it. The fight. Me hurrying after him down the hall. Grabbing his arm to stop him from going downstairs and him shoving me off. Falling halfway down the steps. Seeing the steel in his eyes as he lunged – " She's white as a ghost, and without giving it a second thought, I pull her into a hug.

"Don't hurt yourself like this," I plead. "Don't relive it."

"But if I'd known ... I would have stayed away ... I would have protected the baby."

This makes a deep sadness run through my veins.

She'd have fought for her child. Why not for herself?

"Seth is the only one to blame," I say firmly. "He caused the miscarriage, not you."

Easy for me to say. Impossible for her to accept.

"I hate him," she snaps. "I hate him for everything he stole from me."

"Did you file a police report?"

The question is out of my mouth before I can throw up an iron gate to block it.

And it instantly ends our conversation.

"I can't do this anymore," she says hoarsely. "Thank you, though. For listening. For not looking at me any differently." So is that why she shoves the abuse into a box, because she's afraid of being judged? I get it. There's a stigma attached to so many things in life, too many things, and I can see why, in Serena's mind, she thinks domestic abuse is something to be ashamed of, to cover up. After all, I've been doing the same thing with my homelessness. Nobody wants to feel less than others or expose themselves in an unforgiving spotlight.

So, though I don't agree that the abuse is something to disguise, I don't press the issue with her. "Anytime. That's what friends are for," I add, and when I say it this time, it takes on a new meaning. She musters up the smallest smile and trudges inside with her guitar case dangling loosely from her fingers.

I should go in, too.

But I don't. Instead I breathe in Nashville, drink it in. The hum of cars in the distance. The flash of lights twinkling along the city skyline, illuminating buildings that stand tall like glass pick-up sticks. The rhythmic drumbeat bouncing from a bar across the street. The hooting of an owl as it wakes up to its new day. The *Music City Live Music Venue* sign tacked to a lamppost a couple feet away. The man walking toward me, whistling Keith Urban's new song. He hesitates, looking first at me, then at the shelter, and I wait for it, for the flicker of recognition, the empathy or concern or consternation, but he simply continues on. Something bristles inside me. Relief? No. As I pick up his tune to hum the second stanza, I realize it's annoyance. Much as I didn't want to be noticed in this case, it's also irksome that he didn't seem fazed by my presence. Has homelessness become so accepted that we just pass the people by like they're of no consequence? I'm acutely aware of this now.

I used to volunteer at a food pantry in Portsmouth. It began as an activity with the Interact club in high school – we used to spend two hours there every other week after class, sorting donations – but Kayleigh and I continued the entire summer after we graduated. We stocked items in the pantry and helped with some of their food drives and fundraising events. And I tried to do the same here in Nashville by serving meals at the local soup kitchen. But did I ever tag along when the canned goods were delivered? Did I ever take a seat with the people whose soup I ladled?

Volunteering is admirable in any form, but even that can be impersonal in its own way.

I want to change it somehow.

I want to make a difference. I want to leave a mark on this world.

Where do I start?

With you, my brain answers. *You start with your own world.*

My fingers twitch a little, itching to hold a pen, and I figure, hey, why not? Maybe I don't need a wish to inspire me anymore.

But first, there's another step I have to take.

It's a leap, really.

I open my bag, pull out my phone, and type the text I should have written weeks ago.

Kay: Congratulations on the engagement! You and Gary are perfect together, and I'm happy for you both. If it's not too late, I'd love to be a bridesmaid and celebrate your special day. Things are a bit nuts in Nashville and I can't get away often, but I'll be in Portsmouth in October and can take the train to New York to meet you. Would that work? Hope all went well in London. Talk soon.

My thumb hovers over the digital keypad.

If I send this, there's no going back. I'll have to shell out money I don't have. I'll have to be part of a bridal tea, and a rehearsal dinner, and whatever other fancy festivities Kayleigh's parents throw. This is how they try to compensate for the divorce, by inundating her with expensive gifts, high-class soirees, and exotic vacations. When she graduated from Carnegie Mellon, her mother bought her a Lexus – never mind that she was moving to Manhattan and would be better off taking the subway – and her father surprised her with an all-expenses-paid trip to France. To the best of my knowledge, she still hasn't gone. I once asked her why she accepts these over-the-top gifts when she rarely uses them.

"Because it makes my parents feel better," she said. "It's easier that way."

Is that why Serena stayed with Seth for all those years? Because it was easier that way?

Kayleigh's wrong, though. Easier isn't always better. Easier isn't always best.

Sometimes we have to do the things that frighten us most.

I press my thumb down and send the message.

One down, one to go.

I quickly type another text, close my eyes, and free-fall into the abyss with no safety net in sight.

From: **Eden** *To:* **Wilson**
Does the offer still stand for dinner or a movie?
Would love to see you again.

> *From:* **Wilson** *To:* **Eden**
> *Absolutely. Just name the time and place.*
> *I'll be there with bells on.*

From: **Eden** *To:* **Wilson**
Let's go for dinner. I can do any evening, really.
Whatever works for you is good for me.

> *From:* **Wilson** *To:* **Eden**
> *How about Friday? My sister should be able*
> *to watch Emmalyn then.*

From: **Eden** *To:* **Wilson**
Sounds great. Just so you know, though,
I'm totally cool with you bringing her. She's precious.

> *From:* **Wilson** *To:* **Eden**
> *She is, and I love her dearly, but I'm thinking*
> *it might not make the best impression if you*
> *end up covered in milk or mac & cheese.*
> *Let's just say my Em isn't the neatest eater.*

From: **Eden** *To:* **Wilson**
She's a kid. They're not supposed to be. :)

> *From:* **Wilson** *To:* **Eden**
> *You make a good point. :) That said,*
> *I'm thinking this time should only be us.*
> *How about seven on Friday?*

From: **Eden** *To:* **Wilson**
Sure! I'm looking forward to it already.

> *From:* **Wilson** *To:* **Eden**
> *Me too. It's a date.*

15

*G*etting ready for a first date is always a little bit weird. My emotions are all jumbled, a blend of excitement and nervousness and anticipation, and so many questions dash through my head. Will it be the beginning of something beautiful, or a sour note that's out of tune? Will we have enough to talk about? Will there be a goodnight kiss at the end? Set those questions against the rollercoaster of all that's been going on in my life and you basically have a train wreck in motion. I can almost see myself hurtling toward disaster.

Yet, as I think about Wilson, I'm still smiling.

He wanted to pick me up tonight, but I said no.

"I work downtown," I told him, "so it just makes sense for me to meet you."

"Are you sure? I don't mind coming to get you." I wonder if it's another nugget from his mom – always pick your date up, always bring flowers, always open the door for her and pull out her chair. Or is this one all him? I'm looking forward to finding out.

"I'm sure," I said. Never mind that our plans are for seven o'clock, three full hours after my shift ends. I'll tell him about the shelter at some point, but I couldn't bring myself to say it before we've even gone out once. So, after I finished at work today, I walked the mile back to the shelter, put on a paisley sundress – the first thing in the donation box I've actually liked – and am currently adding a pair of earrings from Serena. "I can't believe you're trusting me with these," I tell her. "I mean, it's probably harder to lose earrings than a bracelet, but – "

"But nothing. The bracelet was an accident, and you tried so hard to find it. It's okay. Let it go now. I have." She watches as I braid the front of my hair and secure it behind my head with bobby pins. "That looks fantastic. Kind of bohemian."

"Thanks." I appraise my reflection in the mirror. Shiny hair. Diamond nose stud. Light makeup. I look like my pre-shelter self again. "I can show you how to do it sometime."

She runs her fingers through her hair. "I always wear mine down," she says. "At least, recently. It was easier to hide the ... well, you know ... that way."

Bruises.

It was easier to hide the bruises.

"Maybe it's time to stop hiding," I suggest gently. She doesn't answer, and I don't push further, because this is her timeline to create and her demon to slay. Before I leave, though, I give her a hug. "You're awesome. I hope you realize that. Thanks again for all the help tonight."

"You're welcome. Have a great time."

Is it strange for her, to watch somebody go off on a date? Does it dredge up memories of when her relationship with Seth was still bright and new, filled with potential instead of tragedy? I think of them as I walk to meet Wilson for dinner. Suppose we're doomed, too? Suppose this ends up being a repeat of what happened with Jared and he leaves me for another woman? I remember that first date with Jared like it was yesterday: dinner at an Italian restaurant, a music festival at the park, and an amazing kiss when he dropped me off at my apartment. I thought we were golden. But gold can lose its luster.

And doesn't history unspool the same thread time and again?

All those worries disappear when I get to the restaurant and see Wilson leaning back against the building with a grin. Again, I feel myself yanked in his direction. What is it about him? "Hi," he says, and a matching grin weaves its way around my mouth.

"Hi."

"You're early."

"You're earlier," I point out.

He laughs, a deep, booming laugh that seems to rush in straight from his soul. "It's incredible how much faster it is to get out of the house when my little tagalong isn't insisting on dressing herself, or scooping up every toy in her toy box to bring with us, or waiting until she's buckled in her car seat to tell me she has to go to the bathroom ... potty training, by the way, was no joke." As soon as he says it, the tops of his ears flush. "Good call, Wilson. Talk about potty training on a first date. How's that for a surefire way to score a second one?"

Now I'm laughing, too. "I won't hold it against you."

"Whew." He breathes an exaggerated sigh of relief and swipes a hand over his forehead. "Your kindness is most appreciated." He opens the door for me – ha, I knew it! – and we go inside, only to come right back out when the hostess asks if we'd like to sit on the patio.

"This reminds me of Portsmouth," I tell Wilson. "There are so many outdoor restaurants. All we need is the waterfront."

"Do you miss the water? It seems like the sort of thing that'd be tough to leave behind."

"I do. Other than my grandmom, it's what I miss most."

"Tell me about her. Tell me about yourself."

"Hmm, let's see ... basically, she's the best woman on the planet. She raised me from the time I was four years old, owns a boutique that's been in New Hampshire since the seventies, and used to be a pretty awesome figure skater. I adore her more than anyone." I pause when the waiter comes to take our drink order – water for me; iced sweet tea for Wilson – then continue. "I wanted her to move to Tennessee with me, but her life is in Portsmouth. She was born there, she met my grandpa there, they began their family there ... " But they didn't finish their family. They couldn't. "We talk on the phone almost every day, though, and I visit a few times per year. For now, I guess that has to be enough."

"I can't imagine being that far away from your family. I think I told you mine lives here? All five hundred of them."

"Five hundred?"

The corners of his eyes crinkle merrily. "Okay, I might be exaggerating a bit. My mom has three sisters, my dad has two sisters and a brother, and I'm the oldest of five. Factor in all the cousins and you've got a lot."

"Wow." Talk about unimaginable. The picture he's painting looks foreign. "That must be really nice. You always have someone to turn to and Emmalyn has built-in friends. Assuming your cousins have kids, that is?"

"Oh yeah. It makes me feel so much better about Em's situation. I was worried at first, whether I was doing the right thing in offering to take sole custody. This is gonna sound backwards, but it felt almost irresponsible. I was twenty-seven when Becky – Em's mom – told me she was pregnant, and I'd just finished graduate school. No job, no prospects, even, because meteorology is a hard field to break into, and the thought of being a parent at that point in my life terrified me. I couldn't provide for myself, let alone a child."

"So Becky wasn't in the picture at all?"

"Nope." He fiddles with the wrapper from his straw and curls it into a pretzel shape. "We were together for three years, until Em came along."

"Don't babies usually bring couples closer together?"

He smiles wryly. "Not when the baby's mother meets with an adoption attorney before she tells the baby's father about the pregnancy, and most definitely not when she tries to forge his signature on the paperwork."

My eyes widen. "Please tell me you're not serious."

"Scout's honor." He holds up his fingers. "Becky was in law school and wanted no part of being a parent. She was too focused on making a name for herself. Honestly, I don't think she ever would have told the truth if I hadn't accidentally caught her in the middle of a bout of morning sickness." A shadow passes over his face.

"You don't have to share all this," I say. "We're only just getting to know each other."

"Which is why you *should* know. It's the most important part of who I am."

"But if you'd rather wait – "

"If I'd have rather waited, I wouldn't have brought it up." We take a break to order dinner, then he leans right back in again. It warms me inside. I like that he trusts me with this already. "To make a long story short, her plan was to transfer schools, have the baby, and stay away until the adoption was finalized. She knew I'd stop her otherwise. And I did. I stopped her. I thought about proposing – it seemed like the right thing to do – but I just couldn't. Not after she'd lied to me. Not after she'd tried to give my child away without me ever knowing. I petitioned for sole custody, we fought it out in court, and I won. Becky hasn't spoken a word to me since then."

"What about Emmalyn? Does she ever see her?"

"Nope, even though I've offered many times. Becky wants no part of her. It's sad, huh?"

Incredibly.

Maybe not now, when that little princess is too young to know any better, but when she's older and begins asking questions … it'll break her heart. Something wells up in me, this surge of tenacity, and it isn't until our food's arrived that I realize what it is. Protectiveness. It feels ridiculous to think about, because I've only met the child once, but still, there it is. I want to shield Emmalyn from that pain, the ache which'll throb below the curves of her heart, the innate sense of unworthiness that'll stem from knowing she was unwanted.

Because I've been there. I've done that. I *am* there. I'm doing that now, doing that always.

In those moments, it won't matter how Wilson stood up for her.

It won't matter how Daddy was her hero.

All she'll be able to focus on is how Mommy wanted something, anything, but her. How she left.

Maybe I can help.

Maybe I was meant to meet Wilson that day, when I was so low, so we could help each other be better. Be whole. I don't voice this out loud, not on a first date, not this soon, but I do acknowledge that, sitting here with him, I feel happy for the first time in a long time. Like there's a glow kindling inside me.

I'm comfortable with Wilson in a way it takes months for me to feel with most people.

But Wilson is different. He's special.

And I think we could be special together, too.

A momentary coil of anxiety twists its way through my stomach. *Then why aren't you being fully honest with him? Why aren't you telling him about the fire, the shelter, the hardships? Why are you hiding information he should know even though he's being so open with you?* The questions nag at my brain, but I shove them aside. Right now, when the date's going so well, they're a gamble I don't want to take. My truth is too shaky to balance on, so I opt for more even ground.

It's nine o'clock by the time we leave the restaurant, and even after two hours of talking, neither of us is ready to go our separate ways. "Give me a minute," Wilson says, taking out his phone, "and then I have an idea where we can go."

"Consider my curiosity piqued." I smile, then avert my gaze as he punches in a number and says hello to, I assume, whoever's watching Emmalyn. I don't want him to think I'm eavesdropping. Still, I can't help overhearing snippets.

"Are you being a good girl for Aunt Melissa?"

"A Play-Doh castle? Take a picture so I can see it when I get home."

"Of course I'll come in to kiss you goodnight, Sweetpea."

"Which animals are joining the slumber party? Bebe, Bananas, Belle, and Bongo?"

And my favorite: "Love you to the moon and back."

It's the cutest.

"If you want to call it a night so you can be there to tuck her in, I totally understand," I say, after he's hung up.

"No, no, it's fine. Em loves my sister. It's a treat for them both to spend an evening together. In fact," he adds, "we should go out again soon so they'll have another chance." We're standing below a streetlight, and as he says this, its murky beams reflect down and make the flecks in his eyes glitter like gold dust.

"I like the way you think."

I also like the way he called Em to say goodnight, and the way he suggests we find an ice cream shop for dessert, and especially the way he reaches for my hand, grazes it with his, then changes his mind and backtracks. It's sweet.

"How goes the songwriting?" he asks, after we've eaten our ice cream and are meandering back along the bustling city streets. "Feeling more hopeful than the last time we talked about it?"

I think of Serena's debut at Noteworthy, of how I sat up in bed that night, holding a flashlight to my journal so I could see the pages, of how I was so optimistic that the tides were turning. Of how I only managed to get down a single verse. "Eh," I say.

"Don't worry," he says. "You'll get there. I'm a big believer in the power of hard work. It has to pay off eventually."

"You sound like my grandmom."

His dimple comes out to play. "Should I be concerned? I'm kinda going for a more manly vibe."

"Keep trying," I tease. "Practice makes perfect."

"Rude." But that dimple creases his cheek even more.

We walk on, footsteps alternating on the sidewalk. "You mentioned meteorology," I say, trying to turn the conversation back toward him. It feels safer that way. "Did you find a job? What sort of thing are you interested in? On-air?"

"Oh no, I'm definitely more of a behind-the-scenes guy. I like to stay out of the spotlight. Same with photography. Put me in front of a camera and I'm awkward. Put one in my hands, and I come alive. That's what I do full-time now," he explains. "Once I found out I was going to be a dad, I knew I needed a way to up my income, stat. Job searching was put on hold in favor of something to bring in actual money. It's not always a lot, and photography isn't the most steady career, but it's enough to provide for Emmalyn. And you know, it was pretty cool, taking a hobby and spinning it into more. That's kind of what you're doing, too, right, with the songwriting?"

"What I'm trying to do," I amend. "If only someone would take a chance on me."

"Maybe you have to take a chance on yourself first."

I'm not sure how to answer that. I think about it as we round the corner and come face-to-face with the fountain outside the Schermerhorn Symphony Center. It has two tiers of water, plus a third level that arcs from the top, and puts the small one at Open Hearts to shame. "You're right," I say to Wilson as we walk over to the fountain and perch on the limestone ledge. "It's tough for me to do that sometimes. My parents left when I was a child. They became Mariah and Joel, philanthropists, instead of Mariah and Joel, Mom and Dad, and I guess sometimes I still wonder ... if I wasn't worthy of their time or love, why *should* I take a chance? Why do I think I could ever be worth it? It's odd," I say, resting my hands against the cool stone. "Like, I feel this push to do it, to put myself out there. And I try, honestly. But at the same time, there's a voice in the back of my head, reminding me that I didn't measure up. It makes me think maybe I never will." Why am I telling him all this? Why am I spilling my rawest fears? Again, it occurs to me that a first date isn't the right time for baring one's soul.

Wilson inches his hand over, and this time, it slowly shelters mine.

His skin is soft, warm, inviting, and when I feel it atop my own, I suddenly want to cry.

"You will if you let yourself," he says.

That's it.

No questions about my parents, no comment about how we define our circumstances instead of the other way around, no attempt to brighten my spirits with overly cheerful platitudes. Just a quiet reminder of the power our inner strength can hold, if only we give it permission. It's exactly what I'd needed to hear. I close my eyes against the tears, against the outside world, and listen to the splash of the fountain.

Maybe we stumbled upon the Schermerhorn tonight for a reason.

Maybe this is where the sheet music flips to a new page.

I open my eyes and smile at Wilson. "Thank you," I whisper.

"Just … thank you."

Maybe this is where more wishes will come true.

ROCHELLE

Love at first listen. Even as a child, Rochelle was enthralled by country music. It was more than the melody, or the lyrics, or the twang humming through each syllable. This genre was *her* genre. It spoke to her in a way she couldn't describe. "I'm going to wear a cowgirl hat and sing on stage," she told anybody who would listen. Growing up in Minnesota, the country music world was far away, so Rochelle did everything possible to bring its harmony to her tiny hometown. She took voice lessons, joined the chorus in school, sang at church, and, when the time came, made a move to Nashville for college.

But it wasn't all glitz and glamour. Surrounded by people who shared her passion, Rochelle was one in a crowd. She didn't stand out in Tennessee like she had at home, and for the northerner who was used to being the big fish in a small sea, finding herself in the opposite situation was jarring. For the first time, she began to question her place. It wasn't until a classmate pointed out the texture in her voice – a texture that lent itself more to soul music than country – that Rochelle really found her niche. She blossomed under it, and when her talent caught the eye of a local producer, she jumped at the chance to sign with his record label. Day after day, week after week, month after month, she worked hard on her debut album.

When it all crumbled around her, Rochelle was determined. She wouldn't let one setback get in her way. She'd still make it in music. Until, slowly but surely, it drove her to the breaking point and brought sadness instead of joy, depression instead of bliss. That's when Rochelle made the change. The life she lives today is one she never would have envisioned.

Is it the answer? Will things get better?

She can only hope.

16

"*U*ntil next time."

Three little words. But as I sit by the fountain, replaying Wilson's kiss in my mind, they make me feel big. It was a light peck, right on my cheekbone, and it instantly invited a coating of goosebumps to the surface of my skin. "Until next time," I murmured back, and then I watched him walk toward his car. He paused about ten feet away to smile at me over his shoulder, and I swear, my heart grew wings. Next time. Wilson wants to see me again.

Tonight's gone better than I had hoped.

Now I want to make someone else's evening better, too.

I look around, searching for someone else who's drawn to the promise of the fountain. The man with a Titans cap, who talks quietly into a cell phone? Nope. He ambles by without even glancing at the Schermerhorn. The woman with a braid that snakes down her spine? Nope. She hails a cab and goes off into the night. The group of teenagers who giggle loudly, clad in their too-short shorts and tank tops? Nope. They blast on by like a tornado of energy. Then I see her. A woman who seems a couple years older than me, with funky black-framed glasses and pink streaks in her hair. She walks alone, head tilted down, and I watch as she slows to a stop by the fountain and removes a coin from her wallet. She stands there awhile, staring at the penny like it's her salvation, or maybe like it's her last hope, and then she releases it. "Come true," she says. "Come true, dammit."

That's my cue.

"Excuse me." I smile as she swivels around. "I'm sorry, I couldn't help overhearing. Everything okay?"

She rolls her eyes sharply. "Okay?" she sniffs. "That word is no longer in my vocabulary. Why? Who's asking?"

I stand up. "I'm Eden. Fountains are kind of my thing."

A snort of laughter spews from her. "Fountains are your thing? Like, you just hang out at them and start conversations with random people?"

Alright, when she puts it that way, it makes me sound like I've lost my marbles. Maybe this was a miscalculation. Granting wishes at the shelter is one thing. Broadening it may not be wise. I don't know whom I'm getting involved with, and neither do they. Really, what would compel someone to reveal their wish to a complete stranger? Plus, didn't I promise I wouldn't meddle if my help wasn't wanted? And what's to say I can do anything for this woman anyway?

"Never mind," I say hastily, backing up a step. "Have a good night."

"Wait." Her voice rings out. "I'm sorry. That was rude." She heaves herself down on the ledge of the fountain and peers gloomily at the water. What do I do? Join her? Leave? I could go back to Open Hearts, tell Serena about my date, and maybe even capitalize on my giddiness to actually write something of value. I would like to capture this excitement, bottle it, in case it's fleeting. But on the other hand, the woman who laughed at me before is currently dropping her head to her hands and talking freely.

I remember the times I prayed for someone to hear me. To listen.

I want to be that person for others now.

So I sit.

"I'm Rochelle, by the way," she says.

"Nice to meet you."

"You must be the fiftieth person to say that to me today, and this is the only time I can accept it. Probably since you aren't wearing a business suit or sitting in a cubicle that sucks the life out of your soul." She curls up her nose in disgust. "First day at a new job," she explains. "Actually, the first day in a torture chamber is more like it. My skin was crawling from the moment I walked into the office. It's suffocating. For real, the people are automatons: they stare at the computer screen, input data with one hand while downing coffee with the other, and spout out quotas like they're programmed to memorize every freaking factoid of information."

"Sounds – "

"Like hell? Yeah, pretty much."

"Then why work there?"

Now her laugh turns bitter. "Because I'm never going to make it doing what I want to do."

"Which is?"

She sighs. "I'm a cliché. I came to Nashville because I've always dreamed of being a singer. For awhile, things were great. I signed with an independent label and the producers I worked with kept telling me I was gonna be a star." She glares at the fountain and the pennies inside it. "Like an idiot, I believed them. I put everything I had into my debut record."

I'm almost afraid to ask.

"And?"

"And the label went bankrupt. If only I'd hired a lawyer to look at the contract before I signed it. But I hadn't, and I also hadn't written any of the songs on the album, so basically I didn't have a legal leg to stand on. You'd think that would have been enough to convince me to back out of this foolish dream, right? But still, I kept trying until I couldn't take it anymore. That brings me to today and the automatons. I accepted a receptionist position at an accounting firm and can already foresee all my creative brain cells dying a slow and painful death."

Is this what I'd turn into if I gave in to the writer's block? The thought makes me shudder.

"I feel your pain," I tell Rochelle. "I moved to Nashville because of my songwriting and have had just about the same success rate as you."

"It sucks. I told myself I'd be happier if I gave up, that it wasn't right for something I love to hurt so much, but God, the corporate world's a beast."

"What did you wish for?" I ask, not really expecting her to answer.

But she surprises me.

"To be able to find one thing each day to make me smile," she says. "It's the only way I'll last."

"Where are you working now?"

Give a company name, please give a company name.

"Blackstone Accounting."

Yes.

I think of my schedule on Monday. Bobbi asked me to switch with her, which means I'm free for the morning and most of the afternoon. Serena and I are teaching a music lesson for the kids at the shelter, but after that I can easily drop by Rochelle's office. The CD I bought last month, the one the veteran threw away, I bet it would brighten Rochelle's day. She appreciates music. She lives it. She gets it.

I felt deceitful at first, telling Wilson I was heading home, too, and then doubling back around to the fountain, but now I know I did the right thing. It wasn't a coincidence that I ended up here. Luck might be shoddy and fortune might be fake, but I can't help thinking that serendipity is real. When I set off for the shelter, the butterflies in my heart flap a little harder. I had a great night with an even greater guy. We have plans to see each other again on Tuesday. I'm on the verge of granting a wish that won't fail, and lyrics hum through my veins, freeform and loose.

Does giving in mean giving up? When do we say that enough is enough?

Can happy-ever-after come in disguise? Or are we missing what's before our eyes?

Reach inside, reach deep, reach true.

Find all that's waiting, all that's waiting for you.

Multiple lines.

With the promise of more.

Those wings my heart grew?

They're carrying me up to the clouds.

* * *

"Miss Eden, can you help me with my xy ... my xylo ... with this thing?" Teresa, one of the kids at the shelter, stretches up her pudgy arms and holds out the rainbow-colored instrument she chose to play for our music lesson. There was a small selection in the toy chest – three triangles, three plastic drums, a xylophone, and a handful of bells – and the preschooler made a beeline for the instrument she's now waving wildly at me. "I want to play Twinkle, Twinkle," she begs. "My mama used to sing me that at bedtime. We sitted in the rocking chair and it was our special song. Can you teach me? I wanna sing it to her when she gets out of the big doctor's office." She looks at me with such hope in her eyes that I can't possibly say no. Teresa's family is new at Open Hearts. They arrived last week with only a backpack apiece, and I didn't find out until today that her mother's in the hospital, trying to recover from a stroke. For a family already struggling with finances, this sent them right over the edge.

"Of course," I tell Teresa. She sits in my lap, and I show her how to hit the wooden rectangles to tap out a song. All around us, children are playing, some following instructions and others not. It's a loud cacophony of noise, but no matter the sound, it's music to my ears. Most of these children had never touched an instrument before today. Seeing the joy on their faces is inspiring. "I have a good idea," I tell Teresa. "How about we record you playing the song and email it to your mom's phone? Then she can watch from the hos – from the big doctor's office." At the suggestion, Teresa jumps up from my lap and spins in a circle.

"Yes, yes, yes!" she cheers.

It's a humbling experience, in a way. Maybe this shelter life isn't so bad after all. The fact that it brings people together who otherwise never would have met isn't something to be ignored. Maybe they're in my life for a reason. Maybe they have lessons to teach. Maybe I do, too. I consider that a lot over the next hour: as Serena and I explain to the kids about melody and harmony; as we remind them to play with each other, not over each other; as we organize them into a band that performs in the community room;

and even as we tidy up afterwards.

"Thank you," Ms. Birnbaum says, coming over to join us. "It was so nice of you to do this for the children."

"Our pleasure." Serena places her guitar back into its case.

"We could do it each week," I offer. "I know it isn't the same as what they'd learn in school, but at least it's – "

"It's wonderful," Ms. Birnbaum says. "My favorite part of the shelter. People helping people."

People helping people.

It's what I grew up around, a notion that we were put on this earth to make it better for others. Even before Mom and Dad started traveling the world to build schools, assist with water purification systems, and bring healthy food to kids who sometimes went days without anything substantial, the humanitarian way was *our* way. We collected money for UNICEF, volunteered at a rabbit rescue, and built houses with Habitat for Humanity. One of my earliest memories is from an icy winter day, snow blanketing the ground and small icicles hanging from tree limbs. Dad was holding me, and we watched as a man received the key to a brand new home that my parents had helped to build. I can still see the smile on his face. I still feel the sense of pride from knowing we – even me, whose role was to draw a picture for the refrigerator – made it possible.

"Like Grandmom says," Mom reminded me, "it's lovely to do well, but it's better to do good."

I think about those words as I deliver the CD to the main lobby in Rochelle's office building. "It's sort of an anonymous thing," I explain to the receptionist. "A random act of kindness, you could say. Can you please not tell her it came from me?"

"Will do, Miss. Have a good day."

"You, too."

As I walk through the lobby, I steal a few quick peeks. Marble floor, swirled with white and gray. High ceilings, oversized paintings, windows taller than I am. Is Rochelle's office that drastic a change from down here? Or is she simply seeing it the way she wants to? I'll never know. I'll never see the woman again, never hear the reaction to her wish coming true – for today, at least – never catch an insider's glimpse into her life. I'll never know whether she sticks it out here or goes back to her true passion. It's odd to think about, because I'm used to helping people at Open Hearts and being able to see the result, but there's no way to follow up with anyone beyond the shelter's walls. Perhaps it should be that way. Granting these wishes isn't about what I gain. It's about what I give.

When a penny's all you've got, a penny is a lot.

A light in the darkness, a clearing in the fog,

A hope for today, a dream for tomorrow,

A break in the reality, a pause in the sorrow.

The words rush at me, swelling and cresting and roaring, and as I grab the journal I always carry, my hands can't move quickly enough to keep up with my brain. This is the part of songwriting I love most, when the lyrics flow fast and furious, almost as though they're in charge of me instead of the other way around. It is the best kind of high, this zap of adrenaline that makes me feel like I can fly. When writing is tough, there's nothing more frustrating. But when it's terrific, there's nothing more exhilarating.

God, I've missed this.

Please let it stay. Please let the spark keep flickering.

My pen skims over the page, leaving a trail of green ink.

Green, like the shirt Wilson wore on Friday.

I think of how it brought out the hazel in his eyes and how it complemented them so well. He joked that Emmalyn picked it out – "Her fashion skills are far superior to mine," he quipped – and ended up telling me a cute story about the day he interviewed with the local branch of the National Weather Service and Emmalyn gave him a crown to wear for good luck. "My parents bought her the game Pretty, Pretty Princess," he explained. "And she was convinced that since the crown helps her win, it'd also get me the job."

"Too cute," I said. "Any chance you snapped a picture in it? I'd love to see that."

"Ha. No." He chuckled. "But the expression on her face when I walked out the door with it on my head ... she just lit up in a megawatt smile. I live for those moments."

You're such a good dad, is what I wanted to say.

"So *did* it bring you good luck?" is what I did say.

"Well, considering I took it off after I left the house ..." He winked. "The interview went well. I liked them and they liked me. In the end, though, they went with a man who had more experience. That's always how it goes." He shook his head. "How do they want you to get experience if nobody will offer a job until you already have it?"

"So you're still looking? I thought you said you put it on hold when you started the photography business?"

"Every now and then a job posting catches my eye. Photography is what pays the bills, though."

"I'd love to see your work sometime."

"I'd love to show you."

And then we sat there, grinning at one another, until the waiter interrupted to ask if we wanted dessert. I'm grinning goofily now, too, just thinking about it. About him. I'm so excited for our date tomorrow. Have I ever felt this way about a guy before? Even with Jared, it wasn't this quick. This big. This all-encompassing. Wilson's different.

I am different.

I'm heavier, but also lighter.

More jaded, but also more wise.

When a penny's all you've got, a penny is a lot.

I'm me.

Finally, I'm beginning to like that again.

July 17, 1982

Dear Diary,

Today is Daddy's birthday. He'd have been fifty years old. I bet Mom would've thrown him a big surprise party down on the beach. That was his favorite place, she says. I have a few memories of spending time with him there, of building sandcastles and holding his hands as he helped me jump over the foamy waves, but sometimes I wonder if the memories are more from Mom telling me about them, instead of remembering. It seems like a lifetime ago. In ways, I guess it was. I was only six when he died. I wish I had more time with him. I wish he were still here. I wish I had a chance to say goodbye.

He's been on my heart a lot today. I guess that explains why I was so distracted at work. This guy came in and ordered a fudge ripple cone, and what did I give him? Strawberry Swirl. It's not like me to screw up the orders. Luckily, he was nice about it. He was nice about everything. And handsome. And funny. I took a chance and wrote down my phone number on the back of his receipt. I hope he'll call. I hope, someday, he can be for me what Daddy was for Mom. Are you up there, Daddy? Are you watching while I write this? If so, Happy Birthday.

Love you always and miss you forever.

~ Mariah

17

"*C*atch." *Grandmom tosses me a can of whipped cream. "Two dollops each, Jellybean. When it comes to dessert, two is always better than one."*

"Got it."

We're in the kitchen of my new apartment, and as I spritz the cream on Grandmom's famous hot chocolate – she has her own recipe that includes a twist of peppermint, a dash of vanilla extract, and a drizzle of mocha syrup – she stands at the counter and slices the cake she baked especially for the occasion. The radio's blaring away, the DJs chatting about the upcoming CMA awards, and a frisson of anticipation ignites somewhere deep inside me as I imagine them sharing my news in a few short minutes.

"I'm so glad you're here for this," I tell Grandmom.

Little wrinkles pop out around her eyes as she smiles. "I wouldn't have missed it for the world."

"You're the best."

"Of course I am." Her laughter is low, tinkling, melodious. She carries over two plates, each with a piece of chocolate chip cake, and makes herself comfortable at the table. "I'm sorry your mom and dad couldn't join us."

Something pinches my chest, but I ignore it. "It's okay, they wouldn't understand, anyway. They never do. You're here. That's the important thing." I bend down to kiss her cheek. "Five minutes to go."

Five minutes until my song debuts. Five minutes until my baby travels over the airwaves.

Five minutes until my words are more than my own.

When the announcement comes, when the DJs talk about the world premiere of the new single, I try with all my might to memorize every syllable. As the opening chords strum their way out, "Oh my God," is all I can whisper.

Grandmom doesn't say anything. She just sits, hand to her heart and tears glistening in her eyes.

"I did it," I murmur.

"I always knew you would." Her fingers curl around mine and squeeze softly. "Congratulations."

My song is on the radio.

Being performed by a Grammy Award winner.

Is this real life?

Is this my life?

No.

I realize that with a start as my phone rings, jolting me from the best dream ever and sending a half dozen heads popping up around the room. I yank my phone from the shelf over my bed. What time is it? Through a fuzzy haze of sleep, I make out the numbers: 5:43AM. "Sorry, sorry," I say in a hushed voice as I silence the ringer. "I thought the sound was off." I stumble into the hall, careful to avoid eye contact with the people snapped out of their slumber, and try to fix my bleary gaze on the display.

Kayleigh? At this hour?

"Kay?" I whisper, slipping, light as a shadow, along the hall and down the steps. "What's wrong? Why are you calling this early?"

The answer blasts out of her. "It's over ... he's cheating ... I'm sorry to call so early ... didn't know who else to turn to ... it's my parents all over again ... " She dissolves into sobs. Is *this* real life? Or am I still dreaming? Did she say Gary's cheating? Perfect Gary with the perfect job and perfect manners?

Is this why she never returned my text about the wedding? I kept checking for her answer, but it didn't show up, and I've been wondering whether to resend the message in case she never got it. I knew there was a good chance I'd burned a bridge, though, by originally declining the invitation to be a bridesmaid. But evidently the silence had nothing to do with me and everything to do with her fiancé. In what alternate universe is Gary unfaithful? "Are you sure?" I ask Kayleigh. "I really can't picture – "

"Well, picture it, sister." She barks out a shrill, staccato laugh.

"He's been working these insane hours lately, and he said it was because of a huge project they were trying to land, but then his boss called last night when Gary was supposedly at the office. He wanted to ask him something about an account he manages. I said Gary was working late on the project, and guess what? Turns out there isn't one."

"But Kay, that doesn't automatically – "

"Not finished yet." She steamrolls right over me. "I waited up for Gary so I could question him, and he comes strolling in at midnight, so intent on texting someone that he didn't even notice I was sitting there. Finally I said something and it startled him into dropping the phone. I got a glance at it before he picked it up. Gabrielle. So basically I'm the worst kind of cliché: the oblivious fiancée who plans a fairy-tale wedding while completely unaware of the deceit going on behind her back." The more Kayleigh reveals, the more angry she sounds.

"Did you ask him about it?"

"God, no. He'd only lie. All men are liars."

"Just because your dad had an affair doesn't mean every man is programmed that way. Maybe it could – "

"What? Be my imagination? I know what I saw last night. I know what I've seen since I got back from London. I think that's when it started. He's been acting strangely, and at first I chalked it up to work stress, but obviously I was right to be suspicious. Good thing I put a hold on the wedding plans until I figured out what was going on. Can you even imagine shelling out all that money when he has no intention of tying the knot?"

"Why on earth would he propose, then?" I ask.

"No idea."

I smother a yawn, not because I don't care, of course, but because it's so early and I was up late last night, working on a new song. "Do you really think he'd throw away a five-year relationship for a fling? That doesn't sound like the Gary I know." Though to be fair, living in a shelter and hiding it from everybody isn't the Eden that Kayleigh knows, either. Sometimes our truths are ours and ours alone.

"What other explanation could there be?" she questions.

"Don't ask me," I say gently. "Ask Gary. He isn't your dad. You aren't your mom."

"I guess."

"Look, Kay, maybe your instincts are right, in which case I'm so, so sorry. But maybe there really is something else going on here. I'd hate to see you throw away the love of your life for no reason. I think you should listen to Gary's side of the story before you crucify him." She agrees, begrudgingly, and I make her promise to update me as soon as possible.

And then I sit.

Alone in the community room, with nothing but the tick of the clock to keep me company.

Kayleigh's father cheated on her mother.

She might be losing Gary now to a similar infidelity.

Serena invested everything in Seth, only to have him put her in the hospital.

Grandmom's heart shattered when Grandpa Rick was killed in Vietnam.

Love breaks.

Mom and Dad ... they're the exception, I suppose.

They met when Dad's family was vacationing in Portsmouth for a summer. He was nineteen and she was eighteen, and from what I've heard, it was an instantaneous connection. "I was working at the ice cream shop in town," Mom said. "Your father came in one night and I fell for him right away. There was just something about him."

"She's painting me in far too good a light," Dad chimed in. "I was sort of a lost soul at that point. I liked a lot of things, but I didn't have a true passion, you know? I was biding time at college until I could figure out what I wanted to do with my life. Then I met your mother." His face broke open in a grin. "She anchored me."

Ironic choice of words, since it was Mom who actually gave Dad his wings.

I wonder how different things would've been if they didn't fly away.

If Dad didn't get swept up in the charity work Mom was already pursuing.

If they were older than twenty-two and twenty-three when I was born.

If the whole stay-at-home, white-picket-fence kind of life hadn't suffocated them.

But there's no sense wondering.

Because those things did happen, and even now, after all this time, Mom and Dad are still head-over-heels for each other.

How about Wilson and me?

Could we be an exception, too?

I look out the glass door, watching as the sun peeks its golden rays over the horizon. I've always thought of the sun as an equalizer of sorts. Same with the moon and stars. No matter where you're living, what you're doing, how you're feeling, the celestial landscape is still there. It used to comfort me as a kid, peering up at the sky and imagining my parents doing the same thing half a world away. That's what inspired "Voyage of the Heart," actually.

What about *my* heart? Is it ready to take a voyage?

And if so, will it float or sink?

* * *

"Check, one, two, three." The singer performing at Sensations tonight raps the microphone and it screeches to life for his soundcheck. "Down in Alabama, where a crimson tide rolls strong ... " His voice is gravelly, gruff, and I listen to its nuances while I wait for Wilson, who should be here soon. We're going mini-golfing for our second date, and since there's no course within walking distance, I agreed this time when he offered to pick me up. Thankfully he didn't question it when I told him my car was out of commission – technically true, since it was wrecked by a burning slab of debris – and gave him my work address.

"You're nuts." Bobbi returns from table nine, where she's just seated a family with five kids, and joins me by the front window. "Who voluntarily spends an evening out in this humidity? On a date, no less. You want to *look* hot, not *be* hot."

"I thought it was a fun idea," I say. "Low pressure. I'm glad he suggested it. It'll be a getting-to-know-you date."

"The only thing he's gonna get to know is your sweat glands."

Of course, because this is the way it always seems to work, that's the exact moment Wilson gets to the café. Oh, please don't let him have heard that. I try to size him up, but he just smiles. "Hey," he says. "Ready to go, pretty lady?"

"Have fun, you two," Bobbi says. "Y'all don't do anything I wouldn't do."

"Friend of yours?" Wilson asks, after we've gone outside.

"Co-worker. She's the other hostess."

"Have you been at Sensations a long time?"

"Only a few weeks, actually. I'm enjoying it, though. It lets me get out there and network a bit with the singers we book."

He holds open the car door for me. "Hey, you never know when something'll change your life, right? How many times has someone been discovered in Nashville's nooks and crannies?" He slides into the car, flicks on the turn signal, and starts off toward the mini-golf place. He's a good driver, I can tell instantly. Confident. Steady. Safe.

He makes me feel that way, too. Like being with him is an escape from all the pain. All the fears and worries. "So, are you good at golf?" I say, as he slows to a stop for a red light. I'm looking down as I ask, answering a quick text from Serena about one of my songs, so I don't realize where we are. Until Wilson doesn't answer and I glance up, confused.

That's when I see it.

Open Hearts.

It's a dozen feet away, halfway between the intersection we're stopped at and the next one, and a woman I recognize is slouching dejectedly as she makes her way inside. I watch her go, my breath frozen in my throat. This is it. This is when I need to tell Wilson the truth. "Is … is everything okay?" I manage to ask. *Come on, Eden. You can do it. Tell Wilson you live there. Tell him everything. You have waited long enough.*

"Yeah," he answers, pressing gently on the gas as the light changes to green. "It just gets to me, when I see places like that." He glances at the shelter as we drive by. "I feel so terrible for people in that situation. Can you imagine?" he asks, and the note of pity in his voice makes my confession do an about-face. "Losing everything? Having to live in a shelter with so many strangers? I wish I could help them all."

I study his face for a moment. The kindness in his eyes, the sympathy.

It reminds me of the reaction I used to get when people found out that my parents had left me. Their body language would change; they'd lean in close and their voices would drop, like it was their duty to let me know somebody still cared. To protect me. But then I moved here, and no one knew me as Joel and Mariah's daughter. No one saw the baggage I was lugging around, and that meant I could finally be free to let it go.

Except I haven't let it go, not really, and the thought of Wilson looking at me that way, looking at me like he looked at that woman going into Open Hearts ... I can't take it. Because, to answer what he said, yes, I can imagine it. I can imagine it all too well. I make up my mind, then and there: I can't tell Wilson about the shelter.

"Me too," I say hastily. "I wish I could help everyone, too." I clear my throat and try to settle my rapid heartbeat. "So you didn't answer me before. Are you good at golf?"

He chuckles. "Not so much."

Talk about an understatement.

The first hole is an easy setup, with only a few scattered bricks as obstacles, and I manage to line up the ball to bounce off one of them and sail towards the hole. "Go, go, go!" I cheer, then groan as its journey slows to a stop shortly before the destination. "Ugh. So close."

"Yet so far." Wilson winks. "Not that I'm one to talk. I couldn't do that if you paid me." As we play on, it becomes obvious that he was telling the truth. Half of the time his ball flies off the green and embeds itself in shrubbery, mulch, or, my favorite, one of the flowing streams that are scattered throughout the course. "Oops?" he offers, as I climb up on a flat rock to fish it out.

"I'm beginning to think you could even lose to a three-year-old," I joke, tossing the ball to him.

He grins. "And I have. Just ask Emmalyn."

I laugh, looking on as he sets up the shot again, stares fervently at the hole, takes a swing ... and promptly gets a hole-in-one.

"Aha!" I exclaim. "So *this* is where you make your move."

"That was a total coincidence." His eyes twinkle in the evening sun. "Trust me," he says, "when I make my move, you'll know it." He steps closer and trails a finger down my arm. Bobbi was right, the humidity is bordering on oppressive, but in this moment, with Wilson holding my gaze like we're the only two people in the world, it's not Mother Nature's heat I feel. It's this connection with him, this chemistry that sets off electrical currents beneath my skin. I want Wilson to kiss me, I want it so badly I feel it in my bones, and I see in his eyes that he's on the same page. His hand finds a spot on my waist, he guides me to him ... and then, suddenly, a neon blue golf ball is flying toward us.

"Watch out!" a boy's voice screams.

We jerk apart just in time to avoid getting clocked, and ten seconds later a woman is standing in front of us, apologizing for her son, who smacked the ball without even looking. "I'll make sure he's more careful from now on," she says, crossing her arms and shaking her head at him. "Jon, what do you say to these nice people?"

"I'm sorry." He winces sheepishly. "Glad it didn't knock you out and send you to the hospital."

I can't help it.

A giggle sneaks past my lips.

Wilson raises his eyebrows, looking at me like *what could possibly be funny about this situation*, and it makes me laugh harder. By the time Jon and his mom return to their game, I'm breathless. "I just ... it's something you'd see in the movies," I sputter, "or some silly sitcom." Pretty soon Wilson's cracking up, too. It doesn't even matter that our moment has passed.

We'll find another one.

We'll make another one.

"Hey," I say, as he writes down his hole-in-one score. "Question: why'd you bring me here if golf is normally your nemesis?"

"Easy." He smiles. "Because if you can't make a fool out of yourself in front of each other, then a relationship won't work. It's all about being comfortable with who you are." He leans in a bit, and I think he might try to kiss me again, but he doesn't. He just brushes a stray hair away from my face and tucks it behind my ear.

Comfortable.

I am with him, scarily so.

But this time, perhaps even for the first time, I'm not going to let the fear stop me. I'm going to let it motivate me, push me, help me. Inspire me.

ROOMMATE WANTED

Date posted: January 2, 2011

I'm looking for somebody to share rent for a 2 bedroom/1 bathroom apartment. The complex is located just outside of Downtown, within walking distance of restaurants, music venues, and stores. Rent is $650 per month, utilities included. Appliances are newly updated, floors are hardwood, and there's a small balcony connected to the dining room.

A little bit about myself: I am a day-shift pediatric nurse at a local hospital. I'm a vegetarian and people always say I'm the most easy-going of everyone they know. I am also an avid reader and the captain of a local volleyball team for twenty-somethings.

If you think we'd be a good fit, would like to schedule a walk-through of the apartment, or have any questions, please feel free to contact me at kristina.grannington@gmail.com.

18

"So, where to?" Wilson jingles his keys and looks at me expectantly.

As the meaning behind his words registers, so does something else: my sheer stupidity. How did I not think about this ahead of time? When I asked him to pick me up at Sensations, how could I not have realized it wouldn't be possible for him to drop me off there? He knows my car is broken, and he's too much of a gentleman to simply leave me off at the café and let me walk the rest of the way. He'll insist on driving me home ... and then what? Ugh. I suppose my excitement about seeing him obliterated all my common sense. And now here we are, sitting in his SUV with Emmalyn's car seat in the back and a pine-scented air freshener hanging from the rearview mirror, and I am just utterly lost for words. "I ... um ... it's ... " I stammer.

His eyebrows pinch together. "Is something wrong?"

"No!" My voices pitches up an octave too loud and I inwardly wince. "It's, uh, well ..."

"If you're worried I'm gonna invite myself in – "

"No!" Higher still. "It's not that. I mean, it's only our second date. We haven't even kissed." I laugh nervously as my mind whips ahead, trying to fabricate a plausible reason for him being unable to take me home. I lost my house keys? I'm having an overhaul done on the property and can't stay there until the renovation is finished? Think, Eden. *Think.* I feel a creepy-crawly sensation climb up my spine, and I have to take a deep breath before I lose it entirely.

"We can fix that."

I jump a bit, startled as he cuts into my silent desperation. "Fix what?"

He shifts closer, the leather seat squeaking as he moves. "We're alone now. No golf balls being lobbed at us. No phone call from one of my clients," he adds, recounting the second time we were interrupted. "No check-in from your boss to ask about working a double shift tomorrow."

"Sorry. I should've let that go to voicemail."

"Nah." His thumb rubs small circles along the inside of my wrist. "This is better. More private."

"Mmm. Yes."

There's something about the repetitive motion of his thumb that's putting me into a trance. Or maybe it's the way he's looking at me, with his long golden lashes surrounding those magnetic eyes. Either way, it's the best kind of hypnosis, like I'm drunk on him, and suddenly it's hard to remember what I was worried about before. It's hard to remember much of anything. Every fiber of my being is full of him.

"Okay?" he whispers.

"Okay," I whisper back. And then his hand is on my cheek and his mouth is brushing tentatively across mine. He tastes sugary, like sweet tea and hope, and it turns my brain to mist. Can this go on forever? Please, don't let it end. My fingers fall to his chest, sheltering the heartbeat inside, and as my eyelids flutter closed, one thought manages to break through the fog: he feels new, yet familiar. Like this is a discovery we've been waiting to make.

"That was ... wow." Wilson pulls back slightly, but he keeps his hand on my cheek and brushes it softly with his thumb. In a way, this gets to me even more than the kiss. Because he isn't running or rushing. He's not locking his mouth on mine again, even though I'm fairly sure we both want him to do exactly that. No. He's looking at me. He's really looking at me, like he genuinely cares about the connection we just wove.

"Wow," I echo.

This time, it's me who closes the distance between us.

There's something about this guy.

It's the way he smiles against my mouth as I kiss him. The way his fingers dance in my hair. The way he makes the moment move in slow-motion. The way he makes me feel special. Worthy, even. Sitting here in his car, it's like we're in a snow globe of promise and potential.

"If only we could stay in this moment," I sigh, as we break apart again.

"But then we wouldn't get to the next one." He kisses my nose. "Or the one after that."

"Would that be so bad?"

Surprise rings his eyes. "Well, I don't know about you, but I'm excited to see where this goes. It seems to me that each moment will be awesome in its own right." I understand what he means. Of course any relationship which stands a chance must be built on a bridge of shared experiences. I do want that. I want to make new memories with him. I'd just like to preserve them all along the way. Reserves, I suppose, for when life returns to its normal speed.

Like now, as I lean over to wipe a smudge of my lipstick from the corner of his lip and he repeats the question I'd temporarily forgotten: "So, where to?"

I know I should be honest. I should explain now, before we are in too deep and the timeline for sharing secrets is in the past. I should trust him. This is a man who stood up and fought for his child, after all. He runs toward responsibility, not away from it. That's part of it, though. I don't want him to feel an obligation. I don't want him to tether his life to mine because he feels sorry for me. He is no longer the stranger who rescued me, but still, I'm drawn to the idea of him being a blank canvas. Is it really so terrible if I control the colors we splash across it? I think of his reaction to Open Hearts earlier and make a decision.

The address I give him doesn't belong to the shelter. Instead, it's for a house in Elliston Place. Kristina and Robert's house. Only once, I promise myself. I will only use it as a decoy tonight. After Wilson and I make things official, then I'll confide in him. He chats easily as he drives, about a photo shoot he has tomorrow and a song he heard on the radio, and I try to keep up. It's difficult, though. How is one supposed to focus when she might be destroying her relationship before it even gets off the ground? Suppose Kristina and Robert are home? Outside? By the time Wilson turns onto their road, my heart's slamming against my ribcage. This is so risky. Too risky.

Is that a light on in their living room?

I squint through the windshield, trying to steal surreptitious glances without being obvious. The closer we get, the more certain I am that, yes, the antique lamp by the window is definitely on. It's similar to one we had in the apartment, and when I see its beige shade with the hanging green pull, a twist of nostalgia spirals through me. Kristina and I might not have been friends, but we did have some fun times when we lived together. I wonder how she is. We haven't spoken since she helped out with Ruby's wish.

"So I was thinking … " Wilson slows to a stop by the curb. "Emmalyn has been talking about the 'lady with the turquoise eyes' since that day at the playground. She really seems to like you. Maybe she can join us next time? You could come to the house," he adds. "I'm a fairly decent cook. I could make dinner?"

"Is that a question or a statement?" I tease.

Another peek at the house.

Is that a shadow moving along the wall?

"A statement." His cheeks redden. "Sorry. Guess I'm nervous. It's been a really long time since I invited anyone over." He clears his throat. "If it's too soon, I completely understand."

"Not at all," I assure him. "It sounds great."

Crap. That *is* a shadow, and a second later, Kristina's springy red hair comes into view. I have to get Wilson out of here before this charade is exposed. But he's asking about my favorite foods now, and there's no way to cut him off without being rude. "Em would live on spaghetti if she could," he says. "So I'm an expert – "

"I love spaghetti," I say hurriedly. "Really, I'm fine with anything. Whatever you want to make is great." I lean over to kiss him. "Thank you for a wonderful evening."

"Right back at you. Looking forward to next time. I'll call you tomorrow to make plans?"

"Can't wait."

I flash him a smile, then hop out of the car and pretend to search my bag for house keys. He sits there, waiting, and it occurs to me that he's not going to drive away until he sees me open the front door. Because that's the kind of guy he is. He wants to be certain I get in safely. It's endearing, but also problematic. I give a wave, hoping it'll prompt him to head home to Emmalyn. No luck. I tiptoe up the porch steps, mind racing as I try to figure out a solution to the mess I've created, and breathe a sigh of relief as an idea comes to me. I can tell him I left my keys at work. Then he'll take me back to Sensations and somehow I can convince him I'll be fine walking back from there. It's terrible to lie to him again, but what other choice is there?

I toss my hands up in frustration, miming annoyance with my own forgetfulness. Then I spin on my heel. Wilson lowers the window, presumably to ask what's wrong, and I steel myself against the guilt. What kind of future is built on a lie?

Mine, apparently.

Or maybe not.

Because just as I've reached the safety of Wilson's car, Kristina's door flies open. "Eden? Is that you?" she calls into the night.

Oh no. Oh no, oh no, oh no, *oh no*.

I freeze, hand tightening around the car door handle until pools of white stretch clear across my knuckles. Perhaps, if I don't answer, she'll leave it alone and go back inside. Except I hear footsteps. "Eden?" As she repeats my name, it fills me with a cold apprehension.

"Hey." I unclench my fingers and force myself to face her. "I thought you and Robert had plans tonight and weren't here. I must've left my house key at work, so I was going to ask Wilson to drive me back there to pick it up." The words betray me before I even have a chance to shut them up. It's far from my proudest moment.

"Your house key?" Kristina wrinkles her nose, confused. "What are you … " But then she stops, glances over at Wilson, and seems to catch on. I see it in the flash of recognition that darts through her eyes. "Oh. Yeah. We were supposed to go out to dinner for our anniversary, but Robert's got a killer migraine so we decided to postpone." She makes a grand show of shaking her head at me. "It never ceases to amaze me how you always manage to forget your key. Guess it's a good thing I was home."

I mouth a thank you to her before swiveling around to Wilson. "This is Kristina," I tell him. "My roommate. Kristina, this is Wilson, the guy I was telling you about." I detest myself for doing this. It is so wrong, and still, I can't make myself utter the confession that will end the lie. Wilson's the best thing to happen to me in forever. I can't lose him.

"Nice to meet you." He smiles amicably at Kristina. "I didn't realize you had a housemate, Eden. Have y'all known each other a long time?"

"Three and a half years," I say.

At least that's the truth.

"I couldn't afford the rent on my own, so I posted an ad and Eden answered." Also true. "We're sorta the yin to each other's yang." Kristina peers at me out of the corner of her eye, and her mouth turns up slightly. "You should ask Eden about her need to clean up other people's messes. One day I hope to return the favor." The underlying message there isn't lost on me, but Wilson is, thankfully, still oblivious.

"Duly noted," he says. A beep from his phone makes him look down, and his fingers glide across the screen, opening the text. "Hey, I've gotta go. Em had a nightmare and she's crying for me."

"Oh, absolutely. Go home to your little girl."

"We'll talk soon. Bye for now." He gives a wave and drives off. Now what?

Kristina's staring at me, I know that without even turning around, and I kind of want to sink into the ground out of humiliation. "What the hell," she says slowly, enunciating each syllable, "was that about?" For a nanosecond, I consider fabricating a story for her, too, just because it seems so much easier than delving into the whole ordeal, but I owe her honesty. She didn't have to cover for me or help with Ruby – who I told her I met in the park – when I asked. But she did. So, after we're inside, I spill the beans. The shelter. The job search. The interview. The day I met Wilson. The facade I've built. God, it feels therapeutic to get it out.

"I … you should have … " Kristina's eyes are wide by the time I'm finished. "Why didn't you tell me?"

"You were moving on," I say simply. "I didn't want to bother you with my issues."

"Your issues?" Her eyebrows dart sky-high. "Pretty sure being homeless qualifies as way more than an issue. You could've stayed with us. In fact, you still can." She leaps to her feet. "C'mon. I'll drive you back to the shelter and you can pack your stuff."

I'm touched by how quickly she extends the offer. Perhaps I was wrong to think she didn't care. But living with her and Robert? I'd be a third wheel. And, it jolts me to realize, I would actually miss Open Hearts. Not the shock of an icy shower, or the sorrow of hearing someone crying into a pillow at night, but the rest of it. The grins on the children's faces as Serena and I teach them notes on the scale. The joy when somebody returns from an interview with a new lease on life. The volunteering we do as a team, like tidying up the flower beds in a park and painting the gym of a local elementary school. But mostly, I'd miss the people. Coloring with Risa, being a confidante for Lainey, playing Go Fish with Tommy, listening to Ruby and Fred reminisce about their "good old days," and strumming the guitar strings as Serena learns my songs … somewhere along the line, these things have become important to me. I've only got so long before we all have to leave Open Hearts and go our separate ways. I'm not ready to lose these people yet. I'm not ready to leave the cocoon of the shelter.

I guess some butterflies need extra time before they can break free.

"Thank you," I tell Kristina. "That's really generous, and I appreciate it, but – "

"But nothing." She taps her foot against the carpeted floor.

"I'm not taking no for an answer."

"You didn't even ask Robert," I point out.

She motions to the ceiling. "He's sleeping. He really did have a migraine. No worries, though. I know he'll be okay with it." She stares at me, perplexed. "Why are you just sitting there? Come on. Let's go."

"I'm fine at Open Hearts," I tell her. "Turns out it isn't such a bad place after all."

"It's a homeless shelter. How nice can it be?"

A month and a half ago, I'd have thought the same thing. Now, I feel a bristle of annoyance, but shove it aside, because I know she's trying to help. I can't fault her for not understanding what she hasn't experienced. "Nicer than you would imagine," I say. "You wouldn't believe how many people it helps get back on their feet."

A dubious look crosses her face. "Doesn't it stifle your creativity?"

"Yeah, it did at first, but I'm making progress."

Slow progress. One line, one chord, one verse at a time.

But the fact that it *is* one verse now? That the cobwebs are disintegrating and the inspiration is returning? That's something to celebrate, and I owe a lot of it to the shelter. To the wishes people shared with me, to the reminder they gave that I can do something worthwhile, that I can matter to someone and touch a life. Sure, there's the fountain outside the symphony center, but Open Hearts is where it started. Suppose I leave and it all ends? Suppose the very place that beat my inspiration down is the only one capable of letting it rise back up? In a way, the shelter is like its own family. I can't leave it now. I can't leave the people who understand, not when we're all going to eventually be separated anyway, after everyone's five months are up and we have to move out.

"Well, our door's always open," Kristina says. "And if you ever need extra cash or anything ... "

There it is.

The shards of sympathy in her voice that I'm so desperate to keep out of Wilson's. The charity I have learned to accept from strangers, but not from those who know me. Suddenly I feel about two inches tall. And yet, at the same time, a surge of adrenaline explodes inside me. "Thank you," I say. "Really, I'll be okay. The only thing I can use is a ride back, if you don't mind."

She starts to say something, then changes course. "Sure."

A ride back.

Back to the shelter.

Back to where, for now, I belong.

June 4, 2003 – yearbook delivery day

Kay –

I can't believe it's been thirteen years since Mrs. P sat us next to each other in kindergarten. I also can't believe we're graduating and going off to college! How nuts is that? I'll miss being your co-president for the honor society, splitting chocolate chunk cookies in the cafeteria, and, of course, winning the badminton championship in gym each year. You'll always be my sister at heart, and I know you're going to do such great things in the world! You truly are the best.

<3, Eden

E –

What can I say, BFF? You are more than my friend, you're my family. From elementary school students who put on a play about Stone Soup to high school seniors who were an hour late to Prom because the limo got lost … you have been my lifeline. Thank you for being there when it felt like my whole world was crumbling. Thank you for being you. I'll miss you so much next year, but I know we'll be in touch. Can't wait to hear how you change the music scene with your songs.

- K

19

Serena's in the lobby when I walk into Open Hearts, singing softly as she scrawls lyrics on a legal pad. "You look at me with eyes so cold. When did they become dangerous black holes? How is this our life? How is this our prison? How did we become everything happily-ever-after isn't?" As I step inside, she stops and glances up at me.

"Sorry," I say. Outside, Kristina's car pulls away. "I didn't mean to knock you out of your zone. I know how frustrating that is."

"I don't mind. Really," she adds, as I look at her doubtfully. "I like to get another opinion while I work. Maybe it's because I'm used to brainstorming with Seth. We bounced ideas off each other all the time. I'd love to hear your thoughts on this." I sit in the rocking chair next to her and she passes over her half-written song. It's littered with cross-outs and arrows, notes about guitar solos and key changes, but through the clutter I see the gems. It's clear from the first line that it's about Seth and the path they've traveled.

"My thought is that you're incredibly brave to tackle a song about this," I say.

She sighs. "We write to heal, don't we?"

I think about that. My entire life, music's been my failsafe. It's been there for me when my dad and mom weren't. Those first couple months after they left, when I'd dissolve into tears at bedtime and ask Grandmom why Mommy and Daddy couldn't tuck me in anymore, she'd climb into bed with me, hug me tight, and sing. Sometimes it was one song – her favorite, Stevie Wonder's "I Just Called to Say I Love You" – and sometimes it took several before I drifted off. But once I did, I would dream of Grandmom's voice and let it take me to places I'd never been. And I'd wake up happy, feeling like all the world was a stage. My stage. Nowadays, it's more of my platform. Music is my way to reach out. Writing is my way to offer the truest parts of myself. "Yes." I nod my agreement with Serena. "We write to heal."

"It's the first time I've let myself go into such a personal space," she confides. "After I left Seth, I wanted to block it out. Block him out. I was scared that dwelling on what he did would prevent me from moving past it."

"What changed?"

"Avery," she says. The therapist she's been working with here. "She helped me realize that by burying my emotions, I was actually strengthening his grip on me. I spent years too terrified to fight back, and then after he put me in the hospital ... that's when I left. The day they released me, I took a cab home, packed my bags, and was gone before Seth even knew I had been discharged. But that wasn't healing. That was running for my life."

"It was courageous," I tell her. "That's what it was. You should be proud."

Her nose curls in disgust. "Of what? Of this?"

In a fluid movement, she yanks at the sleeve of her loose gold shirt. Beneath its glittery thread, beneath the shiny exterior, glares her scar. Up close, I see that it is a good three inches long. What must it be like for her, forced into living with that every day? It's an omnipresent reminder of all she has endured. "Maybe we need our scars, though," I offer, "to show us how far we've come and how strong we are." That's easy for me to say. I'm not the one whose shoulder looks like it fought – and lost – a battle. Is this what Serena's song is about?

You pummeled me, you bruised me, you shamed me, you broke me.
But there is beauty amidst the broken.
I see that more and more each day I'm at the shelter.
Even at our worst, we're also at our best.
Perhaps it's *because* we're at our worst that we're also at our best.

"I'd like to show up on his doorstep one day," Serena says, "and scream the lyrics at him. I'd like to see if anything shifts in his eyes."

She sighs again, pushing her feet against the carpet and rocking lightly. "There was an A&R rep at Noteworthy tonight. He came up to me after my set and asked if I would be interested in meeting his boss." She says this in such a dejected tone, I don't know how to respond.

"That's ... wonderful!" I say. Because it is. It's every singer's dream. So why does Serena look so conflicted?

"Yes," she agrees, "it is. But suppose I'm not good enough on my own? Suppose I can't make it without Seth?"

"This," I tell her, holding up the notepad, "is proof of how amazing you are. It's a haunting song and a beautiful one. I know it isn't the sort of thing you'd sing in front of a crowd, but I'm telling you the truth, it's magic. You have a gift for this and for singing. You make my songs sound the way I've always dreamed they would."

"Speaking of which ... " She peers at me hopefully. "Will you go to the meeting with me? I even thought ... " She smiles half-nervously, half-beseechingly.

"Yes?" I prompt.

"Well, I heard you singing the other day, when you thought you were alone in the courtyard – "

"What?"

Every defense I have races up to create a concrete wall around me.

"It was late," she says. "I'd been having an awful day – it was the anniversary of when Seth and I moved to Nashville together, and I guess the memories got too hard, because each time I closed my eyes to sleep, all I could see was a movie reel of our life. The only thing that seemed like it'd help at all was some fresh air. You didn't see me, but I saw you, sitting by the maple tree and writing lyrics. I don't think you even realized that you were singing along."

I didn't.

Not until this very moment.

"I'm not a singer," I tell her. "Not anymore. I'd be glad to go with you for moral support, but it's not fair to either of us for it to be more than that. Because you *are* good enough on your own. Your talent speaks for itself. You don't need Seth or me for backup."

"How do you know?"

"Because I've heard you sing. I've seen the looks on people's faces as they listen. Even the most vibrant flowers start out with their buds closed," I tell her, repurposing part of a pep talk Grandmom gave me the day I took my first guitar lesson and lamented about how difficult it was. "It takes love and care for the petals to open up. And sunlight. Be your own light." I hope Serena is as inspired by Grandmom's words as I was.

It's tough to tell, though, because she changes the subject. "Enough about me. I need details of your date."

An instant, involuntary grin overtakes my face.

"That good, huh?"

I give a one-shouldered shrug. "It was okay," I say noncommittally. The last thing I want to do is go on and on about Wilson when she's trying to make peace with Seth's sins. Much as I am dying to tell someone about that kiss, about the way it made me feel weightless, it can't be Serena.

"Okay?" She arcs an eyebrow. "You lit up the second I mentioned it." She leans forward. "I get what you're doing. You don't have to worry about me, though. I'm fragile, but the glue is there and I won't fall apart. So let me ask again: how was the date?"

"It was fabulous," I admit. "We click so well. He makes me feel … " I pause, trying to find a way to describe it. "He makes me feel like anything is possible, like there are people whose purpose is to lift us up instead of tear us down." A heat fills my cheeks. "And he kissed me."

She squeals excitedly. "How was it? Fireworks?"

"A whole sky of them."

"Tell me more." So I do. "You should've invited him in," she says, when I've finished. "I want to meet him."

"I'd like that. But not here. He isn't the one who dropped me off, actually. I had him take me to my old roommate's house instead. I don't want him to know about … well … this." I gesture around us.

"Wait … you purposely told him you live somewhere else?"

A coil of guilt reemerges and starts winding its way through my stomach. "He doesn't know I'm homeless," I explain. "I'm trying to keep it that way, at least for a little while longer. I feel like the more he knows about me, the less important this one fact will be. He won't pity me, or judge me, or leave me."

Serena shakes her head. "Not everybody leaves, you know. And relationships are complicated enough as it is. Do you want to make things more difficult by lying? What if he finds out? How will he be able to trust you again?"

"This is a mess." I drop my head into my hands. "All of it. Kristina asked me to move in with her until I can afford a place of my own. And do you know what I said? I said no. I told her I was fine at the shelter." I lift my gaze. "This is gonna sound off-the-wall, but in some strange way I've grown to like it here. I'm not ready to cut ties."

"Yet you're also not willing to be honest about it." She says the words I'm thinking. "Why?"

Why?

It eats away at me all night, spilling its dark ink over the canvas of my dreams and twisting them into nightmares. Flames shooting from my apartment. Calling Mom and Dad for help, only for them to turn me down. Dusty black ash settling atop my journal, smearing the feelings I've poured into its pages. Grandmom begging me to come back to Portsmouth. Wilson getting down on one knee with a glittering promise in hand, then snatching it away when my clothes shrivel up to rags and my past ruins our future. And that veteran. The nightmare about him is what finally snaps me awake, heart slamming wildly and a clammy sweat beading across my forehead.

I pop up in bed, trying to calm myself down, but the walls are closing in. Creeping towards me, squeezing their iron-clad fists. How do I stop the forward advance? I turn to the window, suddenly desperate to grant a wish, and that's when I see it. A stripe of moonlight slips through the curtains, illuminating the nearby watercolor painting. It's different from the other paintings in the bedroom. More abstract. More free. More whimsical.

I focus on it, on the swirls of pastel color and the delicacy of the brushstrokes.

Deep breath in. Deep breath out.

Freeform. Light. Airy. Bohemian. It's soothing. Grounding.

Slowly, my pulse stops thrumming. "They were just dreams," I whisper to myself. "You're okay. Everything is okay." But it's not. It won't be until I tell Wilson.

And what about everybody else? When Kayleigh calls the next day, I decide to test it out on her. Other than my family, she's known me longer than anyone. She was there when I broke my arm on the playground in fifth grade, when I got my nose pierced as a teenager, and when, during my junior year in college, a nurse from Portsmouth Regional Hospital called to tell me Grandmom had slipped off a stool at work and was being admitted for tests. Kay actually flew home from Carnegie Mellon for the weekend to stay with me at the hospital as the doctor ran CAT scans and MRIs to make sure Grandmom's concussion hadn't caused permanent damage. "Not necessary," Kayleigh said, when I thanked her. "Who was there for me during my parents' horrendous divorce? I'm just returning the favor."

Maybe this is how we can bridge the gap. Maybe it'll take something major to bring us together again. She felt comfortable enough to confide in me about Gary. It's time I take a cue from her and do the same.

"So there's something I have to tell you," I start, after she's given me an update on the situation with her fiancé – who is still her fiancé, since it turns out Gabrielle is the sixty-seven-year-old former dancer he'd secretly been taking lessons from to surprise Kayleigh on their wedding day.

"Of course," she says. "Shoot."

So I do. Straight from the heart. I open up the wounds and let their blood flow. "That's why my initial instinct was to turn down your bridesmaid invitation," I finish. "I don't know how I'll afford it. Right now every dime of my paychecks has to go in the bank. Open Hearts is wonderful, but they're only able to have people for a few months since there isn't a lot of room. After that we have to take their transitional housing option or find a place for ourselves. If I have a prayer of managing that on a hostess's salary – "

Kayleigh finally finds her voice. "Stop," she says. "First, I can't believe you didn't tell me before. Second, don't worry about paying for anything. I'll take care of it. My parents have both given me a blank check for the wedding." Ah, here we go. It's Kristina all over again, except this time the sting is even more painful. Kayleigh and I used to be equals. Now she's in New York, with a great job and a terrific life … and I'm in a position where she feels compelled to offer to pay my way. I can almost feel myself shrinking inside.

"Your parents don't have to pay for me," I tell Kayleigh, but she ignores me.

"Why don't you come stay with me and Gary for awhile?" she asks. "Give yourself a breather."

"That's so generous of you. It's just – "

"Think about it!" she exclaims. "We could live in the same place again. It'd be like old times! We can even turn the second guest room into your office."

"I don't need an office. I need to stay in Nashville to – "

"You can go to my dress fittings, and we'll kick Gary out on Thursday nights to watch *Grey's* with a carton of ice cream, just like we used to on our breaks from college – " The longer she rambles on, the more clear it becomes that she's not hearing a word I say. And it isn't that I'm not appreciative, because I am. But maybe, instead of narrowing the distance between us, this conversation is tearing it wider apart.

"Look, Kay," I finally say, "I'm grateful for the offer, truly. It's really nice of you to open up your home to me. This is something I've gotta do on my own, though. I have to be the one who rebuilds. I'll accept a loan for the bridesmaid dress, on the condition that I'm paying you back. That's where it ends, though."

"I don't get it." She sounds genuinely baffled. "Why on earth would you rather wear someone's old hand-me-downs than let me treat you to a new wardrobe? Why would you choose to stay in the shelter instead of rooming with your oldest friend? Why would you make things harder on yourself if I can make it easier?"

I sigh and look around the shelter. How do I help her understand that it's not cold or dingy, that staying here doesn't make me less than anyone else? She's grown up with money. Even before the divorce, her parents were free with it. Their house was the most chic on the block, with landscaping that was flawless and a living room filled with sparkling crystal. They even had a boat. To Kayleigh, a homeless shelter would be the last resort.

Suppose Wilson sees it like that, too?

Suppose he thinks less of me for staying when I could leave?

Confiding in Kayleigh was supposed to pave the way. Instead it's thrown up a roadblock.

And I have no clue which exit to take.

Sensations Café

where music meets munchies

Friday, 8/15/14
8:23PM
Server: Riley K.

Iced sweet tea	$2.25
Iced coffee	$2.25
Orange juice – kids' cup	$2.50
Apple juice – kids' cup	$2.50
Milk – kids' cup	$2.00
Salad Your Way: pasta, carrot, tomato, egg white, cucumber, croutons, Italian dressing on the side	$9.00
Grilled chicken sandwich & French fries	$8.00
Grilled cheese sandwich (cheddar)	$6.75
Side – hush puppies	$3.75
2 kids' spaghetti platters, sauce/no meatballs	$14.00
Side – French fries	$2.50
2 slices – banana cream pie	$6.50
	$62.00
tax	$3.10
total	$65.10

To say it's a long week is an understatement. Bobbi calls out again on Thursday and Friday, due to a sinus infection that's "knocked her flat," which means I'm on double duty for multiple days in a row. It's exhausting, but I'm in desperate need of extra money, so I decline when Dina offers to call the weekend hosts to fill in. Instead, I stand at the podium, I lead customers to their tables, I answer the phone and book reservations. Over and over and over. By the time Friday evening rolls around, I'm operating on auto-pilot. It reminds me of Rochelle and her automatons. I wonder how she is, if she enjoyed the CD. I wonder about the other people who have tossed their hopes and dreams into the fountain by the Schermerhorn. I've been spending my lunch hour there each day since – fingers crossed – making Rochelle's wish come true.

There was the little girl who wanted a baby brother or sister. The middle-schooler who wanted someone to sit with in the cafeteria this coming school year. The teenager who wanted the boy she likes to return her feelings. The baker who wanted a retail shop for her cupcake business. The artist who wanted new paintbrushes. There were all these wishes and others – many more that I couldn't grant than those I could – and as I listened, I realized something: people aren't ever really satisfied. Heartfelt as the yearnings were, they still highlighted the need for more. Then there were the other wishes, like the woman who 'needed' a new smartphone and the man who wanted a flashier set of golf clubs. It made me sad.

"If only you knew," I wanted to say, "what some people would give for the things you're willing to toss aside." But I didn't. I just listened, helped if possible, and tried to remember that everyone's reality is different.

I'm thinking about that now, when a family comes into

Sensations. "Hurry up, I'm starving!" the younger girl proclaims. "My belly is growling!"

"It is," the older girl confirms, giggling. "It sounds like a lion's roaring in there."

"I want a lion! Can we have a lion?" asks the little boy.

The man grins, then swoops him up. "Afraid not, buddy. Where would it live?"

"It can stay in my room."

"Lions are wild animals," the woman explains, fishing in her oversized purse and pulling a phone out. She taps at its screen a few times, then swivels it around to show her son. "See? These are the lions from our zoo back home. Remember when we went to visit them?" The dark-haired boy nods. "Some animals can be pets, but not all."

"*Mommy*." The petite redhead tugs on the woman's hand and looks at her imploringly. "Please, my tummy needs yummies! Ellie's and Jordan's, too! Right?" She enlists her siblings' help and they all clamor loudly.

"Table for five, please." The woman smiles at me. "Maybe in a quiet corner, so the other diners aren't interrupted by my monkeys' antics." This leads the younger kids to squeal and the third one to say she's too old to be a monkey. "I don't know, El," the woman teases, "I have it on pretty good authority that an eight-year-old still falls into that category."

"You're silly." Her mouth curves up and she shakes her head, sending her brown curls flying. "If I could be an animal, I'd pick a gazelle. We learned about them in school last year. They're graceful, and I want to be, too!" She begins to pirouette, her arms out to the sides. "See? Like a ballerina!" She spins around in front of the hostess stand.

"Sorry." The mother casts another smile in my direction. "We just drove in from Georgia, so the kids have been cooped up in the car for hours. Evidently, they have lots of energy to expend. Right, Addilyn?" she asks her youngest daughter, who must be around Emmalyn's age.

"Right," she declares. Then she peers at her parents. "What is that word? Expend? Like when you give money to people at a store?" Slowly, her gaze drifts to me. "Do Mommy and Daddy have to give you dollars and cents before my belly gets food? Is that how it works?"

"I think we should feed your belly first," I answer. "Otherwise the roars might get louder and I'll have to explain to my boss why I invited a lion in for dinner." She laughs and throws a freckle-faced grin at me.

I seat them at a front corner booth, give the kids a pack of crayons to color their placemats, and hurry back to my post by the door. No sooner do I get there than a new group of customers arrives. And so it goes for the next thirty minutes. Customer after customer, phone ringing constantly, and a band setting up in the back to play their set. The sound of their guitars twangs through the air, and I think, for at least the tenth time since Serena asked me to sing with her at her meeting, of the awful open mic night I had during grad school. Of the way I practiced for weeks leading up to it. The way anxiety stirred in my stomach as I took the stage and a sea of people stared at me expectantly. The way a woman came in at the last minute and took a seat in the front. She threw me off completely, because she looked so much like Mom. Same dark hair, same sapphire eyes. As I stood there, guitar pick poised in my fingers, I panicked. I traveled back in time to one of many days I have tried so hard to bury.

It was September of my senior year in high school, and my parents had just gotten back from an eight-month-long assignment in Honduras. "It's unbelievable how much we take for granted," Mom said, filling a pitcher with water in Grandmom's small kitchen. "So many people would give anything to drink this."

"That's what you're here for," Grandmom said. "To make it happen."

That's what she's here for.

In five words, Grandmom summed up Mom's purpose. Dad's, too. I sincerely believe that we're all put on this earth for a reason.

We all have a journey to embark on, a song to sing, a story to tell. For my parents, their story writes the pages of other people's. But not mine. Never mine. They left me to pen my own.

Let's just say they weren't so thrilled with the outcome.

"What do you mean?" Dad asked, when, over Grandmom's lasagna, I announced that I had filled out an early application for Boston's Berklee College of Music. "I thought we talked about this. Your mom and I hoped you'd take a year off and work with us."

"I considered it," I told them. "Honest. It's not for me, though."

"But this is our chance to really get to know each other." Mom's voice dipped down, and I knew she was hurt.

"Mariah – " Grandmom began.

And I finished.

"Get to know each other?" My eyebrows lifted. "The time for that was years ago. It was when I played Rapunzel in the school show and you settled for watching the video six months after the fact. It was when I learned how to play a song on the guitar and you only listened to a few measures over the phone, because your calling card ran out. It was when the boy I liked asked someone else to the Soph Hop and I was so upset I cried in Grandmom's arms." As I ran through a list of times when they hadn't been there, when they consciously picked other children over me, heat burned into my face and left a scorching imprint.

"Eden, that's enough," Dad said quietly. But he looked sad. He looked pained.

Mom?

She was spitting nails.

"Don't be ungrateful," she scolded. "You are so lucky to grow up in an environment like this. To have a roof over your head, clothes on your back, and a hot meal on the table. To have a grandmom who loves you and takes care of – "

That was the final straw. "Grandmom is the best," I said, ignoring the sting behind my eyes as I stood up from my chair. I was *not* going to cry in front of them. "She's there for me whenever you aren't, which, let's face it, is pretty much always. So no, I'm not deferring college. I won't postpone my dreams so you can feel better about yours. If you want someone to blame for not knowing your child, look in a mirror."

I stormed off, accidentally careening into the table on the way and rattling Grandmom's dishes, and spent the night locked in my bedroom, crying bitter tears. Because of what Mom said and what Dad didn't say. Because I adored Grandmom, but I still wished for parents who loved me enough to stay. And, most of all, because I heard the words Mom confided as I blew upstairs: "Sometimes it's like she isn't our daughter at all."

So that night at the café, when the woman settled herself in my line of vision? I just ... couldn't. The lyrics crumbled to dust in my brain, and my fingers, the same ones that knew every string on the guitar like they'd been joined forever, slackened until I dropped the pick. That's the night I stopped singing.

I learned something very important: we aren't all meant to give breath to our own words. It was okay to focus solely on writing, this passion that entrenched itself in the crevices of my heart, and it was also okay to turn my words over to others, to let them find their own interpretation. Every now and then I miss singing. But mostly, I don't. Songwriting is what composes me.

I can't sing with Serena at her meeting. If I freeze up again, I'll ruin things for her, and, honestly, I don't trust that I can get through it. I can't risk another disaster at the microphone. "Never again," I whisper. Then I refocus on work as the phone rings. "Hello, Sensations Café. How can I help you?"

"That depends." I instantly recognize the voice as Wilson's. "Are you asking in a professional or personal capacity?"

I can't hide my smile. "Well, the right answer is probably professional, but for you, either is fine. Wouldn't it have been funny, by the way, if I'd been busy and somebody else answered the phone? Unless you flirt with everyone?"

"I knew it was you." I almost hear his grin. "And no, my flirting's reserved for special people. Or a special person, I should say."

"I like the sound of that."

"Ditto." He's silent for a moment, and I wonder if he's soaking in this conversation as much as I am. "Okay, so question for you: Em and I are going to the grocery store bright and early tomorrow, and we want to be sure to buy your favorite foods for dinner. I can make spaghetti, like I mentioned the other night, or I can go for something different. Any preferences?"

"Oh, whatever you guys normally have is fine."

"I doubt that." He chuckles. "Unless you enjoy chicken fingers dipped in applesauce? Macaroni and cheese topped with celery?"

"Macaroni and ... celery? I ... um ... well ... " I hedge.

"Didn't think so." Another chuckle. "My Em is queen of interesting food combinations."

"Interesting? That's one way to put it."

"Exactly. I'm gonna go out on a limb and say you wouldn't be a fan of most of her favorites. So tell me ... what can I cook for you?"

Something warm settles over my heart.

He wants to cook for me. He wants to make me happy. He wants me to spend time with him.

He wants me for me, not the person he thinks I could be.

"Go with spaghetti," I say. "Or anything Italian is good." I look up as the bell on our door jingles and a man walks in. "I've gotta go; we have a customer. See you tomorrow at six?"

"Can't wait. Ciao, bella."

"Ciao."

I hang up and help the man – he's looking for his fiancée, who arrived a few minutes earlier and is already seated at a table by the front window – and then attend to the group of people waiting to pay their check. Back to the go-go-go. But I'm not tired anymore. Instead I feel like zipping around the restaurant. It's like I've been infused with the best kind of adrenaline rush. It scares me a little, how Wilson has such a profound and instant effect, but more than that, it thrills me. He is a breath of fresh air who's bringing me back to life.

While I work, I sneak peeks at the family I seated earlier.

There's something special about them. It's like they're meant to be. In them, I see what I've never had … and also what maybe, just maybe, I could build with Wilson and Emmalyn. Even more than a career in songwriting, this is what I have always wanted: a family to call my own. People to be there for and people who will be there for me. I want the chaos, the pandemonium, and even the messiness, because a life lived outside the lines means you're painting your own destiny.

Standing there, watching the mother divide two slices of our banana cream pie into five slivers, I realize with certainty that I can't tell Wilson the truth tomorrow. I think I'll wait until I'm out of the shelter instead. It's not like I'll be lying forever. I just have to keep the secret a little bit longer, and this way I won't be risking my future on the past and present.

The tales we tell, the webs we spin
Black and white don't look good on them
The world is gray, shaded in waves
Here and there, right and wrong
It's a murky picture, but still, it's strong

The lyrics come to me out of nowhere, and it's startling, because I'm used to inspiration coming from other people's stories. Not my own. Not anymore. But perhaps that's where I've been going wrong. Perhaps I need to let myself wear my heart on my sleeve again. I pick up the closest piece of paper and jot down the words. They're frightening, these lyrics. They leave me wide open.

Vulnerable.

This is a good thing, I remind myself. There's a quote – "music is what feelings sound like" – that I adore. I used to have a framed print of it in my bedroom, and until this point, I haven't been ready to replace it. The feelings flowing through me? I didn't want to hear what they sounded like. Dark, melancholy. A clash of piano keys, a pounding of drums, a gritty voice layered with nails. Now there is more. Now there is also lightness and anticipation. Maybe a whistle from a flute. A strum of the harp.

I smile at the family in the corner booth.

You can just tell they're the kind of people who live out loud. It's time for me to do the same.

Scrabble score sheet:

Eden		**Wilson**	
star	8 points	cameo	9 points
treble	14 points	sunny	18 points
guitars	22 points	plum	33 points
lugs	12 points	nip	5 points
capers	33 points	zee	24 points
pixie	28 points	meek	39 points
sage	23 points	jig	19 points
ajar	13 points	herd	24 points
ink	18 points	soft	6 points
cog	17 point	oft	7 points
revel	8 points	revelation	26 points
quail	28 points	parted	10 points

21

My eyes dart back and forth as the cab driver makes a right onto Wilson's street. It's in a quaint neighborhood about fifteen minutes south of Nashville, and I immediately fall in love with the neatly manicured squares of lawn, the trellis flower boxes bursting with peonies and petunias, and the cute porches with their outdoor furniture. Every house is different. Some are brick, some are stone, and others are lined with siding. An American flag dangles from a pillar on the corner one, and next to it, a group of kids plays a game of kickball. A lawn mower hums, an ice cream truck parks near the curb as a line of people gather to buy treats, and in the nearby oak tree, a blue jay balances on one of the branches and cocks its head at me quizzically. *What are you doing here? You do not fit the mold*, is what it seems to say.

True.

I don't fit in here, with the chalk-covered driveways and basketball hoops, the flowering bushes and wooden patios, the minivans and fenced-in yards. But I'd like to, someday. I'd like to so much. As we drive on, I touch my fingertips to the window. It's difficult to be on the outside looking in. Or is it the inside looking out? I'm not sure.

"Here we are, Miss." The taxi driver slows to a stop in front of an adorable little house. Most of it is painted white, including the porch railings, but the door and steps are cornflower blue. There's a pastel pink tricycle in the driveway and two flowerpots on both sides of the stairs. It's modest, yet welcoming.

"Thank you." I count out the fare from my wallet – yesterday was payday at work and I actually cashed this check instead of depositing it – and add a tip. "Have a good night," I say, and he wishes me the same. Then he drives off, leaving me alone on the sidewalk. My stomach turns cartwheels. Having dinner here and spending time with Wilson's daughter is a big deal. I hope I don't mess it up.

Live out loud, Eden.

Think of the Jacobs family. I ended up talking with the mom as they were leaving last night, and found out they're in town for an alumni weekend at Belmont. She went there, too, as an undergrad, and decided to bring the whole family for the festivities. "It's more hectic this way," she said with a smile, "but also infinitely more fun."

Infinitely more fun. It sounds like a marvelous way to live.

With that in mind, I hurry up the stairs and ring the doorbell.

"Can I get it?" As the bell chimes, I hear Emmalyn call out. Then the curtains part in the window by the door – Wilson must be holding her – and her cherubic face peers through. "It's her, Daddy," she reports. "And she bringed us a present!" I glance at the apple cobbler in my hands, courtesy of Sensations. Thank you, employee discount.

"Hey." The door swings open and there stands Wilson. "Glad you could make it."

"Wanna play princesses?" Emmalyn asks, sliding down from his arms. Before I can even answer, she slips her hand in mine and propels me into the living room. I barely have time to pass the pie to Wilson first. "Daddy builded me a castle!" Indeed he did. It's wooden, about three feet tall, with a drawbridge, turrets, and a plethora of dolls inside. "You can be Cindy-rella," Em declares, giving me the one with blonde hair.

Wilson lets out a low whistle. "That's how you know you rank. She never shares Cinderella."

Emmalyn picks Ariel for herself. "'Pecially not with Daddy."

"Why not?" The corners of my mouth turn up. "I bet he'd make a super Cinderella."

"Daddy tries hard," she says. "But he's a boy." Her voice drops to a hush, like she's letting me in on a secret. "He needs help."

A swell of laughter rises in my chest. "Well, maybe I can give him some pointers." I take the doll brush Emmalyn gives me. "What happened to her hair? It's not in a bun."

"Daddy," she answers morosely. "He breaked it."

"Hence why I'm not allowed to touch it anymore," he explains. "You've gotta cut me some slack on this, Sweetpea. Daddy didn't know any better, and I offered to buy you a new doll to make up for my mistake. Remember?"

"No need." I twist the doll's hair up, secure it with one of those clear rubber bands, and hunt in the castle until I find her blue headband. "There we go," I say, slipping it into place. "Good as new." If Emmalyn liked me before, this completely endears me to her. Quick as lightning, she wraps me in a hug, literally welcoming me into her world with open arms. I didn't expect that to happen so fast. I thought it'd take time for her to warm up to me. That's how I was as a child. It was difficult for me to let people in. Even with most of my friends, Grandmom stayed at their houses the first few times we got together, chatting with their parents while we played. When she tried to leave, I grew teary-eyed. And I know this is different – Wilson is three feet away and it's not like he's going anywhere – but it still means a lot. To him, too, I can tell. He watches silently, with a soft smile which makes me wonder what he's thinking. I catch it on his face a lot over the course of the evening: when I make Cinderella dance with the prince at the ball, when Emmalyn shows me her toy train collection, when the three of us put on a puppet show, and when I pull a daisy from the vase on the kitchen table and tuck it behind Emmalyn's ear as we sit down to eat.

"This is nice," he says.

"Super *duper* nice," Emmalyn chimes in. "Eden rocks my socks."

Wilson had been scooping spaghetti into her bowl, but at this, he does a double take. "What did you say?" he asks, mouth twitching.

"She rocks my socks." Emmalyn drags the bread basket across the table and manages to tip the whole thing over. "It's a 'spression. I learned it at preschool."

He chuckles. "Cute," he says, grabbing a napkin and using it to toss the garlic knots back into the basket. "Sorry," he tells me. "Don't worry, I won't be insulted if you pass on them." He looks upset, though, and when, a short while later, Em spills her cherry fruit juice and it slides over the table and into my lap, that only intensifies.

"I'm sorry!" Emmalyn's bottom lip juts out. "Was I bad?"

"No, Em," Wilson says, jumping up and hurrying over to grab a handful of paper towels. "It was an accident." He stops to kiss her head on the way back, then kneels by my chair and makes a move to clean up the mess before he realizes how awkward it'd be. I can't help laughing. I just bought the pants I'm wearing from the thrift shop, and no, I'm not particularly excited about the red stain that's spreading across the fabric, but what can I do? So this isn't what I imagined. So it isn't the picture-perfect dinner Wilson wanted. Things don't always go as planned, though, and it doesn't make me like him any less. It actually makes me like him even more.

"I'll take care of that," I say, giving him a quick wink as I stand up. "Which way's the bathroom?"

"Down the hall, first door on the left."

"Got it. Be back in a flash."

It takes a good ten minutes of scrubbing to make myself presentable again, and even then, a big wet splotch covers half my upper leg. I dab at it again, then rejoin my dinner dates. Wilson's wiped up the table now and is standing at the counter with Emmalyn, keeping an eye on her as she scoops dollops of sweet cream onto the cobbler. "Uh-oh," he says, as it drips off the spoon. "I think you've got some on your nose."

"No, I don't!"

"Yes you do," he counters, dabbing it onto her face. "See?"

She squeals. "You're in trouble!"

I shrink back against the wall, not wanting them to see me, and watch as Em jumps off the stool and chases him through the kitchen with the bowl of sweet cream. Around and around and around they go. She finally catches up to him near the refrigerator, which is covered top to bottom with her artwork, and instead of taking the bowl away, he picks her up and lets her retaliate. "You got me!" he exclaims.

"I did!" she cheers, tracing a drippy heart on his cheek. He tickles her and she shrieks with high-pitched laughter. It's beyond cute. Pure, uninhibited joy. That's what it is. What they are.

As I step into the kitchen, Wilson's gaze rises to meet mine, and an involuntary smile grabs hold of me. "How long have you been standing there?" he asks.

"Long enough."

Long enough to know that maybe I *do* fit in here, after all.

* * *

"Wanna join us for story time?" Wilson asks, after Em practically falls asleep on top of the Candy Land board as we're playing. He scoops her up and leads the way to her bedroom. "It's a tradition," he explains, helping her into a pair of Minnie Mouse pajamas before settling into the glider. I perch on the matching ottoman. "I've read to her every night since she was born."

"Tell her the story," Em insists. She looks so cute, her legs dangling over Wilson's and her hair a spring of curls splayed against his chest. "'Bout Grammy."

"My mom bought the original book," Wilson explains. "It was her first purchase after I told her she was going to be a grandmom. She said a child's never too young to hear about all the places she can go."

"Grammy works at the library," Em chimes in. "She says stories live in here – " She points to her temples. " – and here." She turns both thumbs inward to her chest.

"Your grammy sounds wonderful," I say.

"The wonderfulest."

"Most wonderful," Wilson corrects softly. Then he switches gears and opens the book Emmalyn is holding. "Want to take turns?" he offers to me.

"Sure." We alternate pages as we read, and by the time we're finished, Em is fast asleep.

"Now comes the hard part," Wilson whispers. He gets up slowly, edges across the aqua carpet, and lowers her, inch by inch, into bed. Her eyelashes flutter briefly, she murmurs an 'I love you' and a request for her stuffed bunny, then it's back to sleep. Wilson breathes a sigh of relief. "Em usually dozes off when I read," he says, "but sometimes she'll wake up as I move her, and it takes forever to get her settled again." He tucks Em's yellow blanket around her, brushes a kiss to her forehead, and straightens up. "Now, I can't offer an exciting night out, but I play a killer game of Scrabble if you're willing to take on the challenge."

"Challenge accepted."

He switches on Emmalyn's nightlight, closes her door halfway, and we head out to the hall.

"Thanks for joining us. She loved it."

"So did I."

I did, truly. The way they made room for me in their routine was the best kind of surprise. For a heartbeat in time – or maybe several heartbeats, because even now, as we sink onto the sofa with a bottle of wine and the Scrabble board, I feel warm and fuzzy – it was like I could imagine the threads of my life intertwining with theirs. And the tapestry it's creating? I just want to wrap myself up in it for as long as possible.

"I should probably warn you," I tell Wilson, flipping over the Scrabble tiles as he pours us each a glass of pinot noir, "my grandmom and I used to play this all the time, and she didn't call me Queen of Triple Word Scores for nothing. You're going down."

"You wish."

His words immediately make me curious: what would he wish for, if I gave him a penny?

I'm seized by the desire to help his hopes along.

To repay him for the change he and Emmalyn have already inspired in me.

But not yet. Not tonight.

For now, I just want us to stay in this moment.

"Let's see," I murmur, nursing my wine as I shuffle my tiles around. I opt for STAR to start, even if it isn't the highest scoring word I can play, because it feels so appropriate for this date. Being here in Wilson's house, surrounded by the things that make it his home – the stack of meteorology books on the coffee table, the red and white University of Oklahoma blanket draped across the back of the armchair, the toy chest overflowing with board games by the wall, and, of course, the little girl down the hall – it makes this notion swirl through my mind. That finally the stars are aligning. That finally I'm enough. Wilson didn't have to ask me here tonight. He didn't have to welcome me into this life he shares with Em. But he did, and I feel safe here. I even feel wanted.

And when Wilson keeps interrupting the game to steal kisses?

I feel like I might burst with happiness.

"I'm sorry," he says, as he adds on to REVEL to form REVELATION. "I know a lot of tonight was a comedy of errors. The rolls, the juice ... " He smiles ruefully and shakes his head. "That wasn't how I envisioned things going."

I play off his word and tally the points for QUAIL. "Twenty-eight," I count, "and trust me, you've got nothing to apologize for. I'm having a great time."

"You're only saying that to be nice." He adds PARTED to the board.

"I'm saying it because I mean it."

"You wouldn't have been happier going to a concert? Or doing something romantic, like walking through the park under the moonlight?" He records his score, sets down the pen, and fixes me with a serious gaze. "I like you, Eden. I like you a lot. You're the first woman I've brought home to spend time with Emmalyn. And I just – " He drags a hand through his hair, making it stand up a little at the back. "I wanted tonight to live up to your expectations."

"I don't have any expectations." I meet his eyes and let myself be drawn in by their gravitational pull. "At least, not in the way you mean. I don't need grand, romantic gestures. I'd rather have real ones. Like inviting me here and letting me get to know your daughter. I have learned lately that the ordinary is extraordinary, too. Forget the candlelight, or the moonlight, or whatever. This is my idea of happiness, right here." I lean over to kiss him.

Before I know it, the Scrabble board's on the floor, tiles spilling every which way and score sheet upside-down, and Wilson's lowering me into the sofa cushions. A zillion thoughts bombard my brain as his mouth blankets mine, but I can't make any sense of them, because at the same time, a zillion sensations are launching an advance on my body. My heart drums in my chest. My pulse thrums in my ears. I am so aware of his proximity, of the bolt of lust exploding inside and igniting sparks at my nerve endings. "This ... you ... " I give up trying to speak as his kisses move down to my neck, simply snaking an arm around his waist to pull him closer.

"Okay?" he whispers.

Again, checking to make sure I'm ready. Again, making me swoon.

My fingers dance up his shoulders until they're in his hair, and I arch my back slightly, enough to touch my nose to his as he raises his head to look into my eyes. I skate my mouth over his, gently at first, then harder, deeper. I know it's early on, we haven't even made things official, but my God, do I want to be with him right now. I want to feel the blaze of his skin against mine, and the rush of his breath on my collarbone, and the sturdiness of his embrace as he holds me tight. I want to kiss him until I can find a way, some way, to express how fast and how entirely I am falling for him. Which is why, when his fingers play with the neckline on my flowy peasant shirt, I utter a single, certain word.

"Yes."

He slips the sleeve down my shoulder, kissing me tenderly, delicately, and part of me wants him to hurry, but the other part wants to savor every second. Every sensation. He pulls back then, and a smile blossoms on his face as he looks at me. It's like sunshine on my skin. "You're beautiful, do you know that?"

And then, just as he suggests we move to the bedroom, a little blonde head appears around the corner. "Daddy?" Emmalyn asks. "What are you doing?"

GEOFF

Midnight blue sky. Neon orange flames. Acrid gray smoke. Pale green shirt, smeared with black soot. Geoff wants to forget. He wants to banish this horrible palette of colors from his mind, but it isn't possible. It's been seven years since that tragic night, and still, whenever he lets a new batch of flames surround him, he remembers. He remembers the day he married Darcy, their hands clasped tightly as they walked back down the aisle to roaring cheers from family and friends. He remembers the way they ate breakfast together every morning before work and a snack every night before bed. He remembers the scent of her shampoo as she slept in his arms and the glitter in her eyes when he brought her home a bouquet of flowers. But mostly, he remembers the conference call. It lasted an hour longer than it was supposed to, so he was late leaving the office. He texted Darcy to tell her he wouldn't make it for dinner, and she replied with a short and sweet response. He still has that text. He refuses to get a new phone, even though his is on its last leg, because he wants to save those last words he has from his wife.

No problem, hon. Hope the call's going well. I'll wait up. Love you. XOXO

But when he finally pulled into the driveway, Darcy wasn't waiting. Firefighters were. They told him it was too late, that Darcy was already gone, and everything in him sank. He felt that loss like it was his own life. Still, he torpedoed into the house and shrieked for her. The smoke assaulted him, filled his lungs, but he pressed on until the fire chief took him by the arm and led him out.

The next day, Geoff quit his job at the advertising agency. He turned in his badge, boxed up his belongings, and walked out. The day after that, he went to the closest fire company, the one who'd tried to save his wife, and signed up to join their team. He couldn't help Darcy, but he'd help others. He'd battle blazes and rescue people in her honor … in her memory.

22

It is a fitting finale for Wilson's self-proclaimed comedy of errors. He flings himself off me, losing his balance and tumbling to the floor. "Ow!" he yelps, as he lands on a pile of Scrabble tiles, and Em darts forward. She steps on our score sheet, the paper crinkling under her tiny toes, and I quickly fix my shirt sleeve and sit up. My cheeks are still flushed, the tiny hairs on my neck still tingling, but the moment Wilson and I were lost in is now slipping away.

Emmalyn plunks herself down next to him. "You've got an ouchie," she says, pointing to his shin as he massages it. "Does the boo-boo hurt?"

"Just a bit. Daddy's okay."

She's quiet for awhile, scrunching up her button nose, still looking concerned.

"I have an idea," I volunteer. "Why don't you kiss it and make it better? Does Daddy do that to your ouchies?"

She nods. "Like when I falled at Gymboree. Daddy knowed what to do."

"And now you do, too." I ease down to the floor with them. "I bet it'd make your daddy feel so super special to have you take care of him." That's all the prompting the little girl needs. She dives into nurse mode, pressing a marshmallow soft kiss to Wilson's shin and offering him the blanket she carried out with her. It's chevron, yellow and aqua to match the décor in her room, and is fraying at the edges.

"Tell me, little miss," Wilson says, as she drapes it over him, "why aren't you in bed?"

Her face turns solemn. "I had a bad dream."

"I'm sorry." He brushes a wispy tendril of her hair. "Nightmares can be scary, can't they?"

"Super scary. There were lots of monsters. One was blue. One was 'lellow. One was green. Do they live here? Underneath my bed?" She scoots forward until she's tucked between us. "I came to get help. But you were taking a happy nappy with Eden."

Wilson's mouth twitches. "Grown-ups get tired too," he tells her.

"You must've been *really* tired! 'Cause you falled asleep on top of Eden!"

"I just couldn't help myself." He winks at me over the top of her head. "I'm awake now, though. Tell you what, how about we go scout out your bedroom for monsters? They aren't real, but we can double check if you want." He scoops her off the floor, stands up, and extends a hand to me. "Care to join us?"

"Of course." I'm so smitten with Wilson and Emmalyn Graham, I'd join them anywhere.

And, over the next several weeks, I do exactly that.

There's story time at the library and an open house at Em's dance school. Dinners in the city for Wilson and me, picnics in the park for all three of us. Shows at Nashville Children's Theatre and mini golf at Opryland. There are warm days at the zoo and, as summer fades into fall, cool nights outside in Wilson's neighborhood, teaching Emmalyn to ride her tricycle. Coffee dates on my lunch breaks, movie dates after Em's sleeping and we've settled into the living room, hiking dates at Radnor Lake State Park on the weekends. I tell Wilson that my car isn't fixable and I can't afford to buy another one – which is true, really. Sometimes he picks me up at work, sometimes I take the bus, sometimes I walk, and on rare occasions, usually after I've gotten a paycheck from Sensations, I splurge on a cab ride.

Out of all the time we spend together, some of my favorite moments are when I invite Wilson to Serena's nights at Noteworthy so he can hear my songs, and when he asks if I'd like to tag along on his shoots when my schedule allows. Seeing him in his element, snapping photos of tiny newborns, engaged couples, and high school seniors ... I love it. Meteorology might be his first passion, but it's clear that photography is another one. He's terrific at it, too. He's got an eye for details, a foresight about the best ways to frame the world with his lens. Then there's my world. As I tuck Em into bed one night when Wilson's working late, and she asks for "a flutterby kiss," I realize I love this child. I love her father. It doesn't matter that we've only been together for a short while. When something is right, you know.

I know that we've become inseparable.

I know that I no longer want to imagine life without them.

I know that right here, curled into the cushions of Wilson's couch, working on a song as I wait for him to get home, is exactly where I want to be. I have never felt anything like this before, not even with Jared. I love the way my heart flutters when I hear Wilson's key in the lock. The way it settles peacefully when he asks about my day and tells me about his.

And the way it explodes when, after double checking to make sure Em is in dreamland, he leads me to his bedroom for a take two of our first time. After we got interrupted a month and a half ago, we decided it would be best to wait and truly get to know each other. Sure, it tested our patience at times, but it was the right choice. Especially when there's a child in the equation, you want to know how the factors add up.

Tonight?

They tally into something amazing.

"You know," I say, linking my hands with Wilson's as I walk backward toward his bed, "I think we pretty much perfected the whole patience thing."

"Good things come to those who wait." There is something smoldering in his eyes that makes my breath catch. I feel tethered to him in this moment, like there's a line tying the windows of his soul to mine, and all I can think about is how grateful I am. For the fire, because that led me to Open Hearts. For Open Hearts, because that led me to Serena. For Serena, because she led me to have the courage to use "Voyage of the Heart" during my interview. And even for the reality Ginger dropped on my dream that day, because it led me to Wilson. Sometimes, when a dark trail is in front of us, winding around a bend of uncertainty, the thing to do isn't run away. I see now that we must be willing to venture forward anyway. We must blaze our own path and light our own way.

"I think," I tell Wilson, "we've waited long enough."

He says nothing, just captures my mouth with his as I sink down onto the comforter. At first I try to memorize everything. The scent of his spicy cologne. The sound of the clock ticking. The taste of his mouth. The feel of his fingertips as they sneak under my shirt. The sight of his grin as I reach for his belt. But then I stop. I stop trying to paint a picture and let the picture paint me instead. Living love is better than freezing it.

He kisses the corners of my mouth, the end of my nose, the tips of my fingers. It is so gentle, so passionate, that for an instant, I actually think I'm going to cry. Because it's blissful, being here with him. Because I don't have to worry he'll disappear. Because he wants me – in his bed, in his house, in his life. I never thought I was the type of person who needed someone else to complete her, but I consider now that maybe we all need it. Maybe each soul has a hole waiting to be filled by another person.

As our clothes drop to the floor, so do my defenses.

I let myself believe in this. In him.

He blankets my body, leans into me as I trace figure-eights on his shoulder with my nail, and all I can do is sigh. A sigh of contentment. Of hope and desire. My heart floats towards the clouds, and I run my finger over Wilson's mouth, across his collarbone, and down his side. I want to get to know every inch of him. I want us to explore and discover.

I love you, I think.

But I don't say it out loud. Not yet.

Because good things *do* come to those who wait.

* * *

The next morning, as I open the door to Sensations, I feel like I'm walking on air. Wilson taps his car horn, then drives off.

Emmalyn's buckled into her car seat, waving wildly out the window, and I wave back until the car turns a corner. Then I go inside, where, to my surprise, I find Dina watching me with a smile.

"Good morning?" she asks. I think of Wilson bringing me coffee in bed, the steam spiraling in a curlicue, and of Em lighting up when she bounded out of her bedroom and found me at the kitchen table.

"Eden!" she squealed. "You're here!"

I opened my arms for a hug as she flung herself at me. "I am!"

"Does that make you happy?" Wilson strolled into the kitchen from the other direction, his hair still damp from the shower. He was dressed in a Nashville Predators t-shirt and shorts, his feet bare, and there was something so casual about it, so laidback and normal, that I fell for him all over again. I love how our relationship's grown, how we've gotten to the point where it's no longer about a first impression, but rather a lasting one. Did he care that he hadn't shaved yet? Nope. Did I care about throwing my hair into a messy knot instead of brushing it out? Nope. What mattered was the peeks Wilson kept stealing at me as he made breakfast. And the ease I felt, reaching into their cabinets to get plates for the table. And the delight in Em's voice as she answered.

"Super duper happy!" she said.

He met my gaze across the room. "Me too, Sweetpea," he said. "Me too."

Me three.

"Yes," I tell Dina. "A wonderful morning."

Nothing can bring me down today. When a group of businesspeople comes in for breakfast and they change their minds about eating near the windows after their food has already arrived … no big deal, I help carry their dishes to another table. When the credit card machine refuses to recognize a woman's Visa … no big deal, I try again and then call Dina over for assistance. When a toddler drops his bag of cheese crackers and I hit my head on the table as I bend down to retrieve it … no big deal, I take Advil and am as good as new. Never once do I stop smiling.

By the time my lunch break rolls around, I'm starved. It's a gorgeous early fall day, the sunlight still warm, even as a breeze twirls crisp ribbons through the air, and I decide to eat my salad down at the Schermerhorn. It's been a few weeks since the last time I granted a wish and I'm itching to jump back in. Maybe it isn't a lifeline anymore, though. Maybe it isn't a survival tactic. Even without the pennies, the stories, the inspiration, I'm finding myself drawn to writing again. Making a wish come true today isn't about needing to. It's about wanting to.

As I walk to the fountain, I'm hyper aware of the squirrels darting up and down the trees, of the sound of songs wafting through opened car windows, and of the slight chill in the air. It's a promise of chili in the crockpot and football on the television and golden leaves on the trees. I'm leaving for New Hampshire tomorrow, and when I return, it'll be full-speed ahead with the apartment search. I haven't moved on from Open Hearts like I vowed I would before going back to Portsmouth, but it's time now. Then I can finally tell Wilson the truth. I have enough money saved for the first month or two of rent. It'll be lonely, having a place all to myself. As I pass Noteworthy though, an idea occurs to me.

Serena could be my new roommate.

She's been at the shelter for a month longer than I have, so she will need to transition out soon anyway. Doubling the tenants means splitting the rent, plus I think it would be fun, living together. I can picture it clearly, sitting around on the nights she's not at Noteworthy and I'm not at Wilson's, writing songs and playing chords on the guitar. Who knows, if her meeting at the record label goes well today, maybe those songs could actually make it. I'm so excited by the idea that I call her right away.

"Hey, it's Eden," I say, when her voicemail picks up. "First of all, good luck at your meeting later, although I know you don't need it. You'll blow them away. I'm really sorry I couldn't get the day off from work to be there for moral support. Second, I had a brainstorm: we should rent an apartment together. What do you think? We're already friends, we get along great ... this could be perfect!" I exclaim. "Okay, I'll hang up now. Break a leg today. I can't wait to hear all about it."

I've reached the symphony center, so I tuck the phone away and take out my lunch. For half an hour I sit quietly, listening to the chatter around me and trying to absorb the snippets. Two women talk about moving their dad into a nursing home, one man makes a call about a broken dishwasher, and another, wearing a Nashville Fire and Rescue cap, talks to himself. I watch surreptitiously as he slips a hand into his jeans' pocket, removes a penny, and repeatedly flicks it between his thumb and forefinger.

I decide to take a chance. "What would you wish for?" I ask.

His shoulders jerk a little, like he didn't realize I was there, and he looks up at me, half in a daze. And that's when I recognize him. The tattoo beneath his left ear – the name Darcy, written in swirly black ink, with a tiny red heart below it – that's far too unique for two people to have. "I'd wish for something that can't come true," he says, then chucks the penny into the fountain without a second glance.

"I ... I know you." The words fall from my mouth.

His eyebrows stitch together. "I'm afraid you're mistaken. We've never met."

"Not formally, no." I take a breath and reflect on the memories from the night which changed it all. "The fire at Cedarwood Apartments, back in July. I was there ... I lived there ... I saw you rescue that girl and her cat." At this, something flashes in his eyes, but he doesn't say anything, so I opt to continue. "Marlena adopted that cat when it was only a couple months old and she loves her more than anything. Thank you for saving them."

He returns my smile, but it doesn't reach his voice. "Glad to be of service."

"It must be hard, running toward danger instead of away from it. I don't know how you do it."

"Because it's my job."

"I think it's much more than that. The way you all literally put yourselves in the line of fire – "

He grazes the tattoo. "It's worth it to help people."

I want to ask about the ink, about who Darcy is, but I've learned my lesson about overstepping. "Well, please know you've got my endless gratitude. You and your squad were our guardian angels. If there's ever anything I can do to repay you, it'd be a – "

He interrupts me by standing up and shoving his hands into his pockets. It seems as though he's going to leave, but then he heaves a sigh and sits back down.

"I'm sorry if I upset you," I say.

"Not at all. I appreciate the kindness. It's just … what you said before, about my wish. It would be for my wife to come back." I don't let my eyes flit to his tattoo, although it's the natural impulse. "I couldn't save her." His voice breaks. "That's why I became a firefighter. I couldn't protect Darcy, but I can pay it forward."

I don't know how to answer.

Anything I come up with seems inadequate.

"I think she's proud," I finally say, "and that she knows you'd have saved her if you could. She's *your* guardian angel now."

"With me always." He's silent for a long time, staring off into space. Then he says, "I just got off duty. Fought a two-alarmer in Hillsboro Village. You know what gets to me? Pulling people out of a burning building, carrying them to an ambulance, and then never knowing what happens to them. It drives me crazy. Did they survive? Did they heal? I wish there was a way to keep tabs on everybody we rescue, though I'm not even sure if that's legal."

He wishes.

And for this one, I *can* be of use.

"Everyone from Cedarwood's fine," I tell him. "I talked to the landlord a few weeks after the fire and he said the people who were hospitalized had all been released. They're alright, thanks to you." This time when he returns my smile, it's more than surface level.

"I just … I can't even tell you how much you brightened this day. This difficult, impossible day." A flash of pain spikes in his eyes. "Darcy would've been thirty-nine today. I was mourning her … and I still will … but now I can think about those other people, too. The lives that were saved."

Even after he's left, his comment resonates.

No lyrics come this time. I don't need the wishes for that anymore.

Knowing I made a difference, *that*'s all I need.

I love everything about this day.

Then my phone rings.

The fourth grade class proudly presents:

Miracles All Around
A Holiday Extravaganza

Mr. Tenenbaum's class:

~ Candles in December

~ Oh Hanukkah! Oh Hanukkah!

~ Have Yourself a
Merry Little Christmas

Ms. Gowins's class:

~ White Christmas

~ Joy to the World

~ Kindle the Lights
of Hanukkah

Mrs. Dawn's class:

~ Ten Twinkling Trees

~ Ma'oz Tzur

~ Auld Lang Syne

Ms. Johnson's class:

~ Winter Wonderland

~ Light One Candle

~ Feliz Navidad

Finale (all classes):

~ Let It Snow, Let It Snow, Let It Snow

~ Frosty the Snowman

~ It's the Most Wonderful Time of the Year

Please join us in the multi-purpose room immediately following today's performance for holiday snacks, drinks, and cheer. Your children have worked so hard to prepare today's concert for you, and we look forward to celebrating together.

Thank you for coming and welcoming in this season of joy!

❧ 23 ❧

"**Y**our boarding pass is printed? Did you check the size of your bag with the airline's guidelines? You're planning to arrive at the airport two hours before the flight, I assume?" My mother fires the questions at me, slingshot style.

"Yes, yes, and yes."

"Good," she says. "Because it's better to be early than late. Need I remind you of the day your father and I found ourselves stuck at Boston Logan for hours after we missed our flight to Zurich and had to wait for the next one?" No, she doesn't. In fact, the memory is permanently etched into my mind. I was nine at the time, and I had begged them to delay their departure so they could come to my holiday concert at school. My teacher had given me a solo, and I wanted to see their faces in the front row alongside Grandmom's. Dad agreed, but Mom thought it was cutting it too close and said they'd settle for watching the video instead. So when I stepped onto the stage and saw Dad smiling at me, it was the best gift I could've gotten.

I sang my heart out, and when the show was over, I jumped down off the stage and directly into my father's embrace. "You were magnificent," he said, winding an arm around my shoulders. "I am very proud."

"Thanks for coming, Daddy. It's special to have you here."

"My pleasure." He tousled my hair affectionately. "Mom would've been here, too, but she had a last-minute work call." I caught Grandmom's frown as it tipped down the ends of her mouth. "But I've gotta get going," Dad said. "Your mom will be off the phone by now and we have to head to the airport. I'll call you when we get to Switzerland."

As it turned out, the call came way before then. Grandmom

was behind the counter when I got to her boutique after school – I hung out and did my homework there until she was ready to close in the evenings – and the second I pulled open the door, I heard her voice. "Calm down. Yes, Mariah, I know you're upset. I understand that your schedule will have to be shifted." She waved at me with her index finger as I traversed the cozy shop and set my backpack down on a chair. "Trust me, it was worth it."

"What's wrong?" I asked, after she'd hung up.

"Oh, nothing, Jellybean." She straightened a necklace on its display rod, then came over to give me a hug. "Your parents got stuck in some traffic on the way to the airport and missed the plane. It doesn't matter, though, since there's another one this evening. All is well. Tell me," she said, "how was the rest of your day at school?"

I knew she was covering. I knew Mom was annoyed. I knew it was really because of me.

So no, I don't need a reminder now.

"I'll be there, Mom," I say, standing up from the fountain. My lunch break's almost over. "Don't worry. See you tomorrow."

But before the hellos must come the goodbyes. Wilson volunteered to drive me to the airport, but since that would have meant asking him to pick me up at the shelter, I declined. I spend Friday night with him and Emmalyn instead, blowing bubbles in the driveway and curling up on the sofa to watch TV, and ask Serena for a lift the next day. She bought a used car last month, after she'd saved enough from her Noteworthy paychecks to provide a bit of a cushion, and as she drives to Nashville International, she tells me about her meeting the day before. "It went well, I think. Josie – she's the A&R guy's boss – she seemed really interested. She had me sing a few songs a capella and asked for a demo reel of recorded material. No guarantee, but it seems promising." A misty rain starts to fall and she flicks on the windshield wipers. "It isn't too late to join me."

"Thank you, but no. Singing's in my past." I tell her the whole story, all of it, even about melting down at the open mic night. "Not every dream has merit," I muse. "I think some are meant to show us who we're not, so in turn we can find out who we are. Honestly, writing has always been my true love. It's just that most people in Nashville are here to perform, so for awhile I felt like I had to keep up if I wanted a chance to make it in the industry."

She nods. "I guess I never thought about it that way."

"Thanks for believing in me, though."

"Always." She smiles. "That's what friends and future roommates are for. Oh, hey, speaking of which, I saw a sign for a new condo building Downtown. It's probably out of our price range, but I'll look into it and send you the details."

"Sounds good. I'm excited about this," I tell her, as she pulls over to the curb at the airport. The cars fly by as I get out and open the back door to retrieve the luggage I bought from the thrift store. "Thanks a million for bringing me."

"No problem. Have a great time." She waves as I shut the door.

A great time. Is that possible?

I think about it on the three-hour flight. The family dinners. The inevitable questions about how the songwriting is going. The trip down to Manhattan to try on bridesmaid dresses for Kayleigh's big day. The visits with Grandmom not in her cottage, but instead in the assisted living complex. The week without Wilson and Emmalyn. The week *with* my parents. The truth I swore to myself I'd tell them. I wanted to wait until the shelter was in my rearview mirror, but that obviously hasn't happened yet and this is something I'd rather reveal in person. And who knows when I'll see my parents again? It has to be done now.

I try to picture their reaction. I hope it won't be too upsetting for Grandmom. Having me there, seeing with her own eyes that I'll be fine, that I *am* fine, will it provide comfort? That's why I waited until now to break the news to her, so she'd have tangible proof of how I've regained my footing. I don't know about my parents, though, especially Mom. How will my confession be met? With hurt? Anger? Disappointment?

No, I decide. A great time probably isn't possible.

I take out my journal as the plane flies somewhere over Pennsylvania and flip through the pages I've added since arriving at Open Hearts. A line here, a chorus there. Some are good. Some you can tell I was struggling. Still, they are among the truest I've ever written. I uncap a pen and play with a verse or two, but then, as the little girl across the aisle asks her mother if they can "do peek-a-boo," a new melody hums in my mind, composing me instead of the other way around. It's the whisper of a child's secret, the hushed rhythm of her breath as she sleeps, the belly laughter so full of sunshine and innocence. It's Emmalyn's song, and it goes like this:

Sweet blonde sugar plum with your eyes all aglitter,
With your rosy cheeks, curls wild and free,
You're every wonder of the universe, you are the key.
You color outside the lines, you run with arms wide open,
You twirl in circles, and in those moments I'm frozen.
This world can be a crazy place, a confusing place, with more questions than answers,
But one look at you and it all comes together.
You are the strength inside my heart,
The fearlessness inside my soul,
The reason I believe.
You are dollhouses and tutus, tricycles and trains,
You are the brightest rays of sun after the heaviest rain.

I stop there, rereading what I've written. Is it perfect? No. But it will be. I'll work on it until it's a representation of all she is, all she means. Maybe I'll write one for her father, too. Images of them drift through my mind – it's Saturday, their day for music class and lunch at Pancake Pantry – and it's like I feel a pull, down toward the earth. Toward the south. Toward them. But the plane continues on, and soon the pilot's on the speaker to say we're starting the final descent into Boston. I look out the window and think of my parents waiting for me.

Here goes nothing.

Or, perhaps it's more appropriate to say, here goes everything.

We'd planned to meet at baggage claim, so I join the sea of passengers flowing in that direction. Eventually, the forward momentum brings me to my parents. They're standing off to the side, away from the throngs of people searching for suitcases, and I stop for a moment, observing them from a distance. Mom, with her raven hair and slender frame, clad in jeans, a plum shirt, and a lilac blazer. Dad, with his sandy curls and broad shoulders, wearing a Red Sox jersey and khakis. To look at them today, you'd have no clue they spend the majority of their time in areas where it's hard to even find cell phone reception.

It's fascinating, truly, the way we can blend in with our surroundings, and the way my parents in particular can ease seamlessly into the life they so frequently leave behind. I think of my deceptions back in Nashville. Wasn't I also masquerading as someone I'm not? It's a jarring thought that makes anxiety poke at my stomach, so I shove it aside, take a breath, and go over to greet them.

"Hi," I say quietly.

"Eden." Mom's eyes warm with what appears to be genuine delight. "It's so nice to see you."

"Great," Dad agrees, enveloping me in a hug. "How was the flight?"

"Good. Uneventful. I even got some work done."

"For the restaurant?" Mom asks, taking her turn at hugging me. "Grandmom told us you're the hostess for ... " She pauses, pinching her temples. "Shoot. It's right on the tip of my tongue. Why is it I can remember all the details about water purification systems, but things like this always seem to elude me?"

Because we make room in our memories for the facts we deem most important.

Because the brain is a sieve, filtering out the excess to preserve the priceless.

Because some leopards are incapable of changing their spots.

I used to let my hopes fly sky-high when Mom and Dad came home. It'd be a pleasant surprise, I convinced myself. This time would be different. For years after they joined Hands of Hope, I fooled myself into thinking that someday their own child would matter every bit as much. Lesson learned. Now, when we have our annual visit, I suit up in armor ahead of time. "Sensations," I tell my mom. "That's the name, but I wasn't doing work for them on the plane. I was actually tinkering with a few songs."

"How's that going?" she asks.

"Any leads?" Dad questions. "Maybe you can play us some of your new material." My suitcase swings around the conveyor belt then, and I run over to grab it before it passes by. As I roll it across the floor, I see Dad's eyes narrow appraisingly. "Or maybe not," he says, as I return. "Where's your guitar? I thought you always bring it with you."

A picture flares before me, unforgiving orange flames eating away the wood of Grandpa's guitar, and I feel a stab of pain. "It was damaged," I improvise, not wanting to lie anymore but not wanting to explain in the middle of the airport. "Long story. I'll fill you in later."

He looks like he wants to say something more, but Mom takes over, telling me about the nightly campfires they had in the village they stayed in on their last excursion. "You would've loved it," she says earnestly. "Each night, we'd gather around to sing. They taught us some of the local songs and one of our team members played her guitar. The kids were fascinated by it."

I realize this is her way of trying to connect, trying to tie a knot in the string stretching too tautly between us, so I tie one of my own and hang on. "That sounds awesome. There's something special about children experiencing music, you know?" I picture my parents singing with the kids, and smile a little. It's nice to think about them making a difference this way, too.

"It was wonderful," Dad says. "But enough about your mother and me. Tell us about you."

"How's Nashville?" Mom chimes in. "Are you still in love?"

I know she means with the city, but I can't help it, my mind automatically goes to Wilson. At the moment, he seems like a far safer topic than anything else, so as we leave the airport and drive right to Grandmom's, I fill my parents in on him and Emmalyn. "Em's the cutest thing you've ever seen," I gush, "and Wilson is amazing with her. He's been a single father since day one. He even started his own photography business to support them."

"He sounds great," Mom says. "And it's nice to see you so happy."

When I visited them last year, Jared had broken things off only a week before. I was miserable. They tried to cheer me up, but all I could focus on was the fact that, yet again, I hadn't been enough for someone. Wilson's different. With him, it isn't about being enough. It's about being me. Being us.

I've already told Grandmom about this over the phone, but when we get to her apartment, she's still brimming with questions. "First," she says, as I walk in the door, "come here and give me a hug. Then I'm going to need an update on that handsome man of yours. Please tell me you've brought a picture or two."

I laugh, wrapping my arms around her and holding tight. She smells of perfume and hand lotion, irises and love. "I've missed you so much," I tell her. "And yes, of course I have pictures. If you'd let me set you up with an email address, I could send them regularly." I glance at the computer, on the desk beside the window. Mom bought it for her a couple years ago, but she rarely turns it on.

"It's too complicated," Grandmom says, "and I'm too old to learn how to use it."

"You're not old."

"I live in a building of senior citizens." She tosses me an amused smile. "We play canasta, bingo, and mahjong, and have people come around to help with housekeeping. That doesn't exactly make me a spring chicken, dear heart. Besides, technology is too impersonal. I'll always prefer a letter to an email." She motions to the desk, and, next to the computer, I see a stack of the recent mail I sent – a set list from one of Serena's performances; a postcard from the aquarium in Chattanooga, where Wilson and I took Em; the sheet music for a finished song; and more. At first I'm happy to know that she saves all our correspondences. But then I think of how I used to do the same, how I'll never see those notes and cards again, and tears brim in my eyes. Grandmom notices immediately. "Are you okay?" she asks.

I force a smile back on my face. "Sure." I can't tell her now. The time isn't right.

The time is never going to be right, says a little voice in my head. *Stop looking for excuses.*

That voice has a good point.

Mom's puttering around the apartment, tidying things up that are already in order, and Dad's on his phone, tapping the screen as he responds to a message. Grandmom's right, I decide. Sometimes technology leaves a lot to be desired. I wait until he's finished, then reach over to place my hand on Grandmom's. "Actually," I amend, "there's something I have to tell you all."

Three pairs of eyes stare at me steadily.

Save for the tick of the clock, the apartment's swathed in silence.

Waiting for me to break it. Waiting for me to break everything.

I look from face to face, then begin.

BAILEY FISHER
Coastal Reality

FOR SALE:

$225,000 / Single family home in Portsmouth, NH

2 bedrooms
3 bathrooms
1400 square feet
.15 acres

Small town charm makes this cottage a perfect place to call home. Built in 1965, you'll find the quaintness of decades past, but with today's most sought-after amenities. The updated kitchen has hardwood floors, granite countertops, and a tile backsplash. Both bedrooms include a walk-in closet and the master features an en-suite bathroom. Feeling outdoorsy? Venture onto the front porch or into the backyard, which offers a picturesque view of the water. Call today, and this cottage can be yours!

Year Built: 1965
Bedrooms: Two
Full Bathrooms: Two
Half Bathrooms: One
Color: Green
Exterior: Siding
Garage Spaces: One
School District: City of Portsmouth School District
Listing Price: $225,000

"The reason I was upset ... what you said, Grandmom, about sending letters ... " The words stick in my throat, putting up a fight, so I change course. "I wasn't home at the time," I preface. "But this past July, there was a fire at my apartment building." A gasp escapes from Grandmom's mouth, and, in unison, she and my parents turn ashen. "It started in the apartment next door. My neighbor had lit some candles and the match wasn't fully extinguished when she threw it out. The fire spread really quickly. Kristina and I lost everything." My voice quakes as I think of all that was taken. They were only things, but they held meaning. Memories. I loved my aquamarine bracelet not because it was sparkly, but because Grandmom gave it to me when I graduated from college. I loved my collection of guitar picks not because it was extensive, but because it reminded me of the concerts I'd been to and the emotions they spurred in me. I loved my laptop not because the world was at my fingertips, but because it put the world *in* my fingertips. Losing them still stings.

Mom and Dad look stung, too. Flabbergasted. Their eyes are wide, mouths agape, like the wind has just been knocked out of them. And Grandmom? She's so upset, she's basically beside herself. "Why didn't you tell me?" she asks. "All the times we talked ... " She shakes her head, stunned and confused. "This isn't the type of thing you keep from your family."

I sit down on the sofa, pick up a coral throw pillow – one of the items that made the move from Grandmom's house to the apartment – and hug it to my chest. "I knew there was nothing you could do," I try to explain. "It's not like I could live with you here, and with the price you're already paying for this place, you wouldn't be able to send me rent money, too. Kristina opted to move in with her boyfriend, so I was on my own with the expenses doubled." I squeeze the pillow tighter. "It would have broken my heart to worry you. Also," I confess, because if I'm laying my cards on the table, it's only right to play the whole hand, "I was afraid you'd ask me to move back to Portsmouth. As much as I love New Hampshire and miss you, that would have felt like surrendering. Like giving up on my songwriting and acknowledging defeat." I take her thin fingers in mine as she sits down next to me. "I hated myself for lying. Keeping it from you was the hardest thing I've ever done. Are you mad at me?" I can't even look at her. I'm too ashamed.

But, as always, Grandmom is an angel.

"No," she says. "Surprised and disappointed, definitely. You should know that you can come to me with anything. We're a team." I sneak a peek at her. "Where have you been living, then? Your apartment must be uninhabitable."

"Yeah. They knocked the whole building down a couple weeks ago so they can begin to rebuild. I've been – " I inhale a long breath and prepare for the detonation. Then I drop the bombshell. "In a homeless shelter."

My parents have been quiet until now, but at this, they roar into the conversation. "A homeless shelter?" Dad echoes, pronouncing each syllable as though it's foreign to his ear. "For three months you've been living in a shelter instead of calling us to ask for help?" He removes his glasses, rubs the bridge of his nose, then replaces them. "Why on earth would you do that? You've never impressed me as the martyr type."

"I'm not. It wasn't a matter of – "

"It was a matter of foolishness, that's what it was." Mom fixes me with a steely gaze, then starts pacing. "Your father and I see horrific things. Children who are skin and bones, entire families living in a single room who cry with gratitude over something as seemingly simple as a malaria net ... then there are the places where we build schools, teach the kids, and end up learning just as much from them. Do you know what these people would give to have all the options you do? To have parents with the financial ability to help?" Angry red circles appear on her cheeks, and she crosses her arms. "And you voluntarily put yourself into a position of wanting for everything?"

"Calm down," Dad implores. "Take it easy on – "

"No." Her blue eyes flash icily. "I won't calm down, Joel. Not after the things we've seen. She should appreciate the life she was blessed with instead of taking it for granted. Did you ever stop to consider that you were filling a bed in the shelter which could've gone to someone else? Somebody who *legitimately* had no one to turn to?" She rails on me, and I shrink back against the sofa.

"Stop," Grandmom commands. "I didn't raise you to be vicious."

"I'm not." Mom's nose flares a little. "I'm realistic. Honest. Am I sympathetic to her situation? Yes. I'm sorry about the fire. It must be difficult to watch everything you own go up in flames." She addresses this part of her diatribe to me, then returns to Grandmom. "I cannot condone the actions that followed, though. All she had to do was get in touch with us and we'd have helped."

I can't take it anymore.

I spring to my feet and face Mom head-on. "Would you have?" I challenge. "Because you don't exactly have the best track record when it comes to being there in my time of need. What about the day I fell off the monkey bars and broke my wrist? Or the night of senior prom, when all my friends' parents were there to see us off? Or, for God's sake, when I graduated from college? Tell me when I've ever been able to count on you for anything." Her mouth opens, then closes. "Right. There you go. The answer is never. I think it's terrific that you and Dad care about the kids you work with, but I don't understand why it has to preclude you from caring about me."

I have to get away from here. Away from Grandmom, who's crying. From Dad, who's staring at the floor and not doing anything more to defend me. From Mom, who's making my stomach churn. I grab my bag, give Grandmom an apologetic look, and hurry for the door. It slams behind me after I escape. Down the steps, across the lobby, through the entrance. A beam of sunshine bounces over my face as I burst outside, and soon I'm running. I pound my feet to the pavement and don't give a thought to where I'm headed. I just let my legs take me where I need to go.

Familiar sights streak past. The quaint little shopping area Kayleigh and I used to shop at during the summer. Prescott Park, with its boardwalk piers and gardens where the leaves are beginning to change from green into vivid hues of orange and gold. The waterfront and Moran Towing Company. From a distance, I slow down to peer at the tugboats so frequently associated with this town. Then I go on to my next destination, moving by memory, seeking solace in the one place I was always able to find it.

I slow to a stop in front of Grandmom's old home, *my* old home, and stare at it. The white porch railings. The pale green siding. The wicker rocking chairs, the flower boxes, the oak tree where I sat for hours, practicing guitar. There's a birdfeeder hanging on it now, and as I study the cottage more closely, I notice other differences. The flowery curtains Grandmom had in the living room have been replaced with blinds. The seashell door knocker is gone. A boat's in the driveway, and there's fresh grass where Grandmom's vegetable garden used to be.

It's bizarre to see the changes. Unsettling. In my head, I know the cottage belongs to somebody else. I know I'll never sleep in my room again, or play Scrabble with Grandmom at the table, or sit in the backyard, siphoning inspiration from the beautiful view of the river. In my heart, though ... I just want to go inside. I want to forget about my parents and surround myself with the safety of my life here with Grandmom. Memories flit through my mind, each one twinkling fairy dust, and I imagine tossing them up into the air, watching them illuminate the sky like tiny glittering pinpricks. In a way, that's what they are for me: stars to brighten the path, to guide and comfort me. I guess that'll have to be enough for now, because, like so many other things, this home has slipped through my fingers. It's mine, but not really.

I sigh, then turn around to head back. I'm drained from the weight of emotions laying heavy on my shoulders, so I take my time, in no hurry to return to the accusations and vitriol. But when I walk into Grandmom's apartment, using the key she gave me last time I visited, it isn't venom I find.

It's sorrow.

Remorse.

My parents and Grandmom are in the small den, off to the side, so they don't see when I come in. For the first time, being invisible to Mom and Dad works to my advantage. Their voices are loud, raised in discussion. "What's wrong with me?" Mom asks. "How could I be so nasty? Why did I lash out like that?"

"It's your defense mechanism," Grandmom says. "Always has been. You hurt before you can be hurt. It's how you protect yourself."

"Well, do you blame me?"

"No," Grandmom says, a twist of empathy twining through her voice. "Not after what happened with your father."

"When he died, it gutted me." She chokes back what sounds like a cry. "I think ... that must be when I put up the shield. And then when you said that to Eden, Joel, about why she'd choose to live in a shelter rather than turn to us ... how could we not know what her answer would be? We've let her down so often. Why *should* she think this time would be any different? I guess it was just easier to be mad at her than at myself. Easier to feel anger than guilt." Her voice cracks again, and my dad says something to her that I can't make out.

It's bizarre, listening to this conversation I'm not meant to hear.

It's also illuminating.

When Mom apologizes, I accept. "I'm sorry," she tells me. "For the things I said and the things I didn't say. For the headstrong way I reacted. Mostly, I'm sorry for hurting you."

Part of me wants to tell her I overheard her conversation, that I understand now how lasting an effect Grandpa's death had on her, but it's been such a long time since we've had a heart-to-heart, I don't remember how to go to that place with her. Maybe someday.

For the time being, I settle for the effort she and Dad make to connect with me. Does it erase the last two and a half decades? No. But they're trying, and as the week goes on, that helps.

On Sunday, we take Grandmom to a show at The Music Hall.

On Monday, we hop on the boat launch and spend the day on Pierce Island.

On Tuesday and Wednesday, we take on a couple of painting projects at Mom and Dad's house, and though it's strange to be back there again, it's also sort of nice. It's a good reminder that while some things stay the same, others evolve. I have a growing sense of that as the week continues, and by the time I'm boarding a train to Manhattan on Friday – I didn't argue when my parents offered to buy the ticket – I'm actually feeling optimistic. Maybe the visit to New Hampshire was a good thing, after all. Maybe today will follow suit. Maybe Kayleigh and I will be able to bridge the gap between us. I hope so.

I miss our friendship. I miss her.

I'm staying at her apartment overnight, and when the train screeches to a stop, I sling my duffel bag over my shoulder, wiggle my way into the line of people crowding the aisle, and inch toward the door. Kayleigh is waiting by the information booth. She waves as we spot each other, then throws her arms around me in a hug after I make my way over. "It's so good to see you!" she exclaims. "It's been far too long."

"Agreed." I return her hug, then pull back to examine her left hand. "Wow," I say, staring at the ring gleaming up at me. It's French cut, with a square diamond and double band. "That's gorgeous. Gary really outdid himself."

"He's a keeper." A smile blooms on her face. "I can't believe I doubted him."

"I get it." I follow her lead as she heads to the escalator that'll take us up to the Madison Square Garden exit. "After everything that happened with your mom and dad, it was a natural fear." I think about my own parents and how I've been trying for so long to seek out what they couldn't provide. "We're influenced by our upbringing, whether we like it or not. At least we have the opportunity to learn from their mistakes."

"True." She turns to me and her eyes take on a mischievous glint. "In that vein, how would you feel about being part of a wedding today?"

"What?" I stop dead in my tracks. "A wedding … *when?*"

The glint deepens. "Today," she confirms. "Without the Badgley Mischka gown, or the Christian Dior shoes, or the Swarovski-studded veil. Without the cake, or the floral arrangements, or the ten-piece band. Without my mom and dad at one another's throats in their ridiculous attempt to outdo the other." She rolls her eyes. "They've been so obnoxious lately. It's like the wedding has become a war and they're treating every detail as a battle. And you know what? I'm finished. I don't care if this is some misguided way of making up for the divorce. All they're doing is turning my dream into a nightmare." She huffs and puffs as the escalator carries us higher. "Gary and I had a long talk, and decided to forgo the fancy celebration in favor of getting married at a courthouse. It will just be us, you, and his best man."

"But what about your maid of honor?"

She smiles again. "That was always going to be you. I wanted to surprise you with it in person."

"Kay, I … thank you. That's sweet. But what about the rest of the bridal party?"

"They'll understand. Or they won't. At this point, we have to do what's right for us. Gary has a friend who works at the courthouse, and he was able to squeeze us in with a justice of the peace for a three o'clock ceremony. We already have the marriage certificate. All we need to do now is make it official."

"Three o'clock? As in … two hours from now?"

"Yes." She whirls around and grabs my arm. "What do you say? Will you be there?"

"Of course."

And I am. When Kayleigh and Gary pledge their love and lives to each other, her in an elegantly understated white dress and him in a black suit with a red tie that matches the flower in her hair, it's a pleasure to stand at her side. Listening to the justice of the peace as she talks about the sanctity of marriage and the magic of two souls intertwining to create a new union, I'm filled with gratitude. A few months ago, being part of Kayleigh's wedding seemed unfathomable. Today, I can't imagine it any other way.

Maybe our friendship isn't as lost as we thought.

Maybe, when the foundation is there, those bricks can be pieced back together. They might not be arranged the same way now as they were when we were five, or fifteen, or even twenty-five, but that's life. It changes and so do we. I don't know if Kayleigh and I will ever be as close, if we can go back to being, as we used to call it, "honorary sisters," but I have hope now that we can at least try. That, if we put in the effort, we can rebuild.

She wants to, I can tell.

So do I.

I'd like to find room for her in my life again, *create* room, and I'd like for us to figure out what's gone wrong so we can work at making it right. "Congratulations," I tell her after the wedding, giving her a hug as we walk out into the chilly October air. "You too, Gary. I'm thrilled for you two. You're the perfect couple."

"Thanks." He smiles. "I'm glad you're here. You're joining us for celebratory drinks and dinner, right?" He glances from Michael, his best man, to me.

"Please?" Kayleigh says. "It's on us."

It's a show of faith, so I respond with one of my own.

"Yes," I say, smoothing out the pleats of my skirt. Kay bought that, too, at the store we stopped at on the way from Penn Station to their apartment, but I've already promised to pay her back. This time, though, I'm okay with her help. Everything that has happened with my family this week serves as a reminder: sometimes it actually *is* alright to lean on the people we care about and trust that the pillar is steady enough not to crumble.

"This day," Kay says, stopping in the middle of the sidewalk to kiss her groom, "is the best I have ever had." She repeats that later, as the four of us share a champagne toast, and adds on a "Here's to a future filled with only good things."

I tip my glass and sip the cool champagne.

I'll drink to that.

245

October 10, 1969

My dear Lillian and Mariah,

Hello, my loves. How are you? How's everything in Portsmouth? The leaves must be changing color now, into a canopy of oranges and reds. That's always been my favorite part about the fall. When I was a child, I used to get so sad when summer was over and I'd have to say goodbye to the beach for another year. It was – and still is – the best place in the world to me. But those leaves lit up New Hampshire again, and I loved that, too. I wish I was there to see them with you. I wish we could rake them into piles, Mariah, and then take a flying leap right in the center. I promise, baby girl, we'll do that when I get home. We will do so many things when I get home.

We're getting by here as best we can. The days are long, but we lean on each other for support. The soldiers in my troop are a great group of people. It breaks my heart to see the young ones, fighting this war when they should be at home, building a life for themselves. Sometimes I envy them, though, because being a corporal means I see more damage than they do. I know more. Above all, I know this – I miss you both dearly. I think of you all the time and carry your pictures in my uniform pocket. I can't wait to hug you again. One day ... hopefully soon.

All my love, Rick / Daddy

$$\sim 25 \sim$$

I head back to Nashville on Sunday with a hopeful heart. When Mom and Dad hug me goodbye at the airport, I can almost feel the turbulent road we've been traveling ease a bit. There are bumps and potholes still, maybe there always will be, but there's also a lane we can all fit into now. Will my parents stay the course even after they leave for Haiti at the end of the month? I don't know. Their track record says no, so the hope is tempered with caution, but it's still there.

"I want you to promise something," Grandmom says, after she hugs me too. She takes my hand, and I gaze down at hers, with its faint wrinkles etched this way and that. These wrinkles, they're her roadmap.

"Anything," I say. She could ask for the moon and I'd find a way to lasso it to Earth for her.

"I want you to keep me updated," she says, "and if you need help, ask. I'm always here for you, Jellybean."

"I know. You're my rock. Nothing will change that."

She smiles and kisses my cheek. "Call me when you get there," she says, and it makes me smile, too. No matter how old I get, she still says the same thing whenever we part ways. It's endearing. I follow her request after my plane lands, cradling the phone between my ear and shoulder as I reach over to grab my luggage off the carousel.

"Can I ask you something?" I say. "I was hoping to talk about it in person, but Mom was always around and I didn't want her to overhear. I just ... what do you make of her outburst after I told her about the shelter?" I tread carefully, not letting on about the follow-up conversation I heard. I want Grandmom's objective opinion.

She sighs. "I think, in some ways, your mother's still the little girl whose daddy left one day and never came home. That six-year-old is stuck inside her and impacts her more than she realizes. It's why she first got into charity work, you know, because she wanted to honor Rick's legacy and make sure he didn't die in vain. 'He gave up his life to help others,' she said. 'The least I can do is dedicate mine to a similarly worthy cause.'"

"Really? I didn't know that." I imagine her as a child, reading Grandpa's letters and asking when he'd be back. It must have been so hard for her and Grandmom both. And when the knock came on the door and Grandmom opened it to find a military official ... just picturing it makes me teary-eyed. Such agony they went through. I remember what Mom said: *That must be when I put up the shield.* Maybe that's been the issue this whole time. It's too difficult for her to be a mother since she never fully got to be a daughter to Grandpa.

"See, here's what I don't understand," I say to Grandmom. "If she is still grieving his loss all this time later, then wouldn't it stand to reason that she wouldn't want to continue the cycle? Obviously she made a choice to leave while Grandpa would've given anything to stay, but really, the outcome's not so different. If the pain of abandonment cut into Mom that deeply, she shouldn't have inflicted the same thing on me. Whenever I become a mother, I'll never do that to my kids. Never. Because I've learned from what hurt me. Why couldn't she?"

"I don't know," Grandmom answers. "People do things we can't explain and don't agree with. I always supported your mother's charity work, but I was livid when she and your father snuck off like that. It was so wrong. They knew I'd have a problem with them accepting the overseas position and opted to circumvent it by not telling me until they were already out of the country. We fought over it for months afterward, about the effect it'd have on you. I will say, though, honey, that raising you was one of the greatest joys of my life."

"Mine too. I loved growing up with you."

"And I loved watching you grow up. Sometimes it seems like only yesterday you were pushing a doll carriage and building castles out of Play-Doh. Now here you are, sculpting your own life. I hope you know how proud I am of you."

"I do, and it means more than words can ever say." I scan the baggage claim area, where Serena said she would meet me. No sign of her. "I better go," I tell Grandmom. "I have to check in with my friend who's picking me up."

"Okay. Love you, Jellybean."

"Love you more."

It's how we end every phone call.

I hang up and send Serena a text. It isn't like her to be late. I wheel my suitcase to the side, take out my journal, and work a bit more on Emmalyn's song while I wait. Five minutes go by. Then ten. Then fifteen. Still no response. Now I'm starting to get worried. I reach for my phone again and call this time.

She picks up on the fourth ring. "I'm so sorry! I lost track of time and didn't leave when I should have, then there was an accident on I-40 and traffic was backed up forever. I tried to text you back, but that's when the cars finally began moving again and I couldn't finish typing in time. Anyway, I'm almost there. Meet you out front?"

"Sure."

She pulls up to the curbside pick-up area a few minutes later and, even before I get into the car, I know something's up. Gone are the baggy shirt and yoga pants, replaced by dark jeans and a color block top. Her hair's pulled into a loose ponytail, and around her neck is a glittering gold chain with a diamond heart.

"Hi!" The greeting bubbles out of her as I slide into the passenger seat. "How was Portsmouth? How did things go with your family? I bet it was great to sleep in a real bed in a real house with real home-cooked food." She smiles at me. What's with the ebullience? It's radiating from her in waves and certainly seems genuine, but never have I seen her this outgoing, not even when she performs. I wonder if the building downtown ended up being more affordable than she thought and she found a condo for us to move into. She said she would email to let me know, but I didn't hear from her the whole time I was up North.

"It was nice," I say. "Awkward at first, because I haven't stayed in Mom and Dad's house since I was a kid, but also such a relief to do things on my own terms again. Speaking of which: how'd it go with the condo? Any luck?"

"Um, no." She averts her gaze, suddenly staring intently at the road in front of her. "We'll talk about that later, though. Tell me: how did your parents react to the news about the fire? And your grandmom? You told them, right?" It's smooth, the way she changes the subject, but not remotely subtle.

Half an hour later, when we walk into the shelter and I see that the shelf over her bed is empty, I find out why. "What's going on?" I ask. "It looks like you're leaving. But I thought you didn't find us an apartment?" Again, her gaze shifts to anywhere, anything, but me. Her fingers revert to habit, to her wedding ring, and she twists it around while transferring her weight from foot to foot. "Serena? You know you can tell me anything, right?"

"I know." She finally meets my eyes, and I notice something in hers that immediately makes me uneasy. Stubbornness. Obstinacy. Defiance. And I figure it out. Before she even speaks the words, I hear their ugliness. "Seth and I are back together."

All I can do is gawk at her. "I don't understand."

"I don't expect you to. I'm not even sure *I* do."

"But this doesn't ... are you ... " I stop to compose myself before I say something I regret. "Why would you – no, make that how *could* you – put yourself back into such a dangerous situation?"

"I'll be fine."

"You cannot be serious." I stare at the firm set of her jaw and realize with a sinking feeling that she's totally serious. The man's beaten her repeatedly, and she's actually standing here and telling me it won't happen again. It is beyond my realm of comprehension. "What about the sessions you worked so hard on with Avery? And the letter you wrote to Seth? And the miscarriage?" The more reminders I give, the higher my voice pitches.

Serena flinches, but she doesn't back down. "The miscarriage was tragic. It was the worst thing I've ever gone through. That was months ago, though. Seth's changed."

I want to scream in frustration. Nothing I say will matter, I can already see that, but I must keep trying. If Serena's not going to look out for herself, I have to do it for her. "You said you're through with him. You are stronger than this."

She massages her temples, the animated mood from before fading into something more weary. "Being strong doesn't always mean walking away from somebody." As she plunks onto the bed, the diamonds in her necklace – a gift from Seth, I assume – catch the overhead lights and glitter merrily. It's like they're mocking her. Taunting her. "I've spent months trying to move past what he did. I've let myself feel the resentment, the disgust, the rage. But maybe it wasn't the right course. Maybe I need to work on forgiving him instead."

"What he did is unforgivable." My hands ball into fists and I make a conscious effort to unclench them. I might be horrified, but coming off as confrontational won't help the situation. "Nobody has a right to hurt another person. I don't care if he apologized, there's just no excuse for laying a hand on you."

"I know," she says. "I swear, I didn't jump back into this blindly. He called me the day after you got to New Hampshire," she explains. "It was the first time he'd contacted me since I left, and when I saw his number on the screen … honestly, I thought I was going to throw up. I didn't answer, and I had every intention of deleting the voicemail without listening to it, but … " She sighs. "It would've nagged at me, not knowing what he wanted. So I gave in."

"What did he say?"

"That he was sorry. That he hated himself for hurting me. That it was eating away at him."

"Hasn't he said all those things before?"

"Well, yes," she admits, biting her lip. "But it was different this time. He said he's been seeing a therapist and working on getting to the bottom of his anger issues. He has a long way to go still, but his heart's in the right place."

"Maybe it is," I allow. "Some people can turn their lives around. I just don't think you should be rushing into it." I gesture at the bed, which is stripped of its sheets. "You're going back to the house you lived in with him, aren't you?" I watch her face transform into a kaleidoscope of emotion: fear, optimism, shame, conviction.

"Yes," she says, and clears her throat. "I am. He asked if we could meet for coffee, and we had a long talk. A good talk. He told me about the help he's been getting. He's trying, Eden, he really is. We've known each other a long time and I can tell when he's sincere. I'd never have agreed to give our marriage another chance if I thought I was in any danger." It terrifies me, how level-headed she sounds. She believes every word she's saying.

"It's only been a week," I implore. "That isn't enough time to prove himself. How do you know he's really being sincere and not simply telling you what you want to hear?"

I don't get an actual answer to that question.

"I just do." Her voice takes on a pleading tone. "Trust me on this. It feels right. This is where I need to be now. I'm so sorry about the apartment, though. I know I'm leaving you in a lurch."

"I'm not worried about that," I tell her, "I'm worried about you." A thought comes to mind and I decide to go with it as a last ditch effort. "What about 'Broken No More?'" It's the song she wrote in the lobby, the one about Seth, that she said was so cathartic. "What happened to showing up at his door and screaming the lyrics in his face?"

"I did share it with him," she says quietly, "and he cried when he read it."

"As he should have."

"I know how this looks," she says. "You think I'm betraying myself and negating all the progress I've made here. Maybe I am. Maybe this is a mistake, but I don't think so. We took a vow – "

"A vow that he broke repeatedly. God, Serena, he all but broke *you*."

She stands up. "I pieced myself together again. If I can help Seth do that now ... " She trails off, smiling almost sadly at her wedding band. "I never could take this off. Something stopped me every time. Now I know what it was."

"What?"

"Love. I still love him. I can't stop."

"Okay, I understand that. But why not take it slowly? Spend more time with him before moving back. See if his promises are empty or if they hold up in the moment."

"I know what I'm doing," she assures me. "And you have my word – I'll be careful. The first sign of trouble, I'm out of there. He knows that, too. I told him there won't be any more chances."

"I guess there's nothing left to say, then."

"We'll stay in touch, right? You're such a great friend. I don't want to lose you."

"You won't."

"Good. Thank you." She hugs me tightly. "You've helped me more than you know."

"Ditto. I'm not sure I'd have survived this place without you."

"Oh, yes. Yes, you would have. But I'm glad we had each other to lean on."

"Me, too. I'm going to miss you."

"We'll still see each other. I'm holding you to those songwriting sessions."

"Even though you have Seth now?"

"Especially because I have Seth now. We were so close before. Too close. It can't be us against the world anymore. It has to be us *with* the world, and I already told him that we also need to work with other people. Too much of a good thing ruins it. We made that mistake once. I won't let us do it again." She picks up her suitcases. "So ... talk to you soon?"

"Yes. Definitely."

I have such a bad feeling about this. I can practically see the storm cloud billow down from the sky and hover over her head. Dread encases me as I watch Serena walk to the door. Is this why she was late to the airport, because she was distracted by packing? By Seth? She says she's not letting him take over her life again, but if their relationship is already regaining precedence over everything else, what will happen when it becomes her new normal?

Or is it her old normal?

"Hey," I call out. "Remember, you can always come to me for support. Day, night, whenever."

"Thanks. You're the best."

And then, just like that, she's gone.

JEN

From the time she was fourteen, Jen had her life planned out: she would go to the University of Miami, just like her two older sisters, major in education, and build a career as a teacher before she began a family of her own. She already knew whom that family would be with – Joe, the boy who'd stolen her heart when they were only ten. They'd been choosing teams for a volleyball game in gym class, and when he was named as a captain, he picked her first. Even though gym was her absolute least favorite class. Even though she was a slow runner who lacked the kind of upper body strength needed to slam the ball over the net. Even though she was the one normally selected last. Joe was new to school, so perhaps he didn't know these things. Or maybe he did, and he chose her anyway. Jen wasn't sure. Either way, her gratitude grew into more as she and Joe got older.

They were inseparable throughout high school. Wherever one of them went, the other followed closely behind. "When's the wedding?" all their friends would tease. And so, when Joe went to the University of North Carolina instead of staying in Florida, Jen missed him dearly. She knew they'd be together, though. They'd have the life they'd planned. There was never any other option. Until Joe met someone else. Until Jen graduated and couldn't find a job. Until, finally, she grew so frustrated with the situation that she moved to Nashville, enrolled in college for a second time, and worked her way toward a music business degree.

Twenty years later, she has what appears to be a golden life. As the head of her own company, she's both successful and wealthy. But she's lonely, too. She never found another love like Joe and refused to settle for someone who didn't give her butterflies. There are no children running around her expansive house, no little hands to hold hers and no voices to call her Mommy. It's just her and her new dog.

Barney. Barney is her baby.

❧26❧

Within the hour, I'm gone too. I need to get away for a bit. Sitting in Open Hearts, realizing that everyone I've grown close to here has moved on, I feel an overwhelming sense of loneliness. I can't shake the notion of being left behind. Ruby and Fred are back in their home. Sherri and Tommy are in an apartment with Mark, who has finished his stint in rehab. Lainey and Risa are in South Carolina with Denise, after the court approved her petition to adopt them. I'm thrilled for all of them, but at the same time, it hurts to be on my own here. I finally had a concrete plan for how to move forward and transition out of the shelter, and now it's slipped through my fingers. No more roommate. No more Serena.

I can't even think about her without feeling sick. I need to counteract the frustration. I need to do something positive. So, before I even unpack, I'm out of Open Hearts once again and hurrying to the Schermerhorn. Whose wish can I listen to today? I let my gaze wander around. There's a father with a trio of red-haired children, each holding a popsicle, and a guy sitting cross-legged on a bench, doodling on the knee of his jeans with a Sharpie. A teenager walks by, popping her gum and telling someone on the phone that "He doesn't just like me; he *likes* me, likes me." None of them so much as glance over at the fountain. Then I see her. Across the street, a woman is chasing a dog, waving her arms and screaming for it to slow down. As I watch, though, the little white dynamo heads right toward the busy road, dragging its leash behind.

"Barney!" the woman yells. "Barney, stop! Sit! Heel!"

He stops for a second, looks at her, then beelines in the opposite direction. My eyes snap to the traffic light, which is about to change color, and before I can think twice, I dart forward. Horns blare, the woman yells, and my pulse pounds as the dog skids to a halt a foot away from an oncoming SUV. He's suddenly paralyzed by fear. I lunge quickly, hoisting him to safety in the nick of time. "I've got you," I say, my heart body-slamming my chest as I fly back to the sidewalk. "You're okay."

Barney, a West Highland White Terrier, is shaking like a leaf, and by the time his owner reaches me, she is, too. There's a glossy sheen to her eyes, and her dark ponytail is damp with sweat. "You are a lifesaver ... he pulled the leash right out of my hand ... we were on the way to obedience school ... I don't know how he ... it happened so fast ... " She pushes out a puff of air. "Thank you for saving him. How can I repay you?"

"It's not necessary." I give Barney to her and smile as he flicks out a tiny tongue to lick her nose. "I'm glad I could help."

"There must be something I can do," she implores. "That second in time when I knew I wouldn't be able to save him ... everything just stopped. I froze when he needed me most, and I was standing there, praying for a miracle, wishing for somebody to – " A crack forms in her voice. "Can I buy you coffee, at least?"

I let her, not because I need it, but because she seems to, and as she thanks me again, I respond in kind. Little does she know that she's helped me, too. That this was a wish granted in another way from the usual.

After she leaves, I take out my phone and call Wilson. He had a photo shoot today, but it should be over by now, and I can't wait much longer to see him and Emmalyn. Nine days has felt more like nine months. It's odd, though, because once I'm at their house, Em on my lap while we play Chutes and Ladders, it's like no time has passed at all. "Uh-oh, spaghetti-o!" she giggles, as I land on one of the chutes. "Daddy is winning now!"

"Well, we can't possibly let that happen," I say, giving her a tickle.

"Try and stop me." Wilson rolls the dice, gets a five, and triumphantly moves his piece closer to the last space. "Y'all are going down."

I raise my eyebrows. "Shouldn't you be teaching your daughter about good sportsmanship?”

“What’s that?” Em asks.

“It’s when you treat the people you’re playing with kindly,” Wilson explains. “It means being fair and thinking about other people’s feelings. I was teasing before. Winning isn’t important. What we should focus on instead is having fun.”

A smile peeks around her mouth. “I like having fun.”

“Me, too,” he says, brushing a kiss on her forehead. “Especially with you.”

It’s such a sweet moment, so simple and ordinary, yet it’s everything.

I didn’t have this while I was away.

And so, after we’ve ordered a pizza, after Emmalyn’s asked us to read *Goodnight Moon* and *The Lion and the Little Red Bird* for story time, after we’ve tucked her into bed and curled ourselves up in Wilson’s, I opt to delay the inevitable just a while longer. My plan was to tell him about Open Hearts as soon as we were alone, but when his fingers move to the buttons on my cardigan, I instantly cave. “I missed you,” he breathes, and something flies free inside me. It’s one thing to feel that way about him and Emmalyn, and another entirely to know it’s reciprocated.

“I missed you, too.” I link our fingers, needing to feel his hand against mine, needing to reassure myself that we’re in this together, that I won’t lose him when he finds out what I have been hiding. “It’s good to be back.”

“It’s good to have you back.” He stares at me with such intensity that my heart does a two-step. “For the past few years, it’s just been Em and me, and we were fine. We were better than fine. We were the daddy-daughter duo who didn’t need anyone else.” A smile glitters in his eyes and makes its way to his lips. “Then you came along. Em kept asking last week when she could see you again. Her preschool class made invitations for their Halloween parade, and she asked if we could mail you one. We played with dolls, and she said I didn’t do their voices as well as you. I took her to art class, and she painted you a picture.” He pauses to kiss me. “I hope you have room in your house for the best Sesame Street artwork you've ever seen." I know I'm still at Open Hearts, but since moving out soon doesn't seem likely, now that Serena's left me on my own, I decide that this is the perfect time to tell Wilson I don't actually *have* a house. I begin to, but he puts a finger to my lips. "Hang on. If I don't say this right now, I might chicken out." Another kiss. "I love you. I think I have since the day we met."

Oh my God.

Oh my God, oh my God, *oh my God.*

I don't know what I expected him to say, but it wasn't that. My mind goes to a million places at once, but right here, in the arms of this amazing man who actually loves me and misses me when we aren't together, only one thing stands out. "I love you, too," I tell him.

"Hey, hey." He shifts slightly, thumbing away my tears. "No crying."

"You don't get it." I sit up and pull the sheet around me. "What it means to hear that and know you're sincere."

He eases himself up, too, so we're looking at each other eye-to-eye. "I'm lucky, having a family I can count on unconditionally. I know the love is always there. But Eden, that isn't to say I throw the words around lightly. It's the opposite. Growing up, I saw the depth of what my parents shared and that made me hesitant to let myself go to the same place unless I was certain. So I didn't. I dated in high school and college, but I didn't tell a girl I loved her until Becky. Obviously that didn't end well." He takes my hand, traces the outline of my fingers. "Then I had to protect Em. She was the priority. I didn't want her to get close to someone, only to have it taken away."

"But you invited me here on our third date."

"Because I knew."

He says it so simply, like he couldn't be more sure.

"I did, too," I confess. "I just didn't want to scare you by saying it too soon."

He laughs a little, gathering me close.

To his heart.

To his heartbeat.

"I know you've had people tell you they love you and then they leave," he says. "That's not me. I'm not going anywhere." He kisses me, whisper soft, and as we sink into the pillows, I forget about my confession. I can't ruin this beautiful moment. I won't. I've already waited this long. One more day won't hurt.

* * *

When Wilson comes into Sensations the next day, I know this is it. The time has finally arrived. I finish taking a reservation for the man on the phone, then clock out for my lunch break. Wilson has an hour between shoots, and I asked him to meet me so we could talk. My stomach lurches as I join him and we go outside. Suppose he feels betrayed? Suppose he's not able to wrap his head around my choice to keep something so major from him? Suppose, by trying to hang on to him and Em, I'll actually have pushed them away? The thought of it gives me palpitations, and Wilson must notice, because he squeezes my hand.

"What's up?" he asks. "You know you can tell me anything, right?"

I study him for a moment. Jeans and gray thermal shirt. Blue-faced watch around his wrist. As the sun sneaks behind a cloud and drops a shadow onto his face, I notice something new: below his left ear, there's a constellation of freckles. How have I not seen that before? I reach out and graze my fingertips over them. "I didn't realize you had these. You know, I think that's one of my favorite parts about being in a relationship – getting to constantly learn new things about each other."

"Okay, then. Return the favor. Tell me something I don't know about you."

Again, it's the perfect lead-in, and this time, I take advantage.

I rip off the band-aid in one swift yank. "I'm homeless."

His mouth opens, then closes, then opens again. "What did you just say?"

"I'm homeless."

Wilson looks like he's seen a ghost. His eyes widen, and I watch the color drain from his cheeks. "I'm sorry," he stammers. "I'm not ... this doesn't make sense. I saw your house. I met Kristina. Did you have a fight and she kicked you out?"

"No." I steel myself against the rest of my confession. "Kristina was my roommate. We lived in the same apartment for three years, actually, but it burned down in the summer." His mouth falls open. "I've been living in a shelter ever since – the one you saw when we were driving to mini-golf – and I'm sorry, because I know I should have been honest with you from the start. I was going to tell you the night of our second date, actually, but then I saw your reaction to the shelter. It had been a big relief to have somebody look at me and see a whole person. Because society doesn't, you know. It isn't anyone's fault, it's simply the way things are ... when we hear someone's homeless, it defines them instantly. It wouldn't matter that I'm a guitar player, or a songwriter, or a hostess. Instead I'd be categorized by the one thing I lack."

His eyebrows pinch together. "If you think I'd do that, you don't know me very well."

"Not you." Heat rises in my neck, prickling my skin. "At least, not consciously. But these things happen even if we don't want them to, Wilson. Do I think you'd judge me? No. Wouldn't there be a change in our relationship, though? Wouldn't there be empathy in your eyes when you looked at me, just like when you looked at that woman going into the shelter? Wouldn't you refuse to let me treat Emmalyn to ice cream and insist on picking me up at the shelter all the time?" I sigh. "You're a good man. The best I've ever met. And I love that you'd do those things, because it shows what's in here." I put my hand over his heart. "But please try to understand where I'm coming from. I'm so much more than homelessness, and I wanted you to know all of me before I let you– "

"Before you let me in on something this big?" He shakes his head in disbelief. "The night of our first kiss, after mini golf ... "

"I panicked. It was wrong, and I regretted it immediately. That was Kristina's house," I explain. "She moved in with her boyfriend after the fire."

"All this time." Another head shake. "All this time you've been lying to me. How do I know you were being honest about the rest of it? I trusted you with everything … with the truth about Becky, with all the struggles and joys of being a single parent, with Emmalyn." As he speaks her name, life blazes back into his cheeks. "Emmalyn," he echoes. "I let her fall in love with you. I let myself fall in love with you. And now what?"

Now what?

I think I'm going to be sick.

"Nothing has to change," I say, but my voice comes out all wrong. Squeaky. High-pitched. "It's hard for me to share my heart with people. When I do, though, I'm in it a hundred and ten percent. I love you and your daughter. You're everything I've always wanted."

"I just … I don't know."

"You don't know what? That I'm telling the truth now? That you feel the same way? What?" I double my pace to keep up with him as he strides off down the sidewalk. "Talk to me, please. Don't shut me out."

"That's kind of the pot calling the kettle black, don't you think?"

"I didn't shut you out." I'm practically pleading now, and I realize how desperate it must sound, but I don't care. I have to get through to him. "I was honest about everything else. It came straight from the soul. Straight from me to you. Even at the coffee shop that first day, when I told you how scared I am about my songs never making it … " I whirl around, walking backwards so I can face him. "That's been the theme of my life. Never being enough. But with you, I don't have that fear. I feel safe. Secure. I've told you things nobody else knows, not even my grandmom."

"What about her?" he asks sharply. "Did she know about the fire?"

"No." I can barely force the word past my lips. Suddenly I feel so parched it's painful. "Not until last week. She was upset. So were my parents. I think they get it, though, why I kept the secret. It was for different reasons than with you – "

"Please stop." He holds up a hand. "I need time to think." He looks at me, long and sad and so confused, and I hate myself for doing this. I want to apologize again, to beg him for forgiveness, but I am rooted to the ground, paralyzed by my own fear and stupidity. All I can do is watch as he turns and walks away.

MUSIC SCOUT

Job ID: 2014-1874
Location: US – TN – Nashville
Posted Date: 10/22/14

Overview:

Henley Music Publishing is an independent music company with a roster of both local and global songwriters. We take pride in matching clients with musicians, singers, and professionals within the entertainment industry, such as those wishing to obtain rights to a song for promotional, theater, or advertising purposes. Founded ten years ago, Henley Music Publishing has grown into a respected and renowned force in the music world.

Responsibilities:

- Evaluate songs from our clients, providing thoughtful commentary and offering suggestions for new directions the work may take.

- Establish a database of our songwriters and form partnerships between them that will result in exciting, successful collaborations.

- Scout songwriters at a variety of local clubs and music venues.

- Make recommendations on which writers to sign.

- Promote songs to producers, artists, and executives from the tv and motion picture industries.

Qualifications:

- Ability to analyze lyrics and composition, compiling a detailed, insightful evaluation.

- Laser-sharp attention to organization and detail.

- Extraordinary interpersonal skills.

- Passion for music.

- Bachelors Degree in a music-related field highly preferred.

The days that follow are riddled with remorse. I must check my phone a thousand times, breath catching in my throat whenever I see the envelope icon on the screen, but as fast as my heart jumps up, it sinks back down. Because the messages are never from him. There's one from Serena, telling me about the date she and Seth went on: dinner, dancing, and daiquiris. One from Dad, "just saying hi," and another from Mom, saying she found my old Magic Nursery dolls while organizing the attic and is it okay to donate them to the kids she works with? One from Kayleigh, thanking me again for being at their wedding.

But nothing from Wilson.

"I've made such a mess out of everything," I tell Bobbi. It's Monday, a whole week since Wilson walked away without looking back, and even though my shift at work is over, I can't seem to actually leave. My feet feel like they're encased in industrial-strength concrete.

"So fix it." Bobbi pushes a cup of coffee across the table to me. "And drink this. No offense, but you look awful."

I wrap my hands around the steaming mug of espresso, its warmth comforting to the touch. "It isn't that easy," I tell her. "To fix it, I mean. The thing is, I don't blame him for being angry. I'd have the same reaction if someone lied to me for months. He has every right to cut me out of his life and end our relationship."

"I don't think that's what he's doing. To me, if he asked you for time, that means he's not ready to let you go. Otherwise, why not do it on the spot?" She gestures to my cell phone. "Stop staring at that thing and willing it to ring. Just call him. And stop beating yourself up. Seriously, how many people would advertise that they're living in a homeless shelter?"

"It isn't like I'm embarrassed … at least, not anymore. I've met some great people there and I'm proud of the way we've pulled together."

Bobbi is quiet for a minute, pressing her fingertips together in a steeple. "I have a question: why didn't you tell any of us here about the shelter? Even now, I'm the only one who knows, and that's because you needed someone to confide in about Wilson." For a second, I think she's mad, too, but when I meet her eyes, they're curious, not cold.

"Because I hated the thought of you all looking at me differently."

"Did you tell Wilson that?" she asks. "Call him," she repeats. "Or go to his house. Don't just sit and wallow. Do something."

Easier said than done.

I wander the streets for a long time after leaving work. It's a chilly day, cool enough for a jacket and scarf, and as I pass by all the places I've come to love in this city, I'm inspired by their presence. The Hall of Fame, where challenges and triumphs are proudly on display. The Music Garden, where a rainbow of roses blossoms every spring. The Ryman, where big dreams take an even bigger stage. To make it in these places, to make it in Nashville, you've got to fight for what you believe in. That's what I've been doing with my music for years. So why not apply it to Wilson, too? Bobbi's right: we should go out on a limb for the people we love. Even if it's terrifying. Even if it might break. Even if *we* might break.

Some people are worth it.

I pull out my phone, rocking back and forth on the balls of my feet as I press in Wilson's number and it rings in my ear. One. Two. Three. Four. Five. Voicemail. I try not to give in to the sadness I feel. Maybe he's working. Maybe he's not deliberately ignoring my call. Maybe. Hopefully. "Hi," I say quietly, after the beep. "It's me. I know you need time to think and I respect that, but I wanted to apologize again. You and Em mean so much to me, and I promise, I'll do everything in my power to rebuild your trust. To rebuild us. I wish I'd done things differently … " I trail off.

Wish.

Slowly, my gaze travels to the symphony center across the street, and a ping resounds inside my head. Inside my heart. I know how I can make it up to him. How I can fix things. "Please, just keep thinking about it," I say, "and give Em a kiss from me. I miss and love you both." I end the call there, but as I cross over to the fountain, something else is beginning. The idea in my mind is still hazy, but even so, I'm already brimming with a joy that was absent all week.

For months, I've been trying to make people's wishes come true. I've touched their lives. They have certainly left a handprint on mine. But every time, it's been for somebody who started out as a stranger. Why not the people I'm closest to? Why not Wilson? I've thought about it before, but the timing never seemed right. Now it does. Now it feels like the *only* time. And so I remove the penny tucked into my wallet. It's been there since that day at the shelter when I almost convinced myself to take a chance on it, then changed my mind at the last second. *Better to take no risk than to let a risk defeat me.* That's what I told myself. Perhaps it's still true. For all I know, I'm setting myself up for another heartbreak.

But this is a risk I have to take.

Even if it defeats me. Even if it reminds me that luck loses out and fate is for fools.

I stand there for a long time, turning the penny over in my hands.

Heads up, good. Tails up, bad.

This one's for Wilson. For Emmalyn.

I take a breath that fills my lungs with the crisp air, and let the coin fly. Its path is asymmetrical, but aren't all of life's best things? Our roads are not straightforward. They're a jumble, a tangle, an amalgamation.

I watch as the penny slips beneath the water.

Heads up.

* * *

Subterfuge.

That's kind of what it seems like the next evening as I sneak up the walk to Wilson's house. He's at Em's preschool for their *Stone Soup* play, so I know the coast will be clear as I use the key he gave me last month. Am I digging myself a deeper hole? Clearly this wasn't what he envisioned when he pulled me aside one evening, pressed the key into my palm, and said "You should have this." I used to wonder if he thought it was strange that we spent all our time together at his house, or if he just assumed it was because of Em.

Now he knows the real reason why.

Now I know ... what? The spot where his foyer floor will squeak as I pass over it. The triple turn necessary to switch on the lamp in his living room, because the first two settings on the bulb burned out. The spot where he keeps his laptop on the desk. I know all these things with certainty, yet they take on a foreign feeling tonight. It's bizarre, being here alone.

I sigh, opening his computer as I glance around. One of Emmalyn's dresses lays over the arm of the sofa, green with pink and yellow flowers. By the front door, their coats hang on a knob, and two sets of shoes, one big and black, the other tiny and purple, sit against the wall. This is the place they call home. I miss it here so much.

Which is why I double click on the folder marked 'Photography – June 2014.' Wilson has shown me a lot of his work and I love it all, but one picture stands out. It's from an engagement session he shot, and as I open the file to look at the happy couple, silhouetted in black against the sunset over the Cumberland River, it gives me chills. This photo is exquisite, and it deserves recognition. I think I can get that for him. He works so hard to provide for Em, to give her the best life possible, but his business is still a start-up. If I can help it along to the next level ... if I prove how fervently I believe in him, how willing and excited I am to support his goals ... then maybe he'll agree to take me back. It's a gamble, but I have to try.

I open the internet, type in the URL I copied from the flyer posted at work, and upload the photo to the camera shop's website. Then, before I can second guess my decision, I do it. I enter Wilson in the *Show Us the Love* contest.

* * *

I miss you, and I'm ready to talk. I want to work it out. Can we meet for lunch?

My hands shake as I hold my phone, eyes growing damp as I read Wilson's text. It's the message I've been praying for ever since he returned my phone call a couple of weeks ago. He didn't want to see me then, he said he needed to take a step back for awhile, but he promised to be in touch after he took some time to think things through. "I'm not ready to give up on us," he explained, "but I'm also not ready to move forward."

Now he is.

At least, I hope he is.

I blot my eyes with a tissue, glancing around the small reception area where I'm waiting to make sure the lady at the front desk didn't see me tearing up. She's swiveled around in her seat, reaching for a file folder, so I think I'm safe. Turning my attention back to my phone, I start to answer Wilson. I don't get far, though, because the woman stands up and smiles at me. "Ms. Abraham?" she says. "Ms. Henley is ready to see you now."

I send a shortened version of the text – *Absolutely. I miss you too.* – because I can't not answer after he finally contacted me. Then I stand and follow the woman down a hallway lined with framed sheet music. I'd love to stop and study every piece. Memorize their notes and hear their lyrics. For now, I settle for covert glances as we pass by on our way to the office at the end of the corridor. Its walls are all glass, and I can see the back of the woman sitting at her desk. Navy silk shirt. Dark hair pulled into a sleek chignon. A strand of pearls.

Ms. Henley's assistant nods at me as she opens the office door. "Good luck."

"Thank you."

I smooth out my dress, a red and orange paisley print I bought from the thrift shop, and run my clammy palms along the fabric. Then I shoo aside the nerves, smile, and step forward. "Ms. Henley, hi, I'm Eden Abraham and – " She spins around in her chair and my introduction screeches to a halt. No way. It can't be.

She looks as gobsmacked as I feel. "Haven't we met before?"

"Yes." I shake my head a little in amazement. "A few weeks ago, by the Schermerhorn. I'm the one who grabbed your dog when he ran out into the traffic." I think back to that day and can barely believe this is the same woman. She seemed so down-to-earth then, in a t-shirt and jeans, and now she looks more like someone you'd see on a magazine cover. Just goes to show: appearances can be deceiving. I should know that better than anyone.

"Please, sit down." She gestures to one of the white chairs in front of her glass desk. "It's great to see you again."

"You, too. How's Barney?"

A rueful laugh flutters from her mouth. "Still getting into all sorts of mischief. Obedience school is lost on my boy. It's a good thing he's cute. Makes up for the four-hundred dollar pair of shoes he destroyed last night."

Four hundred dollars? For *shoes*? The thought is unfathomable. But for her? It's not a big deal. As she flips through a pile of papers on her desk, moving my resumé up to the top, I take note of her French-manicured nails and the sapphire on her ring finger.

"Ms. Henley, I – "

"Please," she interrupts. "Call me Jen."

I can't bring myself to do that in a setting like this, so I simply nod. "I'm so grateful," I say, "for a chance to interview for this position. It instantly leapt out at me when I read the job description." I stumbled upon the online posting the day after my secret mission at Wilson's house and emailed my application right away. Ever since Ms. Henley's assistant called, I've been spending my spare time in the library at Open Hearts, brushing up on my knowledge about music publishing and preparing for the interview. It would have been a blessing under any circumstance, but with my relationship with Wilson having been stuck in limbo, it seemed like a godsend. I needed something to anchor me, and what better than music? It's always been my light in the fog. This job could be, too.

Ms. Henley leans back in her chair. "So tell me," she says, "what is it that draws you to this part of the industry? I see from your resumé that you're a songwriter."

"Yes." I offer her the portfolio I put together for today. "This is some of my work, if you'd like to have a look." She takes it from me and opens it, seeming sincerely interested instead of just paying lip service like other people I interviewed with over the years. "I know what you might be thinking: why would a songwriter apply for a job on the other side of the fence? Why would I want to work in your creative services department and give feedback to other songwriters instead of spending time on my own material?"

She lifts her gaze and appraises me. "Both very good questions."

"And I have very good answers." The boldness of my response surprises me, but in a good way. "I've been trying to break into the industry for a long time," I say. "I got a Master's Degree. I joined NSAI. I interned with music companies. I support other artists, collaborate with fellow songwriters and singers – " Here, an image of Serena comes to mind, but it's difficult to think of her now, falling increasingly back into step with Seth, so I push it aside. "I've gotten detailed feedback myself, and I use it to help me grow. I'd like to do that for other writers."

She taps a finger on her chin. "You aren't represented by any company, right? Your songs have never been licensed? You haven't had a contract with any major publisher, or an independent one like mine?" Somehow she manages not to make this – or me – seem like a failure.

"It's not for lack of trying," I say. "I've been told my music has merit, but that it isn't marketable enough. I know how that sounds," I rush to add. "Why would you hire me to scout songs if I'm not even there yet myself? Honestly, though, learning about the things that don't work has also taught me what does. You can test me if you want. I'd be glad to evaluate any music you give me."

I can't quite read her smile. "You're right on track. That's actually part of the interview process. Hang tight," she says. "I'll grab a handful of songs from our catalogue and be right back." Her heels click against the floor as she walks out, and the moment she's gone, I exhale a massive sigh of relief. Finally, someone's giving me a chance.

But the universe has a tricky way of balancing things out. Of taking as well as giving.

Because, while I'm waiting for Ms. Henley, my phone vibrates in my bag.

My heart leaps when I check its screen.

Wilson.

Normally I wouldn't answer at a time like this, but I make an exception for him. Just as he did on the day we met, he speaks four tiny words. Today, though, they aren't an answered prayer. They're the opposite.

"What," he says tightly, "did you do?"

Show Us the Love!

Here at Freeze Frame Photo, we believe a picture is worth more than a thousand words. The perfect shot? It's truly priceless. A couple's first look at one another on their wedding day ... parents meeting a new bundle of joy for the first time ... children snuggled up with a beloved pet ... friends supporting each other through thick and thin ... a golden anniversary ... love takes on many forms, and we want to celebrate them all.

For a list of official contest rules and to upload your entries now until October 25th, visit www.freezeframephotos.com. The contest winner will receive a $3000 prize and two runners-up will each win $1000. We look forward to sharing the love!

* No more than three entries per person.
* All entries must be uploaded in JPG format, with a file size no larger than 1MB.
* Photographs must be original work that has not been commercially published.

A pit of dread slides open in my stomach. "What are you talking about?"

For a second, I'm genuinely perplexed. Then I get it. The arrow comes flying at my brain right as Wilson says the words. "Julianna Covington. Brice Taylor. The *Show Us the Love* contest. Does any of this ring a bell? You were the only person I showed their pictures to, so if I didn't enter them into that contest – "

Oh no. Oh no, oh no, *oh no*.

"I can explain." Instinctively, I hop up from the chair and start pacing across Ms. Henley's office. "You know the bulletin board we have at work? Where businesses can advertise? Well, the camera shop sponsoring the contest – "

"They won." Wilson's matter-of-fact declaration stops me in my tracks.

"They did? That's amazing!"

"Oh, no," he says. "No, it is definitely not amazing, and would you like to know why? Because it had to be their decision to enter – or mine, in which case I'd need them to sign a release form first. I can't submit a picture of people without getting their permission. Julianna is well aware of that and just called to rip into me." His voice is sharp, mad, irritated. I have never heard him like this before. Even when I finally confessed about Open Hearts, he was more upset than anything. This is a whole other ballgame, and I feel helpless to catch the pitches as they hurl in my direction.

"Rip into you?" I parrot, as a balloon of panic inflates in my chest.

"Yes. She's less than thrilled about their picture being splashed over the shop's display windows and catalog ... which, by the way, is nationwide. My photo of them will be in households throughout the entire country."

My legs buckle beneath me and I have to dart a hand out to the back of a chair to steady myself.

Be careful what you wish for; you just might get it.

This is what I wanted.

Sitting there in Wilson's still, quiet house, imagining all the good that could come from entering his photo into the contest, this is the very thing which spurred me to do it. I loved the thought of his work being celebrated. He is so talented at what he does, and so unassuming. To be acknowledged for it seemed like the ultimate gift. I couldn't rewrite history, but I could take a pen to his future and give him the chance he was too humble to give himself. If he won prize money in the process? That three thousand dollar check would cover a good portion of Em's preschool tuition. Or buy him new editing software. Or go toward the bills until he could find a job in meteorology. All I wanted was to help. Instead, I've made things worse.

Again.

Visions of that veteran float before my eyes and pierce into my soul. After that disaster, I swore I wouldn't overstep anymore. And now what? Now I've taken it upon myself to do the very thing I vowed I wouldn't.

"I'm sorry," I whisper. "I thought I was doing something good– "

"How did you even pull it off without me knowing?"

I slump into the chair. "That night you had the play at Emmalyn's school, I used – " But that's as far as I get, because Ms. Henley strides back in, a brown accordion folder tucked under her arm. She looks nonplussed to see me on the phone. "I'm in the middle of a job interview," I tell Wilson, trying to suppress the panic in my voice, "but I'll come right over afterward. Maybe if I call the couple and explain that you weren't responsible ... " I pause. Maybe what, exactly? They will magically change their minds?

Unlikely.

Wilson sighs. "You've done quite enough already. This has the potential to destroy my business. Did I mention that they're suing?" he asks flatly, and something pinches my chest. *Suing*? Oh God, what a terrible mistake I've made. I blubber another round of apologies, forgetting about everything else, and tell Wilson I'll be right there. "No, don't do that," he says. "I've gotta go visit Julianna and Brice. Just finish the interview and call me afterward. I thought we had a lot to discuss before; now there's even more." Then, without a goodbye, he's gone.

I just sit silently for a moment after he hangs up, clutching the phone so tightly my knuckles turn white. I feel ... numb. How could this have spiraled so out of control? How could I have thought it'd be okay to sneak into his house and, essentially, steal someone's private property? I'm so upset, the room's spinning.

"Eden?" Ms. Henley asks, taking her seat. "Is something wrong?" She opens a desk drawer and retrieves a spearmint-flavored Life Saver. "Here. These are good for a queasy stomach. No offense, but you look like you're going to be sick."

I feel like it, too.

All the blood's rushed to my head.

"Can I have a minute, please?" I ask. The words come out gravelly.

"Of course."

I jump up so quickly I nearly knock the chair on its side. A bathroom. I have to find one. As I run down the hall, stomach lurching miserably, the plastic wrapping around the Life Saver crinkles in my hand. I should open it. I should slip it into my mouth and let it be a salve. I should throw some cold water on my face and pull myself together before I destroy this interview, this opportunity. I should do all these things. But I can't.

I lunge for the bathroom door, cracking my elbow against the wood as I push it open, and let out a cry of pain. It hurts. Not nearly as bad, though, as the knowledge of what I've done to Wilson. He has worked so hard to grow his photography from a hobby into a business. It puts food on the table for him and Emmalyn. Keeps a roof over their heads. Affords him the flexibility to spend time with his daughter while also paying the bills. What'll happen now, if word gets out about the lawsuit? It could rob him of all of that.

And it would be entirely my fault.

"What is *wrong* with you?" I snap at my reflection.

She stares back at me from the mirror, disapproving and disheartening, and I grasp the porcelain sink, holding on for dear life. One by one, droplets poke out of the leaking faucet. Drip. Drip. Drip. I watch as they splatter, and soon my tears are joining in.

Wilson must hate me.

He was on the verge of forgiving me. Of accepting my apology.

Not anymore, I'm sure.

He'll break up with me now, and I can't blame him for it. I crossed the line. I put his business in jeopardy – him and Em in jeopardy – and it only makes sense to cut his losses. All those nights I laid awake as a child, looking out the window as moonbeams shone down onto the Piscataqua River and made it look like somebody turned on a light bulb below the surface ... all the nights I wondered how Grandmom felt about raising another kid when she had already done it with her own. All those days I had to explain to my friends why my grandmom volunteered in our school instead of a parent ... all the days I turned my heartache into my heart song ... all those days, only last year, when I thought of Jared and pondered what his new girlfriend had that I didn't. All the times I promised myself I didn't deserve to be abandoned. Not until now. There's no reason for Wilson to stay and every reason for him to go.

I lift my head and look into my raccoon eyes in the mirror. Around my neck, my locket dangles, swinging gently back and forth. I watch it for a few moments, transfixed by its motion. I love Wilson and Emmalyn. They mean more to me than I ever thought possible. But love isn't always enough, is it? Love leaves. Love lies.

I graze my fingers over the brushed gold, thinking of Grandmom. Of Grandpa.

Love dies.

* * *

"Thank you, Eden." Ms. Henley stands up and offers me her hand. "I'll be in touch after I make a decision."

There are so many things I want to say to her. That I don't normally interrupt my interviews. That I know my song evaluations weren't the best, but it was difficult to concentrate, given the circumstances. That I'd be honored to work for her and feel like I could learn a great deal here. That I could even add to her catalog, since it seems like she's interested in representing the kind of music I write. My brain's fuzzy, though, and it feels impossible to dredge up the words. All I manage is to thank her, too, and to spout off something about it being nice to see her again.

Not exactly the epitome of eloquence.

Then again, neither was the past hour. The rest of the interview replays in my mind, a horror movie of my own making, as I walk through the building and step into the elevator.

"Here you go," Ms. Henley said, giving me four pieces of paper. "Read them over, jot notes, let me know what you think." She busied herself answering emails as I combed through the songs. The first one I loved. The second had a catchy hook, but the verses lacked staying power. The third was an odd combination of country and rap, and the fourth was what I call a sleeper song – it had a quiet melody, introspective, what I would put on a CD as a bonus track. In my head, I articulated all these thoughts very well.

When Ms. Henley flipped her laptop shut and looked at me expectantly?

Not so much.

"The first one is my favorite," I told her. "'Chasing Rainbows.' The second has a great chorus – "

"Hold on. Let's talk about one at a time."

"Right. Absolutely." I glanced down at the floor as my cheeks reddened to the color of my nose. "The lyrics stood out to me immediately," I said, forcing myself to meet her eyes. "They have such a whimsical quality. It's a song I can see inspiring people, in the vein of Carrie Underwood's 'So Small,' or maybe … " I paused, wracking my brain for another comparison that should've come easily. Ever since I was a child, a track-listing of music has lived inside me. But not today. Not when it mattered most.

That's when the record stopped spinning.

"LeAnn Womack's 'I Hope You Dance?'" Ms. Henley saved me.

"Yes!" I exclaimed. "That's such a timeless song, you know? I remember it was the theme of my high school graduation. The superintendent quoted it in his speech, and – " I broke off. "Sorry. As I was saying, I'd certainly file 'Chasing Rainbows' into that category, especially if the music crescendos up near the bridge. It's whimsical … " Crap. Nothing like using the exact same adjective twice in as many minutes.

"Tell me more about your superintendent," Ms. Henley prompted, when I trailed off awkwardly. I must've given her a puzzled look, because she continued. "That's how I like to gauge songs, actually. Don't talk to me about notes and scales. Talk to me about the music that's part of the soundtrack of your life. That's how I know a hit when I see it. If I can envision a song being part of, for example, a graduation ceremony, if I can feel its impact while it's still words on a page … " She smiles sublimely. "For me it was Taylor Dayne's 'Love Will Lead You Back.' I grew up in Florida, and rather than stay at our senior prom, my boyfriend and I left early and spent the evening at the beach. That song was on the radio at one of the oceanfront restaurants, and Joe asked me to dance. It'll always be special to me because of all the memories entwined with it. Do you think 'Chasing Rainbows' has a similar sort of power?"

Blank.

My mind went totally blank, like someone had wiped it clean with an eraser.

I rambled about sentimentality, about the lyrics boosting people up and encouraging them to go for their dreams, and I think I somehow managed to tie that back in with the anecdote about school and my superintendent. Maybe. Possibly. As the elevator descends, I try to remember, but can't. I can, however, recall quite clearly the idiotic commentary I gave on the rest of the songs. *The chorus is good, but the verses are saggy. It's too jumbled and messy. I love how the writer does that thing with the repetition, like the way those lines repeat themselves.* Ugh. Could I have messed it up any more atrociously?

There's no way I'll get the position. I had my chance; I blew it.

Seems to be the name of my game lately.

When the elevator opens and I step out, I decide to call Wilson and get it over with. I've already lost the job. Now it's time to lose him, too.

His phone only rings once.

"Hey, you've reached Wilson. I'm either off making memories or capturing somebody else's, but if you leave your name and number, I'll return your call as soon as possible. Y'all have a terrific day, and remember: embrace whatever develops."

Voicemail.

Nobody's phone cuts off that quickly on its own, which instantly makes me think he deliberately rejected the call. It shouldn't surprise me, not after what I've done, but it does. It takes me back to that gym class in twelfth grade when we were playing basketball and Mindy Jenkins lobbed the ball right at me. I misjudged the distance to catch it and the thing smacked into my chest, siphoning the air from my lungs and sending me to the ground. The whole class crowded around, and Mindy was in tears, apologizing over and over as the teacher helped me up and walked me to the nurse's office. The entire rest of the day, I was shaky. Unsteady. Straining to regain the wind that'd been knocked out of me.

That's how I feel now.

It doesn't help when Wilson rings back a half hour later. "I was still with Julianna and Brice," he explains. "Trying to talk them down. So I couldn't answer."

"How did it go?"

Please, let them have had some compassion. Please, let them have dropped the lawsuit.

Please, please, *please.*

"No luck. Turns out their families didn't know about the engagement. They wanted to surprise them with the news on

Christmas. Now the plan is ruined, and they blame me for it. They refuse to budge."

I'd been wandering the city aimlessly, but at this, a sickening wave of nausea explodes inside my stomach, and I have to stop. "Let me try," I beg. "I'll tell them it's my fault – "

"No. That'll make it even worse, if they know someone else had access to their files."

He sounds so cold. So upset.

I lean against the nearest building for support. "I'm sorry," I choke out. "I never, ever meant for this to happen. I thought I was helping. I thought I was showing you how much faith I have in you. I thought it would be a way to prove myself and to make up for lying about … " Even as I'm saying the words, I hear how foolish they are. How deluded.

"What you were doing," Wilson says evenly, "was playing God. What made you think you have the right to do that? I love you, Eden, and my life is better when you're in it. That's what I was going to tell you at lunch today. But this? I don't know if I can get past it. They're going after my business. I could lose everything I've worked so hard to build."

Should I explain myself?

Tell him about the writer's block, the wishes, the pennies turned into promises?

Plead my case?

Do I really deserve to do that?

As I slide down the wall, crouching on the sidewalk so similarly to the way I did all those months ago when Wilson and I met, the answer resounds in my head, loud and clear. No. I don't deserve to and I don't deserve him.

"I'm sorry," I say again. "I love you too, and I am so sorry."

Then I do him the biggest favor I can think of.

I hang up.

September 18, 2010

Dear Grandmom,

I started a new song yesterday. Usually I'd wait until it's finished to send, but I thought you might like to see this one now. Hope you love it. Hope Grandpa would've, too.

 xoxo,

 Eden

"You Never Know"

She was sitting on the beach one day, nose buried in a book
He was tossing a football with some friends until he took a second look
Some love is at first sight
Some love needs roots to grow
Some love makes you better, some ignites your glow

You never know what tomorrow brings
Or how your life will change
So hold on to the moments
Don't ever let them wane

She walked down the aisle, bouquet of irises in her hands
He waited with a smile, this fairytale more magical than planned
For theirs was a storybook come to life
Two tales intertwining
Two hearts forever shining

(To be continued …)

$\mathcal{I}$t hurts.

I curl myself into a ball, knees fitting under my chin, and tug the blanket over myself. It's cold in the shelter tonight, the kind of cold that sneaks under your skin and gives you an internal chill, and I burrow into the thin covers, trying to absorb whatever warmth I can. Whatever refuge I can. But it is hard to settle down now, to block out the snoring woman across the room or the cries of the baby as his mother tries to soothe him. If you have to be in a homeless shelter, I suppose that'd be the time for it, when you're too young to understand anything. When that little one grows up, he won't have any recollection of his days here. If only adults had the same capability. If only I could forget about the past four months.

Instead, the memories taunt me, haunt me, and Wilson's accusation blasts through my mind on constant repeat. *What you were doing was playing God.* He's right. All this time, I thought I was doing something good by granting the wishes. Why not grab hold of every opportunity to put a smile back on someone's face?

Because it wasn't my place.

Because actions have repercussions far greater than we can even imagine.

Sometimes good, sometimes bad, sometimes irrevocable.

I shift in bed and rearrange the blanket into a tighter cocoon. I'd like to disappear right now, but I can't. All I can do is think about how horribly I screwed up. What if the judge rules against Wilson, and he has to turn over all his earnings to Julianna and Brice? What if he has to get a second job, or even a third one, so he can afford his mortgage? What if he has to miss Emmalyn's school plays and dance recitals because he's so busy trying to keep them afloat?

What if.

The two biggest words in the world.

They clamp a hold on me in the following days. I make mistakes constantly at work, and outside of Sensations I'm basically worthless. I need to keep looking for an apartment, since Open Hearts only provides shelter for people for five months before they have to move to transitional housing or find a place of their own, but whenever I browse the listings, all I can think of is Wilson's house. His cornflower blue door. His refrigerator covered in Em's artwork. His small backyard, where I pushed her on the swing. His kitchen counter, where we made caramel apples for her to bring to preschool, and his bed, where we exchanged our first I love yous. I don't want a new apartment. I don't want to start the next chapter in my life. I want to edit the last one.

That feels impossible, though. I turned my phone off after talking to Wilson and it's stayed that way ever since. I couldn't take it if he called back to break up with me or Ms. Henley got in touch to say I didn't get the job. I know those things are hanging over me, but to actually hear the words? It would make it all too real. As long as my phone's a black hole, I don't have to face the future. I call Grandmom from the shelter's landline instead, grateful that Ms. Birnbaum has a long distance plan for the people who have no other means of contacting family. It helps a little, hearing Grandmom's voice. It's the only time I feel like I'm not going to shatter.

Otherwise, I'm devastated.

I decide to sit in on Serena's next Noteworthy performance, hoping it'll cheer me up to see her. Except, when I arrive, there's not one microphone on stage. There are two. And when she bounces up to the platform, a man with blonde hair and steel blue eyes follows. His hand is wrapped loosely around Serena's, casual and comfortable, and before they sit down, she leans over to kiss his cheek. I narrow my eyes. So this is Seth. Jeans, white button down shirt open at the collar, gray blazer that matches Serena's dress – the dress that she's wearing without tights, just a tall pair of leather boots, one that accentuates her figure instead of hiding it.

This is good, right? Her petals are growing back and reaching up to grab the sunlight.

Then why does the whole thing feel so dark?

Why do I move to a table in the corner, out of her line of vision?

Is it me? Or is it her?

I am glad she's happy and that Seth appears to be treating her well this time. But the Serena on stage tonight – effervescent, chatty, and buoyant – seems like a stranger. She's not the person who convinced me to stay at Open Hearts, or the one who confided in me about her miscarriage. It's like she's completely shut out that time in her life. It's startling. Scary. Sad.

I'm sad.

I miss my guitar, my book collection, my *I Love Lucy* DVDs, my maxi skirts. I miss my apartment, with its cute galley kitchen, its potted plants by the windows, and its popcorn ceiling that reminded me of the condo in Nantucket where I stayed with Kayleigh's family for three weeks one summer. I miss having a place to call my own. I miss the normalcy. I miss Serena and our songwriting sessions, because, despite her declarations to the contrary, she has fallen back into her old pattern of working primarily with Seth. But most of all, I miss Wilson and Em. I miss what could've been, and that only makes it worse to grapple with what is.

I can't do it.

I can't stay in Nashville. The city I once thought would be a key has become a deadbolt instead. Everywhere I look, all I see is what I've lost. As I listen to Serena sing with Seth, I am convinced: I've got to get out of here. I've got to leave it behind. I hurry back to the shelter, clear off the shelf over my bed, and write a thank you note to Ms. Birnbaum that I slip beneath her office door. Then I call a taxi to take me to the airport, where I head to the ticket counter and reallocate the money I planned to use for an apartment. Instead I put it toward the next available escape. "I can get you on a flight to Boston that leaves in an hour," the ticket agent says. It's the closest airport to Portsmouth.

"Perfect."

Once I'm settled into my seat on the airplane, waiting for the doors to close, I turn on my phone for the first time in days. I type a resignation email to Dina and one explaining things to Serena, and feel the ache deepen inside me, not for the notes I am sending but for the one I'm not. Will Wilson and Emmalyn miss me, or will the hole I'm leaving be stitched up quickly? Maybe I won't even leave a hole at all. The thought hurts my heart. And when I open the waiting email from Ms. Henley? The pain entrenches itself further still.

Hello Eden, it says. *I wanted to call and personally explain my reasoning for going with another candidate for the music publishing position, but your phone keeps taking me directly to voicemail. I think you're a lovely person and clearly extremely passionate about songwriting. It's just that when we moved into the song evaluation portion of the interview –*

I can't read anymore.

I punch the power button on the phone, shutting it off before I can see, yet again, that I've fallen short. Then I toss it – this harbinger of bad news – onto the seat beside me. As we lift off into the starry night sky, I let myself sneak one final peek at the glittering skyline. It is a beautiful place, an inspiring one. But sometimes inspiration doesn't matter. Sometimes we can wish with all our hearts, work day in and day out to create the lives we yearn for, and still, it doesn't happen. Reality isn't like a song, or a book, or a movie, and happily-ever-after doesn't always exist. When we realize that, maybe it's best not to push it. Trying to fit a square peg into a round hole just ends up chipping off its corners.

Better to surrender.

Once I'm in New Hampshire, this will all be easier.

At least, that's what I think until the airplane touches down. By the time I've trudged my way to the taxi line, forked over the last bills in my wallet, and climbed the steps to Grandmom's apartment at the assisted living community, I'm not as certain. I may be twelve-hundred miles away, but it still stings every bit as sharply. I pull out my key, open the door quietly – it's the middle of the night and I don't want to frighten Grandmom – and tiptoe over to the sofa. The living room is silent, dark, and although I'd give anything to wake Grandmom up, to let her hold me like she did when I was little, as I tell her about how I've wrecked everything, that wouldn't be fair. It can wait for the morning. The pain isn't going anywhere. I write a note to Grandmom, letting her know I'm here, and slide it under her bedroom door. Then I unclasp my locket and stare at the pictures inside.

Grandpa. Mom and Dad.

And that's when the tears finally come.

* * *

When my eyes creep open in the morning, there's a blanket draped around me and the smell of cinnamon-infused coffee filling the air. For a couple minutes, I just lie there, listening to the sounds of Grandmom beginning her day. There's the muted murmur of Good Morning America on the TV in the kitchen, the crinkle of the Eggo bag as she takes out two waffles – to have with a glass of orange juice, I know, because this is what she always has for breakfast, even now, when she could go to the dining room and eat with the other residents – and the squeaky shuffling of her slippered feet as she pads across the floor. It's so familiar, so comforting.

"Well, well, well." Grandmom walks over when she notices I'm awake. "Imagine my surprise to find your note this morning." She waits until I sit up, then joins me, holding a steaming mug. "Drink this first. Then tell me what's going on."

The coffee is hot, sweet, and it warms me from the inside out. "I'm sorry," I tell her, then groan, because how many times have I uttered those words lately? "I hope I didn't scare you. I planned to get up early and – "

"I'm fine. Don't worry about your grandmom. I am, however, concerned about you." She rests her hand on mine. "You were crying." This is a statement, not a question. "And I found your locket upside-down on the floor." I blink at her, trying to remember how it got there, but my head is foggy and my sinuses throb like someone took a hammer to them.

"I had to get out of Nashville," I say, pushing the words past my dry, cracked lips. I take another sip of coffee, touched that she added the cinnamon, which she knows I love. "Thank you," I tell her, holding up the mug. "This is exactly what I need."

"I know." Tiny lines appear around her eyes as she smiles. "Grandmothers always know."

"I miss you."

"I miss you, too." She smoothes my hair back from my face. "But you didn't hop on a plane and fly all this way only to see me. This is about Wilson, right?"

Grandmothers always know.

I've told her a bit about what happened, the bare bones scaffolding, and now, pulling the peach and blue blanket tighter around me, I fill in the gritty details. "It was stupid," I say, "and arrogant. It never even occurred to me that I was crossing a legal line. I shouldn't have interfered. Not with him or anybody else. Where did I get off doing that? On what planet did I think it was my right?" I place the mug down on a coaster on her coffee table. "All along, I was telling myself that the wishes were my way of helping people, of making a difficult situation a little better, but maybe I've been fooling myself. Maybe this whole thing has been selfish."

"How so?"

"Well, after the fire, my ability to write just ... ceased to exist." The memory rises up in me, such a bitter pill that I still can't swallow. "It's like the words were trapped behind a wall. It was the most frustrating thing. I already lost so much. The thought of losing my songwriting, too, was absolutely unbearable. But something happened." I flip my hand over so our palms are face-to-face, then link our fingers. "I overheard this boy, Tommy, at the fountain in the shelter's courtyard. He wished for a toy boat, so I made him one with modeling clay, a straw, and napkins. Seeing his face light up was the first moment of joy I'd had in weeks. And then, out of nowhere, a lyric came to me, like granting his wish was the muse. So I kept at it. I thought it was because I wanted to be a positive influence. Knowing I mattered to these people was the best feeling.

It wasn't all selfless, though. Every time I made good on somebody's wish, it inspired lyrics about their life. I wasn't only helping them. I was also helping myself." The realization makes me bow my head in shame.

"You're being too hard on yourself," Grandmom says.

"You're not being hard enough on me."

"Let me ask you something. Did you deliberately exploit those people? Did you ask them about their wishes solely so you'd have writing material?"

"No, but – "

"Did you go out of your way to brighten their days?"

"Yes, but – "

"Did you know ahead of time that Wilson would need a release form from the couple?"

"No, but – "

"No buts. There is nothing wrong with gleaning inspiration from the people around you. That's what creative types do. You have a good heart. Please don't beat yourself up for wanting to matter to people. That's just basic human instinct. It isn't a sin." Her eyes flit to a family photo on the wall, from my fifteenth birthday, one of the few Mom and Dad were home for. "The important thing is to learn from your mistakes."

"Even if my mistakes have cost people everything? How can you still be on my side after that?"

"I love you, Jellybean. I am *always* on your side."

"I love you, too, so much."

"Come on," she says. "Let's eat some breakfast and you can tell me more. We'll figure out what to do about this."

We.

As I trail after her, fastening the locket back around my neck, I realize that even if Wilson never looks my way again, I won't be alone. I'll always have Grandmom. Unconditionally. Unequivocally. Unreservedly. And for that, I am blessed.

* * *

"I'm sorry," the man apologizes. "We still haven't been able to locate it, and at this point, I think we've exhausted all possible channels." The airline's customer service representative is nice, and he has been nothing but helpful since the moment I realized that I lost my phone on the plane, but still, I have to suppress a groan of frustration. It's been a week now since I checked my messages – after breakfast with my grandmom, I felt a lot better about facing things – and discovered the phone wasn't in my bag. Only then did I remember the way I'd tossed it onto the seat. I'd slept the whole way to Boston and was groggy when the plane landed, and I guess, in my stupor, it slipped my mind. Now there's nothing I can do about it.

"Thank you so much for trying," I tell the man. "I really appreciate it."

I hand Grandmom's cell phone back to her after the airline rep hangs up, then open the car door and step out onto the cemetery's quiet grounds. We'd been about to get out of the car before, but that's when the man called with an update. I'll deal with the phone problem later, though. Grandpa should be the one and only focus right now.

"Are you sure about this?" I ask Grandmom, slipping on the pair of gloves she's loaned me. It's a cold, blustery day, the kind you'd expect in January, not November. "I'll be okay. You can stay here if you want."

"Pish-posh. Frigid digits never hurt anybody." She circles a canary yellow scarf around her neck and turns up the hood of her sherpa-lined coat. "Besides, I've been here in much worse weather. It would drive your grandfather crazy if he knew. 'Lillian, what are you doing? Go home, put your feet up, knit one of your masterpieces.' That's what he'd say." She smiles a bit, but it's sad, and I stretch out my hand to hers. Supporting her, holding her steady, like she's always done for me. "Unless this is something you need to do on your own, in which case I understand. Don't worry your pretty little head about offending me."

"I'd actually love to do it together."

For the past week, we've been doing almost everything that

way. Eating meals. Playing games. Watching *General Hospital.* I've slept on her sofa and even tagged along on the days she visited her boutique. It was like old times, folding myself into one of the overstuffed chairs and watching as she chatted with customers. She may not run the place day-to-day anymore, but Sew Stylish will be her baby as long as it exists. And me, too. When I was a kid, Grandmom used to tell me that often: "No matter how old you get, you'll always be my baby."

I feel that now, her constant desire to protect me, as we start through the grass, its blades faded in a reminder that winter isn't too far off. Slowly, we crunch our way across the cemetery, browned and brittle leaves underfoot, until we get to the center. Grandmom's hand tenses in mine. "It never gets easier," she confesses. "You'd think it would after so long, but whenever I come here, it's like I am grieving all over again."

"Grandpa wouldn't want that. He'd want you to be happy."

"I am." She plucks a yellow rose – Grandpa's favorite color – from the bouquet we brought and lovingly places it next to his headstone. "You'd be proud, Rick. I finally found somebody to open my heart to again. It only took forty-four years." She chuckles, and so do I. I met James, the man she's seeing, a couple days ago, and liked him immediately. He's been the best part of the assisted living experience for her. They met during Luau Night in the social hall, when he walked over, lei in hand, and offered "pretty flowers for the pretty lady."

"You'd approve," I tell Grandpa. "He'll be there for Grandmom since you can't be."

"He is there, though." Grandmom turns to look at me. "In other ways. When a yellow butterfly is nearby, or when I page through old photo albums ... when I see your mother, and when I see you. You both have his smile."

"Really?" Something blooms inside me. "I like that."

"He would, too."

She takes a seat on the stone bench and I place the rest of the bouquet down before joining her. "Do you ever wonder how different life would've been if he wasn't killed?" I ask.

"I used to think about it all the time: when your mom would cry out from nightmares; when she had a birthday party and he couldn't be there to celebrate; when she threw herself into charity work in an effort to be closer to the dad she lost." I swivel to Grandmom, watching the breeze sneak past her hood and flutter the sides of her hair. "I was crushed for a long time. And the thing about grief is it doesn't ever disappear, not fully. Even when it's become less a part of everyday life and more a part of the subconscious, it still plays a role in shaping who we are. Like Mariah. I know she has hurt you, and I hate that. I wish things could have been different."

I open my mouth to answer, to tell her I wouldn't trade the times we've shared, but before I say anything there's a rustling behind us. Footsteps on leaves, the soft and measured movement of a person who knows how to be quiet when necessary. Then a whiff of perfume I recognize from long ago.

"Maybe they can be." The voice carries in on the wind, sad and wistful.

A voice I never would have expected.

Mom.

RICHARD WALTER JENKINSON

Corporal Richard Jenkinson, 38, of Portsmouth, New Hampshire, was killed in combat in Vietnam on November 25, 1970. Officer Jenkinson was born and raised in Portsmouth, where he became an integral and beloved part of the community. Known for a hearty laugh and love of all things Boston Red Sox, he was always available to lend a hand to those in need. He was a high school football star who went on to teach middle school history until he joined the army, first in the civil sector and later on active duty. Described by his wife as "a good man with the purest heart of gold and a smile that never left his face," his loss is one that will be felt far and wide.

Officer Jenkinson is survived by his wife Lillian; his daughter Mariah; his parents Paul and Linda; and his older sister Lucille. Those wishing to honor his memory may make a donation to the United Way or For the Love of a Child, two organizations Cpl. Jenkinson championed on a regular basis.

❦ 30 ❧

"**M**ariah." Grandmom's lips twitch a bit at the corners, like they want to sprout into a smile, and she slides over on the bench to make room. But I stay still, gloved fingers clenching into fists. What is she doing here? Why isn't she in Haiti? And where's Dad? All at once, it hits me: something bad must have happened. Why else would she be in New Hampshire, her sapphire eyes brimming with tears?

"Mom. Eden." She nods slightly at the bench. "May I?"

Grandmom scoots over another few inches and opens up a spot between us. As Mom sits down next to me, my nerves bristle. I don't like her getting between us. I keep my gaze averted to a tree across the way, watching as a squirrel climbs its branches, but my ears perk up as Grandmom asks, "Where's Joel?"

Please, let him be okay.

"At the house," she says, and a sigh of relief whooshes out of me. Thank goodness. "He wanted to come, but I thought this was something we needed to do just the three of us." Huh? What does she mean? Since when have we *ever* done something just the three of us? Reluctantly, I relent and sneak a peek over at her. She looks different, I realize. Wearier.

But also determined.

"Why aren't you off rebuilding schools?" I ask.

"Because we're needed elsewhere."

"Oh. I don't remember you switching assignments mid-way before. So where are you heading to next?"

"Nowhere. Well, I mean, eventually we'll go back to Haiti, I suppose, but for the time being your father and I are on sabbatical."

I nearly topple off the bench. "Excuse me?"

"We're on sabbatical," she repeats, and this time Grandmom

does smile. "Because you're going through a hard time and we want to be there for you." She dabs at her eyes, her lashes fluttering as she blinks. "That is, if you'll let us."

I gape at her, my mouth literally falling open, and she winces.

"We've earned that reaction," she says. "There are so many instances when we should've made this decision before. I won't insult you by giving excuses. All I can say is we thought we were doing the right thing. I see now how wrong we were. How wrong I was." She stops, waiting for my reply, but I'm speechless. She continues, "when you told us about the fire and I got angry, that was a low point for me. You accepted my apology, though, and it was a wake-up call."

I think back to that week in October, to the hope I had for how it might change things. But, as I feared, once Mom and Dad left for Haiti, it was a two sentence email here, a five minute phone call there. "Was it?" I ask. "Because you haven't exactly been in touch lately. Why should I believe this will be different?"

"You shouldn't," she says plainly. "Not yet, not until we've proven ourselves to you."

"Why now? Why this time?"

"Because your grandmom called. She filled us in on what happened with Wilson and how upset you are."

"And you came."

My voice cracks on the last word.

They came.

They put their work on hold and flew home. For me.

Mom stands up and walks a few feet ahead, hugging herself, shielding against the biting wind, or maybe against something much sharper. "You sound surprised," she says, so quietly I barely hear it. "I guess that shouldn't come as a shock. We've let you down, and I'm sorry. I'm such a hypocrite. It broke something in me when Grandpa died, and then I – " She trails off, looking at the ground, head bowed. "I basically left you without parents, too."

I glance down, staring at my hands, until Grandmom's creates a shell atop them. She's surprised by my parents' choice, too, I can tell by the look on her face, but perhaps not as much as I am. After all, she's always held out hope that they'd come around. This has to be what she wanted when she called them.

"Listen to your mother," she advises. "I'm not saying you have to give them another chance, but hear her out." If there's anybody in this world I trust, it's her. She wouldn't suggest that unless she meant it.

I raise my eyes and fix them on Mom. "Go on."

She's silent for a minute, kneeling on the ground and grazing her fingers on the engraved letters of Grandpa's headstone. "You'd be ashamed of me, Daddy," she whispers. "When you died, I didn't just lose you. I lost my innocence and my security. So much was taken from me, and I was only six, I didn't understand any of it. All I knew was that Daddy was gone and he couldn't come back." Tears spill over her cheeks again, but she makes no move to wipe them away. "You believed in the cause. That day before you went off to war, when you pulled me onto your lap and explained why you had to leave ... I still remember that. I remember you reading me a book about soldiers and taking me to get ice cream and buying me a stuffed eagle from the toy store." She smiles slightly. "I still have it. I was so proud of you. Mom and I both were. I wanted to continue your legacy after you died, and I wanted to help people, especially overseas, just like you did. I wanted to make sure that other kids didn't feel alone or deserted, the way I had. But what I never realized was that in doing so, I caused my own child the same pain I tried to prevent in others. Charity work made me feel closer to you. It also took me further from Eden."

Before I even realize what I'm doing, I join her on the grass. "I'm sorry you lost him," I tell her.

"I'm sorry we all did."

"For what it's worth, I think he's proud of you, Mariah," Grandmom says. "For fighting for those who can't fight for themselves. For giving your all. And for knowing when to admit you made some errors in judgment." Her fingers grip the seat of the bench, resting against the green vines coiling up its sides. "You too, Jellybean," she adds. "Your grandpa believed in dreaming big and working hard. He's smiling down on you now, watching you write your own song. Your own story." Her voice dips. "He'd be glad you're with Mom and me today. Glad the three of us are together."

Today.

November twenty-sixth.

The anniversary of when he was killed in battle, forty-four years ago.

Grandmom comes here often, and Mom, when she's home, but not me. I always thought it was too sad, too depressing. Now, though, as Grandmom walks over and rests one hand on my shoulder and the other on Mom's, I'm not sad. I'm at peace. Even though I never got to know Grandpa Rick, being at the cemetery today makes me feel closer to him. Like he *is* watching over me. Like his love lives on.

"How did you know where to find us?" I ask Mom.

She reaches into her coat pocket and pulls out three seashells. "I went to Grandmom's, and she wasn't there. On this day, there was only one other place she'd be." She presses one of the shells in my hand and gives another to Grandmom. "Your granddad's favorite spot was the beach," she says. "So now I bring the beach to him." She gingerly places the shell on his headstone. Then Grandmom does. Then I do.

"We miss you," I say, touching the cool stone. "Thanks for looking out for us."

We stay there a long time, until the clouds thicken, and then we stand. Mom wraps her fingers around Grandmom's, and her other hand inches toward me. Reaches out.

Maybe it's foolish. Maybe it's idealistic. But I take it.

* * *

"Oh, I almost forgot!" Mom says, as we walk into Grandmom's apartment. The plan was to look through some old photo albums, to listen to Grandmom's stories about Grandpa, but before we can even open the first one, Mom stops in her tracks and starts rummaging through her purse. A second later, she pulls out my phone.

My eyebrows shoot up. "How did you get that?"

"Someone found it on the plane," she explains. "The man scrolled through your contact list and tried to get in touch with you. He called the 'home' number first, but that was your apartment, so of course the number was out of service. Then he tried me, since it was labeled 'Mom.' I was in a spot with pretty bad reception, though, so I didn't get his call until I checked my messages after landing in Boston this morning. Turns out he lives in the city, so he met me at the airport to give it back." She smiles. "It's nice to know there are still good people out there."

It sure is.

I curl my hand around the phone, thinking of the messages it might hold. Of Wilson. Of Em. Of Ms. Henley, whose email will still be there, right where I left it. Part of me wants to dive in, to finally face everything, but another part wants to put it off just a little while longer. Today has turned into something I never expected, the best kind of surprise, and I'm not ready for anything to tarnish it. If I've already waited a week, one more day won't hurt.

But then the next day is Thanksgiving, and once again, I find myself stalling out of fear. I charge the phone and start to turn it on more times than I can count, but I always find some reason to stop. I have to help out with the stuffing. I have to watch the Macy's parade with Grandmom, like we did every year when I was little. I have to set the table. It's kind of weird, doing that with Dad as Mom and Grandmom cook in the kitchen, but it's also nice.

"Incoming," Dad says, shuffling into the dining room with the casserole dishes.

"I'm pretty sure the food's supposed to go in those before you bring them to the table," I laugh.

"Oh." He peers at me. "Yeah, I suppose that'd make sense."

"Do you see now why your father isn't allowed to cook?" Mom calls from the kitchen. "Ask him about our first holiday together after getting married."

Dad winks. "Salt and sugar look similar, what can I say?"

It's all so … normal.

And yet so monumental at the same time.

I've loved my Thanksgivings with Grandmom, but this is a reminder that sometimes change can be a good thing. Folding the napkins with Dad. Carrying in Grandmom's sweet potato casserole and glazed carrots. Taking a glass of red wine from Mom. Thinking about the people at Open Hearts and hoping they're having a good holiday. Going around the table and saying what we're all thankful for this year.

"For having my whole family under one roof," Grandmom says.

"For second chances," Mom says.

"For the opportunity to make amends," Dad says. He looks directly at me. "You know my family isn't close, and that really affected me when I was younger. When I met your mom … she was like a whirlwind and I got swept up. Her way of life became my way of life and I don't regret that, but I am sorry for not adjusting it when you came into the picture. You deserved much better." I have heard this before – that the pregnancy was unplanned, that they tried the whole white-picket-fence thing until it suffocated them, that they believed I'd be better off if Grandmom raised me. But tonight, it's more.

So, raising my glass, I add "For new beginnings."

Will this one last?

Only time will tell, but for now, my hope's a bit less cautionary than before, especially when talk at the table turns to Wilson. "You know," Mom says, "when you were three, you dragged me to the play-set Dad built in the backyard, climbed up, and said 'Look, Mommy, I can fly.'" She chuckles. "I caught you right before you did a nosedive onto the ground. You just jumped off. You didn't stop to worry about getting hurt. You leapt and trusted you'd land on both feet."

"This isn't the same."

"No," Grandmom agrees. "You already leapt. You already *did* get hurt. So did Wilson. But life's not about how many times we fall. It's about how many times we get back up."

"I wouldn't even know how to try. This isn't some minor offense here. I single-handedly ruined his business and then I ran away."

"Let me ask you something," Dad says. "Do you still love him?"

"Of course."

"Do you miss him?"

I think of him and Emmalyn, sitting around the Thanksgiving table with their family. We may be separated by distance, but, for me at least, we aren't by heart.

"More than anything," I say.

"You should call him," Grandmom tells me.

I want to, God I want to, but suppose he refuses to answer? It's been more than a week since I left. Who knows what he's thinking now? Maybe he'll hang up on me like I did to him. The thought is too much to bear, so I shake my head. "Maybe later." But later comes and goes, until the clock's hands hit midnight and the velvet sky is a backdrop for all the diamonds in Mother Nature's jewelry box. I lie in bed at Mom and Dad's house, staring at the ceiling, wondering why the lessons we learn come too late to salvage what matters most.

Or do they?

I'm here with my parents. I'm trying to forgive them. Maybe Wilson can do the same with me. Maybe I can somehow make things up to him. Maybe all hope isn't lost.

There's only one way to find out. I sit up, reach for my phone, and turn it on.

Three voicemails from him. Ten texts.

Why did you hang up on me? I called you back, but it went to voicemail.

Are you there? Why aren't you answering?

Okay, now I'm getting concerned. Please call so we can talk.

Obviously you're avoiding me. How is that helping us solve anything?

Hiding from our problems isn't the answer. Hiding from me isn't the answer. If you won't return my messages, I'll come find you so we can discuss this in person. P.S. Emmalyn says she misses you and she wants to show you her new "dolly outfits."

My vision blurs. I assumed things were over, that Wilson had cut the ties binding us, but maybe it was a mistake to jump to that conclusion. Maybe I underestimated him and our relationship. And myself, too.

I move on to the next text.

Dina said you quit your job. Serena said you left Open Hearts. Where are you?

Can you please just let me know you're safe?

I don't understand. How can you flip a switch and turn off all we are to each other? Or, at least, all I thought we were …

I get it. You think we're better off apart. I'm still worried, though. I hope you're okay.

And, finally, one from only a few hours ago: *Happy Thanksgiving from Em and me.*

He didn't give up on me.

The realization washes over me and sucks the breath from my lungs. I gave him every reason to walk away. But he didn't. I did that this time. I left.

My fingers hover over the phone. I want to text back, but what would I say? How can I explain myself? And will he even want to hear it anymore? He has to still be angry. Tentatively, I listen to his voicemails. The first is from the day I hung up on him, asking me to please call back. The second is from the next day, saying pretty much the same thing.

The third one is what gets to me.

"Hey," he says softly. "It's been a week since I've heard from you. I know you're upset. So am I. I wish you'd answer me, though. Otherwise, how're we supposed to work through our problems? I do have an update on Brice and Julianna. I met with them again today, and for a little bit, I thought I had actually managed to convince them to drop the suit. No dice, but I've been thinking about what you said, and maybe it wouldn't be a bad idea for you to explain to them what happened. It's worth a try. Call me back and let me know your thoughts."

Now my tears come at full force.

It's too late to call him, so I type out a text. Erase it. Retype it. Delete the end. Hurl the phone onto the bed. I can't do this. I can't face him until I've cleaned up the mess I made. I have to talk to that couple. I have to persuade them to back off. What can I offer as an incentive? The more I rack my brain, the more helpless I feel.

Maybe I should sleep on it. Things always seem more manageable in the morning.

But rest eludes me tonight.

I toss, I turn. I kick off the blanket, I yank it back up. I fluff the pillows, I smooth them down.

Finally, when the first hints of gray light peek around the window shade, I get up.

"Rise and shine," I whisper. "Welcome to a brand new day."

It's how Grandmom always used to wake me for school when I was a kid, and now, as I scoop up my phone and pad downstairs to the kitchen, I think of how true it is. Each day, we're given twenty-four golden hours. To use or abuse. To embrace or waste. To move forward or move backward. It is our decision. And, as I make myself coffee and settle onto the window seat, I choose the former. I choose to tackle my mistakes rather than cower behind them.

Opening the browser on my phone, I research Tennessee state law. Photography release forms. Similar lawsuits that have been filed. I sit, cross-legged, in the light of the rising sun, Mom's notepad on my knee as I jot down anything that seems useful. Maybe it'll help, maybe it won't, but I have to try. Wilson's messages have added color back into my picture. All the dejection I felt has exploded into a desperation that zips through my veins. I shouldn't have given up before. I should've fought harder, pushed harder.

I didn't then, but I will now.

I set my phone down, turning my attention outside as the sun overtakes the sky, airbrushing it in shades of musky lavender and cotton candy pink. There are clouds, too, these wispy puffs that look like they were painted by an artist's brush. Nature's splendor. Nature's enormity. It makes me feel small, watching from below as the blazing sphere assumes its place above, but it also makes me feel big, like I can do anything.

So I do. I pick up my phone again and write from the heart.

Hope you and Em had a great Thanksgiving. I'm okay. In Portsmouth. Will be in touch soon. xo.

Then I send the message.

April 17, 1990

Dear Eden,

Where do we even begin? As we write this, you're playing in the yard, pushing your doll on the swing. It's a sweet sight, and we're drinking it in, because after today, it will have to tide us over for a long time. You don't know this yet, no one does, but we're leaving. Mommy and Daddy were offered a terrific position at work and we have to take it. Starting tomorrow, we'll be helping lots of children in different countries all over the world. Isn't that exciting? We will miss you, of course, but we know you'll adore living with Grandmom.

Things might be confusing for awhile, and that's okay. Never doubt, though, that we love you. The kids we'll be helping won't always have a grown-up to love them. They need us.

Be good for Grandmom. Listen to everything she says. Above all, live your life with arms wide open. Build sandcastles, go on fun adventures, and laugh that sweet belly laugh of yours.

We love you, Eden. Please remember that.

Mommy and Daddy

❦ 31 ❧

*W*hen I board the plane to Nashville this time, I'm not alone. Mom and Dad are with me. It's so surreal, to be returning to the place I thought I'd never see again and to be doing it with the people who've spent most of their lives traveling without me, not with me, but it's wonderful, too. "Thanks for doing this," I say. "You didn't have to."

"We want to," Dad assures me, and Mom pats my hand a little awkwardly.

"We're here for you," she adds.

I thought I was hearing things when they offered to accompany me. I'd just finished explaining about Wilson's messages and how I'd been wrong to leap to conclusions. "Maybe things won't work out," I allowed. "Maybe the hurt and betrayal run too deep. But I have to try. I can't take off when the going gets tough."

Mom bowed her head. "Is that what you think we did?"

"No," I clarified. "I mean, sure, it was tough to understand why you kept leaving, but I never got the sense you were running from something. Just toward it. You wanted to help those children who had nothing. And now, having been on the other side and knowing the families who came to Open Hearts with only the clothes on their backs ... I get it."

"But still, we should've found a better balance," Dad said. "I'll always regret that. Hopefully we can start fresh, though." He makes good on his words when the plane lands in Nashville and he asks if I'd be willing to show them around the city. It's the opposite from when they were here last time, for my graduation. Then, they spent most of the days holed up in the hotel room, attached to their phones and laptops, while I showed Grandmom my favorite places. Now, we visit those same places together. I can tell they still don't get it – Mom's eyebrows pop up when she sees all the neon lights of Broadway and Dad studies the menu at a restaurant, shuddering at the thought of fried pickles – but they're making an effort, and that's what matters.

I do the same.

Over dinner, I ask how things have been going in Haiti. When we're back at Hotel Indigo, where we're staying until Mom and Dad help me find an apartment I can afford, I volunteer to look at their pictures and videos of the school they're rebuilding. And, during breakfast the next day, when we're at Pancake Pantry and Mom's phone rings, I tell her to answer it. "No," she says. "Work can wait. It won't hurt anyone if I call back in an hour."

But it hurt you all those times I answered right away.

I hear the words she doesn't say.

I'm tempted to show her, show them both, the ones they don't know I have written: "Voyage of the Heart."

I think of the lyrics and the way Serena sings them so flawlessly. She asked for permission to use the song on the demo CD she submitted to the record label and sent me the audio file. I could play it for my parents. Part of me wonders if it'd take up residence in their hearts. The other part fears it would be too much to handle, that hearing my rawest emotions would drive them away again. I just got them back. I can't lose them now. So I keep "Voyage of the Heart" close to the vest and opt to show them some of the lyrics I penned at the shelter instead.

"These are fantastic," Dad says. "The way you write, it's like you reach into someone's soul and give it its own song."

"We were wrong," Mom says. "All the times we tried to convince you to follow in our footsteps, all the times we thought we knew you better than you knew yourself ... it was presumptuous." She grazes her fingers across my songwriting journal. "You have a talent that cannot, and should not, be denied."

Their response is more than I could have hoped for.

Unfortunately, that's not the case when I meet with Julianna and Brice the next week.

"Thank you for taking time out of your busy schedules to hear me out," I say. Brice is a personal trainer and Julianna a law student, and as we sit at the café in the office building where she interns, I feel both out of place and out of my league. But I refuse to let that stop me. They're here, after all. Brice didn't hang up when I called after finding his phone number online. Maybe that means they're reasonable.

"Just so you're aware, Wilson already attempted this," Julianna informs me. "He got nowhere."

Hmm. Maybe not.

"I am aware," I say. Then I clear my throat, take a sip of ice water, and delve into the whole tale. I plead my case, honestly and fully. "If you want to sue somebody," I finish, "sue me. I don't have a lot, but you're welcome to all of it." Even if it means not being able to afford rent for an apartment. I'd do that for Wilson. I'd do absolutely anything for him and Emmalyn.

But Julianna won't give me the chance. "We're private people," she says. "And as I told Wilson, our families didn't know about the engagement. Can you imagine how they felt, learning something like that through a catalog in the mail?"

"You hurt us and our families," Brice adds. "So no, we won't reconsider. Wilson clearly violated the terms of our agreement ... or you did, however you want to look at it. Either way, we have every right to sue."

There's more to the story, I can tell. I just don't know what it is.

For the time being, though, they aren't budging.

As I traipse out of the building and into the brisk, sunny air, I puff out a breath in exasperation. I don't feel like I can face Wilson until I have good news. Something to barter with, to trade in return for his forgiveness ... that is, if he *can* forgive me. Judging by his messages, it seemed like he wanted to at least try, but that was before. Maybe he's changed his mind. He never answered my text from the day after Thanksgiving, and I don't blame him. He owes me nothing.

"Could this day get any worse?" I mutter.

Lesson learned: don't tempt fate.

Because, not even fifteen minutes later, my phone rings.

Serena.

But when I answer, she isn't there. At least, I don't think so at first. All I hear is silence. "Hello? Serena?" I ask. Nothing. Then, in slow succession: a sniffle, a whimper, a strangled cry that sounds like a wounded cat.

And, finally, words that make ice crystallize in my veins.

"Help," she whispers. "Please help me."

She squeaks out an address only a few blocks from where I am, and I take off sprinting. I have to get to her, even though I'm scared of what I might find. With good reason, too, because as I dash up the driveway to the house she shares with Seth, I see her sitting on the steps outside, slumped over like a ragdoll. Her head is in her hands, blonde locks hiding her face, and when I kneel down to push them aside, a horrified gasp escapes my mouth.

Oh my God.

My poor friend.

Bloodied. Bruised. Beaten.

"Oh ... oh, Serena." Tears sting the corners of my eyes, but I blink them away, determined to be strong for her. "Where's Seth now?" Looking at her – the circles of black and blue around her eyes, the dripping red snake slithering across her cheek, the swelling near her mouth – I'm filled with rage for the lowlife who attacked her. She isn't even wearing a coat. It can't be more than fifty degrees, and she's sitting there in a t-shirt that's slit at the shoulder, revealing her scar from the last assault. Revealing her secret and refusing to let her hide any longer.

"It doesn't matter where he is." She grabs my hand and clings to it.

"Yes, it does. It matters very much." I shrug out of my own jacket and gingerly settle it over her shoulders. "Did he take off, or is he inside?" I hold her hand with one of mine, and with the other, I reach for my cell phone. "Tell me where he is so I can call the police." I look at her expectantly, sure she'll want to press charges this time, but she just shrinks into herself. "Please, tell me where he is," I say again. "He's not getting away with this."

I hope he spends years behind bars for hurting her. It isn't only her face. As she struggles to her feet, clutching on to me like a lifeline, I see bruises darkening her arms, too. You'd think we were in a horror movie. But this isn't fantasy. It's a terrible reality that happens to way too many victims of abuse.

"He stormed off," Serena manages. "I don't know where he went. I don't care."

"Well, I do."

"Please." Her voice cracks and she staggers a bit, tightening her grip on me to keep from falling. "Can you get me out of here? He just … flipped. He tore me apart, and the house … " She stops and wipes the blood trickling over her cheekbone. "Please."

I'm furious with him, but as Serena's face crumples in agony, I know he's not the important one. We can deal with him later. The crucial thing now is getting her help.

"Okay," I say softly, adjusting my arm so she can lean on me. "Let's go."

She begs me not to call an ambulance and I don't have enough money on me to cover a cab, so I take the chance I never would have even a month ago. I call Mom and Dad. Their rental car pulls up shortly, and they don't ask any questions. They just get Serena to the hospital, and even sit with me while I wait to hear the doctor's diagnosis.

Fractured ribs. Sprained wrist. Bruises to the face, arms, and neck.

They keep her overnight for observation, and release her the next day with a brace for her wrist and a prescription for painkillers.

"Tell me how I can make this easier for you," I implore, helping her into a bed in our hotel room. Going back to her house wasn't an option, and she was too embarrassed to show up at Open Hearts again, so she's staying with us.

"You already have." She lays against the pillows I've propped up, flinching even from the simple movement. "Thanks for coming yesterday, and for waiting with me, and for letting me recover here. I don't deserve it."

"What you don't deserve," I say, perching carefully on the edge of the bed, "is Seth's abuse. Can you tell me what happened? Or if you don't want to – "

She closes her eyes, black-lidded from Seth's blows, then opens them again. "It's alright. I spent too long *not* talking about it. But first, I owe you an apology." Her fingers go to her wedding band, and this time she wrenches it off and heaves it against the wall. We both watch as it springs back and crashes to the floor. A broken vow. A circle that promises infamy instead of infinity. "You've been an amazing friend to me, and I took it for granted. I bailed on you in more ways than one, and that's not what friendship is. I have no excuse, other than to say I sincerely thought Seth had changed. He swore to me he'd been seeing a therapist, and we even went to some sessions together. But he wasn't willing – or maybe even able – to put in the effort or let the therapist help him. It's like he's just wired to have a temper." She sighs, making the fingerprint-shaped marks on her neck do a haunting kind of dance. "Whatever the case, I got so wrapped up in making it work with him that it devalued our friendship in the process. I'm sorry."

I think of how alone I felt when she left me to find an apartment by myself. How eerie it was to see her on stage with Seth. How sad it was to realize we wouldn't be writing partners anymore. But looking at her baggy sweatpants now, and her eyes swollen into slits, and the ice pack she's holding against her ribs, all I feel is sympathy. Serena didn't leave. She was lured away.

"Apology accepted," I tell her.

"Thank you. You're the best."

"You've helped me too, you know. It's a two-way street."

"And Seth is a dead-end." She grimaces. "Things were going well for awhile. I thought we had a shot at salvaging it. We began writing together again, and I even talked the manager at Noteworthy into letting him join my gigs."

"I know," I confess. "I saw you there a few weeks ago. The

night I left for Portsmouth."

"Oh. *Oh.*" She sinks lower into the pillows. "You never should've found out like that. I'm sorry. That's why he erupted, by the way, because of my singing. Remember when I met with Josie at the label? She called yesterday. They want to sign me."

"Oh my God!" An involuntary grin takes control of my face. "Congratulations!"

Even she smiles for a fraction of a second. "Thank you."

"This is the break you've been waiting for!"

"The break he's been waiting for, too," she says, and in an instant, my jubilation for her fades to understanding. To despair. "Obviously when I interviewed with Josie, I was a solo act. Let's just say Seth didn't take too well to the idea of me moving forward without him. I tried to explain and even said I'd talk to her about signing us as a duo, but it's like he couldn't hear me. He just erupted." Her fingers rise and touch the cut on her cheek, one of several that needed stitches at the hospital. "The worst part is that it was my fault," she continues in a low voice. "Not the abuse – I know Seth is the only one to blame for that – but I decided to give him another chance. I chose to forgive, even when I couldn't forget. That was a mistake. I let him hurt me again."

I weigh my words. My options.

Then, hoping I'm not overstepping, I reach for the phone and offer it to her. "Don't let him hurt anyone else. You can stop this. Get justice for yourself and for your baby. Call the police. Tell them everything he's done over the years. File a report." She stares at me for a long time, silent and sad, and just when I'm about to give up, she holds out her hand.

Still silent. Still sad.

But strong. So strong.

* * *

The salty sea air rushes to greet me when I open the car door, enveloping me in its cool embrace and welcoming me to the shore. To New Jersey. To a town called Ventnor, where Serena's parents own a home. "They sold the house in Philadelphia after I moved to Nashville and my sister went off to college," Serena explained on the drive up from Tennessee.

I can tell why. With its oatmeal-colored sand, blue waves, and a boardwalk that stretches far as the eye can see, it's a beautiful place to stay. Rejuvenating. Healing. It's no wonder Serena loves it here. I was hesitant at first when she asked if I'd join her – things are so up in the air with Wilson, and my parents sacrificed a lot to come to Nashville – but in my heart, I knew it was something I had to do. Serena's finally ready to tell her parents about Seth's abuse, and if having me along for moral support will make the difficult experience even a little easier, then I couldn't possibly say no. I drove us up in Serena's car, helping her work through what she wanted to say, and now that we're here, I send a text to Mom and Dad.

Thank you for being so understanding and telling me to go. It's okay if you want to head back to New Hampshire, I type. *Or even Haiti. I know you can't stay forever.*

Not forever, Mom answers. *But for now. We'll be here. Nashville's starting to grow on us, if you can believe it. Your father even suggested a visit to one of those karaoke bars tonight. You may not recognize us by the time you return.*

I grin, still finding it hard to reconcile these people with the ones who missed so much of my life. *Send pictures, please,* I type, then turn to Serena. "Ready?" I ask.

"Not yet." Her gaze shifts to the house, with its cream-colored stucco and wind chimes hanging from a porch pillar. The blinds are open, letting in a flood of December sunlight, but the driveway is empty. "They're not home, which is good, because suddenly I feel nervous again." Instinctively, her hand flutters to her cheek. It's been two weeks since the attack, and the bruises are finally fading, a shadow of what they used to be. Her wrist is weak and it'll be awhile still before her ribs are entirely healed, but she looks much better than that afternoon in the hotel, when she was a battered shell of her former self, telling the police everything she knew.

I hope it'll be enough to send Seth to jail.

I hope Serena's parents will take her under their wing once she finally shares her secret.

I hope she signs that recording deal with Josie.

I hope we can write together again.

I hope for a lot of things.

"Come on," Serena says, motioning for me to follow her. "While we're waiting, I'll show you the best place on the beach. Melanie and I used to play there every summer when we were kids. You'll see, my parents have a zillion pictures of us." She's talking about the fishing pier a few blocks down from their house. It stretches into the ocean, standing sturdy even after all the storms that set their eyes on the Jersey shore over the past couple years. As we walk toward it, wrapped in winter coats on this cold day, I imagine what a pretty scene it must be during the summer, with seagulls flying by and fishermen casting their rods.

"How long have you been – " I stop, mid-sentence, as something catches my attention. There, near the pier. Glinting in the sunbeams. Bobbing up and down, back and forth. What is it? I squint, shielding my eyes with my hand. "Do you see that?" I ask Serena, pointing to the spot in the ocean.

"Yeah." She appraises it for a moment. "I can't tell what it is, though."

We walk closer, curious, and when we're a few feet away, I figure it out. A bottle.

And there's something inside.

June 13, 2014

Fifty-seven years ago, I sent another bottle into the Atlantic's embrace.

Nine months ago, I found it.

Today, we write this letter together, and sometime in the future, we hope the words will inspire. We hope they will convince you to be the best possible version of yourself, to take that leap of faith even when you are afraid you'll fall. That's when you have to be most brave. Continue the legacy and let somebody else's courage push you to create your own. Whatever you want most in this world, grab it. Fight for it. Follow your whisper.

Charlotte Carter & Remi Friedman

❦ 32 ❧

The moment I read the message, I'm intrigued. I want to know more about these women – who they are, why they wrote this, how their story has unfolded. "Follow your whisper," I say. "I like that." Beside me, Serena nods her agreement.

"Me, too. But what happens if the whisper tells you lies?"

"Seth?"

She sighs. "I still don't understand how I could have been so wrong about him. Why did I let myself believe he'd changed?"

"That's what we do. When we love someone, we give them the benefit of the doubt." As I hear myself speak, my mind travels back to Nashville. To Wilson. To the lawsuit. I don't know when the court date is – I asked, but Brice and Julianna wouldn't tell me – and although I want to be there for it, to stand by Wilson as he fights for his business, I'm also afraid it would make things worse. Could their lawyer call me as a witness? Would that be good or bad?

"Hey." Serena touches my wrist, and I jump. "Are you okay?"

"Fine," I say hurriedly. "Just thinking about Remi and Charlotte. How cool is it that one of them found the other's note from all those years ago? I had no clue a bottle could float that long. Hey, do you think we could track them down?" Adrenaline zings through me at the idea. "I mean, obviously they found one another, since they wrote this letter together. Maybe we could ... how did they put it?" I peer at the lavender paper. "Continue the legacy."

Serena arches an eyebrow, and I know *she* knows I'm deliberately changing the subject, but she goes with it. "We could try. Pretty much everybody can be Googled these days," she says, bending to pick up a white pebble from its sandy blanket. "My sister and I used to wish on these and throw them into the ocean. You and I can do that now and wish to find Remi and Charlotte." She scoops a second pebble up and drops it into my palm.

There it is again, that word. *Wish.*

I never told Serena about the wishes. I never told anybody, until Grandmom. Maybe because it felt like a special secret, mine to have and hold, or maybe because I was afraid of how people would react. Meddling with good intent is still meddling, and don't we all have the right to determine the trajectory of our own lives? I understand that now, so I do fill Serena in, starting with Tommy's wish and ending with the one I made on Wilson's behalf.

"You were trying to help," Serena points out, "and no, maybe it didn't always go as planned, but think about all the times it did. All the lives you touched. Be proud of that. You should've told me," she adds. "I would have been your sidekick."

"Really? You don't think I was playing God?" I cringe at the memory of Wilson's accusation.

"I think you were trying to bring good luck to people who had none."

"My dad said something similar. He called it a mitzvah."

"Maybe that's your whisper." She motions to the note still in my hand. "And maybe your voice is supposed to reach others."

It's an interesting perspective. That's what I've always wanted, right? To write the sort of music people can connect to, the sort they can turn to as a reminder that they aren't alone. Over time, so many songs have done that for me. They've lifted me up and wrapped me in their melodies; they've given me an incredible sense of peace when it felt like everything was spiraling out of control. They were there to soothe, to understand, to inspire. Even after all that's happened, I still believe in that. I still believe in music's power to transform. I still believe it's an unconditional ally. I still believe the music is in me.

In Serena, too.

As we head back to the house, she confesses that she's nervous to accept Josie's offer. "Look at me," she says. "I couldn't even protect myself from my own husband. I'm not someone who should be in the spotlight or acting as a role model. She examines the yellow-green bruises on her knuckles and wrist. "Let's be honest, I'm a fraud."

"You are anything but – "

"Seriously," she says sardonically. "What parent would want their child listening to a singer who willfully went back to the man who abused her? I'm sending a great message there." Her nose curls in disgust. "I was so determined to get away from him. So ready to create my own path. When did I go from defensive to defenseless? Why did I ever let someone else's whisper drown out mine until there was practically nothing left?"

I look to the bottle, Remi and Charlotte's note tucked safely back inside. I want to find them not only for myself, but also for Serena. I bet they'd be the best medicine for her beaten-up soul. First, though, it's time to talk with her parents. Their car's in the driveway when we return. Serena visibly tenses, but she still marches to the door and knocks. It swings open a minute later, and I recognize her mother from the picture Serena had at Open Hearts. "Serena," she whispers, dumbfounded, as her hand tightens around the doorknob. "Is that *your* car out front? We thought the neighbors had company." She shakes her head in disbelief. "What are you doing here? It's been so long."

"Too long." She glances at me. "This is my friend Eden. Can we come in?"

"Of course." Her mother holds open the door. "Barry!" she calls. "Serena's here!" I watch him barrel into the foyer and greet Serena with a bear hug. She flinches in pain from the contact against her ribs, but says nothing. She just hugs him back, then moves to her mother.

"I've missed you," she tells them.

"Likewise." Her mother smiles as she looks at her. "Your hair's gotten so long. Melanie cut hers into a pixie style over the summer. I think it's the first time in thirty years you're different in – " Her words drop off and she inches closer to Serena. "What's that?" she asks, staring at her face. There's a tiny scar on Serena's cheekbone, a remnant of Seth's strike and the ensuing stitches.

"It's a scar," she answers, and I'm so proud of her, because her voice doesn't waver at all. She is steadier than she thinks, stronger than she feels. In one fluid movement, she holds up her left hand. The lack of a wedding ring is glaringly obvious. "Courtesy of my soon-to-be ex-husband. He isn't the man I thought he was."

Her mother's gone ghostly pale and her father's gripping onto the bannister like his knees might buckle. They know. I see it in their eyes. "I'll give you time to talk," I say. Serena whirls around and meets my gaze, and for a second I think she's going to ask to me to stay – in which case I will, though I think this should be just between them – but then she mouths a 'thank you.' "Anytime," I answer. I walk outside again, and as I make my way toward the boardwalk, I catch a glimpse of them through the window. On the living room sofa, with her parents bookending her, Serena looks so much like a little girl. I get that. Sometimes I still feel like one, too.

Other times I feel weary, like I've traveled the world twice over.

I slide my hand into my coat pocket as my feet hit the wooden boards. The pebble's still there. Waiting. I run my fingers across its smooth surface, thinking of Remi and Charlotte. Of what Serena said. Maybe the wishes weren't so bad. Maybe I shouldn't regret them. And maybe, even though I swore I was finished, there's one more to grant after all.

* * *

"This is crazy," Serena says, as we walk up to a cute little restaurant a few days later. It's a white building with red awnings, a local place one of our breakfast companions suggested. "It's something you'd see in a movie. Or," she adds, "something you'd hear in a song."

"Maybe we should write one about it," I say. "If this doesn't inspire great lyrics, nothing will." I step toward the door and the adventure waiting inside. "Ready to meet them?" *Them* is Charlotte and Remi. It turns out Charlotte actually lives in Ventnor, so she and her husband were listed in the phone book when I flipped through its pages. She told me that Remi's here for awhile, too, working on a writing project, and suggested we meet for breakfast. As I walk into the restaurant now, it truly does feel like serendipity that I stumbled upon their bottle.

Like it's what I've been looking for.

We find Remi and Charlotte at a table by the window, and I stop a couple feet away, out of their line of vision, to look at them. Charlotte, with her silvery bob and emerald eyes, is obviously the one who sent the original letter. She must be in her mid-seventies now, but there's a spark about her, a glimmer in her eyes, signs of a life well-lived and well-loved. Then there's Remi. With ginger waves cascading down her back and a butterfly locket clasped around her neck, she seems to emanate this aura of being a fireball. She and Charlotte light up as we join them.

"Hi," I say, shaking their hands, "I'm Eden, and this is my friend Serena."

"It's nice to meet you," Serena says. "It was such a surprise to find your bottle. My family's had a house here since I was a kid, and I've never seen anything like that wash ashore."

"That was my reaction, too," Remi says. "I was in Virginia Beach when I found Charlotte's bottle, or I guess you can say when Charlotte's bottle found me. It came in on a wave and literally crashed into me. I could hardly believe it when I read the letter and realized how far and long it'd travelled. All the way from Atlantic City," she adds, resting her arms on the table and folding her hands. "I was so excited when Charlotte called to tell me you'd found our bottle. My greatest hope when we sent it out was that our message would somehow change somebody's life like Charlotte's original one did for me."

The older woman's eyes twinkle. "She gives me too much credit. Remi changed her own life."

"With you as inspiration."

Over the next two hours, I learn all about that inspiration. About Charlotte's choice to run away with Nolan when she was nineteen and he was twenty-one. About the unplanned pregnancy which rocked her world just days before they were due to leave for their great escape. About her terror as she hid the truth from her then fiancé, now husband, and her outlet as she penned a letter to their baby-to-be. "I was petrified," she tells us. "I was a swimmer, you see, and I knew that my dream of competing in the Olympics was in jeopardy. I loved our baby, but I was afraid to tell Nolan about the pregnancy and even more frightened that a gold medal was slipping out of my reach. So I put all my emotions into that note, and on the first morning after we arrived in Atlantic City, I woke up early to toss the bottle into the ocean at sunrise."

"And I found it fifty-six years later." Remi smiles, remembering. "Right when I needed it most. I was the picture of cynicism. I'd been dating this guy for six years and he broke it off because he met somebody else. My novels kept getting rejected, the type of 'close-but-not-quite' rejections that are the hardest to swallow, and I couldn't get a job despite constant searching. I was at my wits' end, in desperate need of a change. Then I read Charlotte's note." They share a look that reminds me of all the ones Grandmom and I have given each other. "She told her baby to follow her whisper. When I read those words ... " She places her left hand over her heart, her engagement ring creating prisms in the light. "They spoke to me, you know?"

I do. "I feel the same way," I say. "It's like I can't shake them."

"Exactly. Neither could I, so I did the most impulsive thing ever. The best thing ever. I bought a one-way ticket to Nantucket and moved six hundred miles away without a job or even a place to live when I got there. Everyone thought I was crazy, but it was the right choice. The fresh start filled me up again. And now ... " Her cheeks flush pink. "I'm engaged to an amazing man who never gave up on me, even when I pushed him away. Eli's the love of my life, and we wouldn't have met if not for Charlotte, so she's wrong about me giving her too much credit. She definitely deserves it. Her letter helped me love again. Write again. That's why I'm here," she explains. "Charlotte and Nolan's story moved me so much, I wanted to share it with other people. I just finished the final draft of the book I wrote about them and brought it for them to go over before

I begin submitting it."

"*All that Glitters is not Gold,*" Charlotte says. "Remember the title. It's going to be a bestseller."

"It sure sounds like it," Serena agrees.

"I don't know about that," Remi laughs. "But it's important to me to get their story out there, to celebrate who they were and who they are. Writing this book was ... " She pauses, looking out the window, trying to find the right words. "It was rejuvenating. Joy-filled. It reminded me why I write and why I can't stop. But enough about me," she says. Tell us about yourselves. We'd love to hear about the people who found our letter."

I go first, then Serena – who, to my surprise, actually tells them the whole truth. I'm so glad she can talk about it more freely now. I guess her story must resonate, and mine too, because as we all stand up to leave, Charlotte asks us to please stay in touch.

We walk out of the restaurant together, an unlikely foursome, but one I believe in. It's amazing to consider how lives can intersect like that, how fate can weave a web of magnificence, how people can come into our orbit for a reason. As I think about that, an idea blasts into my brain. And that's when I know. I know the song that'll be my mark and the one I'm meant to write. I'm not ready for my songwriting journal yet. I'm not ready to turn it into something concrete. It needs to percolate first. To figure me out before I can figure *it* out.

It's there, though.

I feel it.

Meeting Charlotte and Remi was the best inspiration, not because of their story, but because it reminded me of my own. Of the people at Open Hearts. Of the way we can walk alone or choose to take the journey with others. Of the light we can find even when life seems so bleak. And, above all else, of the importance of listening to our own voices. They won't ever let us down.

Serena's learning that, too.

"Can I ask your opinion about something?" she says, once we're back in the car.

"Sure."

"Well, now that my parents know about Seth and I called Mel to fill her in … " She taps her nails against the armrest. "I feel like I can breathe again. Like it's out in the open and I don't have to hide anymore. So I was thinking … instead of covering that scar on my shoulder, why not let it show? It's never going away, and I'm tired of pretending it's not part of me. I don't want it to be a reminder of Seth's abuse. I want it to be a symbol of my freedom. Because I am now. I'm free. This last time, it broke the spell."

"You broke it," I tell her. "You're breaking it every day."

"Which is why I want to do this. I want to own it." She tells me her plan and I instantly love it.

"It's perfect," I say.

An hour later, we're at a tattoo shop, and I'm watching a woman design a lightning bolt around that scar. It's yellow and white, sunshine and strength, and it incorporates the red scar at its center. A bolt of energy. A statement of control. A picture of hope. "He didn't win." Serena says this more to herself than me, but as the woman prepares her shoulder for the ink, I feel compelled to respond anyway.

"Because you didn't let him."

"I almost did. Thank you for helping me take my life back." She looks over and meets my eyes. "I'd be happy to help you do the same. Stop running," she says gently, "stop hiding. Go see Wilson. Get back to the Eden who spilled her heart onto the page and let her own scars show in her songs. I know you can do it."

"I hope so."

"I know so," she repeats, leaning back in the chair as the woman tells her she's ready.

When the needles hit her skin, Serena cries.

But not from the way they jab into her flesh. Not from their sharp, burning points.

The pain she's already been through is so much harsher than any needle.

"I'm proud of you," I whisper.

This makes her tears fall faster.

It is a catharsis, a release, a declaration of more than words can describe.

Later that night, after everyone's asleep and I'm curled into the window seat in the guest room, my tears fall, too. I think of what Serena said, about letting my own emotional scars show, and what Remi and Charlotte wrote in that letter. *Follow your whisper.* My fingers wrap around a pen, and it feels so natural, like coming home again after a long journey. I crack open the window, listen to the ocean, and gaze up at the sky. It seems like a magician's waved a wand and stardust sprinkled from its tip across the celestial blanket. It's cold tonight, but I'm warm. That's what the comfort of music does for me.

I open my journal.

Blank page. Endless possibilities.

Love. Feel. Soar. Play. Live. Learn. Search. Listen. Sing. Write.

Write.

"Watercolors"

Walking down the street one night

Sprinkles of starlight in the sky

When the couple sleeping on a bench can't help but catch your eye

Baby in their arms, tattered blanket a cocoon

Sheltered by nothing but the glow of the moon

Do you turn your gaze, or do you stop?

Do you ask them why they're down on their luck?

Every person has a story

Every person has a song

Appearances can be deceiving

And judgment's often wrong

Blues and pinks, reds and greens

Sometimes a world of difference, it seems

But like the whimsy of a watercolor, so we blend as one

When we reach out a hand

Who knows what we'll become?

The man who's lost his job, the husband and wife

who can't pay their bills

The sisters orphaned far too young,

the battered woman who ran for the hills

They are more than just this chapter, if you look beyond the page

There is beauty in the broken

There is faith inside these faces

You can wish on a penny
Send a prayer to the sky
Or you can take a step forward, offer your heart
For every journey relies on its start

Blues and pinks, reds and greens
Sometimes a world of difference, it seems
But like the whimsy of a watercolor, so we blend as one
When we reach out a hand
Who knows what we'll become?

A ripple in the water, spreading circles wide
We can change the world, if only we try
We get what we give, so let's paint this world bright
Fight for each dream, celebrate each life

Blues and pinks, reds and greens
Sometimes a world of difference, it seems
But like the whimsy of a watercolor, so we blend as one
When we reach out a hand
Who knows what we'll become?

ecember has always been my favorite month of the year. There are rainbows glowing on star-topped trees, flames dancing atop candles, and people gathering inside as the sky's sieve covers the world with icy powdered sugar outside. It's like living in a snow globe. For those thirty-one days in time, even the most practical people are taught to believe in miracles.

When Serena and I get back from New Jersey, Nashville has been infused with the hope of those miracles. The holiday season has sparkled to life. Opryland's flipped the switch on their two million lights, the antebellum mansions have been opened to the public for tours, and Christmas tunes play on nearly every radio station. In fact, as my parents help me look for an apartment, we hear "Silent Night" in both the car and the realty office. The holiday spirit is all around.

Magic is all around.

Grandmom was right about that. I see that now.

I see it when Serena signs a contract with Josie, when Mom pulls me aside during the apartment hunt to say she and Dad are going to help me with rent money until I can find another job, and when I stop by Open Hearts to sign up as a volunteer for their annual fundraiser next March. Most of all, I see it when, finally, I go to visit Wilson on Christmas Eve. As I drive my parents' rental car along his road, goosebumps cover my arms. Oh, how I've missed it here. I park in front, gather the two boxes trimmed with iridescent ribbons, and step into the night. It's a cold one, and I stand for a moment, my breath creating wispy white clouds. Am I ready for this? I thought so. Now I'm feeling nervous butterflies. Suppose he asks me to leave? Suppose the lawsuit has already been settled and he lost everything?

Suppose. The word screams at me, pinging off the walls of my brain.

And I turn around. It's a cowardly thing to do, but I need a little time to collect myself. So I walk slowly, with the wind nipping at my nose and the streetlights illuminating the way, and peek into the houses I pass. In some respects, they're all the same. There are lights twinkling on pine trees, lamps shining brightly, and people celebrating. But, much as these things are the same, others are unique. Like the house with everyone gathered around the television, watching together as a family. Or the one with four children standing on the windowsill, decorating the glass with cut-out snowflakes. Or the one with an elderly couple holding hands as they stand below the mistletoe and kiss each other like they're newlyweds. The one with two men and a toddler. The one with a woman who sits, dog by her side, on a sofa. All their stories are different; all their homes are different. But home is what you make it. Home is where the heart is. I get that now.

So when I wander my way back to Wilson's, I stand my ground this time. I can do this. Honestly, I should have done it long ago. As I walk up the path, my eyes drift toward the living room window, wanting to see what lies inside. A tree with white fairy lights and ornaments galore. Garland draped along the mantel and candles with warm orange flames. The suede armchair, with the University of Oklahoma blanket folded over the back, where Wilson is sitting with Em and reading to her from an oversized book.

I step forward, readjust the gifts I'm holding – a finished version of Emmalyn's song for her and a framed picture of the two of them for him – and ring the bell. Through the window, I can see Wilson look up from the book. He places it on the arm of the chair, lifts Em off his knees, and heads to the door with her tagging along after him.

My heart does a drumbeat. Tap. Taptap. Taptaptaptaptap.

It slams against my ribcage, fast and furious, and when Wilson's face appears in front of me, my legs turn to jelly. "Eden." His mouth opens, then shuts, then opens again. "What are you …

I wasn't expecting ... " He trails off, staring like he doesn't believe I'm real.

Emmalyn, though? She isn't lost for words like her daddy is. "You're here!" she shrieks. "You're actually, really, here!" She lunges for me and wraps her arms around my legs. "I missed you inside my chest. That's where my love lives." Oh, I'm going to lose it. Wilson, too, if the expression on his face is any indication. "Daddy said there was a puzzle in your head and we needed to wait for you to find the pieces."

I rest my hand on her curls, eyebrows raised as I glance to Wilson.

"I told her you were confused," he clarifies. "That sometimes grown-ups have a lot going on and they have to set some pieces aside in favor of others. Remember, Em? We talked about Eden going to visit her family in New Hampshire."

"Right." She squeezes me a bit tighter. "Lots and lots and lots of miles away."

"I was thinking of you," I tell her. "Both of you."

Wilson's eyes bore into me. "Why are you here?" he finally asks. "You said in your last text you'd be in touch soon; that was weeks ago. When did you get back?"

"A few days after Thanksgiving. But then I left again. Serena is ... " I shiver as the wind kicks up and slips inside my coat. "I'll explain later, when little ears aren't listening. That is, if I can come in?" For an instant, I think he's going to say no. His hand tightens around the door, and he looks from me to Emmalyn, then back to me.

"Fine."

Something comes over me as I step inside. It's surreal, almost an out-of-body experience. I see the first time I was here, when Wilson made dinner and I helped put Emmalyn to bed. The last time I was here, when I used Wilson's computer and broke his trust. All the times in between – the game of kickball in the backyard, the Disney movie marathon when Emmalyn had the sniffles, the nights I fell asleep in Wilson's bed, and the mornings I woke up to see him propped on an elbow, grinning at me. And now there is this time.

Christmas Eve. Peace on Earth, goodwill toward men.

If ever there was a moment to get a miracle, this is it.

"I hope I'm not interrupting," I say, setting the presents down and glancing at the armchair. *The Night Before Christmas*, that's what they were reading. "I just ... I was trying to fix things. I met with Brice and Julianna, like you asked me to, and I've been researching similar court cases in the hope of finding a loophole. That's why I didn't come sooner. I didn't feel like I could until I had something to trade for your forgiveness. It's been slow going, though."

The way he narrows his eyes makes his nose scrunch up. "Until you had something to ... trade?"

"Yes."

He gapes at me.

"Em, can you do me a favor?" he asks. "Run to your room and change into those red and green pajamas Grammy and Granddaddy bought you. I bet Eden would love to see them." She nods, then skips off down the hall. The instant she's out of earshot, he grabs my hands. Something swirls in my stomach. The butterflies spiral free. "Let me get this straight. You thought you needed to *barter* for my forgiveness?"

"Yes," I repeat. "Of course."

"Oh, Eden." He closes his eyes momentarily, and when they open again, the golden flecks shine in the light of the Christmas tree. "When I love someone, it's unconditional. No holds barred. Look, was I angry about what you did? Sure. But my forgiveness isn't contingent on you fixing things, and my love's not dependent on anything other than the feeling I get when I'm with you. See?" He puts my hand on his chest. Beneath it, his heart plays a melody. A love song.

For me? I want to believe, but it's tough. "Even now?" I ask.

"Even now. Always. You'd have known that," he says, letting go of my hand and dropping onto the couch, "if you didn't shut me out. Do you know how worried I was?"

"I'm sorry." I sit next to him and shrug out of my red coat. "I am so sorry, Wilson, for all of it. It wasn't fair to you or Emmalyn. All I can say is that I didn't think there was a prayer for us. You were so upset, and I can't blame you, because I screwed everything up. I thought I was doing you a favor by disappearing."

"You thought wrong. Relationships are hard. They take work, but you don't run at the first sign of trouble."

I turn my hands palms up. "I know. Maybe I didn't before, but I do now. And I swear, if you are truly serious about giving this another try, I'll never make that mistake again. Running is ... it's what so many people around me have done. It's the only thing I used to know. The only way out. But I'm not looking for a way out from us." I inch closer, until our arms are touching. "You and Em, you are my sunshine. I love you both so much, and I've missed you something fierce."

"We've missed you, too." The corner of his mouth lifts, just enough for his dimple to flash. "Em was especially disgruntled that she had to settle for me when it came to playing dress-up. Evidently I don't wear a tiara as well as you."

Now I smile, too. "I don't know about that. I happen to think you look quite handsome in one." We fall silent for a beat, and a thought surfaces. I try hard to compartmentalize it, to shelve it into a box in the recesses of my brain, but it insists on being heard. "The lawsuit," I say quietly. "I promise to keep searching for a way to stop Julianna and Brice. I'll do whatever it takes to make things right again."

"No."

"What?"

"No," he repeats, then sighs. "Julianna's pregnant with twins. She told me that when I met with them again last week. But she's spending more money on law school than she makes, and the gym where Brice works is closing next month. They have no idea how they'll afford the baby expenses." I knew it. I *knew* there was something they weren't telling me. "And honestly, they have every right to go ahead with this. The terms of their contract were violated."

"By me! Not you!"

"That's not how the law will see it."

I hop up and begin pacing. Back and forth, back and forth. "I started asking about wishes at the shelter because I wanted to help people," I say. "I loved being able to touch their lives. But this is a one-eighty. I touched your life and made it crumble. Please, you have to let me keep trying. It's the least I can do."

"Eden." He stands up, crosses the room in two long strides, and puts his hands on my shoulders, stopping me in place. "Listen to me. I love you. I love you because you smile in your sleep, and give Em piggyback rides, and play a killer game of Scrabble. I love you because you make me laugh, make me spark, and make me imagine. I love you because you're talented, compassionate, and caring." A grin lights up his face. "I even love you because you steal the covers from me." He keeps one hand steady, raising the other to caress my cheek. "You matter to me for who you are, not what you do. I'll probably lose the lawsuit, and that's okay. But I can't lose you."

His words are more than anything I could have dreamed of.

They're everything.

"You are incredible," I whisper. "I don't deserve you."

"We deserve each other." He dips his head and kisses me delicately, and I clasp my arms around his neck, pulling him close, holding him tight. I never want to let go. Finally, I have found somebody who wants me to stay. Who chooses me. Who loves me.

Make that two somebodies.

As Emmalyn comes prancing into the room and squeezes herself between us, I actually think my heart might burst. I never knew it was possible to be this happy. Maybe sometimes we have to give up on things in order to realize that they're not ready to give up on us. Love is patient. Love is kind. Love is forgiving. Love makes us better, and even though Wilson is right, even though relationships take a lot of hard work, they're worth it. Because, I know now, the four walls of a house aren't what make a home. The four chambers of a heart do.

"Merry Christmas," I say.

"Merry Christmas," Wilson says back.

Miracles all around. Magic all around.

* * *

"Holy cow." Serena peeks around the folds of the stage curtain set up at the banquet hall. "You weren't joking when you said Ms. Birnbaum outdid herself with this fundraiser. There are hundreds of people! It's been forever since I've performed for a crowd so big." She smoothes a crease in her teal dress and readjusts its spaghetti straps. There are no sleeves tonight. No hiding. Only strength. Only a badge of honor. A bolt of pride.

And a treble clef bracelet around her wrist. It's not exactly the same as the one I lost, but it was the first thing I bought after Dina rehired me at Sensations. I gave it to Serena when we got here, as a thank you, both for what's behind us and what's ahead. "So," I ask, joining her at the curtain, "are you nervous?"

She shakes her head. "You?"

"A little," I admit. "Mostly excited."

I still can't believe this is happening. That the song I wrote three months ago in New Jersey has bloomed into something greater than I ever imagined. I knew it was special. I felt it in my bones as the pen raced across the page. I'm proud of all of my songs. Each is part of me; each *has* part of me in it. But this one is my baby, and in a few minutes, after Ms. Birnbaum gives a speech to thank the people attending tonight's fundraiser for the shelter, that baby of mine will be making its debut.

Wilson and Emmalyn are here. Grandmom. Kayleigh and Gary. Serena's family. Even Mom and Dad. They were scheduled to head back to Haiti this week, now that Serena and I are settled into an apartment, but they postponed it for a couple days because, as Mom said, "We wouldn't miss this." She and Dad are in the front row. Having them here makes my heart swell. I know they can't stay forever. I know their place is with the children who need them. That's alright. Even when they are half a world away, we won't be apart anymore. These months together, they've changed us. I even found the courage to finally show them "Voyage of the Heart."

"I can't get over it," I say to Serena. "How different life would be if not for one moment, or one event, or one choice. If my neighbor had double checked that match before tossing it out, if you had never met Seth, if my grandpa had survived the war ... "

"You know what they say: everything happens for a reason."

I never used to believe that. I still don't, not fully, but I can see that it's true in some instances.

Maybe I had to lose everything so I could find myself.

Find my voice.

Playing the guitar for Serena when she sings "Watercolors," hearing the lyrics I wrote, seeing the tears in Grandmom's eyes and the beaming smiles on my parents' faces ... it is, truly, beyond words. *Watercolors.* Like the paintings at Open Hearts. Because, as their colors blend together in a swirl of whimsy, so too must we all join together, not only to create the canvas of our own lives, but also to add brushstrokes to others'. We're all interconnected like the lyrics of a song. Without one another, there'd be such a different meaning. Such a different tone.

That's what "Watercolors" is about.

Maybe it'll go somewhere. I invited Ms. Henley tonight so she could hear the song. I might not have gotten the job at her publishing company, but "Watercolors" could open a different door. Or it could be like my other efforts, who knows? No matter what, though, I'll treasure this song. It's like what Remi said at breakfast a few months ago: it reminded me why I write. It isn't about getting my songs on the radio or on an album. It's about putting my heart in the lyrics and knowing I have a lot to be proud of in the work itself.

Tonight, I am proud.

I am happy. I am whole. I am, finally, where I belong.

Serena gets a standing ovation, but she doesn't take a bow. Instead, she motions to me. "Eden wrote this beautiful song," she tells the audience. The applause is thunderous. Dad, clapping hard, his arms raised over his head. Wilson, holding Em, and looking at me like we're the only ones in the room. Grandmom, blowing me a kiss, just like she used to when I performed in school concerts as a kid. Mom, beaming. And, in a corner, toward the back of the crowd, the man I was worried I'd hurt beyond compare. I can't believe he's here. The veteran who threw away my CD. He tips his hat at me, and later, during dinner, comes over to tell me he's moved back to Open Hearts and is trying to get the help he needs.

It feels like absolution.

It feels like peace.

And when, after the fundraiser's over and I'm alone with Wilson and Em again, it feels like hope.

"Do you have a minute?" I ask.

"For you?" He grins, hoisting a tired Em higher in his arms. "I have all the time in the world."

Even though he lost thousands in the lawsuit.

Even though his photography business is a shell of its former self.

But I'm reminded of what Serena said, that things happen for a reason. Because my boyfriend is now the newest weather producer at Nashville's ABC affiliate, a job which he might never have even applied for if he hadn't lost the suit.

Sometimes when one door slams shut, another swings wide open.

"Good." I smile. "There's something I want to show you. Or rather, somewhere."

I do what I should've done from the start. I take him to Open Hearts. "This is where Serena and I had music classes for the kids," I point out. "And this is where they served our meals. The library is upstairs, and this – " We walk through the community room and go outside. "This is the courtyard. The fountain. This is where it all began."

The night is crystal clear, and I breathe in the air, a hint of spring in its sweetness. I look at the water as a breeze swirls it into the faintest ripples, and think of the people I helped. The ones I hurt. The tiny wishes. The big ones. The selflessness. The selfishness. We're all yearning for something, I've learned. No matter who we are and where we have been, there is always a wish to stir the soul. But maybe the real lesson is this: to stop wishing and begin appreciating all we've been blessed with already.

"Can I throw in a penny, Daddy?" Emmalyn asks.

"Sure thing." He pulls out his wallet and produces a shiny coin, which she promptly tosses in. It plinks into the water and lands in the center of the fountain. Heads up. "What was your wish?" he asks her.

She smiles at me. "For Eden to be my mommy someday."

"I like the way you think, sweetpea."

My world just ... stops. It stops in the best possible way.

Wilson brushes a kiss to my lips. "How about you? Want to throw in a penny, too?"

Follow your whisper.

I knew Remi and Charlotte's note would inspire a special song. They gave me "Watercolors," and "Watercolors" gave me this night. Here with Wilson and Emmalyn, in the very place I sought solace when I had nothing else left. Open Hearts felt suffocating at first, like it shriveled me into the smallest version of myself, but now I see that it was the exact opposite: that it actually helped me grow into a better version of myself.

I lean into Wilson as he encircles an arm around my waist and pulls me to his side. Like the very first time I stood before this fountain, my answer to that question is unequivocal ... but now it's not because I don't believe in luck or risks or love. It's because I do.

"It's not necessary," I say. "Everything I could ever wish for is already right here."

Shari Cylinder believes in the importance of dreaming big, working hard, and embracing our own stories. She is a graduate of Arcadia University and lives in the suburbs of Philadelphia, where she spends her time as a writer, transcriptionist, and a member of the Board of Directors for Luv-N-Bunns Rabbit Rescue – and, thanks to her own rabbits, also a makeshift sprinter and gymnast who tries very hard to keep up with bunnies that run much faster than she does. Sometimes she's even successful.